THE CURSE OF THE THRAX

BLOODSWORD TRILOGY PART I

MARK MURPHY

ISBN 13: 9781491276365
ISBN: 1491276363
Library of Congress Control Number: 2013914585
CreateSpace Independent Publishing Platform
North Charleston, South Carolina

Felicia —
This is an advance
review copy (ARC) of
the book. It has
about 30-40 typos in
it which have been corrected
in the final version.
Enjoy!

World

da says
zim are
ere

Aqueduct

ARK
REST

CAPITUS

TO CAPITUS

Zephyr
Mountains

DRAGON
LAKE

THE
GREAT
SEA

The
Great
Waterfall

The Brightwood

THE GODSWOOD

The
Southern
Islands

The Priest's
Bain

marshes

1

Morning came in the Godswood in a hurry, the sun rising above the dense tangle of forest like an eagle vaulting into the sky. It was summer, and sunrise during the growing season was always greeted by a murmur of insects and the twitter of birds, rays of sunlight pushing back the reluctant shadows. A gentle breeze rustled the leaves and tickled Jaykriss's nose as he slept. The breeze mingled the scent of frying bacon with the sweet floral aroma of jasmine from the tight knot of vines that arched over the doorway of the war chief's bain.

Jaykriss took a deep breath in and smiled. It was Hunting Day. His mother was making breakfast. There would be no lessons this morning.

For a brief instant, he almost forgot that his father was dead.

"Mama says you need to get up and come to eat *breakfuss*!" Annya said.

The five-year-old had burst through his doorway like a little tornado, spinning into Jaykriss's bedding in a blur of arms and legs and hair.

Jaykriss grabbed his sister around the waist and tickled her. She squealed, kicking her feet and pulling breathlessly at his fingers.

"Stop it! Stop it! Mama, he's tickling me and won't let go!"

"Stop tickling your sister, Jaykriss," Mama called from across the bain. Her voice was strained, washed out. She had been that way ever since their father had died. It was like his death had drained all the life from her, as well. She was like a *ghozim*, a shell of herself from the Otherworld.

Jaykriss had not heard her laugh in a long, long time.

"Race you!" Annya said, leaping to her feet.

"You can't beat me!" Jaykriss said. But he tumbled to the floor in a heap, the bedding wrapped around his legs like a deer trap, just in time to see his sister's slim legs sprint through the doorway to victory.

"You're a cheatin' young lady, Annie Bell," Jaykriss muttered, disentangling himself.

Annya was sitting at the table beaming, her fingers grasping the edges of her *plata*. She had woven a strand of jasmine vine into her hair.

"I won! I won!"

"You tied me up!"

"Papa said that deception and warfare are brothers, and that..."

"A trap is as good as a battle-ax. I know. He was my papa too, you know," Jaykriss said.

He kissed his mother on the cheek. Her skin was cool and smooth. "Good morning, Mama," he said.

She placed three strips of bacon and some scrambled duck eggs on his plata. When she looked up at him, her eyes were flat black and dead.

"Not like you to sleep late on Hunting Day," she said.

"I was dreaming," he said.

"What'd you dream?" said Annya. "I dreamed of a dog. A little puppy, wagging its tail."

Mama looked up at her, brows knitted. "There's not enough food for a dog now, Annya. I told you that."

The little girl stared down at her plata, biting her protruding lower lip. "I was only dreaming," she said quietly.

"It's OK," Jaykriss said. "Mama knows." He patted his sister on the shoulder as he sat on the bench beside her.

Jaykriss popped a piece of bacon into his mouth and gazed across the room at his mother, who was absently stirring a pot of vegetable hash.

His father had loved to tell the tale of their courtship. Jaykriss could recite it line by line—how Samaria was the most beautiful thing he had ever seen, more beautiful than sunrise over the sea, and how she was desired by every young man in the Godswood.

"I was the strongest warrior in all the Godswood. Samaria knew what she was getting when she got me," Glyndich would boast. "She knew that she would be the war chief's wife."

But Glyndich, with his hearty laugh and his broad, muscled shoulders, had won Samaria over even before he was made war chief. She had loved him with everything she had. And when Glyndich died, he took nearly all of her love with him into the Otherworld. There just simply was not much love left over for Annya and Jaykriss.

Jaykriss understood this even though he was only fourteen years old. His father's death had left a burned-out hole in his own heart, as well.

Which was why he forgave her.

Samaria spooned the hash onto their platas. Jaykriss noted how pale and bony her hands were. She wore her clothes loosely, the way widows were supposed to, and although her face was thin, he had not realized until now how much weight she had lost.

"Are you eating, Mama?" he asked.

"I ate before you two got up," she said, eyes downcast.

Mama was not a good liar.

"Where are you and Marda hunting today?" Mama said.

"The Brightwood. By the river, I think."

"You're not going anywhere south, are you? Near the Crags? The Thrax was seen there last week, you know."

Jaykriss put his fork down and swallowed. "I'm not going near the Crags, Mama. I promised you I wouldn't."

He chewed his food, staring hard at the plata, eyes fixed and unmoving.

"Look at me," she said.

Jaykriss looked up.

"Promise me."

"I promise," he said, blinking.

Samaria stared at him with her flat, onyx eyes.

"You won't bring your father back if the Thrax kills you, Jay. And if you die, they'll likely make us leave the war chief's bain. We'd then be at the mercy of the Godswood priests unless I took a new husband. Do you want that fate for me, or your sister?"

"There would be honor in avenging my father's death if I were to defeat it. You know *that*," he said.

"There's no honor in dying."

"What if I didn't die? What if I killed the Thrax?"

"Your father was the greatest war chief the Godswood had seen in two generations—and the Thrax killed *him*! You would not stand a chance against it!"

"I am cunning, Mama! I am swift! Papa said so."

"You're a boy of fourteen. You would die, like your father. And then your sister and I would be out of a home. And you might never see us again."

Jaykriss glowered, but said nothing.

"Promise me that you and Marda will stay away from the Crags," she said.

"I promise."

Jaykriss finished his breakfast silently. As he scraped the last of the hash from his plate, he felt his sister's tiny emerald eyes bearing down on him.

"What?" he said.

"Don't die like Papa," she whispered, her eyes filled with tears.

"I won't." he said.

"Promise?"

Jaykriss stood up and picked up his plata and spoon. "I promise. On Papa's grave, I promise."

Samaria glared at him. "Save your breath, boy. You'll need those graveside promises soon enough. Don't use them all up on a mere hunting trip. The gods don't shine their lights favorably on those who don't respect their power enough to save it for…"

"The gods let Papa die."

Samaria looked long and hard at her son, her eyes narrowed. She shook her head slowly.

"Go, then. Just go," she said quietly. "But remember this, Jaykriss: you are not immortal. You have a good bit of your father in you. He thought he would live forever, too. But everybody dies."

"Not today, Mama," Jaykriss said.

He kissed his sister on the head, placed his plata and spoon in the water basin, and sat on the bench to lace up his leggings.

"Safe hunting, Jay," Annya said. She kissed her fingers and placed them over her heart.

Jaykriss repeated the gesture twice, directing it at both his sister and his mother.

"Safe hunting, Annya. And Mama. As always."

But it was not always so. They all knew that.

For that gesture was the last thing they saw all saw Glyndich do before he walked out of the door of the bain that fateful day last winter.

And Glyndich did not return.

Jaykriss strapped on his short sword, snatched up his bow and quiver, and headed out the door of the bain.

The forest beckoned—vast, dark, and full of life. A breeze rustled the trees; birds twittered and cawed. Sunlight dappled the forest floor. The trail that would take him to Marda's plunged though the belly of the wood like a lance.

Jaykriss took a deep breath and closed his eyes, filling his lungs with the sweet scent of jasmine.

"It is a great day to be alive!" Jaykriss proclaimed aloud, to no one in particular.

He had scarcely walked two hundred paces when something hurtled into him from behind, slamming him hard to the rock-strewn earth. The impact stunned him. He saw leaves and sky and dirt and then stars, curiously pulsating stars, and then he realized he was face down on the ground, his mouth in the dirt, struggling to breathe.

A creature was sitting squarely on Jaykriss's back. The thing's breath came in abrupt snorts; it grunted as it worked. It pulled Jaykriss's arms back, expertly binding his hands behind him, cinching the knot so tightly that his shoulders popped.

"You'll make a fine slave, boy," a voice in his ear hissed.

"I am a slave to no man," Jaykriss said, squirming against the tethers that bound him.

"Hah!"

The creature leaned down close to him. It stank like some dead being from the accursed realms of the Otherworld. Jaykriss could feel its hot breath close by his cheek, and flecks of spittle sprayed his ear as the thing spoke. "You are to me, boy. You are to me."

2

Jaykriss's assailant grabbed his trussed arms and flipped him over.

"Honshul," Jaykriss said. "I thought I recognized that voice."

Honshul was a Geshan. Like most Geshans, his thick, muscular torso was built like a barrel, with short, bristly hair all over. His head was piglike, with a short snout, eyes like tiny marbles, and pointed ears that were independently mobile. Honshul's pitted brow was deeply furrowed, the scalp gleaming dully through a blighted crop of scraggly hair that seemed to dribble randomly down from his domelike cranium. He was wearing the traditional Geshan outfit: an eelskin breechcloth that, in this case, was far too short.

The creature glowered at Jaykriss through a pair of alien yellow eyes buried deep within its skull.

"Where's your daddy *now*, little Jaykriss? Or is it jackass?"

Keep him engaged, Jaykriss thought.

The words came into his brain in his father's voice.

He kept on working the trusses with his wrists—wriggling, loosening, fingers working to and fro.

"You know where my father is. He was your protector, same as mine. And he journeyed to the Otherworld in that act of driving the Thrax back into the forest."

Honshul snorted.

"Your father never protected me from anything. And you say he has *journeyed* to the *Otherworld?* How quaint! And how utterly absurd!"

Honshul thrust his ugly face an inch away from Jaykriss. His nose was dirty and snot-filled.

"He's not in some mystical land where brave warriors are honored after death. The Otherworld is a myth created by people like you to make themselves feel better about dying with their honor intact."

"Shut up, Honshul."

The Geshan grinned, shaking his head.

"Your father's *dead*, squirt. And death is death. There is no Otherworld. The mighty Glyndich is gone forever—torn limb from limb by the Thrax. And, if I recall, they never found his head *or* the famous and legendary Bloodsword."

Jaykriss could feel the bile rising in his throat. He had gone to school with Honshul once, years ago. But Honshul had long since left the classroom. He was in his family pirating business now—and with Glyndich gone, and the drunkard Kranin as the new war chief, that business was flourishing.

Right now, if he could, Jaykriss would kill Honshul in a heartbeat.

"Untie him, Honshul," a deep voice rang out from someplace behind Jaykriss.

"Marda, this isn't your fight," said Honshul.

"Your brand of lawlessness may be something Kranin will not awaken from his stupor to control, but Jaykriss is my friend, and this arrow has your name on it. It is trained on your beady little left eye at this precise moment. You know that I can hit a target that small at thirty paces, and this is considerably less than that. So untie him."

"Marda, I was only playing around…"

"*Now*, Honshul."

Honshul stepped behind him. Jaykriss felt Honshul's blade slip by his wrist, and the bindings fell off of his hands.

"That's better. Now leave us, Geshan, before I change my mind and pin your misshapen head to that tree after all."

Honshul muttered a curse under his breath but stalked off, his curled tail poking out from beneath his breechcloth.

"The Geshans hated my father, you know. He sent a number to the prisons at Kingswood," Jaykriss said, rubbing his wrists as he watched Honshul skulk away. "They probably celebrated when he died."

"Your father was worth more than the whole lot. There's not a Geshan in the Godswood that I would choose to break bread with."

Marda and Jaykriss had been friends as long as they could remember. Their families were bound together by blood and by honor; Marda's mother and Jaykriss's mother were sisters, and their fathers had fought side-by-side in the Godswood Guard as young men. Garoth, Marda's father, was gone, too. He'd died of the wasting a few years back, his once rock-hard warrior's body shriveling away to skin and bone. Jaykriss had hated seeing his uncle like that. Garoth had always been a huge, powerful man, jovial and full of life. To see him lying in a dark room illuminated only by the flickering light of his Otherworld candles—eyes sunk deep into his skull, breath rattling in his chest—had been a horror almost as frightening as the Thrax itself.

Garoth's death had hardened Marda. The boy in him was gone; he had an edge like a battle sword, razor-sharp. People respected him. They treated him like a grown man—and, indeed, he was, despite his mere sixteen years. Even the shopkeepers deferred to him, bowing their heads as he walked by.

It did not hurt that Marda was the best bow huntsman in the Godswood. His marksmanship statement to Honshul had been no idle boast.

"Still up for the hunt?" Marda said.

Jaykriss nodded.

The two clasped arms, grinning.

"Safe hunting," Marda said.

"Safe hunting indeed," said Jaykriss.

They turned to go down the path to the Brightwood.

"I heard tell of a herd of deer in the thicket by the river, near the waterfall in the Mist Valley. Small, maybe fifteen or so, but if we get even one it will be worth the journey," said Marda.

"If we get more than one, we'll need to have help," said Jaykriss.

The hike to the Brightwood descended along a stony path that wound among the trees like a serpent. It was an old trail, marked at various points with piles of stone. Firs and spruce at the higher altitudes gave way to tulip poplars and oaks. Jaykriss knew the trail by heart. He and Marda had worn it bare over the years—first with their fathers, and then by themselves.

It was a hike that Jaykriss loved. Every step contained an echo of his father.

"You remember the day we carved that?" he said, pointing at a huge iron-wood tree with his short sword.

Marda nodded.

"You were but five years old," he said.

"Six."

The tree had been carved with the symbols of the four of them: a circle with a square inside it, for Garoth; a bull, for Glyndich; an eagle, for Marda; and a dragon, for Jaykriss.

Marda ran his fingers over the symbols, shaking his head slowly.

"Your father was a skilled swordsman," he murmured. "Each time I see this, I am more impressed with his precision."

"The Bloodsword connected with his soul. It could feel what he was think-ing, could anticipate his needs. It...*helped* him."

"And now it is lost."

Jaykriss nodded. "It was supposed to be mine, you know. It goes to the eldest by birthright. It had been my grandfather's sword, and his father's before him, and so on, going back hundreds of years. I had this dream..."

He stopped, biting his lip.

Somewhere in the valley, a hawk cried out, its thin *screee* trickling in on the wind.

"Go on," said Marda.

"I had this dream that I found the Bloodsword, or it found me. I held it up to a flame and it took, the blade shimmering with fire and light, the ruby in the hilt glimmering crimson, like the setting sun. It lit up the whole of the Godswood. I used it to end the curse of the Thrax."

"A noble dream, indeed. Perhaps it was sent by the gods. Perhaps that is your destiny."

Jaykriss's jaw tightened. "I don't believe the gods help anyone. Papa was faithful to them, honoring their names, and they certainly did not save *him*."

"Do you believe in the Otherworld?"

"I do."

"So perhaps your father was called there by the gods. To help in the Otherworld. Perhaps his death was part of a larger play of fate."

"Now you sound like Harros and the rest of the Godswood priests. I can-not tell you how many times I have heard that sort of thing from them. They told us, 'The ways of the gods are mysterious.' Or 'No man can see the hidden handiwork of the gods.' It was ridiculous—as if those empty words could give my mother any degree of solace."

Marda gazed at the intricate carvings on the ironwood tree once more. "I think we needed your father here more than they could need him in the Otherworld," he said at last.

"Agreed."

"Mine, too. We needed him here."

"The Otherworld has no shortage of great warriors."

"We needed *both* of them. But they're gone now. Now, it's just us."

A red-tailed hawk swooped down from the trees above, screaming right at them. Its dive flushed a huge covey of quail from their hiding place in the underbrush. An explosion of birds enveloped them, blinding them for a moment. But Marda was quick on the draw, and Jaykriss was right behind him. Arrows flew; birds dropped left and right.

It was over in less than a minute.

"How many did you get?" asked Jaykriss. He was picking up birds marked with his red-tailed arrows. He'd shot four.

"Seven. No, eight," Marda said.

Jaykriss shook his head.

"I'll never be that fast," he said.

Marda shrugged, grinning. "You're the better swordsman," Marda said.

"Stop humoring me. I don't need your pity."

Marda stuffed the birds into his game bag and put his blue-fletched arrows back into the quiver. "Four's not bad, you know. Most people would be happy with just one hit in that situation," he said.

"You can say that, Mr. 'Oh, I only killed eight birds.' It comes so easily for you. I have to work at it."

"And I have to work at lessons, while you can do math calculations in your head faster than most people can even read the questions. We all have our gifts."

Beyond the ironwood tree, the trail descended sharply, plunging into the Mist Valley toward the river.

Jaykriss could hear the white noise of the waterfall as it roared, constant and unseen, like a mammoth tiger roaming the dense birch forests of the Brightwood.

"Race you!" Jaykriss said. Just as he started to run, he tripped over a thick clump of rhododendron roots and tumbled to the ground.

In an instant, Marda was gone from sight, the mists swirling about him as he rounded the trail's next switchback.

"Wait up!" Jaykriss shouted.

But his voice was lost, swallowed up whole, the damp, clinging tentacles of fog wrapping tight around his voice and refusing to let it go.

3

The waterfall had always inspired awe in Jaykriss. It seemed incredible every time he saw it—the white waters thundering over the precipice, shorebirds wheeling about in the mist, sunlight playing out in rainbows as the river emerged from the wood, the air pregnant with the indescribable clean scent of the crystal-clear water. He had seen it in winter, when snow capped the black granite rocks at its peak, and in summer, when green willows dipped their drooping branches in the roiling foam of the broad pool at its base. The space around the cataract seemed slightly different each time he came here, but the waterfall itself was eternal, permanent—a three-hundred-foot-high wall of untamed water.

It was his favorite place in the world.

Jaykriss had come here often with his father in years past. It was the best place in all the woods to hunt deer and other large game. Glyndich had killed more than a few elk here, which the villagers never saw anywhere else. Once, Glyndich and Garoth even fought a gargantuan short-faced bear—a massive, stinking beast that seemed all claws and teeth—after it surprised them four of them in a dense thicket of wax myrtles.

Marda and Jaykriss still talked about the bear sometimes. It was the only time either of them got to see their fathers fighting in tandem—and it was something they would both remember until they died. The mists of the water-fall were thick that day, clinging to the earth like a shroud and swallowing up all of the sounds of the Brightwood like a snake. Jaykriss, whose hearing had always been the best of any of them, heard something huge crashing through the underbrush.

"Papa," he had said tentatively.

He had barely gotten the word out of his mouth when the bear lumbered into view and roared at them.

"Boys—climb up that tree. Now!" Glyndich barked, pointing to a nearby elm.

The boys did as they were told. Staring from between the elm's thin branches, they were amazed as Garoth and Glyndich fought as one—spinning, leaping, mists swirling about them. They swung their swords harmoniously, blades whistling through the air, their blows both striking deep into flesh and bone and clanging off tooth and nail. The work of the two warriors was symphonic, almost telepathic, as though each knew what the other was going to do before he did it.

The end came like a lightning bolt. The slavering creature had wheeled its massive bulk about with surprising quickness, a powerful backhanded swipe sending Garoth sprawling backward onto the ground. His battle sword skittered harmlessly across the leaf-strewn forest floor. Looming above Garoth, the enraged monster bellowed, its befanged jaws gaping cavernously as it raised a single great paw to rake its razor-sharp claws across Garoth's exposed belly. At that moment, Glyndich materialized from the mist, wraithlike, his great blade upraised and gleaming. In a single thrust, he plunged the Bloodsword into the great beast's heart all the way up to its bejeweled hilt.

Jaykriss saw the giant bear's eyes dim, flickering once before closing at last. Its enfeebled forelimbs dropped to its sides, and the creature wavered there for an instant, slack-jawed, before toppling lifelessly to the earth in an amorphous heap of blood-soaked fur.

"Praise to the gods for your bravery, Glyndich! I thought he had me for sure," Garoth said.

Grinning, Glyndich pulled the Bloodsword from the bear's body and wiped it clean.

"I thought he had all of us," Glyndich said.

"I knew you would win out, Papa," Jaykriss had said. "You and Garoth are great fighters."

"Never take anything for granted," Glyndich had said, sheathing the Bloodsword. "We could have all died today. That bear was a most worthy adversary. I am far less fearful fighting men than I am defending my child and my friend's child from a wild thing such as this."

The sun came out then, burning away the mists. Jaykriss remembered the thunder and hiss of the waterfall, shafts of brilliant sunlight plunging through the forest like illuminated spears, and his father's clear, slate-gray eyes as he stood there, hands on his hips, simply grateful to be alive.

The four of them had joined hands and said a prayer over the bear's body, thanking the gods for their salvation and for the gift of the bear.

Jaykriss had stared furtively at his father as he uttered the prayer incantation, his heart swelling with pride and love.

I am the son of Glyndich, war chief of the Godswood, he thought.

And he had known at that moment that his father was a great man.

He was still feeling the echo of that long-ago memory as he walked through a dense thicket of willows and saw Marda crouched behind a large boulder at the edge of the pool at the waterfall's base.

"I tripped over a root. That's the…"

Marda placed his index finger over his lips and pointed across the pool.

Jaykriss peered at the shadows among the trees, seeing nothing at first—and then his eyes widened.

The herd of deer was the largest he had ever seen—and at its center was a buck that stood half a head taller than any of them. The rack of its horns looked like the branches of a dead tree.

Marda extended the fingers on his right hand once, twice, and then a third time, before extending a final, single finger.

Sixteen.

Sure enough, the huge stag had at least sixteen antler points. It was proud and majestic—a champion's champion, the war chief of the herd.

"We're upwind," Marda whispered. "They don't know we're here."

"Which one are you targeting?"

"That young piebald buck drinking at the edge of the pool. The fourteen-pointer. We can't kill any of the does because we don't know which ones have babies that are nursing. The fawns are off-limits, of course. And the big stag, the sixteen-pointer, has earned his life. He's off-limits, too. The piebald won't last anyway—he's too easy to see in the woods. A wolf or a bear will get him someday soon if we don't. So I think he's our target."

They set up the shot wordlessly. Jaykriss pulled an arrow from his quiver and sighted the piebald buck over the edge of the boulder. Marda did likewise.

"I'll shoot first," Marda said.

Jaykriss nodded.

The giant stag looked at them then—looked right at them. He was sniffing the air, hyperalert.

"Has the wind shifted?" Jaykriss said.

And then the stag was off, hooves driving, the herd following his lead in an instant.

The piebald buck startled up from the pool and took a few steps, quartering away, but Marda's arrow was true, striking it right between the ribs and dropping it to the forest floor. The rest of the herd had evaporated into the shadows of the deep woods.

"Great shot!" Jaykriss said, lowering his bow.

The piebald struggled back to its feet.

"Finish it, Jay. We can't let it suffer."

Jaykriss let his arrow fly and it was also true to the mark. The young buck crumpled back to the ground.

"What spooked them? Was it us talking?" Jaykriss said.

"Perhaps. That big stag is the reason the herd is so large. He's an old one, and powerful. Probably senses things that other deer cannot."

Jaykriss stood up.

"Let's cross up there, by that stand of river oaks. We can field dress it right there and use some of those branches to make a litter," he said.

Behind them, in the deep woods, there was a cracking sound, like a huge branch breaking, followed by a tremendous crash.

Jaykriss looked at Marda.

"What was that?"

"Tree falling, I think."

Another crash followed—and then a rushing sound, a rumble of something moving through the underbrush.

Something big.

"I don't like this. Let's get across the pool," Marda said.

The shallow water rose to their knees but no more. It was near freezing, but they were not concerned about that now.

Whatever was coming toward them was moving very fast. Branches were snapping and trees were falling, and they could *see* it then, a shadowy bulk thundering through the Brightwood. The forest was collapsing before it. It was at once beautiful and terrible, the largest living thing either of them had ever seen.

"Ye gods," Marda said under his breath as he reached the other side. The piebald stag's body lay lifeless at his feet.

"What is it?" said Jaykriss.

But he knew the answer already, even even before the dire words fell from Marda's lips.

"It's the Thrax."

4

The Thrax erupted into the clearing in a torrent of scales and teeth. Its eyes were blood red, and its cavernous mouth—large enough to swallow a house—was ringed with a thousand white fangs, each as long as Jaykriss's forearm. The creature's obsidian scales gleamed dully in the roiling mist.

"It doesn't see us," Jaykriss whispered.

"Not yet," said Marda.

Each step the Thrax took caused the ground to tremble. Jaykriss did not hear its footsteps as much as he *felt* them. The dragon's feet ended in a collection of razor-sharp claws that it flexed and relaxed as it stood there next to the waterfall, blinking in the sunlight.

The roar of the Thrax reverberated through the Brightwood. It was so loud that it drowned out the sounds of the waterfall. And for a moment after it roared, the twitters and chirps of the forest all fell eerily silent, as if the animals were all afraid to utter any noise at all.

"What do we do?" Jaykriss said.

Marda turned and looked at him. "How do I know?" he said.

The creature took another step forward, sniffing the air.

"Ye gods," Marda said. "It's going to find us."

It was then that Jaykriss saw it.

It was a tiny gleam—the slightest flash of crimson, like a dim star in a moonless sky.

"Marda, look," he said, pointing to the creature.

"What?"

"Look!"

It was barely visible then. The light had to catch it just right. But it was unmistakable; both boys instantly knew what they were looking at. They had seen it for years.

The bejeweled hilt of the Bloodsword was gleaming in the Thrax's left inside shoulder.

"Marda, if you distract it, maybe I can…"

"Are you crazy? Tell me now, Jay, have you gone absolutely *mad?* Because if you have lost your mind, then I shall have to hit you in the head with a rock and drag you home."

"I'm quick, Marda. You know that."

"Not that quick."

"I'm *very* quick."

"You're *thick*, perhaps. I'll concede that point. But that doesn't qualify you to pull a sword from a dragon's breast. It would only qualify you as a dead man. And, ironically, you're not even a man yet!"

"I can avenge my father!"

"You can do no such thing. That creature would snap you up before you came within a boat's length of it."

"But the Bloodsword—"

"Is lost. Forget about it. Let's focus on how we can get out of here *alive*. Perhaps if we escape, you shall live long enough to pluck that blade from between the beast's ribs after it dies of old age."

The Thrax looked right, then left, then lowered its great head to drink from the pool.

"It's drinking! Perhaps we can make a run for it!" Jaykriss said.

"It will not drink forever. If we move, it will find us. We must sit tight. Perhaps it will go away."

But it *did* seem to drink forever. The Thrax drank so much that Jaykriss was amazed any water was left in the pool.

After a few minutes, Marda looked up into the higher reaches of the Mist Valley.

"Maybe if we climbed upward…" he said, leaning on a branch as he looked into the forest.

And then the branch broke.

The Thrax looked up, eyes ablaze.

Its roar was the sound of the tornado, of the swirling vortex of lost hope, of a host of souls condemned to oblivion for all eternity.

It was the sound of certain death.

In a single step, the Thrax was halfway across the pool.

"Run!" Marda said.

Terror seized Jaykriss by the throat and would not let go. His breath caught in his lungs and his chest ached and he dared not look back, certain that the Thrax's needle-sharp teeth would be gnashing right behind him.

And then he had a thought.

"Marda, the waterfall! Run for the waterfall! It's our only hope!"

The boys ran. They ran as their worst nightmare thundered behind them. They ran trying not to think of its claws and fangs, praying that they would be fast enough or fortunate enough to survive another day, another hour, another minute.

This thing killed my father, Jaykriss thought.

He said a prayer in spite of himself.

And then he was at the base of the waterfall.

The cascading water beat him like a war club, nearly knocking him off his feet, but Jaykriss kept going. He had no choice. He would rather drown than face the Thrax.

Suddenly, he was through it. There was a cave behind the waterfall. It was cold and dark, but as dry as a bone. The sheet of water roared in front of him, shielding him from the beast like a vast white curtain.

But Marda did not come through.

"Marda!" he called.

There was no answer.

"MARDA!" he screamed.

The cry of the Thrax was impossibly loud, as though the dragon was lurking right outside the waterfall. It curdled Jaykriss's marrow.

Jaykriss felt his heart sink in his chest. Marda was his best friend. No, he was more than that. He was his brother, flesh of his flesh.

He knew what he had to do.

Steeling himself, Jaykriss plunged back through the ice-cold waterfall.

Marda stood on the other side, shivering uncontrollably. He looked smaller somehow. His hands hung limply at his sides, shriveled and blue-tinted. He was staring at his feet.

And the Thrax was staring right at him, its terrifying jaws agape, not twenty feet away.

"Marda!"

No answer.

"Marda!"

The other boy gave Jaykriss a sidelong glance.

"Listen, the waterfall confuses the creature. There's a cave on the other side. Once we step through that, it cannot see us, hear us, or smell us. As far as the Thrax is concerned, we're *gone* once we step through the waterfall. You follow me?"

Marda nodded.

"Take my hand."

Marda did as he was told.

"Let's go," Jaykriss said.

They crossed the veil of the waterfall, baptized by the frigid water as they entered the cave, and then they waited, shivering, in the half-light of the cave.

Nothing happened.

They waited still.

Then like an avalanche, they felt the deep rumble of movement on the other side.

"It's leaving!" Marda said.

"Shhh."

A few minutes later, they heard the Thrax's unmistakable roar in the distance.

Both boys exhaled sighs of relief.

Marda knelt in front of Jaykriss.

"You saved my life, Jay, just as your father saved my father's. I am forever in your debt."

"Don't be ridiculous, Marda. Anyway, you saved me from the pig boy earlier."

"I would not put Honshul and the Thrax on the same level."

"Look, we're even. You'd have done the same for me. Now get up. You look like you're proposing or something."

Marda stood.

"I will not forget this, Jay. My father always said he could never repay Glyndich enough for saving his life."

Jaykriss clapped his old friend across the back. "Marda?"

"Yes?"

"Shut up. Please."

"OK, but let me ask you one last thing. How did you know about the waterfall confusing the Thrax? Is that something your father told you?"

"Nope. I made that up."

"You *what*?"

"You wouldn't come with me, so I had to think of something to get you to go with me. That explanation sounded logical, so I said it. And who knows? Maybe it *is* true. The Thrax left, didn't it?"

Marda punched Jaykriss in the arm.

"Ow! What happened to your everlasting debt of gratitude?"

"It's temporarily suspended."

Jaykriss sat down on the floor of the cave and unlaced his leggings. He pulled his boots off and emptied the water from them. "OK, indebted one, you tell *me* something. Why didn't you want to go through the waterfall?"

Marda looked sheepishly at the ground. "My father used to say that there were ghozim in here. He told me that the waterfall was the gateway to the Otherworld."

"My father said the same thing. But the way I figured it, if I was going to the Otherworld anyway, I'd rather go on my own than be sent there in pieces by the Thrax," said Jaykriss.

Jaykriss laced his leggings back up and stood facing the waterfall once more.

Suddenly, he felt a deep chill curling around him.

"So what have we here? A couple of fugitives, perhaps?" said a man's voice behind them.

Jaykriss and Marda both whirled around.

But there was nothing behind them but darkness.

5

"Who's there?" Jaykriss said.

His only answer was the thunderous roar of the waterfall behind him.

"*Ghozim*," Marda whispered.

"I wish we had a torch," Jaykriss muttered.

Marda reached behind his back, pulled off his quiver, and plunged his arm into its depths.

"Don't tell me you have a torch," Jaykriss said.

Marda shook his head.

"Something better."

What he pulled out was something wrapped in greasy paper and tied with a string.

"Is that dragonfire?"

Marda nodded.

"It was my father's. I found it in among his weapons. He showed me how to use it once, years ago. He used to carry it in his quiver just in case he needed it. I put it in mine after he made his journey to the Otherworld. I almost forgot it was there—at least until you said the thing about the torch."

"You won't need that," the voice said.

There was a flicker of light, and the cave was filled with the acrid scent of sulfur.

Jaykriss was momentarily blinded as a torch was lit. All he could see was light and smoke and a single gnarled hand as it placed the torch in an iron bracket bolted into the wall of the cave.

As his eyes adjusted, Jaykriss could see a bearded old man standing before them in the small, shallow cave. His hair was a wild tangle of gray; his eyes were a piercing aquamarine, magnified by a pair of wire-rimmed spectacles that had drifted down to the end of his beaklike nose. His dress was odd—sandals, a pair of loosely fitted dark knickers, a top that looked like a rectangle of sailcloth with a hole cut in the middle, and an iridescent silvery cloak loosely draped about his thin shoulders. A large, coal-black raven was perched on one shoulder.

"You're a man," Marda murmured.

"Last I checked," the old man said with a chuckle.

"He thought this place was filled with ghozim," Jaykriss said.

"A convenient legend. It helps to keep out the riffraff."

The old man extended a bony hand.

"Zamarcus," he said.

Jaykriss reluctantly accepted the old man's grip. His palm and fingers were soft and withered, like a piece of old fruit.

"I'm Jaykriss. And this is Marda," he said, tipping his head in Marda's direction.

Marda stared at Zamarcus and then looked around the cave before returning his gaze to the old man. He did not take his hand.

"What are those things on your nose?" he asked.

"Spectacles. To help me see better."

"Are you blind?" asked Jaykriss.

"I've been accused of that before, but no. In fact, with these spectacles, I can see as well as either of you."

"How is it that you came to be here? We did not see you go in. There is no obvious place for you to come from in here. So do you live in here? Did you sneak past us while we fought the Thrax?" asked Marda.

"You fought the Thrax? Today?"

The boys nodded.

"And yet you live."

They nodded again.

Zamarcus clapped his palms together three times, grinning. The raven flapped its wings.

"Well, now, this *is* a cause for celebration. To see the Thrax and live to tell the tale—it's a rarity, for certain. Tell me—did someone tell you about the waterfall?"

Jaykriss furrowed his brow. "Tell us what?"

"The waterfall flummoxes the Thrax. It cannot see past it. I think it is all of the noise and the water—it just renders it insensate."

"Insensate?" said Jaykriss.

"It cannot sense you in any fashion. That's why the entrance to my home is here. When I walk through that water, the creature will not follow."

Marda looked at Jaykriss. "So you *did* know," he said.

"I guessed and got lucky. That's all," said Jaykriss.

"A fortunate guess, lad. Generally, one does not encounter a vermithrax that large and survive very long. They can be ill-tempered beasts."

"Vermithrax?" said Jaykriss.

"That's the species. A type of dragon. There used to be more dragons, of all types. Some even had wings, like bats. But the vermithrax is earthbound. And they are dying out, I fear. You see, it takes a lot to feed a vermithrax—and they won't eat plants. Just meat. Thousands of pounds of it a week, in fact. Paradoxically, they are the victims of their own predatory success. There used to be great herds of elk and deer, and even larger things. I've heard some of the herds were so vast that they could fill the entire Brightwood, and that the great plains had herds that stretched as far as the eye can see. But the vermithraxes wiped them all out. Now, the herds are all smaller—and far more cunning. The stupid animals died out early on. Only the vigilant, intelligent animals survived."

He clicked his tongue against his teeth.

"I personally think that's why the Thrax is so ill-tempered. It is always hungry. Of course, it's been worse in the last year or two. Not sure why that is. The thing even killed a most powerful war chief from the Godswood last season, a fine man named Glyndich."

Zamarcus shook his head. "A good man, that Glyndich. I do miss him."

Jaykriss cleared his throat but hesitated, kicking instead at the dirt of the cave floor.

"What is it, boy? You look troubled."

Jaykriss looked up. "Glyndich was my father," he said at last. His voice was low—almost a whisper.

Zamarcus drew closer, adjusting his spectacles. He took Jaykriss's chin in his hand.

"I can see the resemblance. You have his eyes, and the cut of his jaw. Of course, he was...larger."

"Indeed. I am but fourteen. My father was a man."

Zamarcus chuckled.

"That he was, Jaykriss. That he most assuredly was."

The old man shot a glance at Marda.

"So you wouldn't be Marda, the son of Garoth, would you? Garoth was always with Glyndich. Those two were inseparable—twin sons of different mothers. And you resemble Garoth as a youth—you have the same glint in your eye and the same bold swagger."

"That would be me," Marda said.

"Your father was also a powerful warrior—but with a kind heart. I hope you try to mirror him."

"Every day."

"Good lad. Your father is a fine template for you to follow. And I've heard of you—particularly about your marksmanship. You have a reputation for being quite a good shot with an arrow."

Marda blushed. "I'm OK," he said.

Zamarcus grinned. The flickering torchlight made his face appear lined and drawn; his eyes were set deeply in his skull and glittered behind his eyeglasses.

"Well, I feel I should invite you into my home. Please excuse the mess. I was not expecting visitors."

Jaykriss looked around. "What mess? There's nothing here. It's just a cave."

Zamarcus smiled. "That's where you are wrong. It is *not* just a cave." He turned the iron-torch mount sideways. A huge boulder slid to one side, exposing a long, torch-lit passageway. "Welcome to my home," Zamarcus said, extending an arm into the doorway.

I guess I've got no choice but to go inside, thought Jaykriss.

But he was just a little uneasy.

6

The passageway to Zamarcus's home was long and circuitous, carved deep into the solid rock face of the sheer cliff that the waterfall leapt over.

"What is the bird's name?" Jaykriss said.

"Archimedes," said the bird.

"He can *talk*?"

"Evidently," said Zamarcus.

"How did you come by a talking bird?"

"I found him. He's quite bright—but a bit full of himself."

The bird pecked once at Zamarcus's ear.

"Ow! Enough of that, mind you, or I'll put you in the cage," the old man said.

"Did you do this?" Marda said, trailing his fingers along the rough-hewn walls.

"The passageway? Heavens, no. This was here long before I was ever born. My father found it one day when he was just a little older than you are now— just wandering about in the Mist Valley. He was curious about what was behind the waterfall. I don't know what really made him look behind it—he never made that clear to me. The waterfall used to be much bigger than it is now. I can remember walking up here as a child and being nearly knocked down by the falling water. But despite all of that, my father got through the waterfall, saw the old rusted torch mount on the wall there, and when he turned it…"

The passage opened up into a cavernous room with forty-foot ceilings. Four large skylights allowed light to stream in from above. The room had shelf after shelf, balcony upon balcony, with walkways and stairs allowing access to every level. A mammoth fireplace was built into the stone along one wall; blue and yellow flames licked at a jumble of logs in its gaping maw. Stacks of books were everywhere. A collection of maps littered a heavy oak table in the center, a table that looked as broad and as solid as the deck of a sailing ship. Myriad mechanical devices were stacked on shelves, crammed into nooks and crannies, and piled into wooden boxes.

When they entered the room, Archimedes flapped over to a marble bust in one corner and took up residence.

"Home!" the raven quorked.

The boys craned their necks as they gazed about the cavernous room.

Most of the devices were things Jaykriss had never seen.

"What is all of this?" Marda asked.

"A lot of this stuff was here when I got here. The books and maps mostly came from my father, and some of them belonged to my father's father before him. I've studied the machines that were here and read about them in books, and a number of these things are either machines I've made or things I have acquired, through one means or another, over a long and curiosity-driven lifetime."

"My father had a book on weaponry," Jaykriss said. "It's very old."

"They are quite rare nowadays. And most of them *are* old. Not many people make books anymore," Zamarcus said.

"You must have…thousands," said Marda, his neck craning upward.

Zamarcus nodded, glancing about. "Yes, I do," he said.

Jaykriss picked up a metal implement that looked like a hinged metal V with a small set of lenses on it.

"What's this?" he asked.

"A sextant. It's used to measure the distance between any two visible objects."

"What about this?" Marda said. He was holding something that appeared to be a bow, but with a trigger, a handle, and a large spring underneath.

"That's a repeater crossbow. It fires little arrows called bolts. In fact, it can fire them in pretty rapid succession, once you get the hang of it. The spring on the bottom reloads the firing mechanism between shots."

Jaykriss felt as though he could not catch his breath. "There's so much here that I have never seen! Why does no one know about this stuff?" he said.

"It's contraband. The Dark King has outlawed almost all of it. If the centurions ever found out I had these things, they would probably drag me off to the Kingsguard or Ezahar and imprison me for life. Or worse."

"Worse?"

Zamarcus nodded.

"They might kill me. Or torture me, and *then* kill me, and burn my body into ash, and scatter my ashes to the four winds. Then they would pronounce me a traitor and say that I have met the Dark King's justice. The centurions like to do that sort of thing. Very much into symbolic gestures."

Jaykriss gasped. "The Dark King is our protector. He is the living embodiment of the gods. He has cared for us all for hundreds and maybe thousands of seasons, since the time before time. His centurions watch over us. And the only people the centurions imprison are criminals."

"Like the Geshans," Marda said, sighting the crossbow on the glassy-eyed head of some unfamiliar, horned, bovine creature that was mounted on the wall.

"Exactly! Like the Geshans," Jaykriss said.

Zamarcus smiled, thin-lipped. His bushy white eyebrows arched. "Is that what they taught you in school?"

Marda and Jaykriss nodded in unison.

Zamarcus picked up the sextant and stared at it, turning it over in his hands several times before looking up.

His clear blue eyes were ablaze. "The centurions killed my father," Zamarcus said. "They dragged him from our home when I was sixteen, breaking my mother's arm in the process as she pleaded with them to spare him. I never saw him again."

"Was your father a criminal?" asked Jaykriss.

"In their eyes."

"What was his crime, then?" asked Marda.

"He knew too much. And he had a map. He actually had a lot of maps. But one map he had was a particular problem for them."

"What map? One of these?"

Zamarcus shook his head.

"The map they accused him of having was a map that revealed places like this one. Secret places filled with ancient knowledge, places that the rebels hid things in after the rise of the Dark King. That knowledge is dangerous to them. The centurions thrive on ignorance and superstition. Men who know too much are a threat."

"Did they get the map from your father?" Jaykriss asked.

Zamarcus shook his head.

"He destroyed it before they got there."

"So why did they take him?"

"To torture him. They thought he might tell them about the map and about other things he knew of. But my father was a proud man, and firm in his convictions about right and wrong. He told them nothing. A few weeks after they took him, a centurion showed up at our door with a jar containing my father's teeth, another jar containing one of his fingers, and these spectacles."

Zamarcus tapped his eyeglasses.

"The centurion gave us those things as a warning. He said my father was dead. He also told us if we knew the whereabouts of any maps that we had better turn them over, or else we would suffer the same fate as my father. And then a few weeks after that, they came back and took my mother. I never saw her again."

"I'm sorry," said Jaykriss. "I never heard of centurions doing such a thing."

"Of course you didn't. Because they did not want you to."

Marda looked up from the crossbow. "It's a shame the map was lost," he said. "If this place is any indication, there is so much we could learn from the places on that map."

"That's what they were afraid of. But it wasn't lost," said Zamarcus.

"You said your father destroyed it."

"He did."

"Well, I'm confused. Was there another copy?"

Zamarcus smiled. His eyes danced behind his spectacles.

"Can you keep a secret?" he said.

The boys nodded.

"Come with me, then."

They walked down a well-lit stone corridor that led away from Zamarcus's living space.

"How is this illuminated? Aren't we way underground?" Jaykriss said.

Zamarcus said nothing.

There was a gargantuan metal door at the end of the corridor. It hung on a set of oily, ancient-looking iron hinges that were bolted into the stone walls. A low-pitched thrumming came from behind the door. Jaykriss could feel it in his chest.

Zamarcus opened the door, which groaned deeply. Once the door was open, he reached inside and pushed a button on the wall.

Lights flickered on overhead, illuminating a cavernous room that dwarfed the space Zamarcus lived in. The walls and the ceiling were covered in a yellowed ceramic tile that had buckled and cracked; plants bearded the breaches in the ceiling, hanging down in pendulous stalactites of moist vegetation. On one wall, there was a large map of a dark green continent dotted with glowing red lights, like the embers of a dying fire. Intersecting lines of light crisscrossed between the embers.

Zamarcus extended his hand toward the wall.

"The map," he said.

"Ye gods," whispered Marda.

"Is one of those red lights this place?" asked Jaykriss.

Zamarcus nodded.

"It's that one. By the sea," he said, pointing.

"And where is the Godswood?"

"Right next to it. So close that it is not even marked."

"So what is *that*?" Marda asked, pointing to a star higher on the coast, surrounded by white lights.

"That is Capitus, where the Dark King lives, the largest city in the known world."

"We learned about Capitus in school, but no one ever said how large it is," Jaykriss said. "We always heard about the Great Hall, and the King's Obelisk, but never about the people. How many people live in Capitus? Thousands?"

"Millions," said Zamarcus.

"Millions!" Marda said, his eyes wide open.

Zamarcus nodded.

"Then the world is…huge."

"It is far larger than you could even imagine," said Zamarcus, stroking his beard.

The room also contained three oblong metal cylinders. They were mammoth; each one was larger than the war chief's bain in the Godswood. The cylinders pulsated; a whooshing sound, like water rushing down a stream, seemed to emanate from them, filling the room.

"This is my father's life's work. He found these here and got them working again, eventually," Zamarcus said.

"How old are they?" said Marda.

"Hundreds of years, at least. Older than the Dark King."

"But *what* are they?" Jaykriss said.

"Ah, that is, indeed, the salient question. What, indeed? You see, boys, this is no ordinary waterfall. This is a waterfall that men who lived long before us used to do a great many wonderful things—things that some people would call magic. And these cylinders are the core of that magic. They are what bring light down here. They power many of the devices that I showed you earlier in my home. And it is this sort of power that the centurions fear. *This* is why my father was hauled away and killed. The Dark King's strength lies in keeping his subjects ignorant, making them dependent upon him for power and sustenance. But my father found a way to return power to the people. By restoring these devices, and by getting them running again, he unleashed a force that even the Dark King could not contain: the capacity for understanding, for shedding light on the world."

"Was your father a wizard?" Marda asked.

"No," said Zamarcus. He paused for a moment, wiping a tear from his left eye. "No, my father was a scientist."

7

Jaykriss felt dizzy, delirious, as though he had a fever that burned through all he had thought was real and left it a smoldering pile of ash.

Torture? Murder? The Dark King?

"You make the Dark King sound like a tyrant, or at the very least some kind of charlatan."

"I am only reporting what I know to be true. The conclusions you draw from it are your own."

Jaykriss couldn't breathe; his chest was tight, his heart pounding stuttering hoofbeats within his chest. His whole world had been turned upside down. The thought came to him suddenly, like he'd been hit in the head with a shovel. *The old man's crazy. That's it.*

He began to look for a way out of the room. *Any* way out, in fact. In fact, he would almost rather face the Thrax again than be buried here with Zamarcus and his collection of illicit books, papers, and machines.

The centurions were probably just trying to protect the rest of us from people like Zamarcus and his father.

That thought settled him somewhat, calming the queasiness that had been brewing in his belly. But something nagged at him still, something his father had said to him long ago.

"Stay away from the centurions," Glyndich had said. "Don't cross them under any circumstances. They are outside my authority. If they decide they have a problem with you, I will not be able to help you. And if that happens, I might never see you again."

That recollection hit Jaykriss in the gut.

Papa knew.

Zamarcus was cleaning his glasses, bushy eyebrows raised, his hair a wispy delirium of white and gray, like an irregular halo around his head.

"What are those things called?" Marda asked, pointing at the cylinders.

"Hydroelectric turbines. They take the power of the water rushing through here and convert it into electric energy. Electricity powers all of the lights here. It keeps things warm in winter and cool in summer."

"You are truly are a great wizard, Zamarcus! I have never seen magic such as this!" Marda said.

"It's not wizardry. That's just what people say when they don't understand something. It's science."

"Did the gods build this?" asked Jaykriss.

"No, Jaykriss, men built this. *All* of it. It's called a hydroelectric power plant."

Jaykriss felt another wave of dizziness sweep over him. *Impossible,* he thought. "Men? Like us? But how? How could they put all of this inside the rock?"

Zamarcus chuckled.

"Jaykriss, they *built* the rock. It's a manmade structure called a dam. The dam blocks off the river, creating the lake above it, and then they use the energy from the falling water to generate power with these turbines."

Jaykriss thought for a moment, his chin in his hand, staring at the turbines as they thrummed away. He thought of his father, a powerful man beaten by an even more powerful creature. He had always known that he would never be as strong as his father, never the sort of warrior who could best anyone with brute strength. And the Thrax had shown that brute strength—even the strength of a powerful man like Glyndich—could only go so far.

I could not even best the Geshan. Marda had to help me.

But the things Zamarcus had shown him represented a different sort of power—the power of the mind.

And Jaykriss knew that he could do some good with it.

It was what his father would have wanted.

"Is this the sort of knowledge that is in those books you have?" Jaykriss asked.

Zamarcus nodded. "The books taught my father how to repair the turbines. They can teach a great many things—and not just the basic things you learn in the classroom at school, like math and writing and symbols and weaponry. These books contain ancient things that have been lost to most of mankind for centuries."

Something had turned over in Jaykriss's mind. It was almost palpable, like a fish flopping on dry land.

"If this is what you can learn from books, then I want to learn about it," Jaykriss said.

"The dam? The turbines? What is it that you want to learn?"

"All of it. I want to learn it all."

The world had settled into its new orbit, its spin oriented around a new axis. The vertigo had ceased. *The gods led me here,* Jaykriss thought. He stared at the great map on the wall, its lights winking like so many burning embers.

This is my destiny.

8

Marda and Jaykriss plunged back through the waterfall after bidding Zamarcus goodbye, emerging into the warm rays of the late afternoon sun. The piebald stag the boys had shot was miraculously still there, untouched, beside the pool of water at the base of the waterfall.

"The gods have been good to us this day," Marda said. He tightened the strap on his new crossbow—a gift from Zamarcus—before kneeling to examine the majestic animal. "It's a fine kill—our biggest buck in a long while," Marda said.

Jaykriss saw something in the water just then, glimmering in the shallows.

"Hold on," he said, stepping over a tumble of moss-slick rocks.

An oblong, triangular shell, the color of obsidian, caught the waning rays of the day's sunlight on its edge. It was as big as a man's palm.

Jaykriss picked it up and turned it over in his hands, his eyes widening.

The back of the shell was studded with dozens of tiny, razor-sharp thorns. The thorns had an iridescent sheen; they caught the sunlight from the spray of the waterfall and reflected it into a spectrum of dark color.

This is no shell, he thought. "Marda?"

"Yes?" The older boy was unsheathing his hunting knife.

"I think that this is a scale from the Thrax."

Marda looked up, his mouth open. "Are you sure?"

"Look here," Jaykriss said, holding it up into the sunlight.

The scale was translucent, dark, and hard as stone. Jaykriss held it up, and he could see the disk of the summer sun burning through it like a cyclopean eye, unblinking.

"I think you are right. My father once said that a shield made of Thrax scales would make one invincible," Marda said.

"Had he seen a Thrax-scale shield?"

Marda snorted. "It's the stuff of legend, Jay. Most people have not even seen a single Thrax scale, let alone a full shield made of them. You might as well ask if I had seen a flying man, or done battle with the Green Ghozim of Godswood. They're just stories, that's all."

Jaykriss looked at the scale once more, then slid it carefully into a pocket in his quiver.

The two boys fashioned a litter from a pair of saplings and tied the buck to it. Then they hoisted the litter onto their shoulders for transport back to the Godswood.

"This sort of load always seems lighter when we're on the way home," Jaykriss said, smiling.

And, deep down inside, he knew the load was slighter because the entire world had suddenly become a whole lot more interesting.

The sun was burning its way into the horizon as the boys made their way back through the birch forests of the Brightwood and along the zigzag trails of the Mist Valley. The shadows were longer, coalescing into pools of shade, and the myriad chirps and squawks of the forest were more subdued than they had been that morning.

The ascent out of the valley was not easy. The big buck was a ponderous load, and the trail was studded with rocks and roots. Sweat ran down Jaykriss's forehead and stung his eyes. His lips were as dry as sand. His shoulders ached.

Marda remained silent, his broad shoulders bearing the heavy litter as though it were a feather, eyes fixed straight ahead on the path before him.

The boys startled a dole of doves as they rounded a corner. The birds burst into the air and flapped away noisily, startling Marda and awakening him from his reverie.

"Have you seen Sola lately?" Marda said.

"Only at school. Her father has her working in the bakery when she is not studying."

"She likes you, you know."

Jaykriss stopped walking and twisted his neck to look at Marda behind him.

"What makes you say that? We're just friends," he said.

They had reached the clearing at the spot of the carvings, where the trail leveled out. Marda wiped his brow with his forearm.

"Let's rest a moment. I have a flask of water," he said.

They lowered the litter carefully to the ground and sat down on a patch of grass beside the trail. Marda pulled a flat, greenglass bottle from the side pocket of his quiver and offered it to Jaykriss.

"Thanks," Jaykriss said, pulling out the cork.

He let the water trickle down his throat, savoring its cool essence, then handed the flask back to Marda.

"You don't fool me, Jay. I see the way you look at Sola. I see you staring at her when she walks by, and the way you try to do it so that she cannot see you doing it."

Jaykriss blushed. "I do think she's beautiful," he said. "But she's a full summer older than I am."

"She looks at you, too, you know. When she does not think you are looking."

"Liar!" Jaykriss said, punching Marda in the shoulder.

"Ow! Why are you punching me? I'm serious!"

"You're teasing me."

"I'm not. She *likes* you."

"And how do you know this for certain? Has she told you?"

Marda took another swig of water and shook his head as he swallowed. "She doesn't have to," he said. "I can tell these things." Marda grinned and tapped an index finger to his forehead.

Jaykriss thought of Sola, allowing himself that indulgence for a moment. She *was* small and slim, but beautiful, with huge almond-shaped eyes, dark brown hair that she wore in the modest, braided style favored by the more studious girls, and full, soft lips. She was also the best athlete among all of the young women in the Godswood. She was the only person who came close to Marda in archery, and she could run faster than almost any man. Moreover, she was fearless. By the gods, she was *fearless*.

Jaykriss smiled. "Remember the time she killed the snake?" he said.

Marda nodded.

A huge viper had ventured into Sola's father's bakery once. Jaykriss and his father were at the village well drawing water when they heard some women screaming. Glyndich dropped the bucket back into the well and slid the gleaming Bloodsword from its sheath.

"Stay here," Glyndich had said, but Jaykriss followed him anyway.

By the time they reached the bakery, the screams had gone silent. The silence was unnerving.

The viper's massive red-on-black tail trailed down the steps of the bakery and out into the street. Its scaly body was as thick as Marda's leg.

"*Zharga*," Glyndich had whispered to himself.

Zhargas were spit vipers, capable of blinding a man at forty feet, their fangs like twin icicles. Their viscid green venom was so lethal that anyone bitten by one usually died within the hour. The victims' bodies were rarely found, however, for zhargas had a peculiar taste for human flesh. They would disarticulate their fang-studded jaws and swallow their victims whole, days later vomiting up huge piles of bones, teeth, and hair.

Jaykriss hated zhargas.

He hated them so much that *this* time, when Glyndich told Jaykriss to stay put, he did so.

Glyndich had stepped gingerly over the snake's body as he entered the bakery. He hefted the Bloodsword over his head, waving it in slow circles.

And then he was gone, vanishing into the darkness.

The laughter was unexpected. Jaykriss wondered for a brief moment if the spit of a zharga could cause insanity.

He figured it probably could.

Then Glyndich, Sola, and Hopa, Sola's younger sister, came through the door. Glyndich had his hand on Sola's shoulder. The Bloodsword was sheathed.

And Sola was carrying the severed head of the zharga—a head as large as her own, its cruel fangs dripping with venom—on a wooden bakery plata.

"Did you kill it, Papa?" Jaykriss had asked.

Glyndich shook his head, laughing out loud.

"*She* did," he said, jerking a thumb at Sola.

Sola shrugged. "There was no other choice," she said, and she proceeded to tell them about what had transpired.

Hopa saw it first. The creature had slithered into the bakery, and then raised its ugly head high, peering over the counter at them, its red eyes wide. The little girl gasped. Sola looked—and immediately grabbed the hatchet they used to chop wood for the bakery kiln.

"Stand behind me, Hopa. And close your eyes," Sola said.

Hopa closed them tight.

The snake lunged then, jaws wide, flinging its body across the marble countertop. It was quick, a strike that would have been lethal to most girls.

But Sola was not like most girls.

Pushing Hopa to the floor behind her with her left hand, Sola swung the hatchet with her right.

The viper never had a chance.

Sola severed the snake's head cleanly with a single blow, driving the hatchet blade through its bony spine and deep into the countertop. The snake's decapitated body, spewing crimson arcs across the walls and ceiling, flopped onto the floor and writhed there for a full minute, as though it were seeking to fathom what had happened. Meanwhile, the viper's horrific jaws flexed once or twice, its ruby eyes wide with surprise, before closing for good.

And that was it.

As Jaykriss heard the girl tell her story that day, he realized that he was smitten with her. Not just for her beauty, which was exceptional, but for her toughness as well.

He had loved her ever since.

"She's got the nerves of a war-games champion. That snake would have kicked our butts, Jay," Marda said, placing the flask back in his quiver and hoisting his end of the litter.

"It would have *eaten* our butts, in all likelihood," Jaykriss said.

Marda just smiled and shook his head, picking up his end of the litter and placing it upon his shoulders.

Both of them knew that Jaykriss was right.

As the boys neared the Godswood village, Jaykriss noted something odd. "You hear that?" he said.

"What? I don't hear anything."

"Precisely."

The forest had gone deathly quiet. The silence was thick, as though it was waiting for something.

"You don't think that the Thrax followed us, do you?" Marda said.

"No, It's long gone. I…"

And there it was—the snap of a twig, echoing through the Godswood like the crack of a whip.

Jaykriss and Marda dropped the litter. The stag thudded heavily to the earth, its head lolling backward, eyes white and unseeing.

"Show yourself!" Marda barked, drawing a bead on an unseen foe with his crossbow.

Jaykriss pulled an arrow from his quiver and notched it, his fingers on the bowstring.

"So, girls—back from your picnic?" a voice said.

Honshul!

"We've played this game already today, pig boy. You know how it ends," said Marda.

The Geshan stepped from behind a tree. He was carrying a club.

"It ends differently this time," Honshul said.

He whistled loudly—a shrill, piercing sound that sounded almost like a scream.

His whistle was answered by several more like it, coming from all sides. Jaykriss looked around. At least a dozen Geshans emerged from behind trees and rocks. Some carried clubs; others had short swords. Jaykriss thought he recognized a few of them from times when his father had brought them into the village keep. There was one in particular—a big one, even uglier than Honshul, with a missing left ear and an eye patch—that he knew was Honshul's older brother, a brute named Hammack. Hammack was wearing a short leather cap of the type favored by prisoners. He had a pair of rude-looking tusks protruding from his mouth, a feature typical of the older male Geshans. Those things gave most Geshans the foulest breath imaginable—but they were also a dangerous weapon in close combat. Geshans sometimes used their tusks to gouge out the eyes of opponents during fights, and there were legends that blood-crazed Geshan warriors would disembowel enemy combatants with their tusks, jamming their heads directly into their opponents' bellies and twisting their tusks until their victims' guts fell out.

Hammack's tusks were the longest Jaykriss had ever seen.

I thought the centurions took Hammack away for murder, Jaykriss thought.

"Brought my brothers with me, girls. Not so tough when you're outnumbered, are you, Marda?"

"Looks like they brought us dinner, Honshul," Hammack said. His voice was coarse and guttural, like gravel rattling in a can.

Honshul spat on the ground. "It's probably spoiled," he said.

"Leave us be, Honshul. You don't want this," said Marda.

"What—going to send your fathers after me? Oh, that's right—they're both *dead*."

Marda's eyes narrowed. "Last warning," he said. "Stand aside."

The Geshans were now all in plain sight, encircling the two boys. Their circle was tightening. They were less than thirty paces away.

"Back to back," whispered Marda. "On my mark."

Jaykriss drew a bead on Honshul and pulled his bowstring back.

"You can't shoot all of us," Honshul said. He was slapping the club into a filthy clawed hand.

"Watch me," Marda said.

Hammack let out a bellowing war whoop and charged forward like a crazed water buffalo, a knobbed club held high over his misshapen head.

"Now!" said Marda.

A flurry of arrows and bolts flew into the air. Honshul was struck three times, once in each thigh and once in his right bicep. He hit the forest floor hard, squealing in agony. The other Geshans toppled upon one another as the hail of projectiles struck them.

At the end, only Hammack still stood. Two arrows protruded from his left thigh; a crossbow bolt was jammed into his right shoulder.

The giant Geshan's one good eye was bloodshot. There was a crazed glint in his eye, like that of a rabid dog. Bubbles of spit dripped from his yellowed tusks.

"You don't scare me with your toys. Come fight me hand to hand, like real men!"

He pushed the two arrows through his leg and snapped their shafts, then pulled the bolt from his shoulder. Blood spurted from the wound.

"That's a fool's challenge, Hammack. And we're not fools," Jaykriss said.

"Kill them, Hammack!" Honshul screamed.

The giant took another step toward them. He was a mere ten paces away. Jaykriss could smell the rot of him. He could even taste the murderer's hot, foul breath on his tongue.

"No closer," Marda said.

"I'm not afraid of you," Hammack said, taking another step.

"Kill them! *Kill them!*" Honshul screamed again, his voice breaking.

It happened so fast that it almost seemed like nobody moved—as though the world stood still, the sun freezing in the sky like in the legend of the Battle of Arash-te. The brute moved, bolts flew, knives flashed—and in the end, there was blood.

Lots of blood.

"I'm blind!" Hammack screamed. "You've blinded me!"

"You'll get better, you big lummock. It's just a flesh wound," Marda said. He shouldered his crossbow.

Marda had shot a bolt into the soft flesh just over the Geshan's lone remaining eye, cleanly taking off his hat and ripping a deep gash into Hammack's furrowed scalp. The blood flowing into his eye had temporarily blinded him. Marda then took his time, aimed carefully, and fired two more bolts, one apiece into each of his knee joints, severing the patellar tendons bilaterally and dropping Hammack to his knees.

And now Marda stood behind the Geshan with his short sword at Hammack's broad throat.

"I should cut your fat head off for that," Marda said.

"Go ahead. I'm not afraid to die."

Marda thought for a moment, then sheathed the short sword.

"You're not worth it, pig boy. None of you are. You're just a passel of petty thieves. You're ugly *and* stupid—and that's a bad combination."

"Shut up!" said Honshul. He was crying.

Marda hoisted the litter at the rear of the stag.

"Have fun getting home, idiots. And by the way, the Thrax is out and about. We've seen it this afternoon. Hope you make it in before nightfall," Marda said.

The boys left the Geshans moaning in the woods.

By the time they reached the village, the stars were coming out. The boys hung the stag on the dressing rack in back of the war chief's bain and washed up, then went inside.

Annya and Samaria were sitting by the fireplace. Another man sat beside them—a smallish man, bald except for a thin rim of gray hair, standing behind them in black priest's robes. A gold chain was draped around his waist. His nose was hooked like a vulture's; his tiny eyes, like a pair of silver coins, glittered deep in their sockets. Jaykriss recognized the old priest from various weddings, funerals and other ceremonies in the Godswood, although he had never spoken to him directly.

High Priest Harros, he thought. *But why is he here?*

"You're back!" Annya said, running to hug her brother.

"Safe hunting, like I promised," Jaykriss said, smiling. He picked her up, swung her up into the air, and kissed her on the cheek before setting her down. He then glanced at his mother and High Priest Harros. They were both standing now, side by side.

"Thank the gods," Samaria said. "We feared some ill had befallen you."

"Thank the gods, indeed," the priest said.

The old man extended a withered, bony hand.

"I am Harros, the Keeper of the Gate and High Priest of the Godswood. It is a pleasure to meet you, young man. Your father and I worked together a great deal."

Jaykriss dropped to one knee and took the old man's hand in his own.

"It is an honor to make your acquaintance, High Priest Harros," he said.

The old man's eyes gleamed.

"You may rise, young man. There is no need to stand on ceremony here. This is a social visit. Your father and I knew each other very well. I am merely here to check on your mother."

Samaria smiled, tight-lipped.

"High Priest Harros is most gracious," she said, crossing one knee against the other and bowing her head.

Marda glared at the Harros, his jaw set tight.

"Isn't it a bit late to be visiting, High Priest Harros? Surely there are more needy people in the Godswood than Lord Mother Samaria."

The old priest glanced at Marda, his eyes narrowed, on eyebrow raised.

"Well," he said. "I suppose you're right."

Harros picked up a wooden staff and glided over toward the door.

Marda, who stood by the doorway, opened it for him. For a brief moment, the two of them locked eyes. The boy drew himself up so that he towered over the old man.

Harros worked his jaws vigorously, like a cow chewing its cud, never taking his eyes off Marda He then spat a bloody wad of phlegm into his handkerchief, folded it up neatly, and placed it someplace inside the folds of his robe.

Turning towards Marda, Harros squinted up at him, his head cocked to one side. A row of tiny pearl-like teeth gleamed deep inside his mouth.

"Marda, isn't it? Son of Garoth?"

Marda nodded, but said nothing.

Harros stared at him for a moment, as if he were searching for something.

"You are, indeed, your father's son," he said at last, shaking his head.

And then Harros vanished into the night, leaving Marda and Jaykriss alone with Annya and Samaria.

"Why was he here?" Marda asked. "It's an odd hour to have a priest out making social calls. Especially the High Priest himself."

"He had some things to discuss with me. A proposal of sorts. I told him I'd think about it. But it's no large matter."

"I don't like him. He's a shriveled up old meddler who is always poking around in everyone else's business. My father used to call him 'The Worm.' The term serves him well."

"He's a *powerful* old worm, Marda. One would do well not to cross him." Samaria said.

"My father wasn't afraid of him," Marda said.

"Perhaps he should have been," said Samaria.

"Mother!" said Jaykriss.

Samaria looked at Jaykriss. He could see the dark cloud of worry in her eyes.

"The Godswood Priests are like vipers, Jaykriss. They are sneaky, always hiding in dark places—and they are deadly. One does not cross them. *Especially* not High Priest Harros."

"Well, I'm glad the old man is gone. He smells bad and he's ugly," said Annya.

Jaykriss and Mada both started laughing.

"Come here, Annie Bell," Jaykriss said, sitting down.

Annya jumped into his lap and threw her arms around him.

"Tell us about your hunt!"

"Stars! With the High Priest here, I almost forgot!"

He turned to his mother, grinning.

"Mama, we shot a deer. A big one, fourteen-pointer. We'll need some help dressing it," said Jaykriss.

"Don't forget the quail. We bagged twelve quail this morning," said Marda.

Jaykriss shot him a glance, shaking his head. "I had *completely* forgotten about the quail," he said. "That seems like it was a long time ago."

"Did you forget about the Geshans?" Marda said.

"Geshans! Good heavens, boys. What sort of day was this?"

Jaykriss smiled.

"A long one," he said.

Samaria turned to Marda, placing her hands on his broad shoulders.

"Marda, it has indeed been a long day, and it is late. You must stay with us tonight. It is too late an hour for you to travel back along that dark road alone," Samaria said.

Marda smiled. "Thank you, Lord Mother. I am most grateful for your hospitality," he said.

The four of them spent the rest of the night cleaning the birds and dressing the deer. Jaykriss told his mother and sister about how Honshul had surprised Jaykriss that morning, and how Marda had rescued him. The boys recounted the day's hunting exploits with the quail and the stag. And they finished with the story of the ambush by the Geshans, and their victorious battle against the pig-men in the tangled underbrush at the edge of the Godswood.

But they did not mention the Thrax, nor did they mention Zamarcus. Both boys realized that all of that would be too much for Samaria. It was too close, far too close, to what happened to Glyndich.

And besides, if I tell Mama about Zamarcus, she might forbid me to see him anymore.

As he was putting away his Hunting Day gear and unlacing his leggings, Jaykriss spied his mother standing on the front porch of the bain, staring up at the stars. Her eyes were full of tears.

"Mama, What's wrong?" he asked. But he knew what was wrong.

Samaria put her arms around her son's waist and hugged him tight.

"I miss your father. Jay. I just miss him. And when I stand out here, I feel closer to him, somehow. Like he's out there among the stars, looking down on us from above."

She pulled back, her arms still around Jaykriss's waist, and brushed his hair from his eyes.

"He'd be amazed at how you and Annya have grown, you know. And he'd be very proud."

"I know, Mama," he said.

"Now, you need to run along and get ready for bed. It's late. You've got school tomorrow."

"Are you going to be okay?"

She smiled at him.

"I'm fine," she said. "Really."

That night, as Jaykriss dropped his aching body into bed at last, he thought of all he had seen, if only for a moment. Sleep soon washed over him like the tide of a full moon.

While Jaykriss slept, he dreamt of his father, alive and strong, eyes glinting in the noonday sun. In the dream, Glyndich was polishing the Bloodsword with an oilcloth. He clapped a meaty palm on Jaykriss's shoulder.

Jaykriss could *feel* his father's love flow through him in the warmth of his touch. There was strength in that.

Be the sort of man I would have you be, Glyndich said.

But his voice was all wrong.

Glyndich spoke, and his lips moved, but the sound was but a silvery whisper, the murmured incantation of a ghozim, so quiet that it was almost swallowed up by the wind. And then the darkness stole over them, like an eclipse taking a bite from the sun.

Then Jaykriss saw it. Just over Glyndich's shoulder, lurking in the shadows of a suddenly dark and forbidding forest, was the Thrax, obsidian scales gleaming, its cruel teeth tiny pinpoints of light.

"Watch out, Papa!" Jaykriss screamed.

But Glyndich could not hear him.

9

Jaykriss could not help himself.

The Godswood youth classroom had always been a place of great fascination for him. He would spend hours poring over the contents of a boxes filled with animal bones, bird's nests, exotic rocks, or delicate seashells from faraway places. He had learned so very much there.

But not today.

He could only see Sola's head and shoulders, but that was enough to distract him completely.

Her auburn hair was pulled back and braided, as it always was. It hung down her slim neck, barely covering the bony prominences of her spine. Even though she was seated a full three desks in front of him, he imagined he could inhale the delicious clean scent of her, could feel it filling him up. It intoxicated him, addled him, even though he knew it had to be some cruel trick his mind was playing.

His eyes lingered across the curve of her shoulders. Her posture was erect, her bearing almost regal.

Jaykriss had not wanted to admit to Marda how completely Sola obsessed him. His infatuation was like an illness. When she was near, his chest ached. He felt feverish and queasy; his brain fogged up like the Mist Valley in winter.

"Jaykriss? Your answer?"

Mistress Lineya was staring at him, eyebrows arched, her eyes pinning him to his desk like twin spears.

"Um, Mistress, could you repeat the question?" he stammered.

Mistress clicked her tongue against her teeth. "Daydreams are the idle man's downfall, Jaykriss. Surely you know that."

"I do, Mistress. I'm sorry."

She looked around the classroom, her jaw fixed tight. Her arms held the tattered textbook against her chest. "Anyone else care to answer?"

Sola raised her hand.

Great, Jaykriss thought.

"Sola?" Mistress said.

"The best herb for dropsy is the foxglove. Root wort is used for the darkness and the blue furies. And the wasting disease can be slowed with a draught of pregnant mare's urine combined with the crushed extract of vinca."

Mistress Lineya smiled, nodding at Sola.

"Sola, as usual, is correct. It would behoove the rest of you to prepare better for this class. And I don't want to hear any Hunting Day excuses from you boys. Girls have Hunting Day duties, too, you know."

Marda poked Jaykriss in the back. Jaykriss stared straight ahead, eyes fixed on Mistress, and scribbled notes on the things Sola had said.

Marda poked Jaykriss again.

"Stop it," Jaykriss whispered over his shoulder.

"Jaykriss? Anything you wish to share with the rest of us?"

Mistress had drawn herself up to her full six-pace height; indeed, she almost seemed to be on tiptoe, although her long black robes covered her feet so that Jaykriss couldn't tell for certain. Her chin was thrust forward, eyes blazing. Sunlight glimmered off the jewels set into her instructor's breastplate, dappling the walls with daubs of red, blue, and violet.

"No, ma'am," he said, shaking his head.

"See me after class."

"Yes, ma'am," he said, his eyes downcast.

Jaykriss was careful to stay focused the rest of Herbals class. He took notes on sop algae soup, listed each of the components of the distillate of black ground fungus used to ward off winter cough, and noted where to find the minerals one needed to concoct a really potent blood potion.

He was bored with all of it.

Every once in a while, his eyes strayed to the Sola's loose braid. She was like a lodestone for him, drawing him into her despite his best intentions. He had this sudden urge to draw her picture, to record the curve of her back so that he could look at it when she was no longer right there in front of him. But he genuinely liked Mistress Lineya, even if he was not very fond of Herbals. He did not want to disappoint her.

Reluctantly, he tore his eyes from Sola and scrawled an arcane formula for feverbreak broth. Many of the symbols were calligraphic; his fingers had a difficult time with them.

The gods help me, he thought.

Class ended after what seemed like an eternity. The children gathered their things and filed out quietly, white robes fluttering behind them. There was no chatter until they reached the hallway. Marda gently tapped Jaykriss on the shoulder as he passed, as if to say *I'm sorry.*

Jaykriss nodded, almost imperceptibly. They nearly always understood each other, even when they were not speaking. It was intuitive, almost telepathic—a wink here, a nod there. Their fathers had been the same way—so much comprehended, so much implied, as though they were one soul in two bodies. Jaykriss and Marda were more brothers than any two biological brothers ever were.

Mistress Lineya sat at her desk as the classroom emptied. When the last of the students had gone, she got up and closed the door.

"You have always been one of my best students, Jaykriss. You know that," she said.

"Thank you, ma'am."

Mistress walked over to Jaykriss. She had a bad leg; as a result, her right foot pointed straight out sideways, and her gait was an ungainly, head-bobbing lurch. Rumor had it that she got that way from an old horse-riding accident when she was a young woman.

The chains holding up her breastplate clanked with each step. Bending forward at the waist, Mistress looked him straight in the eye.

Up close, Jaykriss was astonished at low large her nose was. Mistress had a face like a hatchet—angular and sharp-edged. And her nose was a big part of that, to be sure. But it seemed disproportionate, somehow, intruding deeply into his personal space even as she brought her intense seawater eyes on a level with his own.

He recoiled a bit before steadying himself.

"I know your father's death has been hard for you and your family," she said.

"Yes, ma'am."

"And I know it has been especially hard on your mother. Samaria loved Glyndich ever since they were students in my class, years ago. Losing your father was like losing a part of herself."

"Yes, ma'am."

She reached inside her desk and handed him a bundle of roots tied up with a thin leather cord.

"This is root wort. For your mother. It will help keep the darkness away."

"Thank you, ma'am."

She chuckled.

"You know, you do remind me of your father, more so each year. He was a different sort than you, to be certain—less studious, more physical, more... *garrulous*, I guess. He talked a lot."

Jaykriss smiled. "Yes, he did."

"But otherwise, you have his demeanor. He was a leader. People looked up to him. They wanted to be around him. And he was principled, far more so than most boys. About the only time I ever saw him lose focus was when your mother came into the picture."

She smiled at him. "Sola, is it?" she said.

Jaykriss blushed in spite of himself. "What? I mean...I'm sorry, ma'am. I don't know what you are talking about."

"Don't try to play that fool's game with me, young man. I may be old, Jaykriss, but I am most emphatically not blind." She reached inside her drawer again, pulling out a smooth, water-worn stone. "Do you know what this is?" she asked.

Jaykriss nodded. "It's a gizzard stone. From a sea tripe, by the looks of it," he said.

"Very good. You see, it helps when you pay attention."

Jaykriss grinned sheepishly.

She grasped his hand, turned it over, and placed the cool stone in his palm. "Sea tripes are quite particular when it comes to gizzard stones. Did you know that?" she said.

"I did not."

"Well, they are. The stones must a certain size and weight, and be nearly perfectly symmetrical. But that's not all. Look at it closely."

Jaykriss looked. The stone was charcoal-colored, with gleaming flecks of gold and silver. There was a slight concavity on one side. That side was polished to a high gloss.

"See the metallic threads that run through it?"

Jaykriss nodded. "Is that tartrite?" he asked.

"You're very observant. Sea tripes like tartrite gizzard stones, and *only* tartrite. They seek it out. They will fly for thousands of miles along the coastline looking for the right tartrite gizzard stone—and they do it for a reason, not just because it looks pretty. After all, once they swallow it, they never see it again. So what is special about tartrite?"

"Well, the Dark King says that it cannot be held by private citizens, for one thing. He says it is dangerous. Centurions will confiscate it if they find you with it."

She rolled her eyes. "Centurions would confiscate happiness if they could. Go on. What else?"

"It is supposed to give people abilities. Insight and memory, cognition, that sort of thing."

"Precisely. It allows one to *focus*. If you rub your thumb along the concave side, your memory improves. Your judgment becomes sharper, your perceptions more distinct. Even colors seem more vivid."

She closed his fingers around the stone. "You need this," she said.

"But I…"

She placed a long, bony finger over his lips. "*Shhh!*" she said. "Boys of more than ten summers have a hard enough time paying attention without a girl in the picture. With a girl around, it is almost impossible. And you do like Sola, don't you?"

Jaykriss felt his cheeks burning. "She has no idea, Mistress."

"Then this will help you. Trust me. I gave your father one just like it a long, long time ago. It helped him, too."

Jaykriss gazed at the stone and placed it in a pocket. "Thank you, Mistress," he said.

"Run along, boy. You'll be late for archery if you tarry here much longer!"

The archery range was located behind the school, in a field that backed up to a dense, sloping rhododendron thicket choked with flowering honeysuckle. Bales of hay positioned along the tree line held targets in the shapes of various animals. Red target marks showed the locations of optimal arrow placement on each one.

An intense honeysuckle scent drifted across the field. Jaykriss never smelled honeysuckle without thinking of the archery range.

Marda was working at the bear target, and as usual, a small crowd had gathered to see him shoot.

"Do it again, Marda!" squealed Beela.

Beela was a tiny slip of a thing, blonde-haired and blue-eyed. She was one of the village blacksmith's two children, and her mother was widely known for baking the best pies in the Godswood. Beela's small size was an enigma; her father was a burly mountain of a man, with arms like oak branches, while her mother's ample figure was seen on a daily basis waddling about the village market in search of apples, pears, and cherries for her pie-making.

There were rumors that Beela's mother had been small like Beela once, but if that was indeed the case, it was many, many pies ago.

Marda drew back on the bow, his fingers as steady as a rock.

Thwwwwip!

The arrow struck the target dot square in the center, immediately adjacent to Marda's last arrow. Beela bounced up and down, twittering like a chickadee, her golden ponytail flopping about.

"You could be just a little off every once in a while, you know," Jaykriss said.

"What's the challenge in that?" asked Marda.

He held his arm up so that Master Plewin could see him. The master, seated in a twelve-pace-tall observation chair, nodded at his star pupil. His thick black beard and the dense mass of his curly black hair made his tiny dark eyes and thin red lips seem almost irrelevant. Only his nose, thin and aquiline, stood out from the hirsute tangle that wreathed his face. His lips were parted, revealing a jumble of impossibly white teeth.

It was no wonder that the students had nicknamed Master Plewin the "Wolf."

"Everything OK between you and Mistress Lineya?" Marda asked.

"It's fine. She gave me a sea-tripe gizzard stone."

"Really? I thought you were going to be in trouble, but Mistress gives you a gift instead. The gods must love you, Jaykriss. She would have had me mucking out the stables."

"You don't know that."

"I do. I had to muck them out twice last year for falling asleep in class."

A shout came up from the far end of the range. Marda pointed at the group of white-robed students tightly clustered around Sola.

"Your girlfriend has quite a following," he said.

"She's not my girlfriend. And she's the only one out here who is close to being as good as you are."

"That's only part of it. My cheering gallery is much more meager than hers."

Jaykriss grinned. "She's prettier than you are," he said.

"What, you don't think I'm pretty?" asked Marda.

"I think you're *gorgeous*," gushed Beela.

Sola had raised her hand. Master nodded at her, then blew a lusty alto note on the brass battle-horn that he wore around his neck.

"Bows down!" he shouted.

The students went to retrieve their arrows from the targets.

Jaykriss noted that Galabrel, a corpulent young man shooting at the field fox target next to Marda, had managed to hit everything but the target itself, spraying arrows into various spare hay bales, rhododendron trunks, and even the broad dark tail of the adjacent beaver target, the target which had been assigned to Jaykriss.

"Hey, I got one in the beaver's tail, and I wasn't even here. How's that for marksmanship?" Jaykriss said.

"I heard that, and it isn't even a little bit funny," Galabrel grumbled. "I can't even see the target. How am I supposed to hit it if I can't see it?"

While pulling arrows from the bear target with Marda and Beela, Jaykriss thought for a moment. "Marda, do you remember those shiny glass things Zamarcus wore over his eyes?"

"The spectacles? Sure. I tried them on. They don't work, though. I saw worse with them, not better."

"That's because the gods have blessed you with perfect vision. Everyone's vision is different, Marda. People like Galabrel might be able to use Zamarcus's spectacles to improve their sight. Wouldn't that be great?"

"It would be *wonderful.*"

Jaykriss frowned. "I detect a note of sarcasm in your voice," he said.

"Me? Of course not. Why would you think that?" Marda placed his arrows back in the quiver. "Perhaps Zamarcus has a contraption that could get you to stop talking so much."

Jaykriss punched him in the shoulder.

Beela skipped over from an adjacent pumpkin-shaped target. She clutched a brace of green-fletched arrows in her tiny hands.

"I've never understood why they have the non-meat-eaters shoot at vegetables," Marda said. "It's not like the pumpkin is going to fly away or something."

"Master Plewin says that everyone needs to know how to shoot. It's like reading and writing—just something we all should know," said Jaykriss.

"Master Plewin teaches archery. What do you expect him to say?"

"I hit the pumpkin every time!" said Beela, her head bobbing as she hopped in place. Her aquamarine eyes sparkled.

"That's great, Beela!" said Jaykriss. But Beela did not seem to hear him. She was looking at Marda like she could eat him up with a spoon.

Master Plewin raised his arms for attention. His dark robes fluttered in the breeze. Sunlight gleamed off his silver breastplate. "We have two among you who have earned the distinction of Archer's Eagle," he said. "Marda and Sola, come forward."

The students clapped.

"I have taught archery here for thirty seasons, and I can say without any equivocation that you are the two best marksmen I have ever had the privilege to instruct. Moreover, as I have records on this archery range dating back over a hundred summers, I have it on good authority that this season you two have earned the highest cumulative overall marksmanship scores that this range has ever seen. Your exam scores are identical."

The students whooped and hollered. Marda performed an exaggerated bow at the waist, arms extended, while Sola merely smiled, tight-lipped, her eyes dancing, bow slung across her chest.

Gods, she's beautiful, Jaykriss thought.

"However…" Master Plewin began, raising his arms again.

The students quieted down.

"The rules dictate that we name a champion. There cannot be a tie. As you know, each year, the champion's name goes on an engraved plaque in the school's Hall of Trophies. But this season is unique. I cannot simply select a champion based upon the scores alone. So I have decided to have a shoot-off between our two expert archers. The winner will be our official champion— and wins this gold-gilded bow and arrow in honor of his or her designation as the best archer in recorded Godswood School history. The bow and arrow set has a history of its own: it was once owned by the legendary warrior Fyrdhom the Great."

The students gasped.

"But Master, Fyrdhom has been in the Otherworld over a hundred summers! How did you come by this? Was it magic? Did some great wizard conjure it up?" said Galabrel.

"Heavens, no. Do you know any great wizards in the Godswood?"

Galabrel shook his head.

"I don't even know any bad wizards," Marda said under his breath.

Beela giggled so vigorously that she snorted.

"The bow and arrow belonged to my father, who got them from his father. I do not know where my grandfather obtained them, but it does not matter. I am old, and I have no children to pass these things on to. The person who wins the archery contest deserves to carry on Fyrdhom's storied legacy. Either of you two would make a worthy addition to the Roll of Champions—and a worthy heir to Fyrdhom's gilded bow."

"So when is the contest?" asked Jaykriss.

"The morning of the first day of the next full moon. I expect you all to be there," Master Plewin said.

"We wouldn't *miss* it!" Beela exclaimed.

Her voice is so high-pitched it could break glass, Jaykriss thought.

Plewin smiled. His teeth gleamed, white and crooked, in the middle of his vulpine face. "That will be all for today, students! Your assignment for next time will be to find out as much about Fyrdhom as you can. See what you can learn from him. Remember, there are great lessons to be learned from the study of great men." Plewin clambered down the steps that led to his observation chair, his bejeweled breastplate clanking against the oak rungs like a warrior's shield.

"Looks like I'll face an uphill battle," Marda said. "Sola's getting better every time we come out here."

"I'm just trying to work my way up to your level, Eagle-Eye," Sola said, walking up behind him.

Just then, the air was filled with an ear-piercing *Screeeeee!* A shadow crossed the archery range, passing over the students like a ghozim.

"Red raptor!" Jaykriss shouted.

The bird was ten paces across, as big as a wagon, with cruel eyes and powerful talons large enough to crush a man's rib cage into splinters. Its razor-sharp beak hung open, its gaping maw a black portal to oblivion. Red raptors were feared because they preyed on children, spiriting them away to feed their voracious, ill-tempered young in massive nests constructed in treetops near rivers, lakes, and seas.

Marda's and Sola's arrows struck the giant raptor at almost the same exact time, killing it in the air in mid-screech. The lifeless creature tumbled to earth, transformed by death into a misshapen mass of feathers and bones.

"An omen," Galabrel said, reverently. His round face and large brown eyes gave him a vaguely bovine appearance.

Marda wiped down his blood-soaked arrow before replacing it in the quiver.

"That's the first red raptor I've seen in two seasons, and I've not seen one in the Godswood since I was a child. So yes, I agree, it's an omen," said Marda. He gazed high into the crystal blue sky, shielding his eyes from the blazing summer sun. "But an omen of what?"

10

The flames flickered low in the fireplace, dancing along the edge of the burned-out log in sunset shards of saffron and pumpkin.

Jaykriss lay beside the hearth, propped up on his elbows. He could feel the warmth of the embers on his face. It made him drowsy, though. Herbals homework was bad enough on its own; a warm fire thrown in rendered him positively stupefied.

He decided to read the potions out loud to try to stay awake.

"Mandrake root, one, mixed with a couple of medium-sized parsnips and a potato. Add some ashes from the lip of a volcano and grind the mixture with a pestle. Sprinkle in some cinnabar, then add the slightest pinch of sulfur…" He shook his head. "This is the most ridiculous thing ever," he said. "Ashes from the lip of a *volcano*?"

"Your father hated Herbals, as well. He said all of those ingredients made his head spin."

Jaykriss's mother was standing in the edge of the shadows, arms akimbo. It was as though she had simply materialized there. He had not even heard her coming.

"How long have you been there?" Jaykriss asked.

"Long enough to watch you," Samaria said.

"There's not much to watch."

Samaria smiled. "There is when you are a mother," she said.

Jaykriss glanced back down at his scrawled notes from Herbals class that day. They were almost illegible.

His mother glided over, noiseless as a moth. "I was always good at this, you know. It's like a recipe. Your father never liked anything he could not simply beat into submission."

Jaykriss took a sheaf of loose notepaper out and flipped it over.

"What's that?" his mother said.

The page had a sketch of Sola's back and shoulders, serpentine hair trailing down beside her spine. Her head was turned ever so slightly; he could see the gentle proud curve of her cheekbones.

When did I draw that? Jaykriss thought.

"She's quite pretty." Samaria said.

"Mama! Please!"

"I'm serious. She's very attractive indeed."

"This is *so* embarrassing," Jaykriss said, flipping the back page over. His cheeks were burning.

"It's nothing to be embarrassed about at all. Who is she?"

Jaykriss did not look up. He was silent for a moment. "Sola. She's the daughter of Argo, the baker," he said at last.

The fireplace popped and sparked enthusiastically.

"Ah! The snake-killer girl! Your father was quite impressed with her!"

"Papa liked her because she could handle an ax."

"Your father liked her because she could think on her feet. I can remember him laughing at how she lopped off the zharga's head just as it struck at her. He actually thought the snake looked shocked, even in death, as though it couldn't believe that a little *girl* could do such a thing!"

Samaria sat down beside her only son, resting her hand in his hair. "I used to read to you right here, especially in winter. Do you remember that?"

Jaykriss nodded.

"It seems like only yesterday that you were a mere babe in my arms, with jowly cheeks and fat little arms. And now look at you, almost a man— drawing pictures of girls in your classes, killing stags on your own, fighting off hordes of Geshans! It's truly amazing, Jaykriss. Your father would be so proud of you."

"Thanks, Mama."

She rubbed his tousled head absently. "I'm sorry for the way I've been act-ing, Jaykriss. It's been hard without your father. I'm still adjusting. I'll be better someday. But I'll never get over losing him that way. A part of my soul was torn away when he died. That part of me died with him."

Jaykriss felt a vague ache in his chest, like there was a stone there too heavy to remove.

"Oh!" he said. "I almost forgot. I have something for you!" He jumped up and ran over to his pack. Rummaging through it, he found the small bundle of root wort, wrapped in a piece of paper.

"Mistress Lineya said this would help you ward off the darkness," Jaykriss said, handing it to her.

Samaria smiled. "Mistress always looked out for us, you know. She once told your father that it was our destiny to be together. She said the gods had ordained it."

"The gods!"

"I think it was simply her way of saying that we were meant for each other. Of course, we already knew that by then." Samaria got up, the bundle of root wort in hand, and clicked her tongue against her teeth.

"It's a fine day when a boy can say he's made his mother proud. That's something my father always used to tell my brothers. It's the truth, too, Jaykriss. You've had to grow up too fast, I think. Had to be a man before you would have otherwise. But you have made me proud. And I know your father is proud of you, as well, looking upon you from the Otherworld."

"Mama?"

"Mm-hmm?"

"You do believe there is an Otherworld, don't you?"

Samaria's eyes filled with tears. She wiped them away with her fingers. "I do, Jaykriss. I *have* to. I couldn't survive if I thought I would never see your father again. Why do you ask this?"

"Honshul said that there was no Otherworld. He said it was a myth."

"Honshul is a Geshan. They don't believe in anything they cannot eat or steal. That's their nature. They're not exactly the most spiritual creatures in the Godswood."

"So if they don't believe in the Otherworld, what happens to the Geshans when they die? The priests say that if you do not believe, you just...*die*. And that after that there is nothing."

"Your father was no great supporter of the priests. He thought that they exploited the gods for their own designs, using fear to herd people's beliefs in a direction that served their purposes. But I believe on this point the priests may be correct. It's hard to imagine an Otherworld that rewards a nonbeliever with immortality."

Jaykriss felt a great hollow within him, a horrible empty void. And he realized that the void could only be filled with knowledge. He simply had to know the answers to things. A great many things, in fact. Everything, if possible. His hunger for information was insatiable.

"Mama, I'm going to find out the truth," he said. He almost told her about Zamarcus. But something inside him told him not to. *She's not ready,* the voice said.

"The truth? The truth about what?"

"About everything."

Samaria grinned broadly at him. Jaykriss realized how much he had missed that grin. It lit up her face from within. He had not seen it since his father died.

"That's my Jaykriss. Your father always said you were born asking questions." She squeezed his shoulder and unwrapped the root wort. There was a note from Mistress Lineya scribbled on it. Samaria frowned as she read it and crumpled the note in her hand. "That was nice of Mistress Lineya to send this," she said absently as she pocketed the bundle of root wort.

Samaria turned on her heels to leave, but then walked back over to Jaykriss. "Goonight, son," she said, kissing him on the head. "I love you."

She pulled his door closed.

That was odd, he thought. It was as though a cloud had passed over them. The entire room seemed suddenly darker, the shadows longer. *It was the note,* he realized. *Mistress told her something.*

He opened his door. The hallway candles were extinguished. His mother's door was closed tight. Jaykriss lit a candle and walked down the hallway to the kitchen.

The paper had been crumpled into a tight little ball, as though his mother had been simply trying to make it go away completely. It was nestled at the very top of the kitchen rubbish heap, like the unobtrusive egg of some small bird.

Jaykriss opened it. It was unmistakably Lineya's handwriting—simple, direct, and precise.

The letter did not say much. In fact, all it said was this:

Have you told him yet?

—L.

"Has she told me what?" Jaykriss muttered. He carefully placed the note back where he had found it. But the burning curiosity had nearly consumed him. As he turned to go back to his room, he was startled to see his mother standing there in the shadows.

"Mama! I didn't see you there at first!"

She stood in the dark, her arms folded across her chest. He could barely see her eyes, gleaming dully like two flat chips of obsidian.

"Do you remember the story about the old man? The one who came up to me right before you were born?" she said.

Jaykriss could vaguely remember the story. Something about an ancient man with a huge dog. "The blind man?" he asked.

Samaria nodded. "When I was nine moons pregnant with you, an old man came up to me. His eyes were sightless and milky white. A wolf-dog led him about. He stopped in front of me directly in front of the Godswood market, calling me by name.

"'Samaria?' he asked.

"'Do I know you?' I answered.

"His dog sat down right then. It was a huge thing, black with gray markings. It had fangs as long as a man's finger. But its ice-blue eyes were kind.

"Anyway, the old man rubbed my swollen belly with his withered hand. 'A boy,' he said. Not a question, mind you. He said it as a statement of fact.

"I did not know what to say, as I did not know what gender you were then. 'Perhaps,' I said.

"'A boy,' he said again, nodding. He stared off into space, seeing something that I could not. When he started talking again, the old man's voice had changed.

"'I smoked the zale-pipe and stayed awake for three days, and then I had a vision,' the old man said. 'I saw this boy as a young man. I saw him asking questions, always questions. He shall be a Seeker of Knowledge. I saw him becoming wise and strong with the Spirit of the Godswood.'

"The old man coughed then. There was blood on his lips when he spoke again."

"You've told me this before, Mama," Jaykriss said. "I'm always asking questions, just like the old man said."

"Well, there's more. Things I haven't told you," she said.

Glyndich had always said that he did not like this story. Jaykriss remembered Papa telling Samaria that she needed to stop telling it to people, that it was "foolishness," that the old man's ravings amounted to a great steaming pile of nothing. And Jaykriss had never understood that, because the old man had not been wrong. He *did* like to ask questions. What could be bad about that?

And then it hit him, like a club blow to the skull.

It was the other part, Jaykriss realized. *Papa didn't like the part of the story that she's not saying. The part I've never heard.*

"There's something else, isn't there? Something you're not telling me," Jaykriss said.

Samaria began trembling. "It's nothing. Your father was right—the old man was just a crazy old buzzard. He died just a few suns after that—even before you were born. He's long since in the grave now. I should not have mentioned it."

"Mama, what was it?"

Samaria was frowning, her eyebrows knitted tightly together. "I don't believe in prophecy anyway. No one can tell the future."

Jaykriss grabbed her by the shoulders and looked her straight in the eye. "Mama, please. You said I'm almost a man now. I can take it. I *promise.*"

Samaria stared off into space. Her eyes were lifeless. It was though the darkness had crawled back into them.

Jaykriss was instantly sorry he had brought it all up. He could see despair flowing into her, a black tide that could not be stopped. He wished he could take it back, that he could retract his statements and leave it all buried. But he knew that it was too late. The old man's prophecy, whatever it was, had rooted itself deep inside her skull now and would not let go.

Her voice was reedy and small.

"He said that the future was murky and full of shadows, but that you may work great wonders. He even said that you might be the One Who Leads, the one who takes all mankind back into the light. But he also said…"

She swallowed. "He also said that you would die a young man. Of that, he was entirely certain."

11

The next few days were a blur for Jaykriss.

Summer's heat had rolled upon the Godswood with a vengeance. The days were cloudless, the sun a burning coal in the sky, and the air was oppressive, draping itself over the Godswood like a blanket.

The heat was like a sleeping potion. It was all Jaykriss could do to merely keep one leaden foot moving in front of the other.

The sun was relentless. Even when it dropped below the horizon, it was never far away, its heat radiating back from the baked earth like an ember in a campfire. The air was still and thick, and every plant was wilted and lifeless. Even the animals huddled under shade trees and moved as little as they could.

"The gods have cursed us with you, sun," Jaykriss muttered under his breath as he walked home from school along the dust-choked path.

To make matters worse, Jaykriss could not shake his mother's tale. He felt that he was doomed, that each day might be his last. *I am going to die young,* he thought. *The old man saw it even before I was born.* He could not even tell Marda about it. He told no one.

By the day before Hunting Day, he knew he had to do something different. The pressure inside his head was becoming unbearable.

After lessons, he went home, removed his learner's robe, and changed into a pair of shorts. He splashed his some water on his face and set out for the Brightwood, taking the path to the first waterfall on the trail to the Mist Valley.

It was a place he had always loved—quiet and peaceful. His father had taken him trout fishing here on many an afternoon.

"See how the trout's back hides him from us?" Glyndich had said. "It is stone-colored, like the riverbed. It shields him. The raptors can eat him only if he shows himself; otherwise, he is invisible to them. But we humans trick him into revealing himself through our *wits*. We bait a hook with what he sees as food, and he takes it. Then we take *him*." Glyndich snatched his broad hand into a fist.

"The gods gave human beings the ability to reason. It is a gift we should always use for good, like when we are trout fishing. Unfortunately, some people use the gods' gift of reason selfishly, at the expense of others. You should never do that, Jaykriss. You should always do the thing that is right."

"Well, how will I know what is right?"

Glyndich had wrapped a thickly muscled arm around him then. "That's where your mother and I come in!" he had bellowed, laughing.

Standing next to the waterfall, remembering his father, Jaykriss felt things settle in him. The sun spilled through the trees and made a short rainbow in the mist. The air was cooler here.

He sat on a moss-slick rock next to the roaring waters and picked up a small, flat pebble. He skimmed it across the pool at the base of the falls; it skipped three times before sinking.

"What's your record for that?" a voice said behind him.

Jaykriss whirled about and almost fell into the water.

Sola was in a bathing costume, although her shoulders were draped with a large towel. She sat down on the rock beside him.

"I've skipped one seven times," she said.

"My record is eight. But you have to find the right rock."

She nodded, staring out over the water.

The silence between them was almost physically painful.

Say something, you idiot. "You swimming?" Jaykriss asked.

"Not yet," she said, grinning at him.

Brilliant, Jay. "It's so *hot*. I just had to go someplace to cool off," Jaykriss said.

"You and I had the same idea," she said. She dropped her towel on the rock and dove cleanly into the clear water.

Sola swam like an otter. She moved with an easy grace, her legs scissoring precisely, driving her underwater toward the foaming thunder of the waterfall. She made it there in two kicks, her image undulating beneath the shimmering waves, and then she exploded beneath the cataract and surfaced, white water cascading over her head and shoulders.

She was laughing at him, beckoning to him.

He was embarrassed to be looking at her. He felt like he should look away, but he *couldn't*.

"Come on! It's *great!*" she said.

"I'm not in my bathing outfit. And I don't have a towel."

"The two worst excuses of all time. We can share my towel, if that worries you so much. And the difference between a bathing outfit and a pair of shorts is what, exactly? The name?"

She's got a point.

"Get in here. You're making me nervous. I feel like you're just sitting over there *watching* me, like some weirdo."

Jaykriss had no response for that. Pulling off his shoes and shirt, he dove into the pool.

The shock of the cold water was like being slapped in the face. For a brief moment, he thought he had struck the rocks at the bottom of the pool. His chest constricted and his belly knotted up, and then he burst through into the warm summer air, gasping, his arms and legs numb.

"Ye gods! It's f-f-freezing!" he said.

"You get used to it. Trust me. I've been in here at least long enough to tell."

"You've been in here five minutes!"

"That's long enough. Now get over here. I don't want to stand in the waterfall all by myself."

Is this really happening? He had to be dreaming. There was simply no way that Sola was asking him to come be with her.

He swam underwater to the waterfall. He could see her feet on the bottom, pale as a trout's underbelly, the water above them a frothing maelstrom.

And then he was beside her, the cascade pouring over the two of them, icy water pounding his back, the sun overhead casting handfuls of glittering diamonds into the spray.

All of his worries about the old man's prophecy had simply washed away.

"Isn't this great?" she said, her eyes sparkling.

Sola slipped as a foaming gout of water struck her. Reflexively, Jaykriss grabbed her waist.

Touching her skin was like touching fire.

"Whoops! Almost fell there!" she said. "Thanks for catching me."

Jaykriss could think of nothing to say that sounded halfway intelligent, so he just grinned, releasing her when he was certain she had her footing, the memory of her slim waist still alive in his fingertips.

Without warning, Sola dove back into the pool. He wanted to follow her but did not want to seem too desperate, so he just stood there alone for a moment as the sun drifted behind a cloud, and the magic of the moment simply evaporated.

Sola pulled herself back onto the rock. Her dark hair was sleek, her slim body lithe and muscular. Jaykriss had lurched from misery to ecstasy to misery in the span of a few short minutes. Now, he could not take his eyes off of her. She picked up the towel, dried her hair, wrapped it around her shoulders, and then stood there, arms akimbo, staring at him and grinning as he stood in a roaring cascade that had suddenly grown infinitely more frigid.

"Get over here, you big goof! I promised you could share my towel, and you're just standing there freezing to death!"

And so he swam to her, his wait vindicated by her invitation. The summer heat that had been so oppressive earlier was deliciously toasty now. The sun was back out, and he luxuriated in its glow, wondering how he could have ever cursed it to begin with. As she handed him the towel and he dried his hair, he realized that he could smell her scent on it, could feel the warmth of her skin on the cloth.

At that moment, he knew with all of his heart that he loved her.

"You looked miserably cold out there," she said.

I would freeze solid for you, he thought. For one horrifying instant, he thought that he had said it out loud. But she said nothing, and he relaxed, handing the towel back to her.

"I should have come here days ago," he said.

"I come here often, especially when it is hot like this. It clears my head. There's usually no one else here. Not that I mind the company," she said, smiling.

"Have you been practicing for the archery competition?" he asked.

"No more than usual. Classroom work is more important. Win or lose, I'm happy with my archery skills, and Marda is so naturally gifted that I doubt I could beat him even on my best day."

"You're both very good."

"But I have to work at it. Marda seems to have a special ability with a bow and arrow that I cannot match."

"Marda and I have been best friends since we were small. His archery skills are indeed uncanny. But I am impressed with what you can do as well. You don't give yourself enough credit."

"My parents might have something to do with that. They mean well, but they think a girl's place is in the kitchen or raising children. My father always wanted a boy, but they had none. Hopa and I were their only offspring. He's never come out and said that not having a boy was a disappointment for him, but I can tell by the way he thinks. He really doesn't care a bit if I am a good archer or even a good student."

"What? But how can he not care about such things? And you are so good at both!"

"My father told me once that he wants me to run the bakery, find a man, and give him some *grandsons*. Even worse, he thinks I could do those things *now*, as if school is not important at all. 'Give your old papa a rest,' he says. Can you believe that? It's almost as though I have no dreams of my own, or no goals in life beyond those he has for me. I love my father, but he's written my destiny for me, at least in his mind."

Jaykriss thought for a moment, and the thought came tumbling out of his mouth before he could stop it. "Do you believe in prophecy?" he said.

"Which prophecy?"

Jaykriss then told her about what the old blind man had told his mother.

"So he said you would die young," she said, her eyes downcast.

Jaykriss nodded.

She thought for a moment, biting her lip, before speaking again at last.

"The smartest person I've ever met was my grandmother. She's dead now, but she used to be a Keeper of the Dark King's library in Capitus. Grandma was the sort of person I would want to model my life after. She always thought for herself. When the Godswood priests used to talk to her about prophecy, she called it…well, she said words I'm not supposed to say. She didn't like the priests, who were always quoting this prophecy or that prophecy, as though it were fact. Grandma said that preordained behavior robbed us of free will, and she believed in free will."

"As opposed to things being determined by fate alone," said Jaykriss.

"Exactly. She said that she could not believe that the gods would put us here simply to act out some play that was scripted before we were born. What would be the point in that?"

"If I were a god, I would find that boring," said Jaykriss.

"Me, too. Grandma's view was that we are given a series of choices in life. We make the right choices, and we end up where we are supposed to. We make the wrong choices, we end up someplace else," said Sola.

"So if I do the right things…"

"Things will work out the way they are supposed to."

The sun was warming Jaykriss's skin, but Sola's words had taken the chill away from the inside. *Always do the thing that is right*, Glyndich had said to him. Those words came back to him now.

I will, Papa, he thought.

It happened so fast that he barely had time to think. He was very close to Sola, close enough to sense her body's nearness to him, and he still had her scent in his nostrils, and then he looked up and she was *there*, right in front of him. Her eyes, so beautiful that they hurt him, pulled him in, closer than he ever dared, until his lips were brushing hers, and then he was kissing her, his arm encircling her waist. She wrapped her towel around the two of them, and he could feel her body pressed against his, felt her breath on his skin, and he realized that his eyes had closed tight.

When his eyes opened, and their lips parted, he stared at her, eye to eye, their foreheads touching.

"I'm…I'm sorry," he said. "I didn't mean to take the liberty to…"

"You didn't take any liberties. I *let* you kiss me, you big goof. That's the first time I've ever let *any* boy do that. And it was everything I imagined it would be. Now shut up and kiss me again."

Jaykriss closed his eyes again and kissed her, feeling her soft, full lips against his own, savoring the jut of her hipbones against his belly, his arms locked behind her, feeling the gentle curve of her back. His heart pounded in his chest; he was giddy, spots of light pulsating behind his eyes. It was as though the entire world was about to explode into a million tiny pieces.

And, at that moment, he would not have cared if it had.

After the second kiss, she pulled back and smiled at him. "Perfect," she said.

"Perfect?"

She nodded, taking his hand in hers.

They started walking the path back to the Godswood, hand in hand.

"I knew I was going to kiss you today," she said.

"How did you know that? You said you had never kissed anyone like this before."

"I haven't."

"Then how did you know?"

"Because no one else ever said he would freeze solid for me. *That* was when I knew, Jaykriss. That was when I realized that you were my destiny."

Jaykriss shook his head. "I didn't realize that I said it out loud," he said. "You make me crazy like that."

The sun was warm on their backs, the sky a brilliant sapphire blue. Birds twittered in the birch forest; a breeze rustled the tree branches above their heads.

And for Jaykriss, his fingers intertwined with Sola's, the world was forever changed.

12

When Jaykriss was a boy, even before Annya was born, his father liked to tell him tales of bravery and valor.

The pattern was the same every evening. Jaykriss would finish his dinner—every last bit, as wasting even a single grain of rice would warrant a disapproving glance from Glyndich—and wash his plata, stacking it neatly in the drying rack. He would then take a seat by the fireplace—usually on a matted bearskin rug with frayed edges, edges that he fiddled with incessantly—and his father would lumber over, a mead-filled mug gripped in his massive hands.

"Tell me a story, Papa!" Jaykriss would say.

And Glyndich would pensively twist his beard between his fingers, staring off into space as though he were dredging up some arcane secret from the vaults of human history.

"Well, then," he'd say, setting down his mug and wiping his mouth with his sleeve. And then he'd clear his throat with a great, theatrical *harrumph!* before launching into that evening's tale.

Sometimes, Samaria would join them. Sometimes, she would not. Jaykriss came to learn that there were certain stories she did not care to hear—especially the ones where the heroes met a tragic end, like the legend of Xelata the Bold, who ended his life in the jaws of a flying dragon. She particularly avoided hearing any of the stories about the Shadow Men, a race of beings that were said to lurk in the Deadwood. The legends said the Shadow Men brought despair and heartache like summer clouds bring rain.

Jaykriss loved all of his father's stories. They were rich, complex tales filled with brave warriors, damsels in distress, and horrible, stinking monsters with sharp claws and fangs the size of smallswords. Glyndich was a gifted storyteller, adopting the voices of each of his characters so believably that Jaykriss could close his eyes and actually *see* them, weapons flashing, their eyes ablaze.

Among all of his father's characters, Jaykriss's favorite was the legendary archer Fyrdhom the Great.

Fyrdhom was not a typical hero. He was stout and short, "built like a cask of mead," as Glyndich would say. He always wore a feathered cap over his balding head—to cover the deep scars that raked across his scalp. As a child, Fyrdhom had been mauled by a bear. Apparently, the bear had Fyrdhom's head in its massive jaws but could not shatter it. Fyrdhom had stared into its teeth, terrified as the bear huffed its hot breath upon him. When the village archers shot and killed the bear, the creature finally let Fyrdhom go—but not without leaving him with a permanent reminder of just how perilously close he had come to making a premature journey to the Otherworld.

And with that, Fyrdhom became an archer himself.

By the time he was a man, Fyrdhom was not just any archer. In fact, he was the greatest archer of all time, able to shoot an apple off a tree. He once flushed and killed an entire covey of quail, dropping three of them on one arrow. His legend grew when he won the formidable Mortal Challenge of the Priests as a youth of nineteen summers' age, the youngest person ever to do so.

When Fyrdhom won the Capitus archery contest, under the watchful eye of a younger and more publicly visible Dark King, he became famous everywhere. He was known throughout the land by various names: Needle-eye was one. Lancer was another.

But eventually, most people simply called him Fyrdhom the Great.

The Fyrdhom mythology was powerful and extensive. It was said that Fyrdhom ate a dozen raw eggs every morning for breakfast. Before each battle, he polished his bald head until it gleamed and painted the trough-like toothmarks on his skull with streaks of cinnabar to make them stand out in crimson relief. Unlike the other archers, who usually rode into battle on horseback, Fyrdhom almost always skirmished on foot, preferring the use of stealth to vanquish his foes. He shot his enemies dead from the treetops or fired flaming arrows into battle from hidden caves or camouflaged pits. He once killed a feared rebel commander, a giant named Mundrick, as the mammoth warrior drew his great-sword to try to slay the Dark King from behind. The sword clattered to the ground from Mundrick's lifeless hand before he fell dead, an arrow in each eye.

Saving the Dark King's life on several occasions was what eventually prompted the king to give Fyrdhom the title "Defender of the Realm." It was a great honor. Fyrdhom the Great, the Defender of the Realm, was in essence the Dark King's right hand, his enforcer, and confidante. He was the second-most powerful man in the kingdom—at least until he disappeared.

No one really knew what happened to Fyrdhom. The official story was that he was riding on horseback from Capitus to the Godswood, doubtless to right some great wrong, but he never arrived. His horse had been found wandering aimlessly in the Godswood, bloodied and wild-eyed, its entrails hanging from a gaping wound in its side. Something had mauled it badly. The poor animal eventually had to be put down.

After no one had heard from him for over a year, Fyrdhom the Great was finally declared dead. There was a gargantuan state funeral in Capitus, complete with a flag-draped casket and a symbolic funeral pyre. Rumors ran rampant that Fyrdhom was going to make an appearance at his funeral.

But the funeral came and went—and there was no Fyrdhom.

There were legends in the Godswood that Fyrdhom's ghozim could be seen on moonlit nights, lingering around the place where his horse had been found. Strange arrows, with the yellow-and-black "wasp" fletching that Fyrdhom pre-ferred, were sometimes found embedded in the trunks of Godswood trees. But it had been a hundred summers or more since Fyrdhom the Great was last heard from. He was more myth than man now, and certainly dead by all accounts. It was only Glyndich's stories that kept him alive for Jaykriss.

But now there was something tangible to behold—a relic of the great Fyrdhom himself.

The Godswood School archery contest winner was to be awarded Fyrdhom's gilded bow.

Jaykriss awoke early on the morning of the archery contest. His belly grumbled, but he ignored it. Food was not his top priority that morning. He bathed, splashing water everywhere, draped the Thrax-scale necklace around his neck, and dressed quickly, lacing his leggings up in so hurried a fashion that he missed a loop.

"Haste is the brother of chaos, and chaos the handmaiden of death," he muttered, unlacing and then re-lacing the leggings.

It was one of Glyndich's favorite sayings.

When Jaykriss left for school that morning, the birds had barely begun their morning twitter. But he had tossed and turned all night, ruminating over what this contest might mean. And he had decided the night before on a plan— a plan that required him to leave home early.

The way Jaykriss had looked at it, he was in a no-lose situation. Either his best friend or the girl he loved was going to win the Gilded Bow of Fyrdhom the Great. But he had to be prepared for either contingency; the loser was bound to be disappointed. He had to find some gift to cheer the loser up. But then the pragmatist in him spoke up.

Sola's going to lose, he thought. *There's no way she can beat Marda.*

In the end, he had decided to pick a bouquet of flowers for Sola. This was the safest play—if Sola lost, the flowers might cheer her up, but if she somehow pulled out a win, the bouquet would offer her a statement of congratulations.

He plucked some multicolored blooms from the forest around the war chief's bain—a riot of yellow, blue, violet, and red—and wrapped them up with a strand of coarse twine.

Jaykriss met Marda on the tree-shaded road to the Godswood School. He tried to hide the bouquet behind his back, but Marda saw it immediately.

"What's that? Flowers? Are you sucking up to Mistress?"

Jaykriss blushed. "They are for Sola. After she loses the archery contest to you."

Marda rolled his eyes. "What has gotten into you? Have you really gone all mushy on me, Jay?" he said.

"I just...I feel sorry for her. She wants to do something with her life, but her father really just wants her to marry and have babies. He doesn't care if she is good at archery, school, or anything."

"That's crazy! She's just about the smartest person in the school—and the best girl athlete. Why would he not be proud of her?"

"He just isn't. I can't explain it. He wanted sons, and she's not a boy."

They walked past a forest pond rimmed with stands of reeds and cattails. A brace of willows gingerly dipped their drooping strands into the olive-colored water. The pond's gilded surface shimmered in the morning sunlight.

Marda picked up a flat stone and skimmed it across the pond. It skipped six times before sinking into oblivion. "Hang onto those flowers," Marda said. "She's gonna need them."

The excitement in the air was palpable by the time the two of them arrived at the Godswood School. A throng of younger boys immediately surrounded Marda, their hands pulling at his black tunic, seeking to touch him, to be next to him, to bask in his reflected glory.

"This is crazy, isn't it?" Marda asked. But he was smiling.

Sola was already at the archery range when Marda arrived with his entourage. A cluster of white-robed girls stood behind her, talking and giggling.

Jaykriss waved at Sola. She waved back, smiling at him, then notched another arrow, and turned her attention to the rabbit-shaped target.

Thwack!

Sola's arrow struck the rabbit target through the heart.

The breeze changed, and the cloying scent of honeysuckle drifted into the air. Jaykriss took a deep breath.

"That's the smell of victory," Marda said, grinning. Marda set up near the bear target, which was his favorite.

Master Plewin walked up, robes fluttering behind him. His silver breastplate gleamed. He held the gilded bow of Fyrdhom in his hand. Plewin raised his arms above his head, and the students immediately became silent.

"In the long history of the Godswood Academy, only ninety-seven archers have attained the rank of Archer's Eagle. Two of that number are here today— Marda, son of Garoth, and Sola, daughter of Argo. And you two are the best this school has ever seen. But the rules say we must crown a champion every season. And since you two are tied at the end of the season, there must be a shoot-off."

Master Plewin's nose twitched. He blinked, looking first at Sola, then at Marda. His long teeth gleamed.

He really does look like a wolf, Jaykriss thought.

"The competition is simple. Two targets per archer, five arrows each. Each archer must hit the target someplace with each arrow; a single miss of the target with any arrow disqualifies the archer from the competition, although I doubt that will be an issue with either of you. The first criterion is the number of arrows per archer in the kill spot. The one with the highest total number of arrows in the kill spot wins. If there is a tie after the first two targets, there will be a single arrow long-range shoot-off using Fyrdhom's gilded bow itself, with the target set at five hundred paces."

Fyrdhom's bow was huge. It was nearly as tall as Sola. Jaykriss realized that Plewin had elected to use that bow for the long-range shoot-off because it was the only bow that could accurately shoot an arrow that distance.

It's too big for her, he thought. *Sola would never be able to draw Fyrdhom's bow back far enough to get off a good long-range shot.*

Master Plewin had always liked Marda. And Jaykriss had a feeling that he was making certain that his star pupil would come out on top, if it got that far.

The Wolf has rigged it for Marda to win.

Master Plewin clambered up the Observation Tower, battle horn clanging against his breastplate, as he took taking his usual seat there. After settling himself and brushing the riot of hair away from his eyes, he put the battle horn to his thin lips and blew a long, plaintive note.

"Archers, take your places!" the Wolf bellowed.

Marda drew an arrow from his quiver. Suddenly, Beela was next to him, fluttering around him like a moth drawn to a flame.

"For luck," she said, kissing him squarely on the mouth.

Marda's face flushed crimson. He fumbled his arrow before releasing it, nearly dropping it to the ground.

"Looks like Beela is working for Sola," Galabrel said, his eyes shielded against the sun. He was already sweating.

"Beela's working for Beela," Jaykriss said.

Galabrel nodded. He wiped his brow with a sleeve. "Ye gods, it's hot," he said.

Marda notched his arrow again. He looked to his right, then to his left. Beela was hopping up and down like a chickadee, her blonde ponytail flapping, but showed no further signs of impending affection.

Marda drew back, muscles flexing, his arms steady. He released the first arrow. It struck the target with an audible *thwack*! The impact embedded the arrow in the bear's heart up to midshaft.

The crowd gasped.

"Score one for Marda!" the Wolf said.

Sola answered, her arrow striking the rabbit target squarely in the heart.

"Score one for Sola!' Plewin exclaimed.

Sola's gallery cheered.

The next four shots by each were similarly perfect. At the conclusion of the first round, Marda and Sola each had five arrows clustered in their target's heart.

Master Plewin clambered back down the Tower, breastplate clanking. He was carrying a burlap bag. "These targets are no challenge for our two Archer's Eagles. So I have decided to raise the stakes."

Master Plewin pulled a pair of apples from the sack.

"The next round will be like the last, with one exception: the fifth shot for each will be aimed at an apple, which will be positioned on top of the targets. You must strike the apple with the fifth shot to stay in the competition. Any miss counts as a disqualification."

He balanced a fat green apple on top of each target, then scampered back to his Observation Tower.

The war horn's mournful tone echoed across the archery range.

Sola went first this time. Her aim, again, was true.

Marda followed. His arrow was likewise dead center, piercing the bear's heart cleanly.

Sola was perfect on the next two shots; Marda was, as well.

As Sola notched her fourth arrow and pulled back on the bowstring, her eyes widened. She dropped her aim slightly, her arms slackened, and she stared into the rim of spectators standing around the perimeter of the archery range.

Sola blinked and shook her head.

What does she see? Jaykriss thought.

He followed her line of sight.

Argo, Sola's father, was standing in the crowd, hands on his hips. His baker's apron was tied around his rotund waist; his arms were white with flour. Hopa, Sola's younger sister, stood beaming next to him.

Sola lowered her bow the rest of the way and removed the arrow. She dabbed at her eyes with her robe, a stricken expression on her face.

She's crying, Jaykriss realized.

Suddenly, she notched the arrow again and raised her bow, chin thrust defiantly forward, releasing her fourth arrow in a single fluid motion.

The arrow whistled toward the target. It struck cleanly.

But it was lodged in the rabbit's thigh, well away from the target area.

Jaykriss glanced over at Marda. He was smiling, almost imperceptibly. There was a cold look in his eyes. Jaykriss knew that look.

Marda was a warrior at heart. He was at his very best when the odds were against him. But he also had an uncanny sixth sense for that lone chink in an opponent's armor; he could sniff it out and dig it up, like a dog unearthing a long-buried bone. Marda saw weakness as plainly as most people saw sunlight.

It was his gift.

Marda notched his fourth arrow and pulled back on his bow. His aim was steady; his arm was rigid, muscles taut.

He let the arrow fly.

The crowd gasped.

Marda's arrow had missed the target entirely, lodging instead in the leathery trunk of an ancient rhododendron tree behind the range.

Master Plewin said nothing at first. His toothsome mouth gaped like a barn door. Then he cleared his throat. "Marda...has missed the target. He is disqualified. Sola, you are the winner—and the all-time Godswood School Champion!"

The flock of girls around Sola squealed and twittered, hugging both Sola and each other.

Sola looked at Marda, who grinned at her, nodded, then bowed slowly at the waist, arms outstretched.

Sola raised her bow. "Master Plewin?"

"Yes, Sola?"

"May I take my final shot?"

"But why? If you miss..."

She shot a look at her father, who was still standing expressionless in the crowd, his powdered arms now folded across his chest.

"I won't miss," she said. "I want to finish this."

Plewin nodded.

Sola pulled an arrow from her quiver and inspected the gleaming arrowhead. It was a serrated metallic spiral known as a ribbon cutter, designed to cleanly pierce chain mail and lodge deeply into the soft tissues beneath. Sola notched the arrow, drew the bowstring back past her ear, and let the arrow fly.

It struck the apple dead center.

The apple exploded. Seeds, peel, and white fruit-flesh spattered everywhere.

Sola peered into the crowd, eyes searching, her jaw set tight. But Sola's father had gone, taking Hopa with him.

Master Plewin gathered the students around the base of the observation tower. A gentle breeze tousled Sola's hair, bringing with it the intermingled scents of forest and honeysuckle. Sola smiled, her slim hands clutching her bow tightly.

Jaykriss felt just the slightest bit lightheaded as he stared at her.

Plewin cleared his throat, raising both of his hairy arms for silence. "This bow belonged to the most accomplished archer of all time. Fyrdhom the Great, the Defender of the Realm, was both a warrior and a scholar. He was a shining example of all that is just. He lived a life of honor. And this bow, which has been in my family for generations, was his very own bow."

He turned to Sola, eyes bright. "Sola, daughter of Argo, you have earned the right of possession. The gilded bow of Fyrdhom the Great is yours as the all-time Champion of the Godswood School."

Mater Plewin presented the gleaming bow to Sola with outstretched arms, his hands trembling slightly.

Sola took it from him, bowing slightly as she did so. The students whooped and clapped and cheered—even Beela.

The bow was beautiful, intricately carved and inlaid with pearl, gold, and silver. Several jewels were embedded near the nock. Sola ran a fingertip along its edge. She plucked the taut bowstring with a fingernail.

And then she looked up. "We all know who the greatest archer in the history of Godswood School is. And it is not me," she said.

She walked over to Marda. "Marda, son of Garoth, this bow is yours, not mine. Take it."

Marda shook his head. "You earned it, fair and square. It is yours to keep," Marda said.

"It is also mine to give away," Sola said, waving and smiling warmly to the crowd.

"No," Marda said.

Sola leaned in and whispered in Marda's ear. "Look, I know what you did, and I thank you for it. But this should belong to the best, and that's you. That would be what is fair in the eyes of the gods."

"No," Marda whispered back. "You earned it."

"I cannot even use it. It is too big for me."

"You'll figure it out."

Sola looked out into the crowd and leaned in so close that Marda could feel her breath on his ear. "My father will *sell* it, Marda. I know this. The bow means nothing to him. This honor means nothing to him. Fyrdhom's bow belongs with someone who will appreciate its true worth. It belongs with *you*."

Marda hesitated for an instant. He looked about at the crowd. They were silent and expectant, enraptured, their eyes wide.

"*Please*," Sola said. Her eyes were again filled with tears.

Marda thought for a moment, then placed his hand upon the bow, fingers clasped over hers. "I will take good care of it for you," he said.

"I know you will," she said, smiling.

Marda grasped Sola's hand, intertwining their fingers, and raised the gilded bow high in the air with his other arm. The throng of students cheered wildly. Papers flew into the air; one girl turned a cartwheel. Beela looked like she was going to take wing.

The Wolf beamed, clapping his long hands together. "Splendid!" he said. "True sportsmanship!"

Jaykriss was not certain what had just happened, but he looked at the two of them standing there holding hands and was just the slightest bit jealous. It was an emotion he was instantly ashamed of, and he buried it deep.

"I'm so happy for both of you!" he said, putting his arms around them.

"I'm not blind, old buddy. I saw you glaring at us," Marda said.

"What?"

"At least I didn't kiss her. And you know, come to think of it, maybe I should. What do you think, Sola?"

"Suits me," she said. "Come here, lover. Let's give them a show." She opened her arms wide and tilted her head to one side—lips parted, eyes closed.

Jaykriss's head reeled. He felt like he was going to explode into a billion green shards of envy. *How is this happening?* he thought, dropping the bouquet of wildflowers into a mudpuddle.

Marda and Sola burst out laughing.

"Come here, you big idiot," Sola said. She wrapped her arms around Jaykriss's waist and kissed him full on the mouth. "There. Are you satisfied?"

Jaykriss glanced at the mud-spattered flowers lying on the ground. His face flushed crimson. "Was it that obvious?" he said.

"Um-hmm." Sola said.

"You were *frowning*," Marda said. "Everyone in the entire school is going crazy, and you're standing over there with your arms crossed, a big ugly scowl on your face."

"I'm...I'm sorry. I knew I should have been happy for you both. But when I saw you two up there holding hands, and everybody cheering, I just..."

"You were *jealous*," Marda said.

"Yes, I was. I'm not proud of it, but yes."

"I'm a little flattered." Sola said.

"So am I," said Marda.

Sola giggled.

"But I'm not kissing you, big boy," Marda added.

"Thanks for that," said Jaykriss.

He looked at Sola for a moment. She smiled at him, arms akimbo.

Suddenly, Jaykriss had a thought. "Turn around," he said to Sola.

"What?"

"Turn around, just for a moment."

She did as he asked. "What is this all about?" she asked.

"You'll see," he said.

Jaykriss took the Thrax-scale necklace from around his neck and draped it around Sola's.

"What is this?" Sola said.

"A Thrax-scale necklace. It's a symbol of strength and invincibility."

"Where in the world did you get a Thrax scale?" she said.

"He snuck up on the beast while it was sleeping and plucked it like a flower," Marda said, grinning as he shot a glance at the ruined bouquet.

"Really? I'm impressed," Sola said.

"He lies," Jaykriss said. "He always lies."

Marda drew himself up and puffed out his chest. "Begging your pardon, sire. I do not lie. I merely *fabricate*."

Sola giggled. "Well, however you got it, it's a rare and beautiful thing, and I thank you for it," she said, kissing Jaykriss on the cheek. "This is a better prize for me than that old bow anyway."

The three of them walked to class together, their robes fluttering black and white behind them.

"Where am I going to put this thing? My locker's not big enough," Marda said.

"I can tell you where to put it," Jaykriss said.

Marda punched him in the arm.

"Boys, no fighting. We've made peace, remember?" Sola said, positioning herself between them and holding them apart.

Marda grinned. "We're not really fighting. It's just a guy thing, Sola. We punch each other sometimes."

She rolled her eyes. "I'll never understand men," she said.

Sola walked between the two boys, locking arms with each of them. Jaykriss caught her glancing down at the Thrax scale as it gleamed, darkly iridescent in the morning sunlight.

"It's a wonderful day in the Godswood! Wouldn't it be great if we could feel just like this forever?" Marda said.

Sola smiled broadly. "It would, indeed," she said.

They entered the school together just as the morning school bell began to ring. The doors slammed shut behind them.

For that brief moment, Jaykriss was certain that he was the happiest person in the whole world.

13

Jaykriss was awake before dawn on Hunting Day.

He had barely slept all night anyway. When he slept, he dreamt of Sola, and when he was awake, the thought of her consumed him. She was a wildfire burning inside him.

But he kept it contained, kept it hidden deep.

Or so he thought.

He was in the kitchen, already dressed for the hunt, making breakfast for Mama and Annya, when his mother walked in.

"Good morning, Mama!" he said, kissing her on the cheek.

Samaria rubbed the sleep from her eyes and shook her head. "What in the world has gotten into you?" she said.

"It's Hunting Day. Marda and I are going back to the Mist Valley. And yes, I promise I'll stay away from the Crags. On my honor, as the son of the war chief."

"Last Hunting Day I practically had to have Annya drag you out of bed, remember?"

Jaykriss scraped the vegetable hash out of the bowls and placed it onto the wooden serving platas, added a few strips of bacon to each plate, then adorned each one with honeysuckle blooms. "That was last week, Mama. This is a whole new week."

Samaria sat down at the table, shaking her head. "Teenagers," she mumbled, smiling nonetheless.

Annya padded out into the kitchen, bleary-eyed. "Mama, why is Jaykriss making breakfuss?" she said.

"Because he wanted to, dear," Samaria said, pulling her little girl into her lap.

"Has he gone crazy, like that man at the market who barks like a dog?"

"Perhaps."

"I want a dog," Annya said.

"We know, dear."

Jaykriss was ravenous. He could not recall the last time he was this hungry. He ate his food without speaking, shoveling in mouthfuls of hash with his spoon. He ate three strips of bacon so quickly that he forgot for a moment whether he had eaten them or not.

Chewing, he looked up at his mother and sister and noticed that they were staring at him. "What?" he said.

"You're eating like a pig," Annya said, giggling. "A big pig."

"Well, then, you should eat like a little pig, since you're my little sister."

Annya spooned up a mouthful of hash into her mouth. "Num, num, num," she said, chewing vigorously.

"Pigs say oink," Samaria said.

"Num, num, oink!" Annya said, which made them all start laughing.

Jaykriss cleaned up after breakfast, kissed his mother and his sister, and gathered up his bow, quiver, and short sword before lacing up his leggings.

"Safe hunting, Jay!" Annya said, kissing her fingers and placing them over her heart.

"Safe hunting, Annya and Mama," Jaykriss said, repeating the gesture to both his sister and his mother.

"Bring me back a dog!" Annya said as Jaykriss closed the door to the bain behind him.

Marda was waiting for him at the first clearing, crossbow in hand and quiver on his shoulder. The great bow of Fyrdhom was strapped to his back, wrapped up in an oilcloth. Dressed head-to-toe in black, he completed his armaments with Icebreaker, his father's battle sword, strapped to his belt. It gleamed silver in the early morning sun.

He looks like he's ready for war. "Why the battle sword?" Jaykriss said.

"I anticipate the Geshans might have a surprise or two waiting for us along the way, so I thought I might surprise *them*. It would not be the first time my father's sword has tasted Geshan blood."

Jaykriss rolled his eyes at his friend. "You're so dramatic, Marda," he said, smiling.

Marda frowned. "What do you mean?"

Jaykriss bowed himself up and scowled. "It would not be the first time my father's sword has tasted Geshan blood." He mocked his friend's tone.

"I meant that!"

"When you talk like that, you sound like you're quoting the Holy Books, or the Ramallah Prophecies."

"I'm done talking to you, Jay. Leave me alone." Marda's lips were pressed tightly together.

"Marda, relax. I'm just kidding with you."

"There is a time and a place for joking. The Geshans are *dangerous*, Jay. We got lucky last time. We might not be in the future—especially if we are caught off guard. That's all I'm saying."

Jaykriss had to admit that his friend was probably right. They *had* been fortunate before. And Marda's instincts as a warrior were uncanny. He respected them and trusted them, just as he respected and trusted Marda.

"I'm sorry for making fun of you," Jaykriss said.

Marda looked ahead. For a moment he said nothing. "Apology accepted," he said at last, allowing the slightest of grins to crease his face.

But Marda kept his hand on firmly his sword.

The boys descended into the Mist Valley together. There were no races this time, and no games. They talked very little, knowing full well that the forest shadows held many secrets.

And they were surrounded by shadows.

As they neared the great waterfall, Jaykriss could hear the thunder of the water. The air was filled with vapor, tasting vaguely of iron and stone.

"Are you afraid to kill, Marda?" Jaykriss asked.

"No," Marda said firmly, his jaw still set tight.

"Not at all?"

"Not if it is the right thing to do. There is a time and place for everything. If the Geshans attack us again, I am certain that they would have no qualms about killing *us*. We should remember that. And with Kranin as war chief, they would have very little risk. He's a formidable warrior when he's sober, but I doubt Kranin has been sober for more than a week in his life. Drunk, he would be in no condition to bring anyone to justice."

"So you would kill if it was right, but for no other reason."

Marda thought for a moment. "Yes," he said at last. "Right makes might."

"But who determines what is right? What is righteous to one man may not be righteous to another."

"Self-defense is right," Marda said.

"Agreed. But suppose someone had a disagreement with someone else—over whether a branded cow belonged to one man or another, for example. Or suppose a merchant thought he had been cheated by another merchant, and the other merchant denied it. Who is right then?"

"I suppose that is for the war chief to decide."

"But what if there is no real war chief? What if there is only a drunkard? Because that is what we have now."

"You think too much," Marda said. "I know right from wrong when I see it."

"But right and wrong are often colored by one's own perceptions. The Godswood priests called in the centurions on that group of people living in Deep Forest Glen who did not worship their gods. Do you remember that? The centurions killed every last one of them—men, women, and children. Was that right?"

"They were worshipping a false god and plotting a rebellion. It was dangerous. Everyone knows that. They were a threat to all of us."

Jaykriss shook his head. "I used to feel the same way you did, but Zamarcus got me thinking. The priests asked my father to speak to the Deep Forest Glen people before the centurions were called in. He always kept his own records of every contact he had with anyone as war chief. He hid all of his records in a wooden box beneath the war chief's bain. I never understood why he did that, but I am beginning to now."

"What are you getting at?" Marda said.

"I looked up my father's private record of his visit to Deep Forest Glen. Do you know what they were really doing in Deep Forest Glen?"

Marda shook his head.

"Nothing! They were just a bunch of people minding their own business, raising families, and working in the fields! There was no rebellion. They just believed in a different god than the one the priests have taught us to believe in. The only threat they posed was to the Godswood priests."

"So Mistress Lineya lied to us at school? I simply cannot believe that."

"She didn't know any better. She was just relaying the information she had been given by the authorities—but the things she was being told were not the truth. Reading my father's records has made all of this much clearer to me. I never understood why he disliked the priests so much, or why he feared the actions of the centurions. Now I do."

"Hmmph!" Marda said, shaking his head.

"So here's a question: what if the Godswood priests worship false gods? What if the Deep Forest Glen people were worshipping the True God, and the centurions killed them for it? Would that be right?" Jaykriss asked.

Marda rubbed his head. "No, I guess not. But you're giving me a splitting headache, and that's not right, either."

As the valley opened up before them, the waterfall was a majestic sight, as always. A rainbow arced over the frothing water, which glistened gold and silver in the rays of the sun.

"Shall we hunt first or visit Zamarcus?" Jaykriss said.

Marda grinned at him.

"Zamarcus," they said in unison.

They made their way through the stands of weeping willows and clusters of wax myrtles along the path to the waterfall.

Jaykriss could not help but look around him. The memory of the previous week's visit to this place was too fresh in his mind. He could not forget those razor-sharp teeth, those dark scales, or that great, cavernous mouth.

No Thrax this time, he thought, after surveying the valley.

He felt something unclench inside his chest.

The water pouring over them was just as frigid as the boys remembered—perhaps even more so, since the day was hotter.

"Zamarcus?" Jaykriss called after they pushed through the wall of water and into the cave behind it.

"I still think there are ghozim in here someplace," Marda said under his breath.

The cascade roared past the cave's mouth, a continuous tumble of froth and foam. Sunlight began to pierce the cave's damp gloom as the morning sun's rays pierced the veil of rushing water.

"What if Zamarcus isn't here?" Marda said.

"Then we hunt and come back another day," said Jaykriss.

They stood there silently for a few more minutes. Marda squatted to relace his leggings.

Jaykriss sighed. "I guess we should go," he said at last.

Suddenly, a blue light flickered in the cave, and Zamarcus was standing in front of them, dressed in flowing white robes. He was taller somehow; the blue light seemed to tint every fiber of his being. He wavered a bit, flickering for a second or two, steadying only to waver again.

With a shock, Jaykriss realized he could see right *through* him.

"Ye gods, a ghozim! Zamarcus has been slain and now comes to haunt this place!" Marda said. He drew Icebreaker, raising the battle sword menacingly over his head. "Out of here, ghozim! Your spirit is free to journey to the Otherworld!"

Zamarcus opened his arms. "Halt! Who goes there?" he said.

Jaykriss stepped forward. "It is us, brave Zamarcus. And we are sorry that you have met this untimely end."

Zamarcus took a step toward the boys.

"Take this as a warning, ghozim! One more step and you will taste the steel of my father's sword!" Marda said.

"I don't think ghozim are afraid of steel. Even if it is your father's," Jaykriss said under his breath.

"Who goes there? Answer me!" Zamarcus said.

"It is Marda and Jaykriss, Zamarcus. We are sorry to have…"

Zamarcus flickered and wavered, then seemed to resume the position he had been in when they first saw him.

"Halt! Who goes there?" Zamarcus said.

Something's not right here, Jayrkiss thought.

"Leave this place!" Zamarcus said in a booming voice. He raised his arms above his head and took a step forward.

"I warned you, ghozim! I am not afraid of you!"

Marda swung the gleaming battle sword in a perfect arc, slicing Zamarcus cleanly in half at the waist.

Zamarcus did not even flinch.

"Ye gods! The sorcery of this!" Marda said.

He swung Icebreaker again, the blade passing through Zamarcus's neck and striking the wall with a *clang!* Sparks flew as the sword tip glanced off the granite wall.

Zamarcus flickered again but otherwise looked none the worse for the wear. He did not even blink.

"What do you think we should do?" Marda said, Icebreaker still upraised.

"Well, I think swinging the sword at him again likely will do very little good. He's clearly not made of flesh. So for starters, I'd rule out that option."

Marda's sword dropped. "Talk to him," Marda said.

"Why don't you talk to him?"

"Look, Jay, you're the talker between the two of us. So *talk.*"

Jaykriss cleared his throat. "Zamarcus, we recognize that your spirit haunts this place, and that it is dear to you. We pledge to be good stewards of all that you have accumulated here, and we shall uphold the standards of care that you..."

Zamarcus flickered again and went back into his initial pose.

"Halt! Who goes there?" he said.

"It is Marda and Jay..." Marda said.

Zamarcus froze in mid-crouch, then flickered again and went out.

"His soul is freed," Marda said reverently, placing Icebreaker in its sheath. "The gods rest him."

The door in the back of the cave opened. Zamarcus stepped out. "Buggers!" he said, furiously wiping his spectacles. "This thing keeps resetting!"

"Gods be praised! Zamarcus has returned to the flesh!" said Marda, eyes wide.

The old man stared at him, bushy white eyebrows raised over the tops of his spectacles. "What in blazes are you talking about? I never left the flesh. In fact, I never even left my compound. Not today, at least," Zamarcus said.

"Marda thought you were a ghozim," Jaykriss said.

"You did, too!" exclaimed Marda.

A knowing smile crept over Zamarcus's face. "So the image worked?"

The boys looked at each other and nodded slowly.

Zamarcus lit a torch in the wall socket, filling the back of the cave with light. Jaykriss could now see a small metal box tucked away in a corner of the cave. Zamarcus knelt down and began fiddling with it.

"It's a thing called a hologram. I found this projection device almost intact in a box my father left me. I've been working with it for weeks. Figured it might come in handy in case someone stumbled in here and started snooping around."

He looked up and grinned at them. "Like a couple of nosy teenagers," he said.

He snuffed out the torch and beckoned to them with an outstretched arm. "Welcome back!" said Zamarcus. "Truth be told, I've been hoping you would return. Come in! I've got some things to show you."

Once they were inside, Zamarcus took them to a table littered with books, maps and diagrams. "I've decided we shall start your education by teaching you a little history," Zamarcus said.

"We've learned history in Mistress Lineya's classroom," Marda said.

Zamarcus chuckled. "Not the history I'm going to tell you. We are going to go back to tales from long ago, before the Dark King ruled."

"But why should we learn things from back then? Time has moved on. This is a different world now," said Marda.

"Ah, but people are no different. Human beings make the same mistakes again and again, generation after generation. And those who do not learn from the mistakes of the past are doomed to repeat them."

"But I thought that there was no recorded history before the Dark King," Jaykriss said.

"The priests would have you believe that. And they would be wrong. Now, let's see...where shall we start? The Chinese? The Greeks? Or should we review the ancient Holy Books?" He adjusted his spectacles and pulled out a huge, dust-covered leather-bound tome. "Ah. Here's as good a place as any," he said, opening it.

The leather spine of the book made a cracking noise, like distant thunder, as Zamarcus turned to page one. "A long time ago, there was nothing. Nothing at all—no light, no dark, no day or night. No animals, no forest, no man or woman."

"No stars?" said Jaykriss.

"Nothing."

Jaykriss felt his head reeling.

"And then something happened. Something amazing…"

14

"That's enough for today, boys. Quite enough. There's plenty more, mind you—we've just waltzed through part of history, but we've barely touched on science, for example—but you boys need to run along. It's late."

By that point, Jaykriss's head was throbbing. He had heard the old men talking about hangovers, and he wondered if this was what that felt like.

Jaykriss and Marda stayed with Zamarcus until well after sunset. They read the ancient Holy Books, and learned of a god that had no other name but God—and many other gods, too: Shiva and Vishnu, Thor, Apollo and Hera, and a host of other names. They learned of a place called Africa, where man began. They heard tales of David and Goliath, of Odysseus and the siege of Troy, of Romeo and Juliet. There were so many names—Moses and Lincoln, Hitler and Darth Vader, Gandalf and Sauron, and even strange ones, the names of the men with great powers, like Batman and Superman. And, as Zamarcus said, Jaykriss recognized people he knew in each of these individuals. He knew some of the stories before they were told, through legend and fable.

"Truly, my brain is full to the gills," Marda had said as they set out for home.

"You have no gills, Marda," Jaykriss said.

"Apparently our ancestors did, if what Zamarcus has told us is correct," said Marda, grinning.

It was as dark as pitch when the two of them arrived back in the Godswood. The stars were out. Jaykriss knew that his mother would be worried.

That upset him deeply.

He bounded up the steps to the war chief's bain, finding the door slightly ajar.

That's odd, he thought.

There were no candles lit in the house; no fire burned in the fireplace. Everything was left scattered about as though Samaria and Annya had simply vanished into thin air. Jaykriss found an ember left smoldering in the fireplace and lit a candle.

"Mama? Annya?" he called.

There was no answer.

"Where could they be this time of night?" Marda asked.

A foul sense of dread swept over Jaykriss, like a new moon tide. *What if the centurions found out about us going to see Zamarcus?* he thought. *What if they have taken Mama and Annya to the Kingsguard and I never see them again?*

He would get no answers here, he decided. He would need to pay a visit to one of their neighbors. The closest was Galabrel's family. His father was a swordsmith. But the hour was late, and Galabrel's father had a notorious temper. A visit to Galabrel's house this time of night might result in an arrow in the chest—or worse.

He wanted desperately to see Sola, but the baker's home was on the other side of the Godswood.

As he stood there, pondering over what to do, an apparition appeared at his side. "Looking for the widder woman and her young 'un, are ye?" the apparition said.

She was a tiny toothless prune of a woman, barely four feet tall, with a ragged thatch of gray hair. The old crone was dressed in an aggregation of fetid rags that seemed to have no beginning and no end. Jaykriss recognized her from the market, where she sold herbs and potions.

Some people said she was a witch.

"I am. Where have they gone?" Jaykriss asked the old woman.

"Harros and the rest of the Godswood priests rode up here and got 'em. Spirited 'em off just after sunrise. Orders of War Chief Kranin." The prune-faced woman winked at him, shaking her fingers in the air. "Rumor has it that Kranin wants the old war chief's bain for himself—and that he may be after the old war chief's woman, as well."

Jaykriss felt his face flush with anger. "Marda!" he called.

"Over here!" Marda was relieving himself behind a dense stand of boxwood.

"Marda, we must go to the Priests' Bain tonight," he said.

Marda walked toward Jaykriss, frowning. "Why would we want to do that? The Priest's Bain is on the other side of the village, at the edge of the forest."

"This woman told me that the priests have taken my mother and sister!"

"What woman?"

Jaykriss looked around. The old crone had simply vanished into the mist. "It was that old woman in the market that sells potions. The witch."

"I really don't like witches. And anyway, my mother says she's not a witch, only a crazy old lady," Marda said.

"That's not the point. The priests came this morning and took away all that's left of my family!"

"Are you certain that you can believe her? Witch or no witch, she is crazy, after all."

"Well, she may be crazy, but it is nighttime, and my mother and sister are gone. And she has given us our only clue as to their whereabouts."

"Well, if the priests have taken them, that *is* bad news," Marda said. "But why would they do that? Tradition says that the widows of war chiefs can stay in the old war chief's bain as long as there is a viable male heir."

"My father used to say that the priests consider themselves above local law and custom. They use local law only when it benefitted them. Otherwise, they took their orders from the gods alone—or from the Dark King himself. Anyway, according to the old woman, this was all Kranin's doing."

Marda spat on the ground. "He has no right," he said.

Marda drew Icebreaker from its sheath, looking at the light reflected in its brilliantly polished edge. "We should challenge Kranin. If we defeat him, we could then claim the title of war chief," he said.

"You know that is impossible. Challenges to a war chief have to be formally scheduled public contests in hand-to-hand combat. It could not be the two of us together, and it could not be tonight. We challenge Kranin tonight, and we're just attacking him, two-to-one. Then, win or lose, we'd be outlaws, and that would not help my mother and sister one bit. And if

Kranin is sober, neither of us would be likely to beat him in single combat. He's very strong when he's not drinking."

There was a flash of lightning; a throaty rumble rolled in from someplace over the horizon.

"Great," Jaykriss said. "A storm is coming."

Marda sheathed his sword. "So do we go straight to the Priest's Bain tonight? Or wait until the storm passes?"

Jaykriss shot a glance at Marda. "You know how the priests feel about the women under their charge, right?"

Marda nodded.

"So we must go tonight. By dawn, the priests could have sent them anywhere—another Wood, another District, or even to Capitus. Women under their guardianship are the property of the priesthood. If we wait another day, Mama and Annya could be lost forever. Although I have a feeling that there is another agenda at work here."

"What's that?"

"Kranin has never married, and my mother once said that he had a crush on her when they were young. The old woman said that Kranin coveted the war chief's bain—and possibly my mother. I suspect that both of her statements may be true."

"Ye gods, that would be awful! That fat drunk?"

Jaykriss shook his head, thinking of his poor mother. "Awful, indeed," he said.

"Let's go. The storm will be upon us."

15

The village slumbered on, oblivious, its lights extinguished. A fine mist swirled about in the streets. Lightning stabbed the sky at times, followed seconds later by a low growl of thunder. Wind gusts shuddered through the trees. Thankfully, the rain had not yet reached them.

"It's going to be a foul night," Marda said.

"It already *is* a foul night," said Jaykriss. "I can't see a few raindrops making it any more foul than this."

At that, Marda was silent.

The boys left the village and began walking along the Priestbain Road, a narrow trench through dense forestland that wound like a snake among a large wooded tract filled with giant cedars. The cedars had observation posts built within them; even now, Jaykriss suspected that they were being watched. The Priestbain Road was designed so that anyone approaching the priests' abode had to stay within the trench; indeed, it was like an open-topped tunnel, designed to trap adversaries inside. This made them easy prey for defenders of the bain stationed along the way. An old proverb said, "No man flees the Priest's Bain and lives."

Jaykriss could plainly see why this was true.

The Godswood Priests' Bain was a sprawling, ancient structure, originally constructed centuries before of native stone and timber. It had been the home of the high priests long before the village even existed; in fact, the Godswood took its name because of the existence of the Priests' Bain in that district. The high priests served the entire known world at the behest of the Dark King, with the Priests' Bain as their stronghold. The high priests had helped the Dark King solidify his power, years ago, when the world was in turmoil. Some said that the Dark King had once been a high priest himself, while others even said that the Dark King was a god. Reinforcing that notion, the priests always called the Dark King by another name: the God Who Walks.

In any case, one thing was certain: although the Dark King had lived for hundreds of years, the high priests were just men—flesh, blood, bone, and sinew, like the rest of mankind. They could bleed—and they could die.

Jaykriss was pondering the potential implications of this fact as they neared the Priests' Bain. *The high priests are indeed just men,* he thought. But they had powerful resources at their disposal.

"What if they refuse us?" Marda said, as if reading Jaykriss's thoughts.

"What do you mean—refuse to release my mother and sister or just refuse to speak to us?"

"Either one. Both would be failures on our part. If they refuse us, should we try to fight our way in and rescue them?"

Jaykriss looked at Marda and shook his head. "Are you insane?" he asked.

"Well, they are just priests. They are not warriors."

"But they are *guarded* by warriors. There is an entire legion of centurions stationed there. And the priests control the centurions, remember? Or have you forgotten this one minor fact?"

Marda's eyes were downcast. He remained silent.

"They would kill us, Marda, without a doubt. And based on what I have been reading about the priests and the centurions in my father's records, I am certain that they would then kill my sister and my mother, as examples. The priests are ruthless, and they answer to no one. We've been taught to think of them as soft, old men—but they are nothing of the sort."

The Priestbain Road broadened out like a funnel as they neared the bain itself. In the dark, the structure was a mountain of shadow looming above them. Lights flickered in pairs of windows scattered above, myriad sets of eyes staring down at them, unblinking.

"I forgot how creepy this place looks," Marda said.

"Well, neither of us has ever been here at night," Jaykriss said.

The Priest's Bain was surrounded by a massive granite wall tipped with iron spikes. The only breach in that wall was a huge stone arch, ornately sculpted with a plethora of intertwined images. Twin torches flickered at its base. By firelight, Jaykriss could make out the details of some of the carvings. He recognized some of them as gods worshipped by various groups of people; others he was unfamiliar with.

The top of the arch was capped with a heavy spike-tipped crown—the symbol of the Dark King. A massive cast iron gate blocked their progress through the arch.

"What are we going to do now?" Marda said.

Jaykriss ran his hand over the smooth granite surface of the wall. "Well, we certainly can't climb over this thing," he said. "There's not even a crease to get a foothold in."

Jaykriss grabbed the gate with both hands. A shock went through his fingertips, racing through his arms and slamming into his shoulder. "Ow!" he said, shaking his hands. "Don't touch the gate! There's a spell on it!"

The two of them stood before the gate. The Priest's Bain was as silent as a tomb.

Jaykriss had never felt as small and insignificant as he did at that moment.

"What can we do?" asked Marda.

I cannot simply walk away, Jaykriss thought. He knew that if he did that, he might never see his mother and sister again.

Do what you know is right, a voice within Jaykriss's head said.

It was a clear, calm voice.

His father's voice.

Suddenly, Jaykriss knew what he had to do. He grabbed the gate with both hands, once again.

"Jaykriss, no! You said it was enchanted!" Marda tried to pull Jaykriss off the gate but was hurled backward so forcefully that the wind was knocked out of him.

Jaykriss felt pulsations of energy pouring from the gate, lightning bolts ripping up his arms and tearing into his body. He was sweating, heart galloping so fast he thought it might explode, his breaths coming short and shallow, each one a stiletto thrust between his ribs.

Hold on, Jaykriss. Hold on! his father's voice said inside him.

And from someplace deep inside him, Jaykriss summoned up the strength to scream at the top of his tortured lungs, "By the gods and all that is holy, I beseech ye to open these gates, O brothers of the priesthood!"

Pain ripped though him, and yet he held on. He saw stars quivering in a pitch-dark sky. Flames burned within him, searing his flesh from the inside, and yet he refused to yield.

Jaykriss screamed again, even louder this time, his voice breaking. "BY THE GODS AND ALL THAT IS HOLY, I BESEECH YE TO OPEN THESE GATES, O BROTHERS OF THE PRIESTHOOD!"

Somehow, in the middle of a swirling maelstrom of heat and light and pain, he could see his father, whole again. And then his grandfathers and grandmothers—indeed, a whole host of his relatives, standing there around him, smiling at him.

Without warning, his relatives' flesh turned gray and fell from their bones, leaving only a wretched band of open-mouthed skeletons. A hot, sulfurous wind blew up, a wind of smoke and flame, and the skeletons themselves turned to ash, blowing away into oblivion.

And then it was Jaykriss's turn.

His looked at his arms and they were red, clenched tight, the muscles standing out like cords. His fingers seemed to have melted together, fusing around the bars of the gate, blisters forming and rupturing before his eyes.

Hang on, Jaykriss!

His father again.

Or was it his father?

A treacherous wave of despair came over him, despair darker than any he had ever experienced—even worse than when he first found out that his father was dead.

Doubt seeped into his brain, percolating there like some corrosive acid.

They've killed Mama and Annya. They're already dead.

I'm alone in the world.

He realized that the voice he had been hearing had not been his father's after all. It was a trick, an illusion concocted by the Godswood priests. And they wanted him to die.

His arms had turned black, his fingernails falling off like the discarded scales of some dead fish. He could see white bones through the eroding skin of his wrists; blackened tendons snapped, flailing about in the hellish wind. The blackness was migrating up his arms, moving toward his chest, inexorable and relentless. The urge to let the bars go was overpowering.

And yet he did not.

Your mother and sister need you, Jaykriss. Hold on.

And so Jaykriss, his voice tattered to a hoarse rasp, summoned up the strength to utter the incantation once again. It was almost a whisper this time:

"By the…gods and all that is…holy, I beseech ye to…open these gates, O brothers of the…priesthood."

A jagged bolt of lightning struck the crown on the top of the gate. The thunderclap was like an explosion. Jaykriss was hurled back from the gate, arms and legs flailing, blinded and dead to the world.

When he awoke, it was to the gentle pelt of raindrops on his face.

Marda was kneeling beside him, his hood pulled over his head. "Jay? Jay? Can you hear me?"

Jaykriss took a deep breath. "What happened?" he asked.

"You grabbed back onto that gate, you idiot, that's what happened. And I couldn't pull you off. And then a lightning bolt struck the top of the gate, and you went flying backward, and…well, here you are. Are you OK?"

Jaykriss held his arms up, slowly, almost afraid to look at them. But they were not blackened or skeletal. They were instead intact, whole, as if nothing had happened. *Another priests' trick,* he thought, his eyes narrowing.

"Are the gates open?' Jaykriss said.

Marda looked over at them. "No," he said. "No, they're not."

Jaykriss stood up, furious. "I did exactly I was supposed to do! I did *every-thing!*" he screamed.

Jaykriss strode back toward the gate.

"Jay, NO!" Marda said scrambling after him.

Just before he could grab the bars again, the gates began to swing open. A balding, small-statured hook-nosed old man stood behind the gate. He was dressed in the black robes and gold chains of a priest. Jaykriss recognized him instantly.

Harros, he thought.

A giant centurion, dressed in the standard white-and-gold centurion uniform, stood silently behind Harros. His gold-domed helmet gleamed. Jaykriss could not see the centurion's eyes beneath it, but he could *feel* them staring directly at him.

"Well, Jaykriss, son of Glyndich. I must admit you have exceeded my expectations. You have passed the first test," the old man said.

Harros swept his arm inside the gate in an exaggerated gesture, bowing his head as he spoke. The rain was coming harder now, marching through the forest and gusting so that the tree branches flailed about violently.

Jaykriss bowed as well. Marda did not. Jaykriss could almost feel the old priest's eyes crawling over him, as if he were searching for something.

What are you looking for, old man? he thought.

By contrast, Harros absolutely ignored Marda—as if the older boy were completely invisible.

Jaykriss realized that it was not storming inside the Priestbain wall. In fact, there was not any rainfall at all.

The old man stood back upright, silver eyes ablaze.

"Custom dictates that it is time for formal introductions, but I feel I know you both quite well, Jaykriss and Marda. Quite well indeed. And we all met before at the War Chief's Bain a few evenings ago, when I was visiting your mother. So no introductions are necessary."

He tapped his staff twice on the ground. The massive gate closed behind them suddenly, with a metallic *clang!* Jaykriss could feel the massive deadbolts locking into place.

"And so you are here, inside, under the humble protection of the servants of the gods. Welcome, young men, to the High Priests' Bain."

16

Jaykriss and Marda followed Harros and the silent centurion through the Inner Baingate, which closed behind them with a deep *kerchunk!*

The centurion remained at the Inner Baingate. Jaykriss and Marda followed the ancient priest through the Priestbain yard.

"How is it not raining in here?" Marda said, looking skyward.

"We are immune to the vagaries of weather," Harros said. "The gods see to that."

Marda pulled back his hood and ran his fingers through his hair.

"What business brings you to the Priest's Bain at this late hour?"

"His mother and sister are . . ." Marda blurted out.

Jaykriss silenced Marda with a wave of his hand.

"High Priest Harros, my mother and sister are missing. They were taken from our home today while we were out hunting. Do you know where they are? I was told that they were taken here," Jaykriss said.

Harros glanced at him, his eyes ablaze. A cruel frown crossed his face.

"Who told you that?" he sanpped.

"Soneone who saw it happen. A neighbor."

"They are safe here with us. No harm will come to them."

"But why were they taken? The laws are very clear on this—they may stay in the war chief's bain as long as there is a viable male heir. And that's me."

"So you are."

"So why did you take them?"

"The rule you cite applies only if the new war chief is already married. The current war chief, Kranin, has no mate. As such, after the period of mourning for the prior war chief has ended, the new war chief is given the option of first refusal—that is, if he elects to marry the spouse of the former war chief, he can exercise an option on the old war chief's bain. If he does not desire to marry her, then she can stay in her current domicile with her family as long as there is a viable male heir."

"So War Chief Kranin wishes to marry my mother."

The old man glanced up at Jaykriss. "That is apparently the case," he said.

"But why take her out of her home?"

"That is another application of the rule, designed to keep the old war chief's spouse from…escaping, for lack of a better term. A few have run away in this situation. Years ago, we had one war chief's spouse from the Brightwood, a woman named Bathrania, who actually took her entire family into the Great Wilderness after her husband died. She and her children formed an outlaw colony that grew into a real threat to the safety and security of the people serving the God Who Walks. Bathrania's people called themselves the Tribe. We sent a force of centurions into the Great Wilderness to restore order, and Bathrania's tribe butchered them all."

"So what happened to Bathrania and the Tribe? Are they still out there in the Great Wilderness?" Marda asked.

"Sadly, the Tribe was apparently destroyed by a wandering pack of vermithraxes—one of the perils of trying to carve out an existence outside of the jurisdiction of the One True King. The God Who Walks could have protected them. But they chose to live outside his protection—and, as such, they paid the ultimate price for their indiscretion. Their bones are now lining the dragons' nests. Today, there is nothing left of the Tribe or their descendants—not a man, nor a woman, nor a child. Their line was extinguished."

He shot a quick glance at Jaykriss. "An instructive lesson, wouldn't you say?" Harros said.

The three of them approached the door to the Priests' Bain. It was at least ten paces tall, a wood-and-iron construct ornately carved in the same manner as the Priestbain Gate, with all sorts of images, great and small. Twin torches blazed by the doorway. "One moment. I must enter the code to the door. Then you may see your mother and sister."

The priest hunched over an iron box studded with various glowing jewels arranged in a grid. He looked this way and that, insuring that he could not be seen, then tapped a sequence onto the grid with his hand as if he were playing a finger drum. Try as he could, Jaykriss could not see what Harros had entered. Marda, by contrast, was completely uninterested; he was vainly peering at his own reflection in the polished surface of his sword.

After a few moments, the door opened.

Jaykriss gasped.

In stark contrast to its dour exterior, the inside of the High Priests's Bain was the most beautiful place he had ever seen.

An arched ceiling vaulted over a hundred paces into the air. The walls were covered with stone carvings, many of which were inlaid with gold and silver. Panels with bejeweled mosaics illustrating legends of the various gods were placed in alcoves spaced every thirty paces or so. Vast cast-iron lanterns hung from above, each aglow with a curious blue-green light. Black-robed priests, their feet slippered, padded softly about, their murmuring echoing softly throughout the cavernous chamber.

"Ye gods," murmured Marda.

"Indeed," said Harros, managing a thin-lipped smile.

They strode through the central hallway for a few hundred paces before turning down another passage. The ceiling in this one was lower, but the walls were no less ornate. Everything here was inlaid with gold; the entire hallway gleamed with the warm, dull sheen of a polished candlestick.

"The Golden Hallway," Harros said, his palms open and outstretched.

They reached a door in the Golden Hallway that had a large green stone set within its center. Harros turned it three clicks to the right.

The door opened.

Samaria and Annya were sitting on a small sofa beside the window inside a beautiful, spacious room. Samaria was reading to Annya from a picture book. A large canopied bed stood in the center of the room; curtains made of dark green silk brocade covered the windows. A glass bowl of fruit—grapes, oranges, apples, and peaches—sat upon a small marble-topped table in the entrance foyer.

"Jay!" Annya screamed, running to hug her brother.

"Hey, punkin'!" he said, kneeling to wrap his arms around her.

"Mama and I came here for vacation. Are you on vacation, too?"

"No, I'm not, Annie Bell. I'm here visiting you."

Jaykriss stood and hugged his mother.

"I was worried about you. I came home and the house was dark…"

"We're fine," she said, smiling. She cast a warm glance at Harros. "The priests have been most gracious in their accommodations. We are being held here pending a few…negotiations with War Chief Kranin."

Harros smiled back at them, bowing at the waist. "I'll leave the four of you to talk," he said.

The door closed behind him as he left. Jaykriss could hear the three clicks once again, and a soft *clack!* as the deadbolt locked them in.

Jaykriss turned toward his mother. "Surely you are not actually considering *marrying* Kranin!" he said.

Samaria held her finger to her lips. Taking a piece of paper and a pen from her pocket, she scrawled out a few words: *Walls have ears. Must write.*

Jaykriss nodded.

They came with centurions, she wrote. *There was no time to run. Worried about your sister.*

Jaykriss wrote her back: *No warning?*

Samaria shook her head.

Were either of you hurt in any way?

Samaria shook her head again.

I don't want you to marry Kranin. He's awful.

He's not as bad as you might think. We've known each other a long time, she wrote.

Samaria paused, and then added:

And I'd much rather be with Kranin than be at the mercy of Harros.

"Seriously?" Jaykriss said out loud.

Samaria nodded vigorously.

I may not have a choice, she scrawled. *My marrying Kranin would save your sister from these damned priests. Maybe you, as well.*

Jaykriss shook his head, exasperated. *But at what cost?* he wrote.

A price I'm prepared to pay.

The door began making a clicking sound. Samaria balled up the notepaper and popped it into her mouth.

The door swung open. Harros shuffled in, his gold chains jingling.

"Well! I hope you've had a nice chat. It's very late, Jaykriss son of Glyndich, and I'm afraid that I'm going to have to ask that you bid each other goodbye. You can visit again on the morrow, of course. They will be well-kept, as you can see," Harros said.

Jaykriss hugged his mother again and knelt to kiss his sister on the forehead.

"Be good, Jay!" Annya said.

"You be good, too!' Jaykriss said. Standing, he looked back at them. His heart felt like it was going to burst open. "I love you," he said quietly, fighting back tears.

"I love you too, son. Be brave."

Annya kissed her fingers and placed them over her heart. "Safe hunting, Jay," she said.

Jaykriss repeated the gesture to her. "Safe hunting, Annie Bell," he said.

Harros escorted the boys out and locked the door tight behind them.

17

Marda and Jaykriss stood with Harros at the gate to the Priest's Bain. Outside the gate, Jaykriss could see the rain still falling.

Inside, it remained as dry as a bone.

"It seems that you have some powerful magic going on here," Jaykriss said.

"Magic?" the old man said.

"No rain inside? You called it 'the will of the gods,' but it seems to me to be a magic trick."

"Ah," said Harros. "That." Harros waved a wizened hand expansively in front of the gateway. The massive cast-iron gates began to swing open with a deep-throated *gronk!* "Religion and magic are two sides of the same coin," Harros said. "Both seek to explain the inexplicable. But religion acknowledges that there are higher powers responsible for that explanation. Practitioners of magic do not always acknowledge which masters they serve."

He raised his slender eyebrows. "However, there are *always* masters being served, whether one acknowledges it or not." Two giant centurions materialized, golden helmets gleaming. They lined up behind Harros, silent and ramrod-straight. "Have a safe journey back home, Jaykriss, son of Glyndich, and Marda, son of Garoth. May the gods protect you."

The massive gate swung shut with a definitive *clank!*

And when the gates closed, Jaykriss realized that Harros and the centurions were gone, vanished as if they had never been there.

"What can we do now?" Marda said.

Jaykriss held a finger to his lips. "Walk," he said.

They entered the trough of the Priestbain Road once again. Jaykriss could feel the eyes upon his back. He was certain that they were being watched, and maybe even followed.

"My mother and sister seem to be well-cared for," Jaykriss said loudly.

"Yes. The high priests are *wonderful* hosts," said Marda.

Jaykriss rolled his eyes.

The winds and lightning had dissipated, leaving only a gentle patter of rain that barely reached them at all as they walked within the sheltered Priestbain Road.

Jaykriss was so exhausted that it was all he could do to put one foot in front of the other. His muscles ached, his joints throbbed, and his head was stuffed with cotton.

Mama, he thought. *Annya.* He was glad that they were being cared for, but he knew what Samaria was thinking of doing—and the thought of his mother living the rest of her days with Kranin was simply horrifying.

Papa would hate that, he thought.

They stumbled back into the village in the chill of the predawn morning. The night was still and thick. The only sounds were the rustle of trees in the wind and the staccato *drip drip drip* of the waning rain.

"What can we do?" mumbled Jaykriss.

"We could go see Zamarcus. He might have some answers."

"I don't want to walk into the Mist Valley in the dark."

Marda thought for a moment. "You seem to be pretty tight with Mistress Lineya. Perhaps we could talk with her," he said.

Jaykriss clapped Marda on the back. "*That* is the best idea you've had all night," he said.

Mistress Lineya lived in a tiny wooden bain in a wooded area near the school. A large live oak tree draped itself over her rooftop, its thick branches forming a canopy that sheltered the entire home. The tree's thick, tangled roots had wormed themselves beneath the foundation, buckling the house a bit in the middle as they embraced the tiny abode.

No lights were on; the windows were closed tight, like a dead man's eyes.

"She's probably sleeping," Marda said. "Maybe we should wait until morning."

"Oh, come *on*. If we wait until morning, my mother and sister may be gone—or the marriage to Kranin will be arranged. We need to come up with a plan *now*."

They walked up the narrow steps. A small black cat, yellow eyes aglow, arched its back at them and hissed. Marda's eyes grew wide.

"She's not a witch, is she?" asked Marda.

"No more than I am. How is it that you can be so fearless in facing armed Geshans and so bloody *thick* when it comes to anything else?"

"Fighting, I know. Magic and religion are two things I don't really understand," Marda said.

Jaykriss knocked on the door. There was no answer.

"She's sleeping. We should go," said Marda.

"Of *course* she's sleeping. We knew that before. It's just a few hours before dawn."

Jaykriss knocked again, gingerly. "Mistress?" he said. His voice was quavery and uncertain. He had to admit he had a few misgivings about this. Yesterday, he would not have dared to approach a teacher's bain in the wee predawn hours.

But this was not yesterday.

Perhaps Marda is right, he thought, for a moment. *Perhaps we should just leave and come back in the morning.*

But then he thought of Kranin, with his red-rimmed eyes and wretched, rotting teeth falling out of his head. He imagined the man's prodigious bulk pressing against his mother, the foul stench of mead on his lips as he bent down to kiss her...

Jaykriss hammered on the door with both fists. The black cat scampered away, hiding in a gap someplace beneath the home's crumpled-up foundation.

"Mistress! It's *Jaykriss*! I need you!"

There were footsteps inside—irregular, half-dragging footsteps that Jaykriss recognized. And then a lantern flickered on, its pale yellow light catching the boys by surprise.

"Jaykriss?" Mistress called from inside the bain.

"Yes, ma'am."

Locks clicked and tumbled and the wooden door swung open.

Mistress Lineya stuck her head outside. Her eyes were alert, vigilant. She scanned about in the darkness before looking at Jaykriss and Marda.

"Ye gods, boys, what are you doing out there at this hour? And both of you without torches. There are packs of direwolves about in the dark. You know that, right? They come into the village sometimes, when they know the men are asleep, looking for some sweet young thing to eat—and they would make quite a meal out of the two of you."

Jaykriss grabbed her hand. "It's my mother and sister. The priests came and took them to the Priest's Bain."

Mistress looked right and left, then pulled the two of them through the door.

"Get in here, child. These are not the sorts of things we need to say outside of the walls of someplace safe."

She latched the door behind them and shuffled across the room, dragging her bad leg even more than Jaykriss remembered. Striking a match, she lit another lantern, adjusting the flame to a low flicker.

"Sit," she said, motioning over her shoulder.

Marda, mute and petrified, plopped right down on the floor where he stood. Jaykriss found a nearby bench.

Mistress placed a pot of water on top of her massive pot-bellied iron stove and turned up the burner. "We'll make some tea," she said. "You boys are soaked. I'll bet you are chilled to the bone."

After placing the lantern on a rough-hewn wooden table, Mistress lurched her way over to the two of them with a pair of blankets. She handed one to each of them, looking them over as she did so. Her eyes were as sharp as an eagle's.

"So the priests have taken Samaria and Annya?"

Jaykriss nodded, wrapping the blanket tightly around his shoulders.

"I take it that this was Kranin's doing."

"But how did you...?"

"Kranin always loved Samaria. But your mother only had eyes for Glyndich. There was never any other for her. You know why Kranin never married?"

Jaykriss shook his head.

"Frankly, he kept hoping that your father would die. And eventually Glyndich obliged him. Now he's got the priests involved. In doing that, he owes them a debt that will not be lightly repaid. The priests are not altruists. They keep an account of everything, forget nothing, and extract their due payments in blood and treasure."

"But...are they not supposed to be servants of the gods?" Jaykriss said.

"They are servants of their own interests. And the interests of the Dark King, of course."

Jaykriss cast his eyes at his feet. "The priests call the Dark King 'The God Who Walks,'" he said.

"They call him a great deal more than that," she said. She glanced at the pot of water. It had begun to boil. "This should warm you up," she said, pulling a many-fingered clump of sassafras roots from a brass hook on the wall.

She opened the wooden cabinet and took out three battered tin cups, then withdrew a paring knife from the butcher block and began slicing off thin slivers of sassafras bark.

Jaykriss looked around. The room was dimly lit, the lanterns casting shadows on top of shadows, and the low orange flame in the hearth was all but burned out. But as his eyes adjusted, Jaykriss could see that there was very little in the way of furniture—and what was there was spare and simple.

She hardly has anything, Jaykriss marveled.

Mistress had always seemed like such a force of nature at the school—her face as jagged as lightning, eyes as bright and intense as a marmot's. Stories about her abounded. Some might have been true, or at least partly so; others were emphatically not.

Jaykriss looked over to see Mistress gazing intently at him. He quickly lowered his eyes.

"I know what you're thinking, Jaykriss. My place isn't fancy, but I've never needed much—just food, a warm fire in winter, a roof over my head, and stars in the sky. Everything else is just a luxury to me. And I have my books," she said, motioning to a solitary bookshelf on the far wall.

"Were you ever married?" asked Marda.

Jaykriss kicked him.

Mistress snapped off a short purple segment of sugar cane and broke it down to the fibrous pulp, which she then crushed and placed into the cups.

"No, dear. I *almost* was once, long ago. He was a young wizard, of sorts—like his father before him. A young, idealistic chap. I loved him, then. Broke my heart when he left me. But he's long since gone." She sighed, absently smoothing her wrinkled dress with bony hands.

"Anyway, that's that. Here's your tea," she said, handing each of them a cup before sitting down.

Jaykriss sipped at the steaming cup. It was vaguely spicy, with a sweet, earthy scent that filled his nostrils. "So what can I do? How can we keep my mother from having to marry Kranin?" he said.

Mistress frowned. "It will not be easy. The law is fairly clear on this. You could challenge Kranin in single combat, of course—but that's a contest you would not likely win if he is sober. You could appeal directly to the Dark King, but you'd have to travel to Capitus for that—and even then, there is little likelihood that you would even get an audience with him, or that your appeal against a sitting war chief would be successful. And an appeal to the priests would be pointless. The priests are on Kranin's side already. So I think you are going to have to accept that your mother will be married to Kranin. That's just about the size of it."

Jaykriss felt tears stinging his eyes. "There's nothing else? There's no other way to stop this?"

"Well, there's the Mortal Challenge of the Priests, of course. But that's an incredible risk."

Marda's eyes grew wide. "No one has successfully completed the Mortal Challenge in nearly a hundred summers!" he said.

"You *know* about this?" Jaykriss said.

"My father told me about it. Basically, it's a series of tests that the Godswood priests put you through. The tests are both physical and mental. The difficult thing is this: no two Challenges are alike, so it is difficult to prepare for them. A lot has to do with one's ability to adapt under stress. The Dark King was one of the first to successfully complete the Challenge. Fyrdhom passed it, too—in fact, he was the youngest ever to complete the Challenge. But it has been many years since anyone has passed. Many people have died or been seriously injured while trying."

"People have *died?*" Jaykriss said.

Lineya and Marda both nodded. "The tests can be lethal," said Lineya. "Your safety is not guaranteed."

"But why would anyone even risk it, then? What does one get if one completes the Challenge?"

Marda grinned. "Anything one wants," he said.

"Anything one wants that the priests can obtain," Lineya corrected him. "You get to ask for one thing—jewels, land, a position of power, a pardon for a condemned loved one, what have you. You ask for something, and the priests are obliged to fulfill the request. Some say, however, that the choice of reward that the winner makes is also part of the Challenge. It's been so long since someone has completed it that those sorts of specifics are unclear."

"I'll do it," Jaykriss said.

"Are you insane?" Marda said.

"I'm not. It's worth it to me. It could save my mother and sister."

"But how would you even begin to train? I mean, no one is alive who has ever completed the Challenge. You would have no guidance—and you could be killed!"

"I will not have my father's memory defiled and my mother's and sister's lives ruined by having that drunken fool Kranin take my father's place in our home. I would rather be dead than see that."

"You may get your wish there," Marda mumbled.

"Who could train me for the Challenge?" Jaykriss said.

Mistress shook her head. "Marda's right," she said. "The whole idea is just too dangerous. There is no one living who was around when the last Challenge was successfully completed. The only way you might get information of that sort would be from old archives and books. I doubt there would be any such information out here. Perhaps in Capitus, but not in the Godswood—unless you got it from the priests themselves. And I somehow doubt that the priests would yield that information volitionally. You would be going into it blindly. In that setting, you would almost certainly die—and that would accomplish nothing at all. We simply have to find another option."

Jaykriss was silent. He cupped the steaming mug in his hands and stared silently into it, watching the steam swirl off of it like a miniature storm.

"Thanks for doing this," he said at last.

"Well, I just couldn't have just let you boys stay out there half the night. The direwolves might have gotten you—or worse."

"Worse?"

"The Thrax is out and about, too. If that thing was nearby, we'd hear it coming, of course, but we'd be powerless to stop it. Even now, in my home, we could do nothing but pray it if it decided we were going to be its midnight snack. I've only seen the Thrax once, from a distance, but that was enough. The creature's a force of nature. It's like an earthquake or a volcano—a vast instrument of destruction."

Mistress glanced up at Jaykriss. There was a sudden wounded look in her eyes. "But of course, you know that. I'm sorry, Jaykriss," she said.

"It's OK," he said.

"So why did you choose to come to me, as opposed to anyone else?" she asked.

"I trust you. You're honest," Jaykriss said.

His fingers touched the gizzard stone in his pocket that Mistress had given him.

"Do you have any other ideas? Anyone else you could talk to?" Lineya said.

Marda put his cup down and swallowed. "Well, we thought about going to see Zamarcus," he said. "He's really brilliant. He's so far away, though. Through the Brightwood and into the Mist Valley. So we didn't."

"Zamarcus?" Mistress said. Her face drew up, lips pursed, as if she were tasting something bitter. "That's an unusual name. Zamarcus who?" she said.

Ye gods, Jaykriss thought. He did not like the look on Mistress Lineya's face.

Marda was his best friend, for certain. Marda was a great warrior and was loyal to the core.

But sometimes, Marda had a big, big mouth.

"He's just some old hermit we met in the woods. It's nothing," Jaykriss said.

Marda was staring at him. "What are you talking about? Zamarcus is just about the smartest guy I've ever met! And just because he lives behind a waterfall doesn't mean that he's a hermit," Marda said.

Jaykriss rolled his eyes. "Did you ever think that maybe Zamarcus doesn't *want* people to know where he lives? Or do you just always talk before you think, Marda?"

Marda looked hurt. "I just…"

"Tell me more about this Zamarcus. Do they call him anything else?" Mistress said. Her face was stony, emotionless, lips drawn tight. But she had put her cup down and folded her hands in her lap.

"Like what?" Marda said.

"Oh, I don't know. The Secret Keeper, perhaps. Necromancer. Son of Zatheria."

Jaykriss shook his head. "No one calls him anything," he said. "In fact, I've not heard anyone else speak of him. We met him in the Mist Valley one day, while we were hunting. And we've never spoken to anyone about him—until now."

He shot a withering glance at Marda, who was staring intently into his cup.

"He's got all of this...*stuff*, and a lot of it is old. And he has more books than anyone I've ever seen. I don't understand all of it, but it's all pretty amazing."

Mistress was staring off into space, her mind clearly elsewhere. "He lives in the Mist Valley, you say."

"Yes, ma'am."

"Alone. No family."

Jaykriss swallowed. There was a lump in his throat. *Something's not right,* he thought. "No family," he croaked, his voice suddenly hoarse.

Mistress stood up, her jaw set firm. Her eyes were ablaze. "If this man is who I think he is—and by your description, I'm fairly certain that he is Zamarcus, son of Zatheria—then the Dark King has named him a traitor to the kingdom. You should have nothing more to do with him. The kingdom has, in fact, already declared him dead. To associate with him would be treason. It would put both of your lives in danger."

Lineya was shaking. Jaykriss had never seen Mistress like this.

"How do you know him, Mistress?"

She set her teacup in the sink, her hands trembling. "Zamarcus was my betrothed. We were to be married."

Oh, no, Jaykriss thought.

"Years ago, Zatheria—his father—was named as a traitor by the Dark King. Zatheria was executed. It was rumored that Zamarcus was to be next. One night, a few moons after his father's death, Zamarcus came to see me. He told me he loved me, but he had to leave in order to survive. I said I would go with him. He said it was too dangerous, that my life would be at risk. I *pleaded* with him, but his resolve was firm. He left my home and set out for the Great Wilderness, alone."

She coughed and took a sip of sassafras tea. Her hands trembled.

"The centurions followed him. They hunted Zamarcus down. We were told that he had been killed. I never got over his death. He was the only man I ever loved."

Mistress stared out into the darkness. Her eyes were someplace else, someplace far, far away. "But now he's back, after all of these years," she said.

It was dark in the little room, but that did not keep Jaykriss from seeing the tears welling up in Mistress's eyes.

18

*H*e had dared not knock.

Lineya heard the rocks strike her window and knew it was Zamarcus. She felt it in her bones, in the pit of her stomach.

She felt it in her heart, which ached for him.

"You came for me! I knew you would!" she said, her voice a stage whisper.

"Lineya, I…" He looked up at her, his eyes filled up with emotion. She knew the look well. It was the way he had looked at her when he first told her he loved her.

When Zamarcus looked at her like that, she knew he would do anything for her. Anything and everything. That is how deep their love went.

"I'm coming up," he said, his jaw set.

Zamarcus scaled the vine trellis easily, as he had a hundred times before. He knew each iron post as it was driven into the rock wall, knew where the thick vines would hold and where they would not. Lineya's heart thrummed in her chest as she watched him climbing to her, his biceps flexing taut, his hair a tousled mass of blond curls.

She grabbed him about the waist as he clambered through the window.

"Careful now, girl! You'll throw me out," he said, smiling at her.

"I'd never do that," she said. She kissed him. Her lips lingered on his, the bristle of his beard rough against her skin. Her arms encircled his waist. She could feel his body pressing against hers, his muscles hard as iron.

"I've missed you," he said. "You know I would have come if I could. A few days after the centurions took my father, they came back. They wanted me, too—but my mother hid me away in the cellar."

His eyes were ravenous. They drank her in like cool water. She could feel them on her, lingering on her breasts, caressing her face and her hips. If it were any other man, she would have turned away.

But Zamarcus was not any other man.

"They killed him, you know," he said.

It was as if someone had slapped her. "No! But how...?"

"The centurions. By royal decree. They tortured him and killed him."

"But there was no trial!"

"The Godswood priests had said that he was a practitioner of a false religion. The centurions told my mother that the Dark King tried my father himself."

"But the Dark King is honest and merciful! He would not have stood for injustice!"

Zamarcus kissed her on the forehead. She could feel his heart beating in his chest. "That's what they want you to think," he said. "There is much you do not know."

"Perhaps the centurions were simply trying to scare your mother into giving away your whereabouts."

Zamarcus closed his eyes and shook her head. "They took her, too," he said. "She's gone."

Confusion rolled over her, lethal and awful and poisonous. She could scarcely believe what she was hearing, but it was Zamarcus. And Zamarcus would never lie to her.

Not ever.

"My father is dead, Lineya. The centurions brought us a jar with his teeth, and another with one of his fingers. And now my mother is their captive, if she is not dead already."

The room was spinning. Lineya knew what was at stake, but she did not care. She and Zamarcus were destined to be together. She knew this with every fiber of her being.

"We must go. Now," she said.

"No," Zamarcus said.

"But they'll come for you. You said so yourself."

"They already have," he said. "They burned our bain down tonight. There's nothing left. I was sleeping, hiding in the cellar, but I woke up just in time to escape out of a window. That's why I'm here now. I am certain they are looking for me. I have to go."

"That's what I was saying! We can leave now. My parents will understand. They'll have to understand! It's the only way."

He looked at her in that way again. She felt something catch in her chest. "It's not the only way," he said.

She knew what he was going to say before he said it. That was how close their spirits were—she could almost read his thoughts, could feel his feelings.

"You're leaving me," she said.

"Lineya..."

"You're going away without me, leaving me alone."

"It's the only way, Lineya. They'll kill you. I won't have that."

She felt sick at her stomach. "We'll run away together! We can go to the wilderness, into the desert, or maybe sail a boat out onto the Great Sea. Surely the Dark King cannot follow us there!"

"The Dark King has thousands of boats, Lineya. They would find us and kill us."

"I don't care if they kill me. I'll die without you." The tears came then. She could taste them in her mouth, salty and impure. She buried her face in his shoulder.

Zamarcus stroked her hair with his hand. "You will be fine, Lineya. You're smart and you are beautiful. I'll go, and you'll miss me for a while, but you'll forget about me soon enough. Then you will marry some fine young man, and you'll be a great mother to his children."

She looked at him then, her eyes ablaze. "I would rather die a virgin than be a mother to the children of a man I did not love. And I love only you," she said.

"Forget me," he said softly.

"I cannot! I'm going with you!"

"Lineya, please. This is as painful for me as it is for you. You have to let me go," he said.

"I'm going with you!"

"Look at me," he said.

She stared into his eyes. He brushed her hair away from her face, dabbing at her tears with his fingertips.

"I love you more than life, Lineya. But if you go with me, they'll not only hunt us down. The centurions will kill your parents, Lineya. And they will kill your sister, too. I know that this is true. Your going away with me would mean the end of your entire family. And I cannot let that happen. I've seen firsthand what the centurions will do. And they will do anything to get what they want."

Lineya knew that Zamarcus was right. But it hurt her. The pain was searing, like a razor blade gutting her soul.

"I have to go," he said. "They will be here soon, looking for me."

Blinded by tears, Lineya pressed herself against him, burying her head in his shoulder. "I will always love you, Zamarcus, son of Zatharia."

"And I will always love you, Lineya. There will never be another for me."

They kissed once more. Lineya savored the taste of him. She felt his hard frame as it pressed into her. She would have given him her virginity right then if he had wanted it. But *she knew Zamarcus would not have taken it from her. For Zamarcus was, above all, a man of great honor.*

And she knew that honor had its price.

"If there is any way I can come back to you, Lineya, I will. I promise," he said.

She watched him as he climbed back down the trellis, tears streaming down her face.

And then he was gone.

They announced his death a few weeks later. Killed by a pack of wild dogs in the Great Wilderness, they had said.

But Lineya knew better.

When the centurions knocked on her parents' door at last, it was all she could do not to spit on them. Still, she was as silent as a mouse, professing a profound ignorance about Zamarcus's whereabouts. She said she had heard that he was dead. She gave them nothing.

Not even when the lead centurion held her down and shattered her leg.

19

The three of them sat in silence as the gray light of dawn crept slowly into the room. There was a bond between them now, a bond made of shared secrets, a bond both bitter and sweet.

The birds were chirping their morning songs at daybreak. It was a lesson day. Decisions would need to be made. Jaykriss rubbed the sea-tripe gizzard stone in his pocket between his fingers. He felt his thoughts settle out, like silt in a riverbed. His path became clearer. He looked over at Marda and smiled. His friend was sleeping, sitting bolt upright, his hand clenched tight on the bejeweled hilt of Icebreaker.

Even asleep, he looks like he's ready for battle, Jaykriss thought. He was proud to have such a loyal ally.

Jaykriss stood up. "I'm going to visit Zamarcus," he said.

"You cannot," Mistress said. "He is an outlaw."

"I *must*. And you said they had declared him dead, anyway. What is the risk in going to see a dead man?"

Marda opened his eyes and blinked in the half-light. "Is it morning already?" he said. He stood up and sheathed his father's sword.

"Mistress, we value your opinion. But I have to find a way to get my mother and sister back. Zamarcus knows more than any of us about how to deal with high priests and centurions. And he is already outside the law—so much so that they all think he is dead. What is the harm in getting advice from him? And what good would it be to simply go to lessons today, as if nothing had happened? For all I know, Kranin and my mother could be married within a few days. After all, she has agreed to it. So I must go to Zamarcus. He could help me. And I am fairly certain that no one else in the Godswood can."

Mistress sat impassively, saying nothing. After a moment, she set her teacup down on a tabletop. "You trust him?" she said at last.

"I do."

She stood and walked over to a nearby desk, taking a piece of heavy parchment paper out of a drawer along with an ancient, ornate quill pen. She uncorked the heavy glass inkwell, which was filled to the top with viscid ink as black as pitch, and dipped the quill pen into it, swirling it around a few times.

"This stuff gets too thick sometimes," she mumbled.

She put the quill pen to paper at last and scrawled a note, then blew onto it gently to dry it.

"Give this to him," she said, folding up the note and stuffing it into an envelope. "And do not read it. It is for Zamarcus alone. I will excuse the two of you from lessons today—but I expect you to come back to the classroom tomorrow."

Mistress walked the boys to the doorway. The earliest rays of the morning sun were beginning to scatter the shadows. The air was clean and cool.

Jaykriss took a deep breath. For the first time that day, he felt a glimmer of hope.

The serpentine path through the Brightwood was choked with mud. Vines, torn from their moorings by the previous night's storm, dangled from the tree-tops; tangles of roots groped desperately at the soggy earth.

"What happened here last night?" Marda said.

"A storm, I think."

"Not the Thrax, I hope."

Jaykriss shook his head. "The Thrax would cause far more damage than this," he said.

The fog in the Mist Valley was viscid. Jaykriss could taste it on his tongue with each and every breath, moist and vaguely metallic.

I don't like this, he thought. He was filled with a dread that he could not explain. It as though an army of ghozim had surrounded them, watching the two in silence with dead, watery eyes.

"Stay close," Marda said, his voice drawn and tight. His hand, white-knuckled, gripped the hilt of Icebreaker like a vise. The swirling mists swallowed his words whole.

Even the thunder of the waterfall was muted, distant, its powerful roar smothered by the funereal gray fog.

They reached the river just as the dull orb of the sun began to burn away the night.

Suddenly, Marda stopped. He placed a hand on Jaykriss's shoulder. "Hold up," he whispered.

At first, Jaykriss heard nothing—nothing but the waterfall, guttural and primeval, the same as it ever was. But then he heard the other sound, a sound he had never heard before—a whine at first, then a rising scream that filled the Mist Valley with wave after wave of sound.

Through the mist, Jaykriss could see a dark shape moving. It seemed to be floating *above* the crest of the waterfall, drifting over them to eclipse the nascent sun.

The scream grew louder.

"This is bad," Jaykriss said. "Whatever this is, it's not good for us."

The shape materialized then—a vast metallic disc, its base a twisted amalgam of tubes and pipes, with four circular pyres belching flame beneath like a quartet of erupting volcanoes.

"Run for the waterfall!" Jaykriss said.

The shadow drifted over them, unforgiving, stealing the morning light and replacing it with something else.

Jaykriss felt his heart pounding, his breath coming in short gasps as he ran. *Can't...breathe...*

And then suddenly, the waterfall coalesced in front of them, a white pillar incarnated from the enveloping mists.

Jaykriss and Marda plunged blindly through the frigid water. For a moment, the grating scream overhead was drowned out by the cataract's familiar rumble. And then they were through, inside the cave.

"Zamarcus? Zamarcus, it's Jaykriss and Marda!"

The incredible noise outside cut cleanly through the waterfall. It dug at Jaykriss's ears like a targan beetle.

Suddenly, the holographic image of Zamarcus flickered into view. "Halt! Who goes there?" it said.

"Ye gods, *that* thing again," Marda exclaimed, a scowl on his face.

"Zamarcus, open the door!" Jaykriss said.

The hologram flickered again and reset.

"Maybe if we make a little more noise..."

At that moment, a thin, disheveled-appearing Zamarcus strode right through the holographic image of himself.

The old man was virtually naked, wearing only his glasses and a diaphanous pair of shorts shot through with holes. He was painfully thin—a veneer of flaccid skin stretched over a framework of bone. And that skin was covered with a bumper crop of warts, moles, and other things.

Jaykriss tried not to stare at him.

Marda brandished his gleaming sword in front of the old man.

"Why didn't you put some clothes on?" he said.

"Don't tell me what to do, young man! You two came to me at the crack of dawn, making all kinds of racket, and I am supposed to dress in courtly attire to meet you? I heard you out here, hopped out of bed, pulled on these shorts, and could not find a single blasted robe in the mess inside the cave. You sounded so upset that I decided that I should just come outside right away."

It's actually midmorning, Jaykriss thought, but he kept silent.

Marda was staring at the cave's ceiling, studiously avoiding even a glance at the old man. "You sleep in the nude?" he said.

"You don't?" Zamarcus said.

Marda shook his head vigorously.

Suddenly, Zamarcus cocked his ear to one side. "What's that sound? I've heard it before somewhere." His eyes widened. "Come inside, boys. Quickly, before they land."

"Land? But we're on land."

"Before they land the flying ship. That thing you're hearing is a flying ship which belongs to the Dark King—and that ship is filled to the top with centurions."

Marda's eyes grew wide. "The Dark King has a flying ship?"

"He has several. He usually doesn't take any of them far from Capitus. If the Dark King has sent the ship here, to this valley, I suspect that he is probably looking for someone. Because there's no other reason for those ships to be in the Mist Valley."

"Who would the Dark King be looking for here?" said Jaykriss.

Zamarcus was frowning, his eyebrows furrowed. "That's what I'm worried about. No one lives in the Mist Valley but me. So I might be the one they are looking for. But I don't know how they could possibly know that I was here."

Jaykriss felt ill. *I know,* he thought.

Zamarcus led them the boys through the doorway, which closed tight behind them. "Ah, there it is," he said.

He grabbed a robe hanging on a hook in an alcove just inside the doorway and draped it across his thin shoulders.

Archimedes was perched atop a bust of Shakespeare that stood in a corner of the room.

"Nevermore!" the old raven quorked.

"Hush, Archimedes," said Zamarcus.

Archimedes flapped away into an adjacent room, miffed at his rebuke.

"You boys didn't tell anyone about me being here, did you?" Zamarcus asked, tying the sash on his robe into a bow.

Marda and Jaykriss looked at each other.

"Only…" Marda said. He looked at his feet.

"Well, come on, boy, spit it out. Who was it?"

Marda looked up. "Mistress Lineya," he said.

Zamarcus's eyebrows shot upward, his eyes wide.

"*Lineya* knows about me?"

Marda and Jaykriss nodded.

Zamarcus ran his spidery hands through the nest of his hair, shaking his head. "Ye gods, do you know what that could mean?" Zamarcus said.

"We didn't realize you two knew each other. At least, not until she told us," Marda said.

"She was my…girlfriend once, long ago. But she thinks I am dead."

"Not any more," said Jaykriss, firing a withering glance at Marda.

"My stars. Lineya, of all people. And after all of these years. I guess she finally got her revenge against me for leaving her."

Zamarcus started walking back toward the door that led to the cave.

"Where are you going?" Jaykriss asked.

"To turn myself in," he said.

"What?"

Zamarcus spun around. His spectacles had fogged up. Jaykriss could barely see the old man's red-rimmed eyes peering dimly at him from behind them, as if he were staring through a cloud.

"All of my life, I have worked to collect the things you see here. You see the things in this cave as curiosities, as mere relics from some dim time in the past, but they are so much more than that. What you see here is all that is left of human history, Jaykriss. There are secrets here that the Dark King would love to see destroyed, for they are a threat to him. There is so much you don't understand, so much I could teach you both, but there is no time now. No time at all. This…this must be saved. And I shall sacrifice myself to save it."

Zamarcus wiggled his bony toes into his sandals, squatted, and began lacing up the leggings.

"But Mistress Lineya said you would help us! She wrote you a letter!"

Zamarcus looked up.

"Lineya wrote *me*?"

Jaykriss nodded, thrusting the letter at him.

Zamarcus snatched the envelope from him hungrily and ripped open the seal.

The boys stood silently for a few moments as Zamarcus read. Jaykriss simply stared at Zamarcus. Marda picked up the polished white skull of horned, fanged beast and began opening and closing its hinged, fang-studded jaw.

"Well," Zamarcus said at last. His voice was hoarse.

"Zamarcus, I don't have anyone else to help me. My father is dead, and the Godswood priests have my mother and sister. I *need* your help, Zamarcus. I need…"

Zamarcus held a finger to his lips.

"A moment, please. I need to think."

Reaching over to an adjacent shelf, the old man plucked an ornately carved ivory pipe from its wooden holder. He then picked up a small cloth bag, opened it, and dumped the brownish powder within into the pipe's bowl, tamping it down with his thumb.

"What's that?" asked Marda.

"Zale. An old mystic's trick. Supposed to help clear one's mind of clutter."

He took a piece of kindling over to the fireplace, lit it, and jammed the burning ember into the pipe. The pipe's contents popped and hissed. Purplish smoke curled into the air. Before long, the whole room was filled with the rich intermingled odors of frying bacon and baked cherries.

Jaykriss inhaled some of the smoke. It made him dizzy. His tongue felt numb. "What is that?" he asked, coughing.

"Zale smoke," Zamarcus said. "Don't inhale any. You're too young. Now, stop with the questions for a moment. I need to concentrate."

Jaykriss found his mind wandering. It was bobbing along, really, like a cork caught in a spring tide. He thought of his poor mother and his sister, both captives, and suddenly felt as though he were going to cry. He remembered his father's legacy and realized that he had to be strong, to be a *warrior*, by the gods. There were looming shadows of uncertainty—the Thrax, the Geshans, Kranin, and the Godswood priests. He thought of Sola, struggling through her father's indifference. Waves of emotion swept over him, threatening to capsize him, to drown him in the cold gray depths of the white-capped sea.

What is wrong with me? he thought.

It's the zale, another voice—a voice he did not recognize—said from inside his own head.

Purple smoke filled the room, swirling about in iridescent hues that glittered in the candlelight. Or was there a candle? Jaykriss couldn't tell. It might have been a lamp, or the moon, or a comet—for he was certain he was floating about in the night sky someplace, although he couldn't remember how he got there.

Jaykriss glanced over at Marda, who was now engaged in an animated conversation with the horn-studded animal skull he had been holding. Oddly enough, Jaykriss would hear what both Marda and the skull were speaking about. The skull was saying something about hunting, but it was in some sort of low animal dialect that he could not fully comprehend.

I don't like this, he thought.

Jaykriss remembered the sea-tripe gizzard stone in his pocket. He rubbed the stone between his thumb and his forefinger. That helped clear the cobwebs from his mind. His racing thoughts slowed from a gallop to a walk, and the numbness in his fingertips began to fade.

Jaykriss decided that he did not particularly like zale.

After a few moments—or was it a few hours?—Zamarcus folded up the letter and spoke up. "Well. This changes things, I think." He put the still-smoking zale pipe back in its wooden holder. "Lineya has forgiven me. She wants me to help you two. So I guess I've made a decision."

Zamarcus sat down. His eyes danced. He seemed decades younger suddenly, as if he had been infused with new life. He waved the letter in front of his face. "Let me tell you a bit about the Prophecy of the One Who Leads," he said.

"The Prophecy of the One Who Leads says that a man filled with the spirit of the gods will emerge from the Godswood. The One Who Leads will shed light on the darkness, drive evil from the world, and his ascension will usher in a new era of peace and prosperity that will last a hundred generations."

"I've never heard of that prophecy," said Marda.

"That's because the Dark King banned it. He even had the Godswood priests tear it from the scrolls of Ramallah."

"That's not so bad," said Jaykriss. "At least it brings the people hope."

Zamarcus slammed his bony palm on the table. "Precisely! You see, when he first came into power, the Dark King tried to use the Prophecy of the One Who Leads to his advantage. The Prophecy says that the One Who Leads shall come from the Godswood, and that he will have a Warrior by his side who will mete out his justice. So the Dark King allied with the Godswood priests and procured the services of Fyrdhom the Great, the finest archer of all time."

"Fyrdhom!" Jaykriss exclaimed. He and Marda looked at one another.

"What is it?" Zamarcus said, looking at the boys with raised eyebrows.

"I have Fyrdhom's bow," Marda said.

Zamarcus raised his eyebrows. "Do you, now?" he asked, glancing at the crooked homemade bow strapped to Marda's back.

Marda nodded, then noticed Zamarcus's gaze. "Not the one on my back. I keep Fyrdhom's bow covered."

"How did you get it?"

"I won it in an archery contest," he said.

"May I see it?"

Marda unstrapped the huge bow and removed its sheath, then handed it to Zamarcus.

The old man turned it over in his hands, running his fingers across the detail work. "Impressive," he said at last.

"So do you know what happened to Fyrdhom?" he said, handing the bow back to Marda.

"He disappeared," Jaykriss said.

"He did indeed. And his body was never found. But his bow was, obviously. And his horse as well, for that matter, though the poor beast had to be put down."

"Do you know what *really* happened to Fyrdhom?" Marda asked.

"Alas, I do not. But the circumstances were a bit odd, don't you think? People near the Dark King have a terrible habit of either dying or disappearing forever. Like a moth drawn to a flame, I'm afraid Fyrdhom simply fluttered too close. A pity. For he truly was a great warrior. It was his loss that led to the Ramallah prophecies being banned. The Ramallah scrolls spoke of a Great King—the One Who Leads—and a Great Warrior. Without Fyrdhom, the Great Warrior, the Dark King no longer fulfilled the prophecies. And he wanted to eliminate any hope that any rebellious people might have for another ruler, for a savior."

Slowly, inexorably, Jaykriss felt the pieces slide into place in his brain. He rubbed the sea-tripe gizzard stone between his thumb and forefinger.

Click! Click! Click!

"What does this all have to do with you deciding to stay?" Jaykriss said.

"I'm getting to that," Zamarcus said. "Years ago, I knew a prophet. He was ancient when I first met him; some said he was nearly as old as the Dark King. His given name was lost to time, but he was known to all simply as Cha'barro, which means 'the Bringer of the Flame' in the old tongue. He was ancient when I first met him. Cha'Barro was blind, but the gods had compensated by giving him the gift of second sight. He spoke many languages, in tongues that were yet living and tongues that were dead, and even uttered the mystic incantations of the Zora-Jin priests, which have since been lost to all mankind.

"Cha'barro was a guest of the Godswood priests near the end of his life. The priests respected and feared him, and would not silence him for fear of divine retribution. Eventually, he died at the Godswood Priests' Bain, a man as old as the oldest of the great oak trees of the deep forest. It was said that when his eyes closed at last and he took his last breath, his soul flew out of his mouth and into the Otherworld, turning his body into dust in the blink of an eye. A wind came up from nowhere then and scattered his ashes to the heavens."

Zamarcus capped the zale pipe, extinguishing it.

"Cha'barro was fascinated with the Prophecy of the One Who Leads. He was *part* of it, in fact."

"What do you mean, he was part of it?"

Zamarcus reached up on a shelf and pulled down an aged, yellowed scroll covered with the runes from the Old Times. It was tied with a ragged piece of string. Zamarcus loosed the string and unspooled the fragile scroll, flattening it out on the table.

"This is from the lost texts of Ramallah," he said. "It is very, very old."

He cleared his throat and began. "And it shall come to pass that the Bringer of Flame shall take up residence in the Godswood, living there until the end of his days. And he shall be charged with the finding of the One Who Leads, bringing him forth from the Darkness and showing him the Light. And the gods shall see fit for him to identify the mother of the One Who Leads by her countenance, and by her nature, and he shall see her when she is with child and mark her with the Fain Mark, the Glory of the Gods, which shall identify her as the Mother of the One.

"And when the Mother of the One gives birth to the One, the gods shall seek out the Bringer of Flame and transmute his body into dust, for his quest shall at that point have been complete. And the One shall then go and be remanded to the Valley of the Kings, where he shall be taken up by the Keeper of the Flame, and trained in the ways of gods and men. And the One shall bring with him the Warrior, who shall be his Hand, and verily they shalt chase the darkness into night."

Jaykriss felt dizzy once again. The zale pipe was extinguished, but he glanced over at it anyway. He felt a chill trickle down his spine. "Did Cha'barro have a large dog?" he asked.

Zamarcus nodded.

"He did. A wolf dog, with blue eyes and fangs like knives. He called it Striker."

Marda shot a glance at Jaykriss, who was staring at the ground, tight-lipped and pale. "Lineya says that Cha'barro once approached your mother while she was pregnant with you. Were you aware of this?"

Jaykriss nodded slowly.

"Cha'barro said your mother was the Mother of the One," Zamarcus said.

"And that makes me the One Who Leads?"

Zamarcus nodded.

I cannot seem to avoid this fate, Jaykriss thought. "Zamarcus?"

"Yes, son."

"Do you really *believe* in prophecy? Because my mother says she does not. And yet I think she does, just a little. Perhaps she is simply scared of it, like people are afraid of anything unknown. Or perhaps she's worried that if she talks about something enough it will simply come true. But I know that prophecy is not science, and you're a scientist, like your father. So I guess I just want to know if you think prophecy is real."

"It is not absolute. The gods allow us free will, the free will of choice. Free will can make prophecy true or false. Destiny is not firmly preordained."

Jaykriss thought for a moment. "When did Cha'Barro die?"

"Nearly fifteen summers ago. In the Harvest Season." Zamarcus looked up at Jaykriss. "And when do you turn fifteen?"

"Soon. During the Harvest Season." Jaykriss felt ill. He was cotton-mouthed, faint-headed, his vision awash with purplish blotches that pulsated in time with his heart.

"Jaykriss, the time frame fits. You do, indeed, fulfill the prophecy. Cha'Barro was the Bringer of the Flame. I am the Keeper of the Flame—the person charged with preserving the knowledge of the ancients, like my father before me. And it is my destiny, as the Keeper of the Flame, to help you to see and understand why you are here, to help you realize your destiny. That is why we have done all of this. I was placed here to prepare the way for you."

"What does the Ramallah prophecy say about the life of the One Who Leads?" he asked.

"Why, it shall be a virtuous life, a life filled with the pursuit of knowledge."

"Not that. If I am the One Who Leads, how *long* will I live?"

At this, Zamarcus cast his eyes downward. "Your path is not predetermined, Jaykriss. The choices are yours," he said quietly.

"What does the prophecy say?"

Zamarcus read from the scroll once again. "For lo, the One Who Leads shall bring glory and prosperity to all mankind, and it shall come to pass that his glory shall illuminate the earth for a thousand seasons. But the Glory of the Gods shall burn so brightly upon his countenance that it shall consume him completely, rendering him unto ash, and his days will be numbered few."

Jaykriss thought about all of this. He was so still that he could feel his own heartbeat.

I will have to give up so much, he thought.

Including Sola.

Jaykriss had seen the sort of damage his father's death had done to his mother. He had seen how the alleged death of Zamarcus had scarred Mistress Lineya. If Jaykriss was marked for an early death, he could not do the same cruel thing to Sola. She deserved a better life.

He would have to give her up.

"It is my choice? I can choose to be the One Who Leads, or I can choose not to be?"

Zamarcus nodded. "The gods gave us free will."

"And if I choose not to be the One?"

"Then there will be another. The gods will see to that. There are many paths to the future."

Jaykriss's thoughts swirled in his head. He could feel his father's presence, someplace close by.

Do the right thing, said a still, small voice someplace deep inside him.

His father's voice.

"Have you chosen your way, Jaykriss?" Zamarcus asked.

"I have," Jaykriss said hoarsely.

And just like that, the world shifted on its axis once again, spinning into new and different directions in the cosmos. Jaykriss thought of something else his father had been fond of saying.

All choices made by men are reflected in the eyes of other men, and in the heavens, and in the stars themselves.

20

The next morning came and drifted languidly into afternoon, eventually falling backward into the cool of the evening, and Jaykriss simply endured it.

He was more surprised at what did *not* happen than he was at what did.

Jaykriss half expected to be arrested and hauled off to some dismal children's prison camp in the Deep Wild—either that or made to face the Thrax once again, perhaps naked this time, and unarmed. He fully expected the worst nowadays. Indeed, that was all he had seen of late—his father and uncle were dead, and his mother and sister were still held in captivity. He was too wired to read and too anxious to explore the cave, and so he slept, paradoxically, most of the day, waking up only to eat, use the bathroom, and worry silently.

Zamarcus fed the boys some dry, cracked bread and a handful of scuppernongs each, wild grapes with tart rinds as thick and tough as leather.

"Sorry I don't have more for you two. I don't usually have guests," Zamarcus said. He cocked his head to one side, raising one bushy eyebrow. "In fact, I *never* have guests," he said.

Jaykriss and Marda dared not go out during daylight hours, pausing instead behind the waterfall to see if they could hear the thrumming engines of the Dark King's flying ship, or see the waves of centurions as they swept through the valley in their gleaming white and gold armor, searching for Zamarcus—and possibly for them, as well.

But as the sun dipped below the horizon at last, Jaykriss, Zamarcus, and Marda stood on a rocky ledge beside the waterfall and gazed into the inky void of the Mist Valley. There were no ships and no centurions—only the throaty roar of the waterfall, the sonorous buzzing of insects, and the staccato hooting of horn-birds as they sought their furry prey in the depths of the forest.

"The flying ship is gone," Jaykriss said at last.

"I agree. They would not tarry here long. The Dark King likes to keep his ships close to Capitus," Zamarcus said.

The fingernail moon emerged from the trees like a thief in the night. The three of them watched the phosphorescent water tumble past them for a few more moments. Jaykriss felt a knot relax inside his gut.

"Well, that's that. Time to go inside for the night," Zamarcus said. They went inside the cave and closed the door.

Jaykriss's stomach growled. "Do you have something else to eat besides bread and grapes? I mean, they were good, but I'm feeling a little more hungry now," he asked.

Zamarcus grinned. "As a matter of fact, I do," he said. "I've got just the thing for you."

The old man removed an old black pot from the fireplace with an iron hook. Jaykriss had not even seen it there before; it had been surrounded by flames. "My father's recipe," he said. "Rabbit stew. Been cooking all day." He set the boiling pot upon a stone and shuffled around the room, eventually coming up with three wooden bowls and three spoons, which he set upon the table.

"Here you go," he said, ladling the steaming stew into their bowls.

Jaykriss looked at his bowl. It was filled with chunks of meat, carrots, potatoes, and onions in a thick brown sauce. Its rich, meaty aroma made Jaykriss's mouth water.

"Thank you," he said.

Zamarcus nodded, then sat down between the two boys. He bowed his head and took one hand from of each boy into his own withered grasp. "The gods be praised," said Zamarcus.

"The gods be praised," the boys echoed back.

The three of them ate as if they were starving—which they were, in fact. None of them had had any appetite the entire day. But it had returned now, with a vengeance. They emptied their bowls and each got second helpings. Marda went back for a third.

"This is some great stew," Marda said, smiling broadly between mouthfuls.

Jaykriss had been on edge all day. He had been hungry and scared and tired and anxious, but that was all gone now. Now, he was full—and sleepy. His eyes were heavy. His thoughts drifted to his mother, and his sister.

"Don't nap now! We've got to clean up!" Zamarcus said.

Jaykriss's eyes snapped open. "I'm sorry. It's just..."

Zamarcus held up a long, thin hand. "No need for excuses. We've all had a long day. But chores come before rest. I'm sure your fathers taught both of you that."

The boys both nodded. After scraping the last bit of sauce from their bowls, Marda and Jaykriss helped Zamarcus clean the bowls and spoons and wash out the stewpot. They dried their hands on a few towels hanging from wooden pegs next to the washbasin.

Afterward, Zamarcus headed over toward the fireplace. He motioned to the boys to follow him. There were two bedrolls laid out next to the hearth.

"This is where you will sleep. Tonight, we rest. Tomorrow, we shall begin talk about strategy," he said.

Marda looked at Jaykriss, one eyebrow raised.

"Strategy?" Jaykriss said.

Zamarcus rolled his eyes. "Were you even *listening* to all the stuff we were talking about before? About the One Who Leads and the Warrior? About me being the Keeper of the Flame? Remember all that?"

The boys nodded.

"Well, was I just talking to hear myself speak? And do you think that sort of stuff just *happens*? That you two boys will simply show up and the Dark King will yield, bowing his knee to you because of some musty old *prophecy*?"

"Well, I just..."

Zamarcus whirled around so that he was face-to-face with Jaykriss. Their noses were almost touching.

"Prophecy is meaningless if the proper choices are not made. Poor choices will incinerate prophecy like the morning mist. You must *prepare* if you are to fulfill what might be your destiny. You must plan. You must build up your strengths and eliminate your weaknesses. Otherwise, prophecy means absolutely *nothing*. It's smoke, an illusion, a gimmick. And the Dark King slices through gimmickry like a Valerian sword slices through butter. He would kill you both if he thought for a moment you were a threat. And what happens then? No more prophecy."

Zamarcus spun away again, his robe trailing behind him, and strode forcefully toward the fireplace. "Strategy, then. Bright and early, first thing in the morning."

Marda raised his hand.

"Marda? You have a question?" Zamarcus said.

"What exactly did Mistress Lineya's letter say that changed your mind?"

"That's between us."

"But you read it and decided to stay. It was only after you read it that you took out the zale-pipe and began thinking about the Ramallah prophecies. I think we deserve to know what she said."

Zamarcus rolled his eyes. "You are one persistent young man," he said.

He pulled the letter out of his tunic and opened it once again. "Her handwriting is still impeccable," Zamarcus said, shaking his head. He cleared his throat and began reading.

Dear Zamarcus,

These boys came to me for help. They mentioned your name, and I was astonished. At first, I was angry. I remembered how you left me, how you walked away from us. But age has brought me some capacity for reflection. I now realize that you did what you did for the sake of me and my family. And while the pain of losing you wounded me for years, I am grateful that you have survived, and that these boys have found you. They are both fine young men. In fact, they remind me of you, long ago, when the two of us were young.

There is something important you must know. The mother of the young man named Jaykriss once confided in me that she was tapped by Cha'Barro with the Fain Mark while she was pregnant with him. I have seen the Fain Mark on this woman, Zamarcus. It is real. Her son is the One Who Leads. I have been watching over him in the village, but his father was killed by the Thrax, and his mother and sister are now captives of the Godswood priests. Things have become too dangerous for him here. I feel that his destiny lies with you. I know that you will guide him well.

I have forgiven you for leaving me. These boys have need of your counsel. They are fine young men. Teach them all you know. Please give your knowledge to them with my blessing.

I want you to know…

Zamarcus coughed and cleared his throat.

I want you to know that, true to my promise, I never married. And I realized tonight that I still love you, even after all of this.

Zamarcus folded up the letter suddenly, stuffing it back into the envelope.

"Anyway, that's enough of that mushy stuff. She's forgiven me. That's the main thing. The rest of it is just a bunch of flowery words and memories and the like—things you don't need to hear."

Zamarcus took off his spectacles and wiped them clean with his robe, then sniffed, wiping his nose with a sleeve. "Truly an amazing woman," he mumbled. "Now where were we?"

"Strategy," said Jaykriss.

"Ah, yes. Strategy. A great place to begin. That's where we'll start in the morning."

He tottered across the room aimlessly, as if buffeted by some unseen current, his white hair an unruly halo around his face.

I need to talk to him about how to go about freeing my mother and sister, Jaykriss thought. But the timing was not right. He knew that. Zamarcus had his mind in another place and another time, at that moment.

And Jaykriss understood completely.

21

J aykriss drifted in and out of sleep all night. He awoke once and was momentarily disoriented, the looming shadows of Zamarcus's cavernous abode towering above him like the walls of a canyon. He was unable to figure out where he was until he saw the low flames dancing in the fireplace nearby. He awoke a second time to Marda's sonorous snoring.

And then, suddenly, his eyes fluttered open and he was being stared at by Zamarcus, who was only inches from his face.

"You're awake. That's good. We've got work to do. But first, breakfast. I've made eggs. Lots and lots of eggs."

Jaykriss sat up. The flames in the fireplace were low, mere flickers of blue and orange, and the air was chilly. He grabbed a leather vest off of a nearby chair and put it on. Marda, as usual, was already fully dressed, except for his leggings. He had gathered his weapons up and was strapping his longsword's scabbard to his belt.

The old man had ambled over to a table littered with papers, charts, and books. He rolled up the papers and stacked the books to make room for them, ducked over to the stove across the room, and returned with a couple of platas piled high with scrambled eggs, bacon, and vegetable hash.

"Where was all of this food yesterday?" Marda said.

Zamarcus cocked his head. "Why, it was right here."

"But I thought you said you only had a little bit here to eat, and that you never had guests."

Zamarcus arched his bushy eyebrows. "This is breakfast. That's different. I always have plenty of food for breakfast," he said.

The boys ate ravenously, without looking up. Zamarcus stood watching them, arms crossed.

"You're not eating?" Jaykriss asked at last. "You're making me nervous, just standing there looking at us like that."

"I've eaten," Zamarcus said. "The hour is late for me. There are only so many hours in a day, and at my age, I can almost see my time running out. So I sleep very little, arise early, and eat when I can. I had roasted fish and cracked-pepper bread before sunrise."

"Oh, that's just *awful*," said Marda, making a face.

Jaykriss grinned at him.

The boys cleaned up after finishing their meal and took their seats back at the table.

"Now, the time has come to talk strategy," Zamarcus said.

"Speaking of that, Zamarcus, what can you tell me about the Mortal Challenge of the priests?" Jaykriss said.

"Why would you want to know about that barbaric old custom? It has nothing to do with defeating the Dark King."

"Lineya had mentioned it as one way that I might be able to keep Kranin from marrying my mother."

"*What?*" Zamarcus stood up, eyes blazing. His sudden movement sent Archimedes flapping toward the opposite side of the room. "Surely she did not suggest that you use the Mortal Challenge to do this? Lineya is wiser than *that*, I hope."

Jaykriss and Marda looked at each other. "Actually, she didn't. I wanted to do it, but she thought it was a bad idea," Jaykriss said.

"There is no one living who has any experience with a successful Mortal Challenge. It is a dangerous, nearly impossible quest, and it would not help prepare you for dealing with the Dark King in the least. I am glad that Lineya had the sense to discourage it."

"So how can I save my mother and sister?"

"You cannot. They are Kranin's now. It's as simple as that."

"*That's* your solution? That's all that the great scientist can come up with?"

"Didn't you say that they were with the Godswood priests right now?"

"I did."

"And isn't Kranin the new village war chief?"

"He is, but…"

"Then it is settled. Custom gives him the right to claim her. Your mother and sister are in the safest place in the Godswood. They will be well provided for, I can assure you. No harm will come to them because Kranin has deemed that a priority—and the priests need his cooperation as much as he needs them. Besides, we have far, far greater things to attend to. You have much to learn. Learning all you need to know to defeat the Dark King might take five summers' time."

"Five summers! Why, that's…that's *forever*. I came here to get help from you for my mother and sister, to seek your advice, and you have somehow turned the whole thing into the fulfillment of your life's work. That's all well and good, but it doesn't help rescue my mother and sister."

"Well, I…"

Jaykriss brushed away a tear. "I will not let my father's memory be dishonored by letting my mother marry a drunkard! I have to get them away from him somehow. It's…it's just *wrong*. Kranin does not deserve to be living in my father's home, married to my mother!"

"The law says he does."

"And you, of all people, are lecturing to me about the *law*? Zamarcus, you've been running from the law your entire life!"

Jaykriss stood up. "I'm going to do the Mortal Challenge to save my mother and my sister. I've made my decision. So as the Keeper of the Flame, you can either help me, or not. But I'm doing it either way. This is important to me. They are all I have left, and family comes before anything else. Even prophecy." Jaykriss's fists were clenched tightly. His heart thrummed in his chest. "It's what my father would have done. Of that, I am certain."

There was silence for a moment. When Zamarcus spoke again, his voice was low and steady.

"The Mortal Challenge of the Priests is not a boy's game, Jaykriss. It is a life and death challenge. If you fail, you get nothing. You could be maimed or killed. You could be rendered armless or legless or blind. It could alter your destiny forever. Do you understand this?"

"I do."

"And yet you plan to proceed."

"I do."

Zamarcus nodded slowly, his chin in his hand.

At long last, he sighed.

"You're certain this is the path you wish to take?"

Jaykriss nodded. "Even if it means my death."

"Very well then. I will try to help you fulfill this quest. If it is that important to you, it is imperative that you at be prepared."

Jaykriss sat down. "Thank you," he said quietly.

"I have no books or scrolls on the Mortal Challenge. The Godswood priests keep those, and no one but the priests are allowed to even look at them. Still, I know a place we can get some more information about all this. It will be difficult, but I will do my best to help you. I will need to ask a few questions so that we can know what to expect."

Jaykriss was puzzled.

"Marda said that no one living had any experience with a successful Mortal Challenge."

"Marda spoke true."

"Well, how will you ask questions of someone if no one who has even seen a Mortal Challenge is alive?" asked Jaykriss.

"Who ever said that all consultations had to be with the living?" Zamarcus said.

22

When Jaykriss awoke, he gasped out loud. His heart was galloping, and he was slick with sweat.

That awful dream again. The great room was dark, but he could again see the pulsating garnet pinpoints of light given off by the dying embers in the fireplace. They glowed at him, like the cruel eyes of a hundred tiny demons.

They stared at him even now, unblinking.

The dreams had come to Jaykriss every night for over a week now, stealthy and insidious, like grave robbers. They were volatile, evanescent, evaporating from his consciousness so rapidly that he could only remember a shred here and a fragment there after an hour or so—just a vague residue of a whole night's torment.

But he always, without fail, remembered the Wall of Skulls.

He remembered the Wall as an unspeakable horror illuminated in flickering torchlight. The guttering torch he held with a death's grip, black smoke streaming from it like an ancient curse, only added to the palpable fear Jaykriss could taste in his gullet at the nearness of the Wall.

What if the torch goes out? Jaykriss thought.

Then I will be alone in the dark—with them.

By the dying light of Jaykriss's flame, the Wall of Skulls was simply that: a massive edifice of human skulls that snaked off into oblivion, impossibly long and piled as high as Jaykriss could see. Sightless, their long-dead mouths mute and gaping, they towered into the darkness, threatening to topple in a clattering avalanche of teeth and bone.

Jaykriss intuitively knew that there were stars someplace above him. That gave him some comfort, some sense of relief. Still, he could not see them—not a single one.

In the haunted dream-world that now constituted his nightly curse, Jaykriss was forced to take the presence of the stars in the sky on the basis of pure and undiluted faith. That was a task far more difficult now.

With all that Zamarcus had taught him about the Old Times, the gods that had seemed so all-powerful his entire life now seemed like mere puppets of fate—empty shells, lifeless and impotent, acting out a scripted drama written by mankind. And Jaykriss had lost his faith. He no longer believed in anything he did not see with his own eyes or touch with his own hands. Everything he had been taught over the years had been a lie, or was based upon a lie, or had a lie at its roots. For Jaykriss, the edges of reality were frayed and cracked. His entire world, in fact, seemed to be a fragile concretion of dust and memory, an aggregation that seemed somehow less than the sum of its parts.

The nightmare of the Wall of Skulls was not merely in the Wall itself. That was unnerving enough, but it was only a dream, after all—and he could wake up from a dream.

But what the Wall represented was another matter entirely.

These were people, Jaykriss thought. *People like me, with hopes and dreams, people who loved and laughed and stared at the stars in the sky.*

And then the despair would creep up on him, filling him with darkness as his torch sputtered and dimmed.

And now they are gone.

Jaykriss looked around. The Wall of Skulls receded into the world of dreams. He sat up and took a deep breath as his heart rate slowed to a more normal pitter-patter.

Peering across the room in the darkness, Jaykriss he could barely make out Zamarcus. Clad in flowing white robes and hunched over a table in the corner of the room, he looked for all the world like a ghozim. He was thumbing through a massive leather-bound book by the eccentric light of a dim candle that had tilted nearly sideways in sheer defiance of gravity. His eyes were a finger's breadth away from the page.

It was a wonder Zamarcus could see anything at all.

Jaykriss arose, splashed some water onto his on his face, wiped his face with a hand towel so rough that it felt like a sheet of bark, and padded quietly over to where the old man sat.

"Zamarcus?" Jaykriss said.

The old man glanced up, startled, his caterpillar eyebrows raised. "I thought you were sleeping," Zamarcus said.

"The nightmare came again. The one with the Wall of Skulls."

Zamarcus clicked his tongue against his teeth. "I told you to drink some warm milk before bed," he said.

"I tried that. I also tried reading, exercise, and that bending-around thing you taught me," Jaykriss said.

"Yoga."

"Yes, that. And the nightmare still came, same as always."

Zamarcus took off his spectacles, huffed a breath to fog them, and began diligently cleaning the lenses—as he often did when he was thinking.

"So what do you think this nightmare means?" the old man said.

"I was hoping you could tell me."

Zamarcus fished around in his robe and retrieved a translucent green vial. "Put out your hand," he said.

"What is it?" Jaykriss said.

"Go on," said Zamaracus. "I promise it won't turn you into a toad or a chicken. It's sleeping powder. To help you rest."

"So it will not help me understand the dream?"

"It will help you avoid the dream. And that's good enough for now. Understanding can come later." The old man tapped the edge of the vial. A few greenish-gold flakes fell onto Jaykriss's outstretched palm.

"What do I do with them?" he asked.

"You *eat* them. Then lie down, quickly. The sleep caused by those flakes will not creep up on you, but instead will come upon you like a roaring flood in the Mist Valley."

Jaykriss settled down by the fireplace again, resting his head upon a pillow. He tasted one of the flakes initially. It tingled on his tongue.

"OK, here goes," he mumbled, putting the rest of the flakes in his mouth. They tingled there for a moment. He felt lightheaded. Dim stars pulsated someplace behind his eyes.

And then he was gone.

When Jaykriss awoke the next time, it was with the odd sensation of breaking the surface of a dark lake—as though he had been submerged the lake's shadowy depths and then released, like a shimmering air bubble, to find his way back to the rest of the world.

And Zamarcus was right—there had been no dreams at all, not even a flicker. Only darkness and oblivion.

Jaykriss rubbed his eyes and looked around. Marda was snoring, as always. The fireplace embers winked at him once more. But something was different. The air was decidedly cooler, for one thing. And the room was now suffused with a strange green-blue glow, phosphorescent and pulsatile.

Jaykriss stood up.

The glow seemed to be coming from an area near the wall, behind the furious jumble of shelves and artifacts that populated the room.

What could that be?

The lantern at the table where Zamarcus had been reading was extinguished. He supposed the old man had gone off to bed at last.

The glow beckoned him. It beseeched him to follow it, to find its source. Jaykriss could not help himself.

There were two huge wooden shelves that loomed ahead of him like the walls of a canyon, shelves that contained scores of rocks and minerals and jars filled with various dark liquids. There were a few rows of jars on those shelves with the preserved remains of various animals within them— snakes and lizards and fish, mostly, forever motionless unless one turned the jar to look at them. Then, they would turn slowly in their tiny prisons, eyes flat and lifeless, staring out as if to see who had disturbed their eternal slumber.

Jaykriss did not like to look at the dead animals. He did not like the blank way they gazed at him, their fins and legs moving ever so slightly as the dark liquid swirled around them.

But he would have to pass them to find the source of the light.

"Great," he said under his breath, shaking his head. He took a deep breath and moved quickly past the shelves, past the jars and the stones and yet another jumble of books, and then we was by the wall, at a place he had walked past a hundred times.

But something was different this time. A bookshelf against the wall had slid to one side, revealing a passageway carved into the rock behind it.

The green-blue glow was coming from the passageway. The air pouring from the passageway was frigid, as cold as icewater. He could see thin tendrils of mist curling from the opening, gossamer and diaphanous, like the beckoning arms of some long-dead phantom.

Leave, his instincts told him.

He walked closer.

Run, a panicked voice inside his brain screamed at him.

Jaykriss ignored it.

Everything about this seemed wrong. *There could be creatures living inside the rock who stole away with Zamarcus,* he thought. *Or perhaps the centurions came under cover of darkness.*

But centurion raids were never quiet. And somehow he doubted that there could be creatures living in the walls of this place that Zamarcus did not know about after all of these years.

He knew he would have to go into the passageway. His curiosity would not let him do otherwise. But he would not do it alone.

He went to wake Marda.

Marda was lying on his back. His snoring was like the buzz of a gigantic cicada.

"Marda!" Jaykriss whispered.

"*Marda!*" he said again, more loudly this time.

The older boy was on his feet in a heartbeat, his hand gripping Icebreaker's scabbard.

"What is it? What?" he said.

"Shh! I've got something to show you," Jaykriss said.

He led Marda back to the passageway. The green-blue light was even more intense now. It pulsated ever more rapidly, playing little tricks with the shadows in the corners of the room.

"It looks like there might be ghozim in there," Marda said. Marda had always hated ghozim. He had never actually seen a ghozim, but he hated the *concept* of the ghozim—the spirit of a dead person walking the earth. He would face a screaming red raptor armed with nothing more than a stick, and he was no more afraid of Honshul and his stinking band of outlaws than he was of a family of forest toads.

But the dead? Another matter entirely.

"If there are ghozim, would it not be better to face them head on, as opposed to simply waiting here for them to enter the room from the passageway?"

"That sounds strangely logical, somehow, but it doesn't make me feel any better."

"Then let's go. Zamarcus is gone, and that passageway is open. It stands to reason that that's where he went. We need to make sure he's OK."

"Zamarcus is *gone?*" Marda said.

Jaykriss nodded.

Marda's eyes narrowed. He picked up Fyrdhom's bow, his quiver, and the crossbow, and began strapping them all on.

"Well, that's completely different. Why didn't you say that in the first place?"

Jaykriss shrugged.

Taking a deep breath, Jaykriss entered the passageway to find the source of the light. Marda unsheathed Icebreaker and followed right behind him.

The air had a sharp metallic tang, like water running over rusted iron. Reflexively, Jaykriss trailed the fingers of his free hand along the wall beside him. It was uncomfortably cold and moist, and as smooth as glass.

Touching the wall sent a chill into Jaykriss, a chill that pierced deep into flesh and bone. It was as though a jagged shard of ice had lodged inside his forearm.

"This place is *f-freezing,*" said Marda.

Jaykriss put his index finger to his lips.

The boys wandered through a twisting corridor that seemed to turn back on itself over and over. Jaykriss could feel the oppressive weight of the atmosphere above him as the corridor spiraled downward, winding deeper into the bowels of the rock.

At long last, the passageway began to broaden. The phosphorescent glow was more intense now. It throbbed like the pulse of a beating heart, insistent and unrelenting. Jaykriss did not merely see it; he *felt* it, thrumming in his chest, seeming to match his own pulse.

The passageway opened up into a room that seemed to have no beginning and no end—so large the walls and ceiling were invisible. In the distance was a brilliant green orb illuminated from within, a sphere floating in space like a tiny planet circling an alien sun. Glimmers of light squirmed restlessly beneath the sphere's smooth surface as if something were alive inside it. Once, a shaft of light broke through to the outside of the sphere, a beam that pierced the gloom like a battle sword.

The brilliant beam made something tighten up in Jaykriss's eyes, like the turn of a tiny screw. But it showed him something else.

A dense blanket of fog that hugged the invisible floor of this place.

If there is a floor, he thought.

As the beam broke through, he saw that there were things moving about in the dense mist. They were shapeless things, shrouded in fog, but with the vague forms of men.

Ghozim!

Jaykriss was sweating despite the cold. It trickled in rivulets down his back.

He pointed to the fog-shrouded forms moving about. Marda's eyes grew wide. Neither of them said a word, but they each knew what the other was thinking.

Garoth was right. There are ghozim in this place.

Jaykriss felt a lump in his throat.

The green orb was throbbing, its pulsations now matching his heartbeat, *lubDUB, lubDUB, lubDUB,* over and over.

It knows me, he thought.

And then he saw Zamarcus. The old man was standing waist-deep in the mist, his long robes flowing around him. A horde of ghozim surrounded him, enveloping him completely—dozens of them, it seemed, with more coming from every direction. They were *flocking* to him, it seemed. In a moment, he would not see the old man at all.

The ghozim are taking Zamarcus, he thought. *We are lost.*

Jaykriss looked over at Marda, but Marda's eyes were staring, wide open but unseeing. Marda's grip on Icebreaker loosened. The gleaming longsword slid from his hand and clattered to the ground.

Jaykriss was paralyzed. He could scarcely breathe. He thought about running, but couldn't. His limbs felt like they were made of stone.

He felt something coming from the orb—a force of sorts, insistent and probing, like an invisible finger swirling about in the mist.

It's looking for me, he thought. *It's going to find me, going to pull me in like it did Zamarcus.* Terror filled him, clutching at his throat with icy claws, choking off his very breath.

And then the orb erupted.

The beam of light blinded him, piercing him through the eyes and wriggling deep into his brain. The sheer force of it dropped Jaykriss to his knees, but the beam stayed with him, tearing memories and thoughts from him with a thousand greedy tentacles.

No, no, no, he thought, but it was far too late for protest. The orb had pinned him to the ground like an insect, and it stayed on him, boring relentlessly into his consciousness like an ice pick.

He could feel the memories being torn from him—forcefully, as though the orb were ripping them from within his skull. He could not stop it, could not block the orb's violent intrusion. Once again, Jaykriss felt the despair of his father's death, the pain of watching his mother descend into hopeless sorrow—it was all there, fresh as a new wound, searingly raw and painful.

His last thoughts were of his family. He saw an image of each of them flicker someplace behind his eyes, like pictures scribbled in flashes of lightning.

And then there was nothing.

23

When Jaykriss awoke, he was completely blind.

He was drained, his body drenched with cold sweat. His head throbbed; his muscles ached. He fumbled about in the frigid darkness until he found Marda.

The older boy lay on the ground nearby, unconscious but breathing. Jaykriss could hear his heartbeat, still intact.

Thank the gods, he thought. *Marda lives.* Jaykriss drew in a deep breath. The air was so cold that it hurt.

He blinked. Light and dark flickered in front of him. His vision began to return, the room growing brighter by the minute. Jaykriss could now make out the outlines of a round chamber with pristine white walls and a vaulted ceiling studded with hundreds of ivory stalactites, poised like spear points above his head.

Ice, he thought. *It's all made of ice.*

The cavern was filled with thousands of shapes like those that had surrounded Zamarcus earlier—an entire legion of phantoms swaying gently in a cavernous chamber, a chamber that seemed to stretch on to the edge of eternity. He could not see the end of it.

"Jaykriss?" a voice behind him said.

A *human* voice.

Jaykriss scrambled to his feet and whirled about. It was Zamarcus—or something that looked like Zamarcus.

Jaykriss backed up, eyes shifting right and left. "Zamarcus? Is that really you? I thought I saw the ghozim take you," he said.

"They aren't ghozim. They are the stored memories of people long dead—and anyway, I was speaking to them. They are so starved for human contact that they swarm like locusts when anyone asks questions of them. They are harmless, I can assure you. What are you doing down here? You were sound asleep when I left you. I had hoped that the flakes I gave you would keep you sleeping until I could finish my work here in the repository."

It is him. Thank the gods, Jaykriss thought.

"I'm sorry, Zamarcus. I did not mean to intrude down here. I just...I awakened and saw this...*light,* and I followed it, and the bookcase had slid over to one side, and there was a passage, so Marda and I followed the light into it, and I came down here, and..."

He looked about. "What is this place? You called it the repository. What is that? Have we entered the Otherworld?" Jaykriss asked.

Zamarcus chuckled. "I am sorry you had to find it this way. And no, this is not the Otherworld. I doubt that a journey to the Otherworld would be quite so easy as striding through a hidden door and down a corridor. But it *is* a repository, of sorts—a storehouse of the ideas and thoughts of people long dead. My father called it the Library of Souls."

"But I do not understand. How can this be?" Jaykriss said.

"The room is a thought and memory recording device. The recording apparatus is housed in that orb you see there in the center of the room. It dates back to the Old Times, and even to the Time Before, long before the Reckoning. People left their thoughts here before they died, their dreams and ideas and knowledge, and the room recorded them so that they could be kept forever. The shapes you see are the representations of those people. Each one left something here for future generations to see. In that way, it allows one to have a conversation with the dead. Only the technology had been lost for centuries when my father rediscovered it."

"So the orb recorded *my* thoughts?"

Zamarcus nodded. "It sensed that you were here and sought you out, as it does everyone who enters here, and then recorded everything in your mind. That's how I knew you were here, in fact. The orb told me."

"This is great magic!"

"It is not magic, boy. Surely I have taught you better than that. It's *science*."

Zamarcus waved his arm across the vast expanse of the room. "Most of these people you see here date back to the Old Times," he said. "They have taught me a great many things. But there is one person in particular that I want you to meet." Zamarcus rapped his cane on the ground twice, took a step backward, and vanished.

"Zamarcus?" Jaykriss said out loud. His voice was muted. The icy walls seemed to chew it up and swallow it whole.

There was no answer. He looked over at Marda, who was beginning to stir. The room seemed to be growing even colder—if that was possible.

Jaykriss sensed movement on his left. He turned and saw nothing. He looked right—and saw nothing. He tried to recall which direction the exit was, but his mind was still scrambled from the orb's intrusion. He was not even certain that he was standing in the same place.

It was foolish to come down here. We're just children, not warriors. Zamarcus was wrong, Cha'Barro was wrong, they all were wrong. I am not the One.

His fears splashed over him, chilling him to the marrow.

I'm just a boy, he thought again. *A boy with no father.*

"Zamarcus?" he said again.

"I'm coming," the old man said.

"I cannot see you," said Jaykriss.

And then, suddenly, he could.

Zamarcus was striding through the billowing mists, materializing from the realm of arctic nothingness that seemed to reign in this accursed place.

Jaykriss exhaled. *Thank the gods,* he thought. Just seeing an actual flesh and blood person helped Jaykriss breathe more easily.

But then he saw the creature that was walking beside Zamarcus and his breath caught in his throat.

It was a wraith, a ghozim. It simply *had* to be. And although it was as colorless as steam, was considerably more well-defined than the other apparitions. It was obviously a man—or what had once been a man. Jaykriss swallowed. His mouth was as dry as dust.

The ghozim was grinning broadly. Although the image was amorphous, forming and re-forming like tangled wisps of smoke, Jaykriss could actually see the phantom's eyebrows, a set of crooked teeth—and a bald scalp with deep furrows carved across it.

Could it be?

"I often seek counsel from the images here. My father, for one. His memories live on here, like those of the others in this place. But this one here is special—a former pupil of my father's, one who can teach you a great deal about the Dark King *and* the Mortal Challenge of the Priests. You see, he knew the former—and he won the latter."

Jaykriss looked again at the phantom standing before him. "Who are you, then?" he said.

"They call me Fyrdhom, young man," the shade said. "And I have heard a great deal about you."

24

When Marda awoke, he sat up and rubbed his forehead, blinking.
"Ye gods, what happened?" he said. "My head is killing me!"

"You two curious little ferrets have stumbled into the Library of Souls," said Zamarcus.

Marda stared at Zamarcus, his eyes still struggling to focus—and then he recoiled as he saw the glimmering shade of Fyrdhom standing behind him. Jumping to his feet, he grasped the bejeweled hilt of Icebreaker, unsheathed the great sword, and raised it menacingly above his head.

"Zamarcus, I must warn you—there is a ghozim standing directly behind you. And he is a particularly ugly one at that."

Fyrdhom glided right *through* Zamarcus toward Marda, shifting and swirling about in the mist as he did so.

"Stop right there, ghozim, or you will feel my steel!"

"If I am an ugly ghozim, as you have suggested, then I am already dead. Why should I then fear your steel, Marda, son of Garoth?" Fyrdhom said.

Marda's arm dropped a bit. "How do you know my name, phantom?"

Fyrdhom motioned toward the orb. "The device knows everything and everyone in here. No one enters this room without being sampled."

"Marda, is that any way to speak to Fyrdhom the Great?" Zaamrcus said.

Marda's eye widened as he recognized the shade of the famous warrior. He dropped to one knee. "Forgive me for calling you ugly, sir. I did not mean it in a negative way. You have been my hero since I was a child."

Fyrdhom chuckled. "I am not aware of a positive way that a man may call another man ugly. But I'll tell you this—I was never known as a handsome man. The bear that tried to eat me when I was a boy myself saw to that. And, as a warrior, being ugly can be a helpful thing. So rise up, Marda son of Garoth. It is difficult to make eye contact with a man who is kneeling."

"But how are you here? Why would you haunt this place? Why not some battlefield, or the woods that you perished in?"

Fyrdhom glanced at Zamarcus. "I perished in some woods?"

"Vanished, sir. They found your horse, but not your body."

"Ah. That's better. I was concerned for a moment that something had transpired that I was unaware of."

Marda looked thoroughly confused. "If you are a ghozim, how can you not be aware of the nature of your own death?"

"You don't understand, Marda. They aren't actually ghozim. They are just collections of memories that have been stored there," said Jaykriss.

"Can you see through them? Are they made of mist?"

Jaykriss nodded. "We can all see that."

"Ghozim, then. Pure and simple. There's just no other term for them."

"Look, Marda, it's not what you think. The place isn't haunted. They are just memories, preserved in an unusual fashion."

"My father was right. He *knew* there were ghozim in here," he said.

"Perhaps I can set your mind at ease, young Marda. I understand that you have my bow," Fyrdhom said.

Marda nodded. "I am not worthy of it, sir. I know that."

"Why not? I certainly do not have much use for it right now. It seems fitting that it should come to you, seeing that you are the Warrior. That smacks of fate to me. I thought once that I might be the Warrior, you know. But I served a false king. And I paid dearly for my lack of perception."

"But the Dark King was—and is—king, after all. So how is he a *false* king?"

"The Dark King is a tyrant who feeds on ignorance and fear. He is cunning, I'll grant that. And he can be quite charming when he needs to be. But his words mean nothing. No matter who he once was, he is now a creature of deception and cruelty. His kingdom is built upon a foundation of lies. There is no honor in him. I discovered these things too late, after our destinies were too deeply intertwined."

Fyrdhom glanced at the sword, which was now back in Marda's scabbard.

"I see you wield Icebreaker. I know that weapon. It's ancient and legendary—fine steel, honorable and true."

"It was my father's, and his father's before him," said Marda.

"Did you bring my bow with you as well?"

Marda nodded.

"Might I see it?"

Marda unwrapped the bow carefully before presenting it to Fyrdhom, arms outstretched.

Fyrdhom gazed at the bow for a moment. "It is indeed mine. It is nice to see it so well cared for after all of this time."

He ran a ghostly finger down the bowstring. "Do you see the pair of blue and red stones in the center of the bow, next to the nock?" Fyrdhom asked.

Marda nodded.

"Press them in together with your thumb."

Marda did as he was told. The two stones began to glow intensely, taking on a violet hue.

"Ye gods," Zamarcus said.

"Can it be?" Fyrdhom said, his eyes wide.

The orb had awakened, it surface roiling with swirls of light. Green-blue shafts of light pierced the mists. The rock beneath their feet rumbled, as if something were about to erupt.

"What is it?" Marda said. "What does this mean?"

Fyrdhom's ghostly hands passed through Marda's, caressing the illuminated stones with fingers made only of vapor.

"This…this means that I still *live*." Fyrdhom looked at Jaykriss, then at Marda. "You will need to go to the Dead City. At once."

A chill went down Jaykriss's spine. "The Dead City? That place is forbidden! Why should we have to go there?"

Fyrdhom came in close. Jaykriss could feel the wraith's cold vapor on his face. "Because if I am indeed still alive, that is where you will find me."

25

Like most of the children in the Godswood, Jaykriss was familiar with the legend of the Dead City.

He vividly remembered the first time his father had told him the story. They had just finished dinner one night. As usual, his mother had taken Annya to the womens' bathing pool in the back wing of the bain, leaving Jaykriss and Glyndich to clean up after dinner.

"Have I ever told you the tale of the Dead City?" Glyndich asked, drying his hands. Jaykriss shook his head. "What is the Dead City?"

Glyndich put the last plata in the drying rack, picked up the Bloodsword, and poured himself a fresh mug of mead before taking his usual seat beside the fireplace. "Bring me the sharpening stone, and I'll tell you the tale. Mind you, it's a dark one, so it is best that your sister not hear it. She's too young. It will keep her from sleeping."

It was storming that night; the winds howled outside like packs of dire-wolves. Sheets of rain spattered fiercely across the roof of the war chief's bain.

Jaykriss brought the sharpening stone over to his father and sat down on the bearskin rug. The flames in the fireplace were crackling and spitting like a nest of zhargas.

Glyndich cleared his throat, as he always did before he began a tale.

"Years ago, in the Oldest Times, there were a great many more people in the world. They lived all over—in great cities, like Capitus, or in small towns and large ones. And times were good. There was food for the hungry, medicine for the sick, and the people were generally happy."

"But people are happy now," Jaykriss said.

"Things were different then. I was not living, so I cannot tell you anything except what I have read in books, and what my father told me. But there were many more people, and the people were nonetheless blessed with great riches."

"What happened to all of those people, then? Did they move away?"

For a moment, Glyndich said nothing. His thick arms worked the edge of his sword deliberately, rhythmically, sharpening its red-tinted steel to a razor's edge.

"They died, Jaykriss. The people died," he said at last.

"They did not all die. We are still here. And grandfather survived to have you, so he did not die."

"This was many years before your grandfather. It was even before the Dark King, before Fyrdhom and all of the other tales I have told you. This started in the Time Before."

Jaykriss felt a chill. "The priests say we are not to speak of the Time Before. Not ever. It is forbidden."

"The priests do not govern this house, Jaykriss. It belongs to me, and I can speak of the things that I choose to speak of within its walls. But you are never to speak of the Time Before to anyone outside this home. Is that understood?"

Jaykriss nodded.

"The men in the Time Before had everything, but they became greedy. They wanted even more. They became envious of one another. And what have your mother and I taught you about envy?"

"Envy is a corruptor of one's soul."

"Precisely. Envy corrupts the soul. And so these men in the Time Before were all envious of one another, each wanting what other people had, and thus was the seed of evil planted among them. They began fighting among themselves to get those things they coveted from each other. This was wrong, of course, for there was more than enough to go around."

"The gods would frown on that," Jaykriss said.

Glyndich nodded. "They would indeed—and they did. War broke out around the world, pitting brother against brother. Ultimately, the causes fell away, and men simply battled one another for power, and riches, and more power, until the fight itself became more important than anything else. For a time, there was nothing but war. Many men and women died."

"Did the war kill all of the people?"

"Some of them. But others still lived. And a number of the living took refuge in a large and beautiful city on a river, the largest city in the Southern Provinces. It is a city whose true name can no longer be spoken—for speaking its true name was forbidden by the Dark King himself, years ago. That was when the true name was still known to some. It does not matter now, for no one living in this day knows the true name. The city is now called the Dead City."

"Why is it called the Dead City?"

Glyndich squinted and looked along the plane of his sword, staring intently to gauge any slight imperfection in the finely honed blade. He then looked up at Jaykriss.

"Because it is truly dead, son. No men, women, or children live there anymore. Its people were all wiped clean by the Hands of the Gods during the Reckoning."

Jaykriss cocked his head to one side. "What is the Reckoning?" he asked.

"They did not teach you about the Divine Reckoning in school?"

Jaykriss shook his head.

Glyndich rolled his eyes as he sheathed the Bloodsword. "I'm surprised, but I'm not surprised. The old stories are being lost to time. No one cares about them anymore. But everyone should know about the Reckoning. It was an example of the power and fury of the gods, an event that changed everything."

Annya sprinted into the room in her nightgown and threw her arms around her father's neck.

"I love you, Papa!" she said.

"I love you, too, punkin'!" he said back, pressing her face close into the tangled scruff of his beard.

Samaria was drying her hands on a towel and smiling. "OK, enough is enough, you two. Annie Bell needs her beauty sleep."

"I don't want that old beauty sleep! I want to hear Papa's story, like Jaykriss!"

"Perhaps—if the story is not too filled with monsters and ogres and people getting their heads chopped off. What is your story tonight, Glyndich?"

Glyndich flushed. Jaykriss could see the color blazing in his cheeks. "I'm telling him about the Dead City and the Reckoning."

Samaria's eyes blazed. "Annya does not need to hear about that. And I'm not so sure it is good for Jaykriss, either," she said.

"There is no strength in ignorance, Samaria. The boy *does* need to know of it. The priests no longer let them teach about the Reckoning in school."

"And so you take it upon yourself to instruct your son in things the priests have forbidden? What's next? Are you going to tell him tales from the Time Before?"

Jaykriss piped up. "Actually, Papa said…"

Glyndich placed a calloused hand on Jaykriss's thigh. "No, Samaria. But the Dead City is not from the Time Before."

"Actually, it was. And that is why it is now dead," she said.

"I want to hear about the Dead City!" Annya said.

"Absolutely not!" said Samaria. "It's bedtime for you."

Annya's bottom lip poked out. "That's not fair," she said.

"It's fair if I say so, little lady. Now run on off to bed. If you hurry, I'll read you the story about the magic chicken," Samaria said.

Jaykriss smiled. That story was one of his sister's favorites.

Annya's eyes brightened. She ran over and kissed Jaykriss on the cheek. "Mama's going to read the magic chicken story!" she said, beaming.

"I know, Annie Bell! Have fun!"

"Goodnight! Goodnight! Goodnight!" she squealed as she sprinted down the hall.

"Goodnight!" Glyndich and Jaykriss said in unison.

After she left, Glyndich shook his head, smiling.

"What is it, Papa?" Jaykriss asked.

"Your sister is a fireball. I was just thinking what an even bigger fireball she will be when she's grown. Gods be praised, she's strong-willed. Got a wee bit too much of me in her, I'm afraid."

"That's not such a bad thing," Jaykriss said.

Glyndich tousled his son's hair. "So, where were we?"

"You were telling me about the Reckoning. And it made Mama mad."

"Ah, yes. That. Perhaps your mother is right. The Godswood priests do not like us to speak of it, so maybe we should not."

"The Godswood priests do not govern this house. Isn't that what you said earlier?"

Glyndich sighed. "You've got a bit of your mother in you, Jaykriss—outsmarting me with my own words. Fine. I'll tell the tale." Glyndich took a long swig of mead, wiping his mouth with his sleeve.

"The wars lasted for years. Brother fought against brother. One side would win one battle, and the other would win the next. Things were going nowhere, but people were surviving, somehow. Men were making do, you see. Despite all of the selfishness and narrow-mindedness in the world, despite the wars and the pettiness of human governance, most people were still able to carve out a life. But one day a vast and sudden rainstorm rolled in out of the east and poured forth a foul-smelling oily deluge that stank of chemicals and excrement. The rain lasted for day after day and night after night, without letup. It was as if the bowels of the sky had opened. By the time the rain finally ended, a plague was unleashed upon the world, a plague that killed man, woman, and child alike. It tore through the cities like lightning. Millions upon millions died. Crops failed because there was no one to tend them. The people caring for the sick became ill themselves, and they died, too. There was not enough water and not enough food. Before long, gangs of people were fighting and killing each other in the streets. People foraged for food in the abandoned buildings. Thousands took to the forests, stripping them of game. That event—the Rain of Death, they called it—changed the world forever."

Glyndich finished his mug of mead and belched loudly.

"Was that the Reckoning? The storm?" Jaykriss asked.

Glyndich shook his head. "The Godswood priests had retreated into the Priests' Bain by then, surrounded by their centurions. They proclaimed to all who would listen that mankind had sinned, and that the gods had exacted their wrath upon mankind through a Divine Reckoning as retribution. As the priests could walk among the dying with impunity, never once becoming ill, the people took that as a sign that the priests were favored by the gods, and that their idea of the Divine Reckoning was true. They listened to the priests, and their power grew. Still, it was a dark time in the world. The planet was consumed by death and chaos. Whole villages were burned to the ground as the outlaws searched for food and clothing. Roving packs of wild men moved like packs of wolves, killing people indiscriminately. Some whispered that the wild men were cannibals, eating the flesh of their victims."

The thought of this made Jaykriss queasy. The lamb in his stomach felt like it was trying to climb back out. "So the Reckoning was what happened after the Rain of Death?"

"Aye," said Glyndich. "The priests said it was the gods choosing who would live and who would die. And they were the messengers of the gods."

"So what happened to the Dead City?"

"It was once a beautiful and vibrant place, teeming with people and filled with shining buildings that soared into the sky, but it was poisoned during the Rain of Death and turned foul. Almost everyone died. Those who did not die left. Over time, the forest grew over it and around it, leaving it a tumbled-down ruin. There were legends that it was cursed. Some said that evil creatures roamed the ruins during the day, and that the legions of the dead rose up and walked the streets at night. There were also legends of great treasures hidden among the vast destruction and waste. The dreams of these riches caused some misguided people to journey to the Dead City to hunt for artifacts. Most never returned, and the few that did had suffered gruesome injuries—arms or legs missing, horrific burns over most of their bodies. Many died shortly after returning home. Survivors spoke of being attacked by monsters, of demons that sprang suddenly up out of the earth, or giants who rode dragons the size of mountains. No one ever returned from the Dead City with any treasure—not a single, solitary soul."

"Have you been there, Papa?" Jaykriss asked.

Glyndich shook his head. "When the Dark King came into power, he decreed that all roads into the Dead City should be destroyed, and that the rivers that once ran through it should all be diverted forever. To this day, the Godswood priests will not even speak the city's name. Even the centurions avoid it. Some even say that it is the true gateway to the place of punishment in the Otherworld, and that to go there provokes the wrath of the gods. Any way you look at it, it is truly a poisonous and evil place—to be avoided at all costs. That much is known. Most people are too frightened to even speak of it, much less go there."

And yet now he was going there. Jaykriss sighed.

I miss Papa, he thought.

It had been several summers since Jaykriss had even thought of the Dead City. It had remained buried, a memory of a memory, something he could not even speak about with anyone else but his father—and Glyndich, of course, had been gone over a year now.

Which was why he was shocked when Fyrdhom said that they must go there.

"My father always said the Dead City was haunted. Monsters and ghozim live there," Jaykriss said.

Fyrdhom waved his hands dismissively. "Rumor and innuendo. I've been there. There are some strange sights, to be certain, and a few unusual creatures, perhaps. But there are no ghozim."

"Not that you've seen," Jaykriss said.

"Look, the Reckoning was hundreds of years ago. Insurgents journeyed to the Dead City when the Dark King was hunting them precisely *because* the centurions did not like going anywhere near the place. The Dead City was the only place the insurgents were truly safe. I've been there. I've seen it. And while it may be strange, it is *not* haunted," said Fyrdhom.

"So why don't you just go with us?" Jaykriss said.

Fyrdhom smiled. "You forget what I am. There is no man speaking here in front of you. I am simply the echo of a memory—a mirage, at best. And that mirage cannot leave this room—not ever. But if I am still alive somehow, and you find me in the Dead City, *that* Fyrdhom—the real flesh-and-blood one—can probably help you."

"Then it seems we must go there," said Zamarcus, his thin lips set. "Pack up your things, boys. We must prepare for a difficult journey on the morrow."

Marda began wrapping up Fyrdhom's bow; Zamarcus was stuffing random things into his knapsack. But Jaykriss stood and thought for a moment. There was something nagging him, something deep and insistent—an aching, somewhere, that he could not place. "Fyrdhom, do you know what exactly happened after the Reckoning? My father told me about it, but he was never clear about what came later."

The phantom Fyrdhom drew close in to Jaykriss. A fine tendril of vapor hung in the air, still and cold, like the tail of some earthbound comet. "The Reckoning was the beginning and the end of it all," he said. "After the Rain of Death, it took less than ten summers for most of mankind to die off. In the cities, thousands of bodies were piled up into mass graves. Tumbled mounds of human skulls and bones littered most cities; in the later days, people even made barriers out of them, forgetting in the process that those dry bones had once been people, too."

I know what that looks like, Jaykriss thought. He cast a glance at Zamarcus, who nodded at him slowly.

"The Godswood priests put forth an edict that the first man who could pass a rigorous test of wits and skill of their design would be crowned king. That was, in fact, the very first Mortal Challenge of the Priests. Dozens of people tried the Challenge and failed. A handful even died. Nevertheless, a single man emerged victorious from all of this. No one had heard of him before the Mortal Challenge, but everyone knew who he was after it. The winner's real name has been long lost to time, but the Godswood priests began calling him *Dhatzah-il,* a name that meant God-King in the old tongue.

"Dhatzah-il worked with the centurions and the priests to bring back some sense of order. He caught most of the wild men, killing a few and taming the rest, eventually transforming the survivors into his most elite guards, the Capitus Brigade. He clamped down on all the gangs and crushed every rebellion. His power grew wild and tall and broad, like a stand of bamboo. It was a power rooted in his control of the people, and soon Dhatzah-il began to control everything—water, food, and even knowledge. And as he tightened his grip on power, the people began to call him by another name: The Dark King."

"So the Dark King ended the Reckoning?"

Fyrdhom nodded. "As the Dark King grew more powerful, the secrets of the Time Before were lost to most men. Computers, medicine—he kept these things for his own use, and the use of those under his command. No one else knew of them. Before long, virtually all memory of them was gone."

"But why would the Dark King want such things suppressed? Why would he want to keep things like computers and medicine away from the people?" Jaykriss asked.

Zamarcus stared off into space.

Fyrdhom spoke up. His image flickered a bit before stabilizing. "You've seen wolves, right? Direwolves, perhaps?"

Jaykriss nodded.

"The Dark King is such a wolf. He is a wolf who keeps a ready flock of sheep—all of us—at his disposal. He thrives on ignorance, staying in power by keeping his sheep in the dark. He uses the priesthood to maintain superstition, and uses the centurions to promote fear. He keeps the population dispersed, keeps communication at a minimum, and the only large city left in the world is Capitus, a city he runs with an iron fist. He knows that even sheep can tire of being sheep—and sheep armed with information can be dangerous in numbers."

"But you were with him for so long. You were his friend, his ally, and yet you speak of the Dark King as though he cannot be trusted."

"The Dark King *cannot* be trusted," said Fyrdhom.

"But why? Ultimately, if the people are living in peace, why is having the Dark King so in power so terrible?" Jaykriss asked.

Fyrdhom looked at Jaykriss. His eyes shimmered a bit, wavering like a desert mirage. "The good man I once knew as Dhatzah-il was my friend. We fought side by side to restore peace and order. I saved his life in battle many times, and he saved mine. But that man, my friend, is long dead, no matter what the priests would have you believe. The Dark King has replaced him. And the Dark King will do *anything* he must to stay in power. He has no conscience and no remorse; he is a creature corrupted by his lust for power and control. It's because he wants that power so much that it must be taken from him—before it is too late."

"There's one more thing," Fyrdhom said. "The roads have all been erased, but you may still travel to the Dead City via the old aqueduct, at the top of the waterfall. When you get there, you need to speak to the queen. She can be a formidable ally if she finds you worthy. S-s-s-he is…"

Fyrdhom's image flickered again, his mouth open as if to speak, and then froze up completely. It was as if he had turned to ice.

"Fyrdhom?" Zamarcus said.

In that instant, Fyrdhom melted, evaporating completely into a few scant wisps of vapor. The lights in the room flickered, irregular and unsteady. Jaykriss heard a deep rumbling noise beneath him, like huge boulders were tumbling someplace beneath his feet. A *whoosh* of frozen air filled the room.

And then it all stopped, plunging them into utter darkness.

Jaykriss realized he was holding his breath. His heart was pounding in his chest. "What just happened?" he said.

"I...I don't know," Zamarcus said. "That has never happened before."

The lights flickered, stuttering a bit, before slowly coming back on.

The shades had completely vanished. Their disappearance transformed the mysterious Library of Souls into an empty cavern of bare ice. The orb slept, dim and silent as a rock, its lights fully extinguished. Even the exit pathway had been transformed into a simple corridor, dimly lit but unassuming.

It was as if nothing had ever been there at all.

"Well," Zamarcus said, his magnified eyes blinking behind his spectacles. "I guess the orb has spoken."

"So what do we do now?" asked Marda.

"There is nothing left for us here. Perhaps that is what the Library is trying to tell us. We must journey at first light to the Dead City," Zamarcus said.

The old man turned and made his way back toward the passageway.

Jaykriss and Marda followed Zamarcus, looking behind them at the extinguished orb, as they moved back into the world of the living.

The tip of Marda's sword scraped erratically against the icy walls as he walked, sounding for all the world like the grating of steel against living bone.

26

Jaykriss stood tight-lipped, gazing out over the Mist Valley as the sun rose and burned its way through the morning. At once, some unseen cue caused great flocks of spoonbills and killdeer to take to the sky in flapping, cackling masses of feathers and bone.

"Did you remember to bring the Dragonfire?" Zamarcus asked.

"It's always with me," Marda said. "It stays in my pack."

"And your crossbow bolts?"

"I have it all, Zamarcus. I promise."

Zamarcus reviewed his own inventory one last time. "It's all here, I think. I keep a drybox next to the boathouse at the entrance to the aqueduct, but the food in there is pretty awful stuff—pemmican and wax-wrapped hardcakes, and some canned preserves. That's really for emergencies, like that hard freeze a few years back."

Jaykriss looked at Zamarcus with a puzzled expression. "My mother said the last hard freeze was before I was born."

"Was it? I suppose it was. Must have been your father I was thinking of. A hard freeze is nothing to make light of, now. Men have died during a hard freeze just gathering firewood. Why, a whole company of men once fell through the northern ice shelf when it collapsed on the Dragon Lake. The poor fools didn't even realize they were standing on ice. They all froze solid before anyone could get to them—mouths agape, eyes wide open, like they didn't even have time to grasp what was happening before the end came."

Zamarcus strapped up the last of the straps on his pack. "There. That does it. I think we're ready to leave."

"How long will we be gone?" Marda said.

"It will take us a day or so to get to the boathouse and load things up, then another day of travel to get to the Dead City—unless the boat motor's not working. Then we'll have to paddle. That'll take longer—maybe three days' time or more, depending upon how high the water in the aqueduct is. It should be OK this time of year. We're still getting some snow runoff down from the mountains. That helps."

"Have you ever been to the Dead City?"

Zamarcus shook his head.

"I have heard the old legends, just as you have. But I have never visited that place, not even once."

"Fyrdhom mentioned something about a queen. What was that all about?"

Zamarcus leaned his pack against the rock.

"There were stories, years back, about the Queen of the Dead City. It's all largely campfire gossip—rumor and innuendo, the sort of things you scare children with. But Fyrdhom has traveled many places—far more than I have, for certain. And he has indeed been to the Dead City. Still, it has been many summers since I have heard anyone speak of the queen at all."

The old man stroked his snowy beard.

"Of course, before you two came along, I had not spoken to anyone at all in quite some time. Except Archimedes, of course."

Marda rolled his eyes. "Archimedes is a *bird*, Zamarcus. He's not a person."

"Don't try and tell him that," Zamarcus said.

As if on cue, the old raven flew down from his perch on top of a dead tree next to the waterfall and landed squarely on Zamarcus's shoulder. "Quiet!" squawked the jet-black bird. It averted its beak from Marda, clearly miffed.

"OK, I have one question: How can any queen of the Dead City who actually knew Fyrdhom still be alive? She would be hundreds of years old!" said Marda.

"Stranger things have happened. Remember, the Dark King is even older than that," said Zamarcus. The old man rapped a dark rock beside the waterfall with his cane and the flow of water ceased almost immediately. He then ducked back into the cave behind the waterfall to make one final check of their supplies. The waterfall resumed flowing just as soon as Zamarcus was inside.

Jaykriss and Marda, packs strapped on tight, stood looking out over the Mist Valley in silence. Marda picked up an irregular chunk of granite and hurled it into the foaming froth of the waterfall below, where is disappeared.

"Our days used to be like that," he said, gazing wistfully down toward where the rock had been.

"Like what?"

"Like that rock. Remember when we were kids? A day would go by and would simply disappear, to be replaced by another day. We would explore the forest, and we'd hunt, and we'd joke around with friends, and life was wonderful. Now, everything we do seems to have some cosmic meaning. Life became so bloody serious all of a sudden," he said.

Marda gazed out over the valley in silence for a moment. "I miss having things not matter so much," he said at last.

"Me, too," said Jaykriss.

"So what if we just left? What if we just told Zamarcus that we were not going to the Dead City? What if we went back to the Godswood and walked into Mistress Lineya's classroom door like nothing had happened? Do you think we could go back to the way things used to be?"

Jaykriss looked at his old friend, shaking his head. "My father is dead. Your father is dead. My mother and sister are being held hostage by the Godswood priests. We're not kids anymore. That's over."

"But things were so simple then," Marda said.

"They were never as simple as we thought they were. We were just blind to the complexity, like all children are," Jaykriss said.

Marda sized up another rock, this one round and smooth like a goose egg, and hurled it into the air, trying to clear the froth at the waterfall's base. "So do you really believe it?" he asked.

"Believe what?"

"All the stuff about the prophecy, Fyrdhom and his bow, that sort of thing."

"Sola believes that we choose our own destiny. The prophecies exist, but the gods let us select our fate."

"Well, here's another question: Even if the prophecy is right, are we up to it?"

Jaykriss was silent on this. The waterfall thundered and the shorebirds called and the sun climbed higher in the morning sky.

A deep, booming voice echoed from the jumble of rocks behind them. "A better question would be this: if the righteous path were hard and the path of the coward were easy, would you choose the righteous path over the easy path?"

In an instant, Marda drew Icebreaker from its sheath. "Who is that?" he said, looking around warily.

The waterfall stopped flowing for a moment, and Zamarcus stepped out onto the rock ledge. He had changed into different attire—round, purple-tinted sunglasses, a hooded sky-blue poncho, and a loose pair of tattered black breeches tied with a twist of frayed rope. He was carrying a canvas backpack stuffed nearly to the point of bursting.

Archimedes was perched on Zamarcus's shoulder, onyx eyes glittering as he peered at the boys.

"Was that *you* just now?" Jaykriss said.

Zamarcus nodded. He waved a white cone-shaped device that he held in his right hand. "Loudspeaker. Another ancient toy I've been playing with."

He walked toward them, stepping gingerly over rocks and other assorted debris. "What makes you boys think you might not be up to the challenge of the prophecy?" Zamarcus asked.

"It's just…our fathers were great warriors, of course. But we are just two *boys*," said Marda.

"Remember, all great men and women were mere children once," Zamarcus said.

The two of them stood silently as Zamarcus hoisted his pack onto his shoulders.

"Zamarcus, I have another very important question," said Jaykriss.

"What's that?" said Zamarcus.

"Where did you get those *pants*?"

Both boys started laughing out loud.

"Oh, *really*," Zamarcus said, striding past them, his aquiline nose up in the air. "And to think the Dark King might have something to fear from the two of you."

The old man tapped the dark rock at the edge of the waterfall with his staff. The cascade of water started back almost immediately, resuming its tumultuous journey to the sea. "Now let's get moving, boys," he said. "We have a long journey ahead to the Dead City."

Zamarcus led the way down a rock-strewn path that wound around the base of a huge boulder. Within moments, the three of them were climbing through wiry clumps of grass beside the edge of the cliff, the ragged edge of the forest looming heavily above them at the very top of the waterfall. The sun was brilliant, sailing through an aquamarine sky.

"Adventure!" crowed Archimedes triumphantly.

"Yes, Archimedes," Zamarcus said. "Adventure, indeed."

27

Zamarcus, Jaykriss, and Marda hiked through the upper forest along a footpath that wound through vast thickets of rhododendron. It circled around piles of gigantic gray boulders—tumbles of rock that seemed to have fallen right out of the sky—and meandered past silent stands of massive redwoods that stood like rigid sentinels in a forest floor thick with tree ferns and drooping lianas as thick as a man's arm. The sun blazed high in the sky now, a brilliant orb that dappled the path before them with myriad iridescent butterflies of light. Archimedes flew up ahead of them, soaring from branch to branch on iridescent ebony wings. A gentle breeze murmured deep forest secrets through the soaring arc of the trees overhead—secrets as old as time itself, known but never uttered aloud, the sort of thing you just felt someplace deep inside when things were *right*.

And Jaykriss knew that things were, indeed, just right. He could sense it in his heart.

At the outset of their journey, Marda had hooked his thumbs into the straps of his pack and begun singing an old Farming Day song, a little ditty about a clever rabbit caught in a farmer's trap who escaped by tricking the farmer's wife. He sang it loudly and lustily—and rather badly off-key.

"You'd be best to stop that racket," Zamarcus said.

"But why?"

"Awful singing attracts dragons. It is like a dinner gong to them. Surely you knew that," the old man said.

Chastened, Marda abruptly ended his boisterous rendition of "Little Brown Bunny."

Zamarcus turned and winked at Jaykriss when the older boy turned his back.

Throngs of forest birds twittered about in the high, needle-studded branches of the giant redwoods, but they were almost invisible—chirps and shadows, with a rare flash of blue feathers or a red wing. In fact, three of them scarcely saw any animal life at all—save a few pesky blackflies that stubbornly flew suicide missions directly at their heads.

"Why does this path wander about so?" Jaykriss said, swatting at a vagrant blackfly.

"It's an old path. My father walked it, and his father before him. That's just the way it goes," the old man said.

"But why can't we cut through the ferns?"

"There are things hidden in the world that you cannot see. The path is a known thing—safe and reliable. We need to stay on it."

"They are just *ferns*, Zamarcus. What could possibly be hiding in a stand of ferns?"

Zamarcus raised the knob-studded tip of his walking stick and gently pushed back the thick green fronds of one of the tree ferns. There was a hiss, a glint of gold, and a flash of movement, almost too fast to be seen.

The gold-and-black-striped creature launched itself out of the tree fern and into the air—scaled wings spread wide, its cruel mouth open to reveal a mouthful of vicious fangs.

Marda rolled left, unsheathing Icebreaker in a single fluid motion. He dropped to one knee in front of Jaykriss, encircling his friend with his left arm while the other hefted his gleaming blade in front of his eyes.

"Here is the sort of thing that lives among the tree ferns," Zamarcus said, holding his staff aloft.

The serpent had buried its razor-sharp teeth deep into the walking stick's polished shaft. The snake refused to yield, its unblinking blood-red eyes boring into the three of them. The reptile coiled about the staff in a slow and deliberate constriction that caused the sunlight to shimmer across its scales like summer lightning. Its short wings flexed rhythmically as the coils tightened.

"Danger! Danger!" crowed Archimedes, circling overhead.

"It's beautiful," Jaykriss murmured.

"And quite lethal," Zamarcus said. "One bite of a reticulate zharga can kill ten men. And it's the birthing season for them right now. She would snap those jaws around your throat, paralyzing you in a heartbeat, and then drag your half-dead body back into that thicket to feed her babies. Because that's what reticulate zhargas do."

The old man drew his short sword and sliced off the serpent's triangular head with a single stroke. Its black-and-gold striped body fell limply to the forest floor.

Zamarcus struck his walking stick against a redwood's massive trunk to dislodge the snake's stubborn head, snapping off a couple of the of the creature's fangs in the process. The zharga's crimson gleam of an eye flickered one last time before its eyes—and its jaws—closed for good.

"Did you have to kill it?" Jaykriss said.

"She would have killed us."

"Would she have?"

"Without a doubt. We were in her territory. Invaded her space. And with her babies nearby, she would have defended them to the death."

"How did you know it was a female?" Marda said, sheathing Icebreaker once again.

"Did Lineya not teach you *anything* about snakes?" Zamarcus asked.

Both boys shook their heads.

"Male reticulate zhargas are solid brown and green, for camouflage. They hibernate among the tree fern fronds until mating season. During mating season, they turn all black and seek out a female. The females, which are twice as large as the males, mate only once before they kill and eat the male—often while they are still coupled with them."

"Why would they do that?" asked Jaykriss.

"Because the males are lazy. They would loll around in the trees until the young were born, and then would simply consume their own babies. Only the female reticulate zhargas actively hunt. And they teach their female offspring to do the same—while the males skulk off into the fern fronds to rest, to eat whatever unsuspecting animal crawls down their branch, and to wait until the next mating season. It's the same way with the vermithrax, you know. They produce a litter only once in a dozen years or so—and vermithrax females routinely kill the males during mating, too. Lots of reptiles do that."

"I'm glad I'm not a reptile," Marda muttered.

"I think we're all glad of that, Marda," Zamarcus said.

"So I guess we'll stay on the path," Jaykriss said.

"I thought you might say that," Zamarcus said, grinning.

The forest deepened as they hiked on, the path becoming narrower and less distinct as tree roots encroached from below and branches crowded in from the sides. Jaykriss felt a sudden wave of claustrophobia wash over him, as though all of the air around him was being sucked up. He shuddered as he recalled the zharga and its needlelike teeth. Even the touch of a wayward branch on his arm caused him to flinch. Cold sweat trickled down his back. He wheezed softly with every exhaled breath.

Zamarcus glanced over his shoulder at Jaykriss. "Are you OK?" he asked.

"Just a little jumpy, with the snake and all. I'll be fine."

"The trail opens up again once we reach the waterhole," Zamarcus said.

"When is that?" asked Jaykriss.

"A bit ahead of here, over the next ridge."

"That snake really bothered you *that* much?" Marda said.

"About as much as the ghozim bothered you," Jaykriss said.

Marda's eyebrows furrowed, but he was silent after that.

They hiked further. The sky was growing darker. Through the treetops, Jaykriss could see clouds gathering. A cold wind had kicked up. Archimedes clearly did not like it. He huddled on Zamarcus's shoulder, his feathers puffed out for warmth.

"Perhaps I should tell you a story to keep things moving," said Zamarcus.

"This doesn't look like a place a dragon might frequent. Perhaps I could sing," said Marda.

"No!" said Jaykriss and Zamarcus in unison.

Marda poked out his bottom lip. "Very well," he said after a moment. "Tell us a story."

The old man ran his fingers through the tangled mane of his snow-white hair and pulled his hood up over his head. "We've been talking a great deal about snakes today. Have you boys heard the tale of the Serpent King?" he asked.

Both boys shook their heads.

Zamarcus smiled and cleared his throat.

The Tale of the Serpent King.

There was a great war chief once, long ago, who was blessed by the gods with many skills. He was a valiant warrior, strong and swift of foot. He was also brilliant, with an uncanny ability to discern what an opponent might do in battle. And he relied on his wits and his strength and his speed to become the most decorated conqueror the world had ever seen. Over time, he defeated all of his enemies and could retire from the field of battle in peace. The people in his lands chose him as their king, and he built a great city, as a monument to himself. Within that great city, he constructed the most wonderful palace the world had ever seen. It had seven levels, each with its own lush gardens, with plants and animals from all over the world. The great walls of the palace were gilded with gold leaf, inlaid with jewels, and were carved with ornate details of the king's victories.

It came to pass that the king was not merely a great warrior. He was, in fact, a very good king—as good a king as he had been a war chief. His rulings were just, his people had all the water they needed to drink and plenty of food to eat, and there was order throughout the kingdom. The people paid homage to the Great King in song and dance. They loved him and revered him. Some thought he might even be a god.

After decades of peace, the Great King received word that a hostile army had landed on the seashore ten leagues from his city. Hungry to defend his lands, the king mustered his fearsome army, strapped on his battle sword, and took the reins of his chariot.

He arrived at the seashore to find entire villages of his subjects slaughtered, the houses burned. Even the animals were killed.

"This is an affront to the gods!" he shouted. He vowed to seek revenge.

He came upon the invading army as they were brutally overwhelming yet another defenseless village. The army was led by a tall, powerful warrior who stood astride a golden chariot emblazoned with a twisted serpent, the symbol of the invading army. Flags bearing the same twisted serpent emblem flew with every regiment of the invading army. The warrior was tattooed with images of serpents from head to toe, and his skin was pierced with gold chains with serpents' heads. The Serpent Warrior hurled insults at the Great King.

"You cannot defeat us!" he snarled. "We will take your lands and your riches from you!"

The Serpent Warrior's taunts enraged the Great King. He pursued the Serpent Warrior's army, driving them before him to the banks of a river swollen with floodwaters. The Serpent Warrior's army was trapped. They tried to cross the river and could not. Their horses drowned and their chariots overturned, and so they turned back, facing the Great King's army. They begged for mercy. But the Great King was blind with rage, and he slew them all so that the floodwaters ran red with blood for days. In the end, as the battle was won, the Great King took the Serpent Warrior's life himself.

The Serpent Warrior had been towing a wagon with a small jail cell in it as part of his retinue. Inside the jail cell was a withered old man dressed in rags. His eyes were crusty, his skin pockmarked and scarred, and he was bearded and filthy, covered in dirt from his bare feet top of his bald scalp.

"Who are you, old man?" the Great King asked.

"Why, that should be obvious to such a great man as you. I am a prisoner," the old man said.

Smiling, happy to have one last victory over his now-slain enemy, the Great King gave an order.

"Release this man," he said. "Give him a bath and warm clothes, and let him join me at my table."

The Great King's servants obliged. That evening, the Great King and the now-released prisoner dined together.

"Who imprisoned you?" the Great King asked.

"Why, it was the Serpent Warrior," the old man said.

"How long have you been imprisoned?"

"For weeks, now. I come from a land far, far away."

The Great King smiled. "Well, you have a home here, if you like. You are welcome to join us and live among my people. What is mine is yours," the Great King said.

"Thank you, kind sir," the old man said.

The next morning, the Great King gathered up his things and gave the order to return to his beautiful capital city. Upon his triumphant entry into the city, the citizenry lined the streets, singing the Great King's praises to the heavens and showering him with flowers. It was obvious that they loved their king.

The morning after he arrived in the city, the Great King noticed an itchy spot on his forearm. He looked at it and saw a single reddish bump.

Hmm, he thought. *Must be an insect bite.*

By that evening, there were a few more bumps.

By the following morning, the Great King was covered in them.

The Great King called in his wizard to ask about the rash. To his horror, he saw that the wizard had the rash, as well—and that it was even worse in the wizard than it was in the Great King, covering the old necromancer with oozing scabs and angry red pustules from scalp to ankles.

"You cannot fix this?" the king asked.

"I do not even know what it is. I have never seen the likes of it," said the wizard.

The first palace guard died before lunchtime that same day. The rest followed soon after, along with the wizard, all of the king's ministers and everyone else in the palace. In time, only the Great King was left.

As night stole upon the Great King's dying kingdom, there came a rapping at the castle door.

The Great King ignored it at first. He was feverish, almost delirious. His eyeballs throbbed, his head pounded, and his joints and muscles were aching as though he had been stretched on the rack. In his confusion, the illness tormenting him from his scalp to his feet, the Great King simply forgot (or did not realize) that there was no one else left alive in the palace. Instead of answering the door, he sat motionless in his favorite chair and focused on his breathing. There was a glass of sherry beside him, but he was too weak to raise it to his lips.

Rap rap rap rap!

The knocking came again.

"Someone has come for me," the Great King muttered. He could taste his own foul breath on his tongue, bitter and hot.

The Great King got up and tottered down the cavernous—and now empty—hallway. Corpses, their faces frozen in death, pale skin pockmarked and blotchy, lay propped against the gilded walls and sprawled out across the polished marble floors. All of the dead were friends and acquaintances of the

Great King. He knew each and every one of them. But the king stumbled around and over the bodies, too ill to pay any of them much attention.

When he opened the great wooden door of the castle, he saw the old prisoner, his crooked feet bare in the virgin snow.

The prisoner was still bony, his rib cage all hollowed out and stark, but he was no longer filthy. His beard had been shaved, and a heavy ermine robe rich with the musky scent of woodsmoke was draped across his narrow shoulders. The myriad pockmarks that studded his thin visage were drying up and crusting.

"We meet under different circumstances now, Great King, do we not?" the former prisoner said.

"How is it that you still live? Everyone else is dying of the pestilence!"

The old prisoner smiled. "The pestilence is mine. I delivered it to you. But I am merely a carrier, immune to its lethal effects. I am a ruse, a phantom, a myth. I have brought you Death, in all of its rank glory. And Death is waiting patiently for you. His appetite is relentless, you see."

The bald prisoner, grinning toothlessly, rolled up his sleeve and revealed the tattoo there, on his forearm—a writhing serpent with needle-sharp fangs and ruby-red eyes, wearing a gleaming crown of gold.

"Who exactly are you?" the Great King asked.

"Why, I am the Serpent King. And as you promised, what is yours is now mine."

And the Great King fell dead as a stone in his own doorway, ultimately overcome by his own failure to observe, his once-great kingdom defeated and lifeless, lost to pestilence and ruin.

Jaykriss had stopped walking, his eyes wide, open-mouthed. "That's a terrible story," he said at last.

"But what does it tell you?" asked Zamarcus.

"That even great men can made mistakes?"

"That is true. But here is another lesson here. What was the Great King's failure? What mistake did he make?"

"I'm not sure what you are asking."

Zamarcus leaned forward and looked Jaykriss right in the eyes. "How did the Great King fail?" he said.

Jaykriss thought for a moment.

"He was too nice?" said Marda.

"No. Something specific—and lethal."

"He trusted the old prisoner?" said Marda again.

"You're getting closer. What did he fail to do?"

At that moment, an idea blossomed in Jaykriss's head, opening up like a morning glory. "I think I know."

"Enlighten us," Zamarcus said.

"The Great King did not pay enough attention to detail and jumped to conclusions that he should not have. The real answer was right there in front of him the entire time. Had he noticed the snake tattoo in the beginning, he would have realized something was different about the prisoner. He could have avoided the pestilence, saving himself and all of the people in the city, by locking the prisoner back up."

Zamarcus pointed a crooked finger at Jaykriss. His amethyst ring glittered in the half-light.

"Bull's-eye," he said.

"So what does that teach you?"

Jaykriss was puzzled. "I…I'm not sure," he said.

"Attention to detail, Jaykriss. You have to notice every little thing, and you *cannot* make assumptions without adequate data. Things are rarely the way they seem at first glance. They are, in fact, almost inevitably far more complex than anyone realizes. Understand?"

Jaykriss and Marda both nodded.

After they had crested the next ridge and marched down into the valley, the clouds began to break up, and the trail did indeed open up so that the three of them could walk abreast of one another once more. They reached the waterhole in the early afternoon. It was a beautiful spot—a deep blue pool rimmed with weeping willows and river oaks, fed by a broad, stone-filled creek burbling in from the edge of the forest.

Jaykriss was parched. He took a swig of water, wiped his brow with his sleeve, and took a seat on a hollow log.

"How much further to the boathouse?"

"A good way yet. Two more ridges at least."

"Shouldn't we stop and rest? This seems like as good a place as any," said Marda.

"I suppose we can break for a few hours. We've made outstanding time so far, and we'll still make the boathouse well before sunset if we do that. That's as far as we're going to go today, anyway."

Zamarcus cast a glance at a stand of bamboo next to the shoreline. "You know, this is usually a pretty good spot for bass fishing. I always carry some line and hooks in my pack for emergencies. We can try our luck at bass-catching for a bit if you are interested."

"You don't have to convince *me*," said Marda, grinning. The older boy dropped his pack to the ground and immediately began assessing pieces of bamboo for a suitable rod length.

Jaykriss and Zamarcus sat on the log and ate an apple each, tossing a third to Marda. After eating, they rolled the log over and began digging for grubs in the soft earth.

"I've got some!" Jaykriss said, placing a handful of grubs on a large plant leaf that Zamarcus had laid out.

Marda had been very efficient, using the hooks and fishing line that Zamarcus had brought to construct three passable fishing poles in short order.

"Good work!" Marda said, beaming, when he saw the collection of grubs laid out on the leaf.

Unfortunately, that was when the excitement ended. The three of them fished the waterhole for nearly an hour without a bite.

Finally, Jaykriss noticed some flashes of white in the froth of the creek near the blackened, water-slicked trunk of a downed tree. He knew what that meant.

"Look over there," Jaykriss said.

"What?" said Marda.

"There are trout swimming in the current near that tree. They like flies, not grubs. I can make some artificial flies out of a few of these feathers around here and see if we can catch a few," he said.

Jaykriss put down his cane pole and walked through the rushes beside the riverbank, plucking a few stray orange and red feathers from among the tall blades of grass. He then took a fishhook, unwrapped a bit of string from his shirtsleeve, and bound a few tufts of feather tightly onto the hook. He sealed the tie with a bit of candle wax that he retrieved from his pack.

Zamarcus inspected the fly. "It looks good to me—but I know nothing about fly fishing. Who taught you this?"

Jaykriss grinned. "My father," he said. "He loved the water. We spent many an hour fishing."

Jaykriss cast the lure right next to an eddy pool by the downed log. It bobbed on the water's surface, hanging there a mere heartbeat or two, before something struck it in an iridescent flash and yanked it under.

"Got one!" Jaykriss said, setting the hook. Within a few moments, he had hauled in a wiggling brown trout, its scales gleaming in the dappled sunlight.

After stringing his catch and tossing it into a nearby pool of water at the river's edge, Jaykriss made two more flies while Marda fished. The flies were delicate blue ones this time, which Jaykriss made by using a few tufted feathers from a tricolored heron that had snagged in the rushes.

"I got one, too!" Marda said, his rod bowed nearly double with a shimmying rainbow.

Zamarcus inspected the new flies admiringly. "Those are splendid!" he said. "See how the colors shine? That's because of light refraction. There are tiny air pockets in each of the feathers that scatter the light just so."

Jaykriss cocked his head, staring at Zamarcus and grinning. "What was that again?" he said.

The old man arched his eyebrows. "Hand me the fly, boy. I suppose that lesson can wait."

Jaykriss, Marda, and Zamarcus fished for another hour, hauling in eight beautiful trout before they quit—three stubborn browns, four sparkling rainbows, and a single glittering golden.

After they had finished, the three of them propped their rods against the trunk of a nearby cedar and pulled the string of fish from the pool of water. Jaykriss opened his pack and unsheathed an elkhorn-handled steel boning knife, its blade gleaming like a mirror. Silent, his fingers moving expertly, Jaykriss sliced through each fish's head and tail and incised it cleanly along the trout's white-scaled belly, gutting it. As he filleted the fish, he was reminded of the many times he did this exact thing with his father. It seemed like a lifetime ago, and yet it seemed like only yesterday.

Marda had built a roaring fire, which they used to roast the trout fillets on sticks made of sharpened, fire-hardened oak branches.

Jaykriss thought that the trout might have been the best thing he had ever eaten in his entire life.

After their meal, they put out the fire and hoisted their packs to their shoulders once more. The rest of the hike was the easiest bit of the day. The three of them loudly sang a collection of obscure old fishing songs right along with Marda and did not worry about the Thrax, the Dead City, or Kranin—or anything else, for that matter.

Jaykriss felt a curious joy in his heart when they hiked around the Great Round Rock and first beheld the shimmering waters of the aqueduct. They had made the boathouse well before dark. Zamarcus exclaimed that it was record time, and the boys did not doubt him. Even cranky old Archimedes seemed jubilant. As they hiked up the last hundred paces, the old raven flew in broad circles against the late afternoon sky, squawking "Glory! Glory!" as loudly as his avian lungs would let him.

Somewhere, somehow—today, Jaykriss had felt it: a palpable shift in the universe, a sudden redirection of the stuttering lodestone that heretofore had guided him in his meandering journey through life. There was direction now, a purpose. He could not explain it, but he could feel that shift in his gut, could feel something deep and vital tugging at his soul. The earth felt full and substantial under Jaykriss's feet. The sky seemed absolutely limitless.

He had not felt this way in a long time.

Not since Papa died, he thought.

If he closed his eyes, Jaykriss could see Glyndich smiling at him from the Otherworld, his broad ruddy face beaming with pride and love. And that made Jaykriss very, very happy.

28

When Zamarcus had spoken about the boathouse, the structure had been built up in Jaykriss's mind to the degree that he had imagined it as a sort of fortress—replete with hewn stone walls, flickering torches and a shimmering moat.

What he actualy saw as they approached it was something else entirely.

The long passage of years had seen it overgrown by the forest, and the jumble of stones that it was constructed from appeared gray and ancient, surely dating back to the Time Before.

Or maybe even the Time Before the Time Before, if there was such a thing, Jaykriss thought.

The path that Zamarcus had used to bring them around the Great Round Rock approached the aqueduct side of the structure. From that vantage, the boathouse was a plain, unornamented, arch-shaped building made of a curious weathered stone that vaulted across the aqueduct itself like a bridge. Its roof had been reclaimed by the forest; small bushes and green shocks of forestgrass covered it up, as if hiding it from the gods. There were four small boat slips on the aqueduct side, although only one held a one held a boat—and a tiny one at that.

Marda hiked around to the top of the boathouse to survey the lake, pushing his way through the grasping riot of underbrush before stopping at the lake's edge.

"This is amazing!" he said, grinning.

Jaykriss joined him.

The other side of the boathouse abutted the lake's edge. It was bearded by bulrushes and grown over by the rambling tendrils of vines, rendering it nearly invisible from the water. But large trees could not find sufficient root depth over the hard stone roof of the structure, and would not grow there. This afforded the boys an unobstructed view of the body of water known in the Godswood as Dragon Lake. And Dragon Lake was majestic, stretching across the valley almost to the horizon.

"So much water!" Marda said.

"You see the mountain range on the other side, the ones with the snow on the peaks? Those are the Zephyr Mountains. The road to Capitus winds around the other side of them," Jaykriss said.

"Someday, we will go there," Marda said.

Jaykriss nodded.

"If you boys are done sight-seeing, we have a little work to do before dark!" Zamarcus called from below.

Jaykriss and Marda raced each other down the path to the back of the boathouse. Marda slipped once, nearly tumbling headlong into the water, but he caught himself on a root that had conveniently grown its way out of the edge of the trail.

"Where are you, Zamarcus?" Jaykriss called from the back of the boathouse.

"Over here," the old man said. Zamarcus was crouched beside the doorway to a single closed room at one end of the boathouse. The doorway was padlocked from the outside, with rusted iron bars on the plain square windows.

It looks like a jail, Jaykriss thought when he first saw it.

"I know it looks like a jail," Zamarcus said—a statement which caused Jaykriss to raise his eyebrows. "Still, it's dry and clean—and it is by far the safest place in this portion of the upper forest. There's food here, too, and a wood-burning stove. It's a palace compared to where we're headed."

"Where we're headed is worse than *this*?" Marda asked.

"We are headed to the Dead City, a place where no man has journeyed in years and lived to tell the tale. Or have you forgotten?"

Zamarcus opened the padlock with a key on his belt. "Boys, listen. This is the only key to this lock. If something happens to me, make certain that you *get this key*. This is a wild place. There are no villages in the upper forest. No one can save you if things go wrong."

He patted the key with a bony hand. "*This* could be the difference between life and death," the old man said.

And Jaykriss believed him.

Jaykriss and Marda gathered some wood and Zamarcus started a fire in the stove as the sun edged toward the horizon. As they prepared to eat their supper, Jaykriss glanced at the aquamarine sky. Evening was approaching; shadows had begun to coalesce. A few glimmering stars were already out, suspended like brilliant grains of sand in the heavenly firmament, as night advanced across the upper forest in a breathless rush. With the darkness came bone-chilling cold. A bitter wind whistled in from the lake, relentless and unforgiving.

Splat! Sush-AT!

Jaykriss could hear waves slapping against the boathouse; water from Dragon Lake dropped over the wall and into the aqueduct channel in a chaotic, staccato rhythm. It was irregular enough to be disconcerting—Jaykriss felt his pulse quicken momentarily the first few times it happened, before he realized what the sound was—but it was also soothing, in some strange way.

Water is life, Jaykriss, his father had once said. And Jaykriss realized that this was true.

They dined on leftover trout from lunch, and some apples and bread that Zamarcus had brought along. Marda wanted to try the pemmican and dried fruit that was stored in the boathouse drybox, but he only got through one bite of each.

"Who can eat this stuff?" he said, his face twisted sideways as he chewed.

"Starving men," Zamarcus said. "Which, thankfully, we are not."

When Jaykriss finally bedded down for the evening, he was bone tired. A thought came to him as he huddled beneath his blanket, inching closer to the stove. "Zamarcus, why do they call it Dragon Lake?" he asked.

"Because years ago, there used to be a great many dragons here. Sadly, there aren't any dragons left at Dragon Lake. Most of them died, or flew away. Or something," the old man said drowsily.

He removed his spectacles and rolled over on one side.

"I do miss seeing dragons," he mumbled.

In an instant, Zamarcus was asleep, his mouth agape. His snores were almost deafening.

I hope I don't dream about dragons, Jaykriss thought. But there were no dreams at all that night.

It was still dark when Jaykriss first heard the howling.

It awakened him with a start, like a bucket of cold water being dumped upon him. The sound was distant at first—high-pitched and mournful, the wail of a grief-stricken woman whose child had died.

And then it was closer.

The first wail was soon joined by another, and then a third. The chorus was a crescendo, growing louder by the minute.

Marda slept on, oblivious.

"Marda!" Jaykriss whispered.

The older boy snored on.

"*Marda!*" Jaykriss said again, shaking his friend by the shoulder.

In an instant, Marda was on his feet, sword in hand. "What *is* that?" he asked.

"Direwolves," Zamarcus said from the darkness on the far side of the room, his voice thick with sleep.

"But what are they doing?"

"They have caught our scent. They know we are here. And they are coming."

The pack of direwolves drew nearer with each passing second, their hellish chorus growing louder and more insistent as they approached. How many were there now—ten? Twenty? Jaykriss could not count their voices anymore.

"They are here," Zamarcus said at last.

In the dark, Jaykriss could see almost nothing at first. But then he caught the blood-red reflection of a pair of eyes in the darkness and saw a flash or two of bone-white teeth.

The howls came from all around them now. There was a cacophony of other predatory noises—deep growls, grunts, and occasional short barks, as though instructions were being given.

"We should fight them and drive them away," Marda said.

"You cannot even *see* them, Marda. They would tear you apart before you could land a single blow," said Zamarcus.

"So we're trapped here?" Jaykriss said.

Zamarcus nodded. "For now," he said. "Until they lose interest."

"Thank the gods for this boathouse," Jaykriss said.

"This is only a small bit of what we may encounter on our way to the Dead City. There are other things out there even more fearsome," Zamarcus said.

"More fearsome than a pack of Direwolves?" Marda said.

Zamarcus nodded.

"But what if the Direwolves don't lose interest? What if they stay here, surrounding us?" Jaykriss asked.

Zamarcus stroked his beard thoughtfully, silent for a moment. "That would be a problem," he said at last.

"So how can we get rid of them?" asked Jaykriss.

"Well, they can't swim, and they are deathly afraid of fire, but that won't do us any good. We can't exactly set ourselves aflame," Zamarcus said.

"Not in the usual sense, we can't. But I do have an idea," Marda said.

He explained his plan to Zamarcus and Jaykriss. Zamarcus agreed that it might work.

"Let's wait until daybreak," Zamarcus said. "Perhaps they will just go away."

A cold, gray dawn came soon enough, but the direwolves had not left them. Jaykriss could see them now—gray and black and silver, padding about on huge paws the size of a man's fist, their wicked fangs dripping with saliva. He counted at least twelve; there might have been more. Some of them were huge, as large as bears or small horses, and they moved about constantly, stopping every so often to howl—which they preferred to do in unison, their voices rising up among the trees and echoing across the vast reaches of the Dragon Lake.

"Shall we try now?" Marda said.

Zamarcus nodded. "It's as good a time as any," he said.

Marda put on a pair of eelskin gloves and removed the Dragonfire from his pack, unwrapping the paper that surrounded it.

"Careful, now. Don't smear any of that on your skin, or you could catch flame," Zamarcus said.

They slathered it onto the arrowheads and shafts of several arrows and generously over the blades of their swords before carefully wrapping it back up and re-sealing it.

"Light one of the arrows for me," Marda said.

Jaykriss put the tip of an arrow into the opening of the stove. The arrow-head erupted into a blaze of silvery flame as bright as the noonday sun.

Marda notched the arrow, pulled back on the bow, then let it fly. The arrow zipped past the head of the largest direwolf—a majestic black-maned male with a graying muzzle—and lodged into the trunk of a tree behind him, setting the trunk aflame.

"Another," Marda said.

He fired the second into another tree—and then a third, and a fourth, setting up a perimeter of flame around the boathouse that kept the direwolves at bay.

Frustrated and hungry, the howls of the wolves grew louder and more urgent. A few tested the flames but pulled back, tails tucked, as the blaze raged.

"Light the swords," Marda said.

The three of them left the safety of the boathouse, their burning swords held in front of them.

At the sight of the three of them out in the open, the wolves grew bolder. One leapt into the fiery perimeter and found itself trapped between the flames and the waters of the aqueduct.

"Hurry!" Zamarcus shouted.

Flaming swords aloft, the three of them sprinted down the ramp to the tiny craft that bobbed in the boat slip—a battered wooden skiff that rode low in the water, white paint peeling off of the hull. At the back of the boat was an ancient motor, flecked with rust.

Marda rolled his eyes when he saw the boat up close. "We're going to drown," he said.

The flaming arrows were sputtering and losing their flames, and the direwolves were edging closer.

The three of them boarded the craft and Zamarcus untied the ropes that bound it to the boat slip. The current in the aqueduct was far from brisk, however, and they drifted away from the boathouse at a pedestrian pace.

Zamarcus had squatted at the stern and was fiddling with the motor, trying to get it to start. "This thing is always balky," he muttered, shaking his head.

"Now he tells us," Marda said.

As they cleared the top of the boathouse, the large black male direwolf looked above their heads as if he saw something, then turned and began galloping up the path to the top of the boathouse.

With a shock, Jaykriss realized what the wolf meant to do.

"Zamarcus! Get that motor running! The big one is going above to jump down on top of us!"

"I'm trying! My father restored this thing years and years ago. It's probably a hundred summers old!"

He pulled the starter cord. The engine coughed once, but that was it.

The black direwolf had reached the top of the boathouse and was *sprinting*, full-bore, for the edge of the roof.

"Zamarcus…"

"I'm working on it!"

Marda held his flaming sword above his head, but the great wolf was undeterred.

It won't matter, Jaykriss thought. *If the wolf jumps on the boat, it will sink, and we'll either drown or be eaten. Or perhaps both.*

The wolf leapt into the air in full stride.

"Got it!" said Zamarcus. He yanked the starter cord again—and the engine roared to life at last.

Marda tumbled backward in the boat as the prow of the little craft rose up in the air, but he never lost his grip on Icebreaker. The gigantic direwolf splashed headlong into the aqueduct just behind them, paws outstretched, kicking up a huge wave that lapped at the edges of the aqueduct. As they sped away from the boathouse at what seemed like a ridiculous rate of speed, Jaykriss could see the wolf's dark head bobbing above the roiling water, ears folded back, as it paddled furiously back to shore.

"I thought you said that direwolves couldn't swim!" Marda said.

"I guess I was wrong," Zamarcus said, shrugging his shoulders.

Archimedes soared down to them from a treetop someplace, alighting with some difficulty on Zamarcus's shoulder as he sat at the tiller guiding the skiff.

"Nevermore!" the old raven quorked hoarsely.

The waves slapped at the low-lying front of the skiff as the little craft putted down the arrow-straight channel of the aqueduct—straight into the heart of the forest.

The vegetation around the edges of the aqueduct was closing in, stealing more and more light. Even the water was becoming dark, stained with a mixture of tannins that gave it the look of oversteeped tea.

Jaykriss drew his arms around his knees, feeling a chill stealing its way into his bones.

"How long until we get to the Dead City?" Marda said.

The body of some large creature, its black scales gleaming, breached the water ahead of them. Jaykriss caught a brief glimpse of an enormous eye and an impressive array of needle-sharp teeth—and then the animal was gone, vanishing back into the murky depths.

"Don't be so anxious about our destination, Marda. This is no pleasure cruise. All eyes must be on the river, at all times. There are things in this part of the upper forest that would frighten even the bravest warrior out of his skin."

"What sorts of things?"

"Strange creatures. Monsters. Leeches and dragons. Even ghozim, if the legends are to be believed. It is a region that has long been fraught with all sorts of strangeness, a place filled with magic and mystery—and death, to the unaware. Do not take it lightly."

Tendrils of green-gray moss hung down like the beards of hirsute old men. Vines draped heavily across the channel like serpents, their thick bodies laden with dead leaves and blackened fruit.

An amorphous dark shape tumbled out of the canopy of trees and landed on the back of Jaykriss's neck with a *thwack!*

"Get it off, Zamarcus! Get it off!"

Zamarcus reached over to Jaykriss and snatched a viscid blob from behind Jaykriss's ear. He looked at it briefly before tossing it overboard. It sank beneath the dark water without a trace.

"That was one of the lesser threats of the aqueduct, Jaykriss," the old man said.

"What was it?"

"Detritus. A whole wad of it, half-decayed."

"Detritus! Ye gods, that sounds foul! What does that mean?"

Zamarcus grinned, his eye crinkling up as he did so. "You were attacked by a rotten plant, young man. Nothing more."

Jaykriss flushed crimson. *Soon, I will be brave, Papa,* he thought to himself. *I will be brave just like you. I promise.*

29

The aqueduct shot through the dark heart of the upper forest like an arrow. *I have never seen a river like this,* Jaykriss thought.

But then he remembered that it was not simply a river.

"This was built by men?" he asked.

Zamarcus nodded. "In the Old Times, aqueducts like this one fed water to many cities around the reservoir lake. But this one is important because of where is leads. The rest of the paths to the Dead City were wiped out by the Dark King."

"Did he just forget about this one?" Marda asked.

Zaamrcus shrugged. "Who knows? Perhaps it is fate," he said.

The sky had been obliterated by the dense canopy of forest overhead. Jaykriss knew that it was still morning, but it seemed like dusk—as though the sun had been eclipsed. The air was dense and chilly and was permeated with a peculiar organic tang—the sick-sweet odor of decay. The water had grown darker still, and was now oil-black. Lizards, their leathery, dark-green skin glistening in the half-light, clung to the vines draped overhead, and fat-bodied water snakes longer than their skiff slid silently into the depths as the little boat approached.

"I wouldn't drink *this* water," Marda said, shaking his head.

"You would if you had to," Zamarcus said.

They cruised past another docking station, much like the one they had departed from earlier that morning. The forest had almost completely overgrown this one. River oaks and weeping willows had sprouted through the concrete landing, their massive roots grasping the crumbled pilings like the hands of giants. A gout of crystal clear water, steam rising from it like smoke, cascaded over the top of a spillway and coursed among the tortured maze of tree roots before spattering into the dark channel below.

"Why is that water steaming?" Jaykriss asked, pointing.

"That stream is from the Hot Springs," Zamarcus said. "Legend says that the Hot Springs were blessed by the gods with healing properties, and that those who bathe in its waters can be cured of any malady."

"What do *you* say about it?" Jaykriss said.

Zamarcus turned the tiller to guide the boat around a fallen tree. "What do you mean?"

"Well, the science of it. You're always giving me a scientific explanation for the mystical. So what does science say about the Hot Springs water?"

The old man grinned. "You *have* been paying attention, haven't you?"

Jaykriss nodded.

"The Hot Springs are volcanic. The waters are warm and filled with nutrients. Certain species of thermophilic bacteria and algae—bacteria and algae that like warm places—live there when they cannot live anyplace else. And those organisms produce chemical substances that can kill bad bacteria, thereby healing injuries and eliminating infections in wounds."

"So there is truth to the legends."

"Aye. There is indeed," Zamarcus said, nodding.

"So who is to say that the gods did not merely bless the Hot Springs with those thermo-things you talked about?"

"Thermophilic. Heat-loving. And yes, I suppose you could look at it that way."

"Just because there is a scientific explanation does not mean that the gods are not involved, right?" Jaykriss said.

Zamarcus rubbed the boy's head. "Your father would be proud of you, young man. I hope you know that."

Jaykriss nodded, but kept his eyes fixed on the waters of the aqueduct.

Their journey through the aqueduct continued for hours. The water continuously slapped against the hull in a staccato rhythm, the engine hummed its steady droning tune, and Jaykriss was *tired*, bone tired. He soon found his eyes closing in an inexorable way that defied all resistance. He splashed some water in his face, but the water stank, so he did that only once. He tried propping his eyelids open with his fingers, but that hurt after a while, and then he became drowsy, and his hands fell away. He pinched himself, but the effect lasted only a moment, and he couldn't pinch himself all day.

He did not realize that he had fallen asleep until he heard Marda shout.

Jaykriss barely had time to open his eyes before he tumbled to the floorboards of the skiff in a heap. As if a giant hand were lifting it, the boat heeled up on its starboard side, engine whirring desperately as the propeller broke the surface. Marda reflexively launched himself over to the skiff's port side in order to steady the craft.

"Hold on!" Zamarcus yelled.

The hull slapped back down in the water with a hollow thud.

"I don't know where that wave came from," Zamarcus said.

"That was a *wave*?" asked Jaykriss.

They were now idling in a pool of choppy water bridged by a massive gateway made of sculpted grayish stone. The aqueduct continued on the other side of the gateway, but their passage through the gateway arch was barred by a heavy iron gate that blocked the entire channel. Granite boulders extended steeply up on either side of the gateway all the way to the top, creating a funnel of stone leading into the gate.

"Danger!" Archimedes called out hoarsely as he circled overhead.

That foul-tempered bird is usually right about things like this, Jaykriss thought grimly.

The boulders were covered with a layer of dark green slime and were pockmarked with myriad holes and crevices—orifices that were crammed full of leaves, sticks, and other debris. Broken canoes, the shattered spines of wooden rowboats and other ruined watercraft littered the rocks. A splintered mast, its tattered sail flapping forlornly in the frigid breeze, was wedged awkwardly askew against one of the pillars of the gateway arch.

And there were other things.

"Is that a skull?" Marda asked, pointing.

"It is," Zamarcus said, his jaw tight.

And it was then that Jaykriss realized what he was seeing.

Those aren't just sticks, he thought. *They are the bones of men.*

Piles of bones, both whole and in fragments, were crammed into every crack and crevice. They were strewn across the rocks and stood in random heaps against the immutable stones of the mammoth gateway arch.

"What is this place?" Marda asked.

"It's the aqueduct's entrance to the Dead City. They call it the Widow-maker Gate."

Marda shook his head. "That is not our destiny. We shall make no widows today," Marda said.

"None of us are married, Marda," Jaykriss said.

"Precisely," Marda said. "No widows."

"Is there no other way in?" asked Jaykriss.

Zamarcus shook his head. "Not for us. This is it."

"Well, how do we get past this?"

At that moment, there was a deep mechanical sound from someplace far beneath them—metal on metal, a sonorous aching groan, as if a slumbering giant were awakening someplace in the deep.

"I don't like that," Marda said.

On the other side of the gate, beyond the iron bars, the water's surface bubbled and roiled—and then a wall of solid stone rose up from the depths of the dark water.

"What in blazes is *that*?" Marda said.

"Hang on again!" Zamarcus said, turning the boat's tiller. The old man throttled the engine up and wheeled the boat in a rapid about-face.

But it was too late.

The skiff's exit from the pool was blocked by a second stone wall that had risen behind them in tandem with the one on the other side of the gate. They were sealed in the pool now.

And the water inside the pool was rising.

A rhythmic clanking pounded incessantly deep below them like a war hammer, again and again, funereal and somber.

The skiff had risen halfway up the gate now. Jaykriss could see a weather-worn inscription in one of the old languages carved upon it, the faded words covered in slime and studded with clusters of mussels that had wedged themselves into the myriad folds and cracks in the rocks.

A sightless skull stared at him from a crack in the boulders before him—first from above, then at eye level, then from below, as water filled its mouth and nose and eye sockets once again for perhaps the thousandth or ten-thousandth time, reenacting the owner's death in a neverending tragedy of sorrow and unfulfilled dreams.

"What is going to happen?" Marda said.

"I don't know," Zamarcus said.

As they neared the top of the arch, the idea came to Jaykriss like a lightning bolt. "Zamarcus, get the boat over next to the gate, next to where that iron ring is. And hurry."

"Why?"

"It's our only chance. Marda, hand me one of those ropes and get ready to tie off the one at the stern."

They maneuvered the skiff over by the gate next to a series of thick, rusted rings of solid iron that protruded from the stone wall near the top of the gateway arch. Jaykriss tied one rope to the gunwale at the front of the skiff and instructed Marda to do the same at the rear. They then secured the ropes to two of the iron rings.

"Now tie yourselves to the boat, under your arms and in front of you—tightly, mind you, with no slack. And hurry. I don't know how much time we have."

At that moment, then clanking stopped.

"Are you tied in, Zamarcus? Because I think our time is up."

The old man's crippled fingers were fumbling with the knot. "I'm trying, but I can't…"

Jaykriss reached over and laced him in tightly with a sheepshank. "My father taught me that," he said.

"Hey, the water's stopped rising!" Marda exclaimed.

"Hold on. Here it comes," Jaykriss said.

Somewhere beneath the waves, there was a loud and sonorous *clank!*

Zamarcus looked up, his eyes wide.

"I don't know how I did not see this. You're right, Jaykriss. You're absolutely right."

The water level began to drop—slowly at first, but then faster and faster, the current spiraling into the center of the pool like the arms of a maritime galaxy.

"Blast! It's a vortex!" Zamarcus exclaimed.

And then the water fell away from them like a stone tossed into a well.

30

Marda was screaming.

The swirling water had opened up beneath them like the cavernous mouth of some great water beast—a kraken, perhaps, its tentacles grasping upward for them even as it sank away beneath the earth. Bones and logs and bits of debris were all sucked into the ravenous maw and disappeared into the vast forever as the nightmare rush of dark water pulled everything into oblivion.

But Marda's screams were screams of pure joy.

The three of them, still roped into the skiff, were suspended a hundred feet up the hard rock face of the ancient gateway. In his enthusiasm, Marda hugged Jaykriss tightly about the shoulders before pulling away and smoothing his dark, wet hair back from his face.

"That was *brilliant*! How did you know?" Marda said.

"I just did—I could see how it was all coming together. Now hurry. It's not over yet, and we don't have much time. We need to untie ourselves, use the ropes, climb up onto the gateway, and get out of here. Soon, the walls will drop, the aqueduct will fill the pool again, and the whole process will start over."

"I should have seen it," Zamarcus said. "I missed the signs." His face was a rigid mask of perturbation.

"You can't see *everything*, Zamarcus. And we're alive. Isn't that the ultimate goal?"

He untied himself with trembling hands. "That is the goal, of course. But I should have seen it coming."

The top of the gateway was only a few feet above them. Archimedes was prancing along the gateway arch as though he owned it, head bobbing as he walked. He peered at his human counterparts in the dangling skiff, cocked his head at them, and cackled, "Out of the boat! Out of the boat!" so loudly that it echoed.

"Archimedes, quiet!" Zamarcus hissed.

The old bird flew away in a huff.

The three of them clambered out of the suspended skiff and soon stood atop the gateway arch, staring down at the aqueduct. Just as Jaykriss had predicted, the walls were submerged once again, and the pool was filling up with water once more.

"I guess we're leaving the boat here," Marda said.

"We're *definitely* leaving the boat here," Jaykriss said.

Jaykriss could see the silhouettes of a jumble of ancient buildings beyond the rocks—soaring marble obelisks straining to reach the sky, toppled spires, and vast temples collapsing in on themselves, their spent columns leaning against one another like a league of wounded soldiers. The upper forest had been inexorable and relentless in its march to take back what was rightfully its own. Massive banyan trees, their roots splayed out like the hands of giants, sprouted in the middle of ancient roadways. Dwarf palmettos studded with fan-shaped leaves with razor-sharp edges and river oaks with thick trunks now sprouted from the venerable old rooftops, and clusters of wax-leafed shrubs threaded their grasping roots deep into the crumbling rock. A cat's cradle of ropy vines draped over the buildings and trees alike.

The Dead City is far from dead, Jaykriss thought. Indeed, the forest seemed to have infused it with life.

A well-worn pathway atop the gateway arch led to the edge of the rock face up ahead. A drape of dry, pinkish lichen and soft, dark green moss clung stubbornly to the arch's top; wiry sprigs of grass sprouted from the cracks between the massive blocks of stone. Still, the path was clean and arrow-straight. It led straight toward a doorway arch decorated with worn carvings of the sun, moon, and stars. The passage inside the arch, cut into the very face of the rock, seemed filled with an impenetrable darkness.

"We should head that way," Jaykriss said, nodding at the moon-and-stars doorway.

"Well, I don't see many other options here, chief. I'm *certainly* not jumping back into that boat," Marda said.

Zamarcus remained silent. He was gazing out over the vast wasteland of the Dead City, his thin lips pressed into a deep scowl. "Whatever we do, we cannot remain here. We need to get down off this gate," he said at last, his voice hoarse.

"Why is that, Zamarcus?"

The old man pointed to a billowing plume of coal-black smoke that had arisen in the distance. The smoke twisted up on itself as it rose, spiraling around a monstrous tangled ruin of concrete, steel, and glass before drifting up into the sky and dissipating among the low-hanging clouds.

"We're too exposed, too much out in the open. They can see us here," he said.

In the distance, a drumbeat began thrumming—slow and steady, like a warrior's beating heart.

"Ah, too late. They've found us," Zamarcus said.

"Who are *they*?" Marda asked.

"I don't know," said Zamarcus.

The three of them began walking toward the moon-and-stars doorway. A stiff breeze had kicked up, bringing with it the smoke plume's dense odor of charred wood and some other acrid tang Jaykriss could not quite place.

I know that scent, he thought.

Jaykriss glanced about him for another way off the arch, but there was none—the water was high on both sides, the dark waves chopping in the breeze, and the water was beginning to swirl as the ugly vortex threatened to yawn open once more. The face of the rock was smooth and slick. Apart from a few sets of the sort of rusted handholds that they had used to clamber out of the skiff, there was no other pathway down. Save for the moon-and-stars doorway, they were prisoners of the arch.

Jaykriss glanced again at the moon-and-stars doorway.

"Air! Air!" Archmedes squawked, circling overhead.

They want us to go that way, Jaykriss thought. The idea made him uneasy. His stomach burbled a bit in warning. But no other options were available to them.

As the three of them neared the moon-and-stars passageway, Jaykriss could feel an unseen river of cool air pouring from it. The passage was wide open and impossibly dark—so dark that it seemed that the passageway had stolen the light, absorbing it from the atmosphere so that there was simply none left.

"There's an inscription," Zamarcus said. "It's in one of the old tongues."

"Do you recognize it?" asked Marda.

Zamarcus nodded.

They paused at the doorway. Zamarcus ran his shriveled fingers across the runes and symbols carved deep into the rock.

Jaykriss noted that the clumps of vegetation that had previously crowded the path vanished near the moon-and-stars doorway. In fact, there was a sharp line of demarcation extending about fifty paces in any direction from the passage. The vegetation near the line was dead; beyond it, there was nothing at all—not even a single blade of grass.

It's as if even the plants are afraid of it, Jaykriss thought.

The distant drumbeats had picked up the pace. Jaykriss could feel them in his chest somehow, as though their rhythm had wormed its way inside him. They were not so distant anymore.

What is that smell? It was a strange intermingling of scents—fascinating, really. Wood smoke from all sorts of trees, with a hint of ocean grass.

Why would they use that? Jaykriss thought.

But there was that other scent. The bad one. That was one he could not place at first, the one that filled his brainpan with ice water and rendered him numb.

His head was swimming, bobbing along the current of cool air emanating from the passageway like a cork on the spring tide.

"Zamarcus," Jaykriss said weakly. His entire *skull* felt numb; his eyes had filled up with tears.

Marda was crawling blindly, sword in hand.

I know that odor. I know it.

"It says 'And who shall enter here shall find himself inside.' I wonder what they mean by that?" Zamarcus said, his eyes intent on the inscription.

The smoke column had found them. It swirled around them, its stinking breath thick and hot—so thick, in fact, that for a moment Jaykriss could not see anything but smoke.

And it was then that he realized that the smoke was not actually black. It was, instead, a deep and intense purple.

It was very powerful—so powerful, in fact, that it almost took him.

Jaykriss felt his knees buckle. *I know that odor,* he thought, one last time. But the world was spinning away from him.

"It says here that this is the Door of Sorrows. I wonder what that means?" Zamarcus said.

It was then that the realization came to Jaykriss, like a thunderclap—but the thought was almost too late.

Zale!

He fumbled for the sea-tripe gizzard stone in his pocket. When his fingers found it, he wondered if it was already too late, if he had already failed everyone. His thoughts drifted to his father and mother, to his sister, and to Marda.

He felt like crying. A dark tide of despair washed over him and threatened to drown him. It filled up his soul; indeed, he felt incredibly, completely lost. Jaykriss rubbed the stone between his thumb and forefinger, feeling its bitter tingle penetrate his skin. His senses sharpened suddenly, as though a razor had cut away the haze of the zale smoke and made him whole again.

Marda! he thought.

The wind shifted and Jaykriss spotted Marda just as the older boy reached the edge of the arch. Marda's right hand clutched Icebreaker; his left hand was scrabbling along the steep stony edge of the arch.

Below them, the deadly vortex was alive once more, sucking everything into its hungry maw.

Jaykriss grabbed Marda by the foot and pulled him backward.

"Let *go!*" the older boy said, kicking back at him. "You cannot have me!" Marda brought Icebreaker down in a deadly arc. The sword clanged hollowly against the stone—a mere hand's breadth from Jaykriss's head.

"Marda, it's me! It's Jaykriss!" The wind blew the zale smoke away from them. Jaykriss could see that the older boy's face was streaked with tears.

"They were coming for me, Jay! They had no faces, their eyes were empty, and their hands were made of bones, and they were *coming* for me! They tried to take me away!"

Jaykriss put an arm around Marda's shoulders. "Come on. We've got to get Zamarcus."

They staggered toward the old man, the world swimming around them, as the purple smoke swirled and an invisible host of nightmares continued to gallop about in Marda's head.

Oblivious, Zamarcus was still kneeling down at the doorway's edge, reading the inscription with his spectacles perched precariously at the very end of his long nose.

"Jaykriss—see here? 'The Door of Sorrows is the bringer of Darkness to all who enter.' What do you suppose they meant by that?"

Dense clouds of purplish zale smoke intermittently enveloped them. Jaykriss felt like his head was a big, fat balloon bobbing along on the end of a very long string. His lungs burned, his eyes watered, and he seemed to be outside of himself looking at the three of them from above, or beneath, or from behind.

He rubbed the sea-tripe gizzard stone furiously, feeling its deep prickle in his fingertips. "Are you just *immune* to this stuff?" Jaykriss asked.

"What stuff?" Zamarcus asked, his eyes blinking large behind his spectacles. Jaykriss pointed.

Zamarcus stared at the thick column of purple smoke that danced around them like some living thing. Sparks and ash winked within it like the eyes of demons. "Ye gods," he said. "That's zale!"

"Air! Air! Air!" Archimedes screeched overhead.

The old raven soared past them, flying directly through the gaping mouth of the doorway, and vanished into the impenetrable darkness.

Zamarcus had told Marda and Jaykriss numerous stories of the crafty old bird's uncanny knack for survival. Archimedes had survived volcanic eruptions, forest fires, floods, and a host of other calamities by the sheer force of wit.

We would do well to follow him, Jaykriss thought. "We need to go inside. There are awful things in that smoke. Marda almost crawled over the edge of the gate."

Marda was now completely unconscious, his eyes rolled back into his head. A thin stream of drool hung from his mouth. Zamarcus picked up his staff, placed it under the crook of his arm, and hooked his other arm under the limp Marda's shoulders.

"We must go inside, by all means," said Zamarcus, nodding.

The two of them dragged Marda through the doorway. Immediately after leaving the furious purple riot of the zale smoke, Jaykriss felt his head begin to clear. A dull ache throbbed behind his eyes. *I don't like zale*, Jaykriss decided.

They lay Marda down on the ground just inside the doorway's arch. His right hand still clenched Icebreaker in a grip so tight that neither of them could loosen it.

"It's getting darker. The sun must be setting," Zamarcus said, glancing out of the doorway.

"It's not time for sunset," Jaykriss said. His eyes had not yet adjusted; he could see nothing but shadows. "Where are we, exactly?"

"They call the entrance the Door of Sorrows. The inscription is ancient; I was having a hard time with the translation. It seems that this is one of the passages into what we call the Dead City—but where it ends up was not entirely clear to me."

The air inside the Door of Sorrows was cool, clean, and moist—and the passage itself was even darker now, as black as the midnight sky. There was a gentle breeze; crickets chirped someplace behind them.

Marda began to stir. "How long have I been out?" he said, sitting up. He rubbed his eyes and looked around.

"A couple of minutes," said Jaykriss.

"Well, how did it get to be nighttime so fast?"

Jaykriss looked up. He could no longer see the Doorway of Sorrows; it had vanished completely into the black. It was as though a giant hand had scooped them up and dropped them into another world. The night now extended around them in every direction. A cool breeze rustled in a brace of unseen trees. A pair of barn owls hooted at one another in the distance.

"It's too dark. We need some illumination," said Zamarcus, hands fumbling invisibly in his pack.

Jaykriss touched Zamarcus's shoulder. "Hold on," he said, pointing above his head. "Look up there."

Overhead, an array of stars glittered across a nighttime sky like a handful of diamonds. The slim crescent of a fingernail moon hung low over a distant horizon.

"Where are we?" said Marda. "I don't recognize any of those constellations."

Jaykriss shook his head. "I don't know where we are—but wherever it is, I think we may be stuck here for a while."

At that very moment, Jaykriss heard something moving behind him.

Something big.

31

Marda was on his feet in an instant, swinging Icebreaker right and left in broad arcs before bringing the great steel blade up in front of his face. "Who's there!" he said. "Show yourself!"

Jaykriss heard a rustling of arms and legs and feet, and the staccato clinking noises of chain mail and weaponry. These were familiar sounds of impending battle, and he knew them well. There was a ragged breathing sound, as well— *chuff! chuff!*—and Jaykriss could sense a large animal moving in the shadows. Its breath smelled like smoke and embers.

But he saw nothing.

"I have a light!" Zamarcus said, fumbling about in his pack. His fingers emerged wrapped around a small glass orb. "Behold!" he said, thrusting the orb aloft.

The orb suddenly illuminated from within, and it threw splashes of light everywhere—but then it sputtered and faded away, dimming almost as fast as it had lit up, leaving them nothing but orange scuffmarks on their retinas and an even more impenetrable darkness than before.

"Well, I'll be. That didn't go well at all," Zamarcus muttered, tossing the spent orb back into his pack.

Jaykriss drew his short sword, but it seemed puny and ineffective against a faceless foe that seemed to be everywhere at once.

"There's more than one of them!" Marda said.

"How do you know? Can you see them?" asked Jaykriss.

Marda shook his head. "I cannot see anything. But I can *feel* them. They're out there, all around us."

And then Jaykriss saw it—the slightest wrinkle in the static river of stars that winked near the horizon, as though something was moving there.

Got you, he thought. Jaykriss sheathed his short sword and nocked an arrow, aiming it at the wrinkle in the horizon.

Thwip!

The arrow's aim was true.

"The little one has shot me!" a voice cried from the darkness.

Jaykriss watched amazed as the horizon parted, as though a curtain had been withdrawn—and then a huge armored creature was simply standing there in the half-light, tugging at an arrow that had lodged in the tiny gap between his broad armored shoulder plates and his chain mail tunic.

And the creature was a reptile—a phenomenally large and ugly one at that.

"Take the Nightshield down," said a gravelly voice from behind the shadows.

Jaykriss, Marda, and Zamarcus were suddenly surrounded by a company of armored lizard soldiers, many of them holding flickering torches. The largest of the soldiers sat in a metal-studded boiled-leather saddle astride a fearsome-looking creature with glowing ruby eyes, a mouthful of razor-sharp teeth, and a long, scaly tail studded with bony plates. The creature's tail whipped about like a zharga looking for prey.

A dragon! Jaykriss thought. He was certain that it was a fire-breather by its smell. *But they are supposed to be extinct.*

The largest reptilian soldier dismounted, handing the reins of his dragon to a nearby footman. He stood over ten paces tall, with gleaming obsidian scales and a protruding crocodilian jaw filled with white teeth as long as Jaykriss's index finger. An iron helm covered with metal spikes covered his massive skull. A pair of cruel topaz eyes glittered from beneath the helmet's protruding brim.

"Who are you, and why are you here?" the reptile soldier demanded. He spoke the guttural Old Tongue, a language that always had sounded like a dog growling to Jaykriss.

Zamarcus stepped forward. "I am Zamarcus. These two lads are Jaykriss and Marda. We have come here to seek an audience with the Queen of the Dead City," he said.

The reptile soldier chuckled—a noise that sounded like mud boiling.

"The Dead City has no queen. Her tale is but a myth told by Outlanders to frighten their children into behaving—a bedtime story, a fairy tale, nothing more. You need to leave this place, old man. And take the two infants with you. They do not belong here, either. If you leave now, no harm will come to you. If you stay…"

"We have no intention of leaving now. We have come to seek an audience with the queen."

"I told you once, old man. There is no queen. I am in charge here."

"And who might you be?"

The giant crocodilian pounded his broad chest with a mailed fist. "My friends call me Zarg, Lord Commander of the Stygian Militia. My enemies call me Death."

Zamarcus extended his hand. "Greetings, Lord Commander Zarg. It is a pleasure to make your acquaintance."

Zarg stared blankly at Zamarcus's hand as though he might eat it—but he left it there, in midair, unmolested. "You need to leave. *Now*," he said, baring a mouthful of jagged teeth.

The vermithrax, crimson eyes flashing, let out a *chuff!* Jaykriss could taste its stinking sulfurous breath in his throat.

"We were told to come here by Fyrdhom the Great," Jaykriss said.

Zarg cocked his head and stared at Jaykriss with a baleful eye. "Fyrdhom is in the Otherworld," the reptile said flatly. "Everyone knows that."

"He's not. He's alive. And he's here."

"Why do you say he is here?"

"Because his shade at the Library of Souls told us to find him here," Zamarcus said.

"And because his bow says he is here," Marda said. He unwrapped Fyrdhom's bow and pressed the blue and red stones beside the nock together with his thumb. The buttons began to glow with an intense violet hue that pulsated like a heartbeat.

"See? He's alive," Zamarcus said, nodding at the bow.

"That means nothing," snorted Zarg. "You don't even know where *you* are, old man. How can you conjure up a dead man from the dust?"

The still air was abruptly disturbed by a gust of wind, which brought the sharp tang of ozone to the air. The great dragon's ugly head began agitatedly moving from side to side as the creature began shifting its weight from one forelimb to the other. Its gargantuan mouth gaped open to reveal row upon row of needle-sharp fangs.

"She's coming," the footman whispered to Zarg.

Zarg waved him off.

The whirlwind blew in out of nowhere, a glowing funnel of light that buffeted them to and fro before settling down into something else—something oddly static, a standing column of dust and noise and illumination.

And from it, a woman's voice.

"Zarg, are these the friends of Fyrdhom?"

"They claim to be, your Majesty," Zarg said.

"Bring them to me, then."

"But they are intruders! We caught them in the Valley of Shadows after they entered the Aqueduct Portal!"

"They possess Needle-Eye's bow, do they not?"

Zarg nodded.

"Then bring them to me. Now."

Zarg sighed, placing his massive fist over his chest with an air of resignation. "Yes, your Majesty."

The glowing column dissipated, throwing off tendrils of light and vapor and becoming less and less defined, until it was gone. When it vanished, they were alone in the night once more.

All was quiet after that. Jaykriss even heard a few crickets someplace in the distance.

"I thought the queen did not exist," Jaykriss said, eyebrows raised.

Zarg shrugged. "I lied," he said.

Zarg turned and barked some orders to his company in a sibilant tongue that Jaykriss had never heard before. The reptile soldiers began to gather their things and line up, and Zarg took the reins back from the footman and mounted his dragon.

Jaykriss marveled as the crocodilian soldier wheeled his mount about with a ponderous, fluid grace, as though they were one creature. The Stygian commander stood tall in the saddle. His eyes flashed like jewels in the torchlight.

"We must journey to the Dead City. You heard the queen's decree. She has commanded your presence," Zarg said.

Zamarcus tottered up to Zarg, his beard whipping about his face in the dragon's hot breath. The mounted militiaman towered above the old man like a mountain.

"What is it that you want, grandfather? A laxative?"

Zamarcus traced his fingertips across the dragon's scaled flank. The dragon shifted its weight, its head moving about to see who was touching it. "It's a fire-breather, isn't it?" he asked.

Zarg nodded, sitting a bit taller in his saddle. "Of course. All Stygian commanders use fire-breathers as their mounts. We are paired with them at birth."

Zamarcus stroked the creature's neck, speaking to it softly. The dragon turned and looked at him, red eyes blinking in surprise.

What is going on here? Jaykriss thought.

The dragon lowered its great head to allow Zamarcus to scratch it between its horns.

"You know Dragonspeak," Zarg said.

"My father was a trainer once, years ago. I grew up with them. At least the tame ones. The wild ones have forgotten the ancient trainer's tongue—or are not patient enough to listen."

"There aren't many men left who know Dragonspeak, either. These are new times. It saddens me," said Zarg.

"New times, indeed," said Zamarcus.

Jaykriss and Marda watched, amazed, as the fearsome creature closed its eyes in bliss and lolled its head like a puppy.

"It has been many seasons since I have seen as fine a creature as this one," Zamarcus said. "What is her name?"

"Ancalagon. An ancient name."

"Indeed. A storied name for a fire-breather," Zamarcus said.

He said something else to the creature in Dragonspeak. Ancalagon licked Zamarcus's face with her great black tongue.

Zamarcus looked up, catching the Stygian commander's eye. "She's beautiful. But I thought fire-breathing vermithraxes were extinct," Zamarcus said quietly.

"They are everywhere else. Killed off by the Dark King, who feared they might be used as weapons against him. But not here."

"Where is here?"

Zarg chuckled. "I like you, old man—and anyone who is a friend to Ancalagon is a friend to me. But you are full of questions."

"I just don't have any idea how it became dark so suddenly—or how we ended up here."

"You are now in the Valley of Shadows. It is always dark here. That is why it is called the Valley of Shadows," Zarg said.

"How did we get here?"

"You took the portal from the top of the Water Gate, didn't you? The Doorway of Sorrows?"

Zamarcus nodded.

"Then *that* is how you came here—through the Doorway of Sorrows. Why would you ask me such a silly question?"

"But we were outside in the daylight, and we stepped into this portal thing, and the next thing we knew we were here—at night, under a strange sky."

"I told you before: the Valley of Shadows is in the Nightland, where it is always dark. I know nothing more than that."

"So is the Dead City in the Nightland?" asked Marda.

Zarg shook his massive head. "Of course not," he said.

"I'm confused," Marda said.

"There are only two ways one can enter the Dead City. Both are portals— the Aqueduct Portal and the Overland Portal, on the far side of the city near a cliff. You recall that the Aqueduct Portal, where you entered, is called the Doorway of Sorrows. The Land Portal is called the Doorway of Doom. Both portals lead into the Valley of Shadows, which is patrolled by the resolute forces of the Stygian militia at all times."

"How do the portals work?" Zamarcus asked. The old man was stroking Ancalagon under the chin. The dragon had rested her fearsome head on Zamarcus's shoulder, her eyes now blissfully closed.

Zarg chuckled again. "You ask that question of the wrong person. I am a Stygian guardsman—a soldier, serving the needs of my queen and my people. I do not know how the portals work, nor do I care. I only care that they do. They keep the Dark King's forces at bay. Anyone who seeks to enter the Valley of Shadows must first face our wrath." Zarg pounded a scaly fist into his chest twice.

"Aren't you a little frightened of the centurions?" asked Jaykriss.

Zarg spat on the ground. "We live for the day when the Dark King brings his puny centurions here to face us. They are infants, not fit to leave their mothers' breasts. We would tear them apart and feed them to our dragons." Zarg raised his sword in the air and bared his teeth.

The screech that came next from Zarg's closed mouth was unearthly— a cross between an eagle's cry and a Myrish war-whistle. Jaykriss felt it ripping into in him—a thin knife-blade of sound that seemed to pierce his skull. Ancalagon snapped to attention at once and arched her armor-plated back, belching a column of flame into the pitch-black sky. The Stygian militiamen brandished their weapons overhead.

And then it ended.

Zarg resheathed his weapon, as did all of his men. He turned about in the saddle and looked back at Jaykriss. "Do you doubt our ferocity, young one?" Zarg said. He was actually grinning.

"I do not, Lord Commander. Not in the least," Jaykriss said.

"So now we are off to the Dead City. May the gods be with us!"

With that, the company of reptiles picked up the pace of the march. Zarg soon led the soldiers in singing an unusual marching tune—a wordless, rhythmic cacophony of grunts, shrill tweets, and loud hisses.

Archimedes flapped in from someplace, landing on Zamarcus's shoulder, and immediately began a perfect mimicry of the company's bizarre song. It was as though he had known the tune his entire life.

"You never cease to amaze me, Archimedes," Zamarcus said, shaking his head.

Jaykriss could have sworn that he saw the old raven smiling as he twittered away by the half-light of the crescent moon.

32

The Dead City was as quiet as a tomb.

The quiet was dense, almost palpable—and that unnerved Jaykriss, for reasons that he could not fully explain.

When the Stygian militiamen reached the Portal gate, Zarg ordered the rest of his company to stay behind in the Valley of Shadows. He left Ancalagon with them. This disappointed both Zamarcus and the sulfurous old dragon, who had taken quite a liking to one another.

"The Dead City makes Ancalagon anxious," Zarg explained. "An anxious fire-breathing dragon can lead to unfortunate events."

"Unfortunate events?" said Zamarcus.

Zarg nodded. "She burns things. It can get out of control sometimes."

"Ye gods," Marda muttered.

The four of them walked down a broad avenue inside the ruins of the Dead City. Jaykriss marveled at the great stone buildings with collapsed columns, some of which looked like burned-out skulls. He craned his neck to gaze up at the gleaming towers of metal and glass that soared into the lead-white sky. Many of the glass panes in the towers were gone, leaving gaps in the dim mirrored surfaces of those buildings that looked like missing teeth.

"It is obvious that this was once a vast dwelling-place."

Zarg nodded. "Millions of people once lived here, I am told. I cannot fathom that. Even a few humans can make lots of noise. With that many humans, this must have once been the loudest place in the world."

But on this day, it was quiet everywhere.

"The hair on the back of my neck prickles. I feel like we are being watched," Jaykriss said.

"You are, of course," said Zarg.

At first, as they walked, the ruin of the Dead City was broken up by the occasional bit of foliage—a palm here, a few shrubs and weeds there. As their journey progressed, larger and larger trees began to encroach on the edges of the avenue. At first, they were mostly gargantuan live oaks, with moss-draped branches that arched over the roadway like the arms of giants and snakelike roots that ruptured the sidewalks. The oaks were soon accompanied by braces of red-barked cedars, phalanxes of tall pines, and dense clumps of white birch. There were mimosas and cypress and dogwoods and hosts of others, including many trees that seemed strange to Jaykriss. He was certain there were some he had never seen before. Various vines and ferns and shrubs filled in what little space remained. Before long, the once-broad avenue was merely a path through a dense jungle. Indeed, the vegetation seemed to be crowding them, funneling them in, stealing what little light remained.

"She is near," Zarg said, nodding, as though this explained everything.

Jaykriss was not prepared for what he saw next. As they crested a broad hill, the ground simply opened up in front of them, creating a gaping black wound in the earth.

It was, in fact, a cave—a hole gouged deep into the face of a rocky cliff. Its mouth was surrounded by a verdant riot of trees and vines and shrubs of all types. Flowers bloomed everywhere—roses and tulips and oleander, and a thousand others that Jaykriss did not recognize. A heavy floral perfume hung in the air. Jaykriss could make out the scents of honeysuckle and jasmine, but there were others intermingled, as well.

"I…I don't understand this," Jaykriss said.

"There are species of plants here from different climates and environments, and yet they are all flourishing," said Zamarcus. "It's truly extraordinary."

"This is all because of her," Zarg said.

"Who? The queen?" Zamarcus said.

Zarg nodded. "She is life. She sustains us all."

"You talk as if she is some sort of goddess."

"She would be the first to tell you that she is no goddess. But we all revere her. She has given new life to the Dead City."

As they neared the entrance to the cave, Marda unsheathed his sword.

"You'd best put away that weapon, boy, or I will take it from you. You'll have no need of it here," Zarg said.

Marda looked at the giant, armor-clad, jagged-toothed crocodilian looming above him, opened his mouth to say something, then thought better of it. He placed Icebreaker back in its sheath.

"There's a good lad," Zarg growled, patting Marda on the shoulder.

As they entered the cave, Jaykriss heard scuttling noises all around him. *There are things moving around in here,* he thought. But he had no idea what.

His eyes took a moment to adjust to the darkness, but he soon realized that the cave was not truly dark at all. A greenish glow suffused the air. The glow seemed to intensify as he moved deeper into the cave.

The three of them came around a sharp turn in the passageway, and Zarg stopped walking. The scuttling noises stopped with him. The four of them stood bathed in waves of blue-green light.

"We are here," Zarg said.

Marda stood open-mouthed.

"Is this real?" Jaykriss said.

"I have heard tales of this, but I never imagined that it was true," said Zamarcus.

Before them, in a cavern the size of a castle, was the largest tree any of them had ever seen. Its trunk alone was large enough to swallow the war chief's bain that Jaykriss had grown up in. The tree's branches, as thick as a man's waist, spread out for hundreds of paces in every direction. Each branch held a thick canopy of broad, flat leaves as large as the serving platas Jaykriss's mother used. The leaves were phosphorescent; most glowed a dim green, but a few were either a violet or a blue color. Tiny pinpoints of white light gleamed like stars along the branches. The tree's roots were the dense color of basalt; they clutched at the rock beneath the massive trunk like a giant hand, plunging deep into the cave's soft limestone floor. Jaykriss could hear a faint trickling sound everywhere around him; the sweet intermingled scents of chlorophyll and pure water filled his nostrils. An underground river flowed gently around the tree, isolating it on a small island.

Incredible, thought Jaykriss.

They walked closer to the tree, moving to the edge of the river. The ground was spongy and soft; Jaykriss could feel it yield beneath his feet.

Marda poked Jaykriss in the ribs and nodded to his right. "The walls are moving," he whispered.

Jaykriss turned and saw that Marda was correct. Behind them, above them—all around them, in fact, the walls were indeed moving, undulating in rippling waves.

"The walls are moving because they are *alive,*" Jaykriss said. Suddenly, he felt vaguely nauseous. *This isn't right,* he thought.

Marda took a step backward. His foot came down upon on a snakelike creature that writhed beneath his shoe for a moment before slithering away.

"We are surrounded, Jay. They are all watching us. And we are terribly outnumbered," Marda said. He had placed his hand on Icebreaker, as if preparing to cut his way out of the cavern if he needed to.

As Jaykriss peered into the river depths, he could see ghostly shapes hovering in the clear water. *Fish,* Jaykriss thought.

But these were no ordinary fish. They were phosphorescent, like the tree. When they moved, even their path through the water glowed, making them look like tiny comets arcing beneath the surface.

"Is it safe to cross the river to get a better look?" Zamarcus asked.

"Only if the queen allows it," said Zarg.

"And if we decide to cross anyway?"

Zarg smiled, showing a hundred or more teeth that glowed an eerie greenish-purple in the half-light. "The anglerfish are always hungry. They would whittle you down to a pile of bones in a matter of seconds."

As if to prove his point, a large glowing anglerfish pushed its snout above the water. It lolled its ugly head to one side, staring at them with a huge, round eye, and opened its awful mouth wide to display an impressive collection of needlelike fangs. After a moment, the fish snapped its jaws shut and slipped warily back beneath the waves.

"The river is filled with them. There's not much to eat in here, so they are always looking for prey. And humans are much more tender than a Stygian warrior in full battle gear."

"Point made," said Zamarcus.

"So how *do* we meet the queen?" asked Jaykriss.

At that point there was a great shuddering sound in the rock beneath them. It felt as though the whole cave were going to split in two.

The tree's branches shook. Its light blazed up as brilliant as the stars in a midnight sky. The trunk of the tree began to glow more intensely. The half-visible creatures that had been scuttling around the four of them seemed to draw back into the shadows.

Zarg knelt down, his eyes averted.

"Is she coming?" Jaykriss said.

"She has been here all along," Zarg said.

"Welcome, friends of Fyrdhom the Great. I am Bathrania, Queen of the Dead City," a woman's voice said.

"Who said that?" asked Marda.

"Kneel! The queen is speaking to you!" hissed Zarg, his eyes still averted.

Zamarcus, Jaykriss, and Marda all knelt, their knees pressing into the spongy earth.

"Who is talking? I can't see anyone," said Jaykriss. He could hear movement all around him, could feel thousands of eyes staring at them. The immense tree was sparkling now, its branches a galaxy of lights so brilliant that it made his eyes ache.

"I think..." Zamarcus began, his voice a hoarse whisper. But he stopped himself.

"What?" whispered Jaykriss.

Zamarcus shook his head in disbelief before speaking again. "I think that the voice is coming from the tree itself."

33

*B*athrania.

Jaykriss had heard his father speak that name long ago. He could vaguely remember something notorious about her. But what?

"So you remember my name, Jaykriss? And you as well, Zamarcus?" the tree said.

How did she know that? Jaykriss thought.

"There are no secrets here. I can hear your thoughts are surely as I can hear my own. You may all quit kneeling. That's really quite unnecessary, Zarg. They are guests here, not prisoners."

"Yes, your Majesty," Zarg said, standing and straightening his spiked helmet.

They all could see the queen clearly now.

Zamarcus gasped.

Bathrania's human body had become integrated within the giant tree itself. Her face was at the top of the trunk, and her voluminous hair was interwoven into the foliage. The trunk itself had a woman's curved form; he could make out her shoulders and hips. Her arms spread wide, fingers having been transmuted into branches, and her feet had grown into the tree's vast system of roots.

She is the tree, Jaykriss thought.

"I am the tree, yes," she said.

"They said that you were dead. That you were killed by dragons," said Zamarcus.

"A lie, of course. The Godswood priests are filled with them."

"It was said that you fled to the Great Wilderness after your husband died. That you and your followers butchered a force of centurions."

"That part is all true, unfortunately."

"You *killed* a force of centurions?"

Bathrania sighed. "That was so long ago. But yes, we did. We had no choice. One does what one must."

"You had *no choice?*"

"When my husband died, the Godswood priests decreed that I was to marry some fool, a lackey of the Dark King, who had desired me for my looks. As you know, the priests view women as mere property, like cattle. It was a viewpoint that I refused to accept. I told them that I was not a farm animal to be bartered for political gain. As a result, I refused their 'offer.' I preferred to live out my life as a single woman. I would not leave my people in the Brightwood, nor would I leave my children, who were young then, to be corrupted by the priests. As payment for my lack of cooperation, the Dark King sent a man to kill me."

Jaykriss felt another wave of nausea sweep through him. *I hope Mama and Annie Bell are okay.*

He had not thought of them in days. A pang of guilt tugged at something deep inside his chest.

"But you survived," Zamarcus said.

"The Dark King's emissary was a man of great honor. He realized that I was no criminal and did not carry out the sentence. Instead, he arranged for us to depart to the Great Wilderness. The entire village fled in the middle of the night, leaving the fires burning in the hearths. A couple of older women stayed behind as they felt as though they could not survive the journey. Those old women helped maintain the deception that we were still living in the village. As a result, it was several days before anyone realized we were gone."

"So why did the Dark King not leave you alone then? Everyone knows that the Great Wilderness is a trying place to live," said Jaykriss.

"We were outlaws. The Dark King does not tolerate outlaws. I believe you know something about that, Zamarcus, son of Zatharia."

"I do, indeed. But how did you kill a force of centurions with a collection of freemen, women, and children? And why?"

"The centurions pursued us to the edge of the Great River. They came upon a group of our children bathing. The Dark King's soldiers slaughtered them all in an attempt to try to break our resolve. My own children were among them. I lost both a son and a daughter that day."

"Horrors!" said Zamarcus.

"The Great River was too wide for us to cross, and we knew that if we did not make a stand they would rush in and kill us all. It was kill or be killed. As I said, one does what one must."

"But how *did* you do it?" asked Marda.

"We had the assistance of a brave and noble warrior—the very man the Dark King had sent to kill me, in fact. He baited the trap, and we sprung it."

The realization struck Jaykriss suddenly, like a stone tumbling from a cliff's edge. "It was Fyrdhom, wasn't it? That's how he fell out of favor with the Dark King."

Bathrania smiled. "I may not be the only mind-reader here, Jaykriss," she said. Bathrania's leaves glowed even more brightly; her branches sparkled like jewels in the sun. "It was indeed Fyrdhom the Great who was sent to kill me. And it was Fyrdhom who set the trap to wipe out the force of centurions who had killed the children."

"But where is Fyrdhom now? We were led to believe that he was here, in the Dead City," said Zamarcus.

"I am here, Zamarcus," said a man's voice.

Fyrdhom! Jaykriss thought. He knew the voice well from the Library of Souls. But he could see no one.

There was a great rumbling once again—the sound of stone against stone, coming from deep within the earth. And then the little island that the great tree stood upon turned on its axis.

Fyrdhom was part of the great tree as well, occupying the reverse of the trunk. Bathrania and Fyrdhom were, in fact, a single being, fused back-to-back. Fyrdhom's face was also at the top of the trunk; like Bathrania, his arms and fingers were branches, and his feet and toes were roots. The scars on his skull, left by the fangs of the bear that attacked him when he was a child, were still plainly visible.

"You have found me," Fyrdhom said.

"You are a tree," said Marda.

"So I am."

"But you were a warrior," Marda said.

"So I was," Fyrdhom said.

"Your cunning was legendary. You were an archer, but now you cannot even move your arms."

"That was another Fyrdhom, in another life. I am here, bound to the woman I love for all eternity. And what is more important in life? Battlefield glory or true love?" Fyrdhom said.

"You were lovers?" Zamarcus asked.

"Not at first. But I saw in Fyrdhom the same things I saw in my late husband—a dedication to honor and duty, and a sense of fairness. And over time, I fell in love," Bathrania said.

"She grew on me," Fyrdhom said, smiling.

"Your jokes have always been terrible, Fyrdhom," Bathrania said.

Jaykriss found himself smiling nonetheless.

"So how did this happen? If you don't mind me asking, that is. I've never met anyone who has become a tree before," said Marda.

"We knew if we stayed in the Great Wilderness that the Dark King would find us. Fyrdhom knew that the Dark King avoided the Dead City at all costs. So he decided we should come here," Bathrania said.

"The Dark King was hunting us," said Fyrdhom. "Moreover, despite my many years of loyal service to the crown, he was still determined to have me executed for treason. The Dark King's trackers searched for us everywhere, and some of them eventually found us. We were attacked by a regiment of centurions in the Brightwood while we were on our way here. I served as a decoy, which allowed Bathrania to get away, but the centurions shot my horse out from under me and wounded me gravely. I escaped, barely, on foot. By the time I got to the Dead City, I was dying."

"One does what one must," Bathrania said.

"This is known," said Zamarcus.

"Bathrania knew that this city had once been a city of healing, in the Time Before, prior to the Reckoning. She found some medicine here that saved my life. But the medicine exacted a heavy price. I survived, but the cure turned me into this."

Fyrdhom raised his branches into the air.

"But Bathrania, you are now part of the tree as well," said Zamarcus.

"The tree is immortal. Eventually, I grew old and ill. I was dying," said Barthrania.

"I could not bear to see her die," Fyrdhom said. "I begged her to join me, to become one with me in this form. And now we are one, for all eternity."

For a moment, there was no speech—merely the burble and splash of the river, and the vague rustle and murmur of the mass of barely visible creatures that surged behind them like the tide.

"Tell me, Fyrdhom and Bathrania—is it true what they say? That the Dead City was where the Reckoning started? Is that why the City is now Dead?" Zamarcus asked.

"Does this city look dead to you?" Bathrania said.

"No," said Zamarcus.

"This city has its secrets, to be certain. The Zeedezee, the great palace of the scientists from the Time Before, was here. And there was the great wizard M, whose works are the stuff of legend, although his exact role has been lost in the mists of time. M and the Zeedezee both were part of the work that made the Reckoning, but the Reckoning itself was the work of one group of evil men bent on taking power for themselves."

"Do we know any of those evil men? Have we heard of them?"

"You have indeed. For the Reckoning was the work of the Godswood priests."

Jaykriss felt dizzy. "You're saying that everything that happened—the Rain of Death, all of it—was the work of the Godswood priests? How is that possible? They are nothing but a superstitious collection of old men!" Jaykriss said.

"Did they benefit from the Reckoning?"

Jaykriss nodded.

"Did they *name* the Reckoning?"

Jaykriss nodded again.

"And at their direction, the Dark King destroyed the entrances to the Dead City, forbidding anyone to ever come here again, because those secrets were here all along," Zamarcus interjected.

Fyrdhom smiled. "I journeyed here once before on behalf of the Dark King. He had asked me to make certain that no men yet lived within the walls of the Dead City. My mission was simple—if I found anyone here, I was to kill him. And I did find men—freemen, living here to escape the wrath of the king I served. There were other creatures, as well—outcasts, mutants created by the scientists from the Time Before, beings deemed unworthy of salvation by the priesthood. The freemen and the outcasts were the ones who told me of the Zeedezee and of M, both of whom had been here, in what is now known as the Dead City, during the Time Before. I did not believe them at first. But they took me to the Zeedezee. They showed me the ruin of the palace of M. The evidence they had was so overwhelming that it made me realize that I was serving a corrupt regime. But I had to be careful. The Dark King had spies everywhere. I could not tip my hand, or he would have had me killed. But when he sent me to murder Bathrania and the Tribe, I had no choice. I had to declare which side I was on."

"And you picked the side of right over might," Bathrania said.

"I did, indeed," said Fyrdhom.

"So it was indeed as my father said: M and the Zeedezee were both here, and they had been forces for good, working to create medicines to make people well," said Zamarcus.

"Aye, that is true. But the Godswood priests corrupted their research, ultimately creating the Rain of Death. And then the priests called it a Divine Reckoning on the sins of man, took advantage of the chaos it caused, and used the vacuum created by that chaos to put one of their own number into power," said Fyrdhom.

"Dhatzah-il. The God-King."

"Precisely. And that same Dhatzah-il, now known as the Dark King, rules the entire world with a fist of iron," Fyrdhom said.

"Just as the Godswood priests designed it," Zamarcus said.

"Given that the Dark King is more powerful than ever, and considering that he is immortal, I would say by that token that the priests have won," said Marda.

"He is *not* immortal," said Fyrdhom. "He is a man, and he can be beaten."

"He shall be beaten. It is inevitable," Bathrania said.

"Which leads me to why we are here, Queen Bathrania."

"I know why you are here, Zamarcus. You have brought us these boys in hopes that they will breathe new life into the ancient, dusty Prophecies of

Ramallah. Jaykriss, the One Who Leads, and Marda, the Warrior. And yet I see only a pair of callow youths."

"The prophecies fit them. If you can read my mind, you can see that."

"Prophecies are like currents in the sea, old man. They can be channeled into any direction one wishes—for good or for evil. Men use them for their own purposes. The power of prophecy, you see, is not in the prophet. It is, rather, in its ability to galvanize people to follow a cause, making it a useful tool for insurrection. Prophecies that never come to pass are conveniently forgotten. Prophecies that are fulfilled are the rallying cries of war. So, if you would have these boys fulfill that age-old document, the question remains—is this boy the One Who Leads, or is he simply the latest pretender? So how do you propose that we answer that question?"

Zamarcus was at a loss for words.

"Very well, then. We shall settle this in a time-honored fashion—with combat. The gods will see to it that the victor wins justly. The loser shall be rightly judged as inferior. Your Jaykriss and your Marda shall fight Lord Commander Zarg."

"With all due respect, Queen Bathrania, that is hardly fair. They are young men, not seasoned warriors like Zarg," Zamarcus said.

"Save your excuses, old man. You have come here for some sort of blessing. Very well. Those are my terms—if the boys battle Zarg and win, Jaykriss and Marda will win the full support of the inhabitants of the Dead City."

"And if they lose? Will we be free to go?"

"You do not understand, old man. This is not some Hunting Day training session. This is a Warrior's Challenge in the old tradition—by mortal combat, hand to hand. To the death."

34

"That is not acceptable!"

Zamarcus looked less like an old man and more like some vengeful spirit. His eyes blazed like embers; the vast cloud of his white hair seemed to be standing on end.

"Who are *you* to tell me what is acceptable, old fool?"

Bathrania was fully illuminated now. Every leaf, every branch, every fiber of her being burned with a white-hot intensity. Indeed, Jaykriss could hardly look at her; it hurt his eyes somewhere behind the retinas—in the depths of his brain, perhaps, in places that could not be seen by mortal men.

In the supernova brilliance of Bathrania's fury, the creatures of the cavern were now plainly visible. There were thousands upon thousands of them, crowding the entire room. Some appeared to be men—or crude representations of men, in any case, but with coarser features, and more powerfully muscled bodies. Some of the creatures were reptilian, like Zarg. And there were hybrids of all sorts—a few Geshans, which he recognized, but also bird-men with wings, creatures with the faces and fangs of tigers but the bodies of men, and several elephantine behemoths, standing on two feet, with human hands but also with a pachyderm's tusks, trunks, and large flapping ears.

The creatures filling the cavern now erupted with a deafening cacophony of sound—squawks and roars and hoots and screams of the most unearthly sort. Marda reflexively covered his ears—an action which brought a dark chuckle from Zarg.

"This child is afraid of *noise,* old man," the crocodilian said. "I will soon teach them both the true meaning of fear."

"*Silence!*" the queen shouted, and the room was instantly quiet again. Even the anglerfish stopped moving.

"I must reiterate, Queen Bathrania—with all due respect, we came here to seek the wise counsel of your consort, Fyrdhom. We did not come prepared to do battle. The boy is not yet ready. He will need to acquire more skills to battle the Dark King. He…"

"Do you think that we have survived in the face of the Dark King's hatred of everything we stand for by being *soft,* old man? That we have learned through fear and cowardice to endure the Dark King's wrath? I know you feel strongly about these young charges of yours, and that sentiment is, on some level, commendable. But challenging the Dark King is not a schoolyard fight. It is real life. People live, and people die. And at the end of the day, I must serve those you see here—the outcasts, the half-men created by the Zeedezee, mutant creatures deemed defective and unworthy by the all-powerful priesthood. Every single being in this room would battle the Dark King one on one to save the rest. And the Dark King would kill each and every one of them. He is not immortal— that is certain. But he is quite powerful—more powerful than even you know. You have heard me say that to survive, one does what one must. This is the creed we have lived by for centuries—and we shall do the same for centuries to come. So tell me, old man—if your young charges cannot defeat one lone Stygian commander, how can they *possibly* hope to survive the limitless fury of the Dark King?"

There was a palpable silence in the room.

Water trickled someplace. Jaykriss could hear the muffled breathing of thousands of souls crowded around him. The air tasted metallic; it was hot and moist, like blood.

This was a mistake, Jaykriss thought. *We should never have come here.*

But then he felt a hand upon his shoulder.

"I stand with you in this, Jay. We can defeat him." Marda had one hand on Icebreaker. He was grinning. "Tell me—is he stronger than a dozen Geshans? Can he outrun the Thrax? Does he have the spirits of the fabled Glyndich and Garoth guiding him from the Otherworld in battle?"

Jaykriss shook his head.

"Well, then. Let's do this. I have a feeling that if we do not fight this big ugly lizard, we will never leave this place alive."

He's right, thought Jaykriss. *We've seen their secrets. We know the way into the Dead City. If we are not allied with them, we will be forced to stay here forever—or die.*

Jaykriss stepped forward. "Queen Bathrania, Marda and I accept your challenge. We will fight Lord Zarg in Mortal Combat. To the Death."

The legions of creatures in the room erupted in a chorus of cackles and grunts and screams once again—even louder this time, in fact. But Marda did not cover his ears this time. Instead, he unsheathed Icebreaker and held it over his head, acknowledging the roar of the crowd.

"Show-off," said Jaykriss.

"Just winning the audience," he said.

Zamarcus, who had appeared so imperious and imposing a moment earlier, now seemed to have shrunk two sizes. His bushy eyebrows were knitted together with worry. "You cannot do this. Zarg will kill you both."

"Zamarcus, they are going to kill us anyway. We know too much now. So we might as well try to win the support of an army in the process," said Jaykriss.

The old man placed a hand upon each of their shoulders. "Truly, I am sorry that I have gotten you into this. You are both fine young men. You do honor to both of your fathers. I just wanted you to know that," he said.

"Zamarcus, you must remember: We came to *you* for help. And you have been an excellent teacher. So there are no regrets here," Jaykriss said.

"Besides," Marda said.

He flipped Icebreaker end over end twice before catching the battle sword cleanly by the hilt and holding it high above his head once more, bringing another ecstatic roar from the crowd.

"We've got this," he said, beaming.

35

When Jaykriss was a young boy, he had dreamed of fighting valiantly for the Godswood, like his father.

In his dreams, Marda was always at his side—and they always won.

And in each and every dream, Glyndich was there at the end, his beard plaited with rings of gold, silver, and copper as he often did in times of ceremony, beaming with pride as he clapped a firm hand on his son's shoulder.

I could sure use Papa's help today, he thought.

The word had spread among the Dead City residents about the impending Warrior's Challenge. The Queen's Cavern in the Dead City seemed even more full now, if that were even possible. Creatures of all sorts filled every level; there were bat-people hanging upside down from stalactites on the ceiling, purplish blobs with eyes and mouths that seemed to ooze along the walls like they were made of some sort of jelly, and many, many more that Jaykriss could scarcely see in the perimeter of light around the giant tree that was now Bathrania and Fyrdhom.

The queen had called Zarg, Jaykriss, and Marda onto her island in the middle of the cave. A land bridge emerged that allowed them to cross unmolested by the anglerfish; the bridge sank back beneath the water after they crossed over.

"The rules are simple; all combat is hand-to-hand. One cannot shoot arrows, as that confers an unfair advantage to persons firing from a distance," Bathrania said, casting a glance at Marda. "You may not leave the island. You may use anything on the island as a weapon, including whatever weapons you have on your person at present. The match will end with the death of one side or the other. You kill Zarg, you win. Zarg kills the two of you, he wins. May the gods see the true champion through to victory."

Jaykriss looked out into the cavern. The denizens of the Dead City crowded into every space of the cavern—but they had cleared a five-pace perimeter around Zamarcus.

They fear him, he realized. *They think Zamarcus is a wizard.*

Jaykriss smiled and waved at Zamarcus. The old man waved back, trying to smile—but the smile appeared forced. His brow was deeply furrowed, his eyes drawn tight with worry.

Jaykriss drew his short sword. *Father, help me be brave.*

"Begin!" said the queen.

"Try to get behind him," Marda said. "If you can cut his ankle tendons, he will fall. I can then finish him from the front."

"He's wearing mail!" Jaykriss said.

"There are gaps. Find them."

The Stygian Lord Commander advanced on the boys in long, purposeful strides. He brandished a massive curved scimitar in each clawed hand. "I can kill you both cleanly right now and give you an honorable death," Zarg said. "It will be swift, I promise. Just hold still. A clean decapitation is painless."

"We have no intention of dying today," Marda said.

Zarg raised both scimitars over his head. "Then I must have you know that I take no pleasure in killing children. I do my queen's bidding in this, as she commands it," he said.

Zarg brought the swords down quickly. Marda dropped and rolled left; Jaykriss rolled right. The tip of one of the swords ripped open the front of Jaykriss's tunic, drawing blood.

"He's quick for a big guy," Jaykriss said breathlessly. His heart was pounding.

"Are you OK?" asked Marda.

"I'm fine. Here he comes."

Zarg charged at them like a bull. Marda realized that he could not avoid contact this time and raised Icebreaker to parry the blow. Light flashed as the swords collided. The impact buckled Marda's knees, driving him to the ground.

He's strong, too, Jaykriss thought. *No one drives Marda down like that.*

"You will die now, insolent one," the crocodilian hissed. His fangs were mere inches from Marda's face.

Jaykriss had scrambled around behind Zarg when he saw it—a tiny space in the chain mail, just above the ankle.

His short sword was small but razor-sharp.

Jaykriss sliced into Zarg's ankle, driving the short sword as deep as he could. Dark blood spurted out of the wound.

The crocodilian bellowed, toppling sideways. One of Zarg's clawed hands struck a stone as he fell, and he dropped one of the huge scimitars, which clanged harmlessly against the cavern floor.

Zarg righted himself quickly, bearing most of his weight on his uninjured leg. "An unworthy tactic," he grumbled.

"You are in mail, with two swords," Jaykriss said. "Any tactic is fair."

"Very well," Zarg said.

He charged them again—but then, just as he neared the two of them, he dropped to the ground and spun, bowling both Marda and Jaykriss off their feet with his arms and his long, thick tail.

"Now we'll see what's fair, boy," Zarg said. His breath was foul.

Jaykriss realized that the crocodilian's face was right next to his own. He could not budge the creature's massive bulk, so he instead turned his face away. Zarg sank his sharp teeth deeply into Jaykriss's shoulder.

If he bites all the way down, I'll lose my arm. Jaykriss closed his eyes tight.

But then there was a furious rush of something moving past him—a fluttering of wings and claws—followed by a metallic *clang!* And then the weight of the crocodilian was lifted off of him.

"I'm blinded! I cannot see!" Zarg was screaming.

The crocodilian had stood back up and was flailing at his eyes—and at a tiny assailant, a feathered thing flapping furiously about his helmeted head.

"Archimedes!" Jaykriss said.

The old raven was flying about the giant crocodilian like a wraith, pecking and clawing at the giant warrior's eyes.

"What sort of demon is this you have unleashed on me?" Zarg screamed.

Jaykriss stood up again, but he saw spots pulsating before his eyes. His knees buckled beneath him. Looking at the ground, he saw a large pool of blood.

His blood.

He knew that the battle had to end quickly. He was bleeding a lot. He would not be able to stay conscious for very long.

"Hold still, you foul beastie!" Zarg bellowed.

Where's Marda? Jaykriss thought. Then he saw Marda crawling toward the Stygian, Icebreaker in hand.

Jaykriss shook off the dizziness and sprinted over to help his friend. At the precise moment that Jaykriss arrived, Zarg wrapped his fingers around Archimedes's small body.

"Got you, demon," he said. Zarg crushed Archimedes in his mailed fist. The bird seemed to disappear completely within his grip.

"And that's that," Zarg said, dropping Archimedes's lifeless body to the ground.

The bloodthirsty crowd howled.

Jaykriss blinked back tears as he saw the tiny black body fall. "He was a *bird,* not a demon!" Jaykriss screamed.

Marda, at ground level, sliced cleanly through Zarg's other ankle tendon with Icebreaker just as Jaykriss leapt from his feet, striking Zarg fully in the chest. The giant crocodilian toppled over like a redwood. His bloodied helmet clattered away and fell into the river. Flashes of phosphorescence went off like lightning as it sank into the deep.

Zarg was trying to rise up but he could not; his legs would not support him. Marda brought Icebreaker down through his right hand and pinned that limb to the ground. But the crocodilian was unbowed. He flailed at Jaykriss with his left arm and gnashed at him with his teeth.

"I'll tear you open, boy. I'll kill you just as I killed your pet," Zarg screamed at him.

Jaykriss looked at the clawed left hand that clutched at him. *The hand that killed Archimedes,* he thought. Jaykriss leapt off of the crocodilian's broad chest and onto his left arm, forcing it down with all of his weight.

Forcing it into the river—and right into the school of hungry anglerfish.

The water began boiling as Zarg's hand was thrust beneath the surface. There were flashes of light and glimpses of teeth and fish scales and the crocodilian began screaming—a horrible sound that sounded like a cross between a woman's shriek and the roar of a wounded lion.

"My hand! You've destroyed my *hand!*" He drew the arm out and stared at it through his bloodied eyes. What little flesh remained on the skeletonized limb hung in grim tatters from the bone.

The cavern was utterly silent.

"Finish him," said the queen.

Jaykriss stood up. He eyed Bathrania with a cool gaze and gazed back at Zarg, who muttering and cradling what was left of his left arm to his chest.

"No," he said, sheathing his short sword.

"I gave you a direct order! *Kill him!* Those are the rules!"

"Zarg is beaten. Anyone can see that. There is no need to end his life."

The queen then turned her gaze to Marda, eyes blazing. "You, then. Finish what you have started!"

Marda pulled Icebreaker from Zarg's right hand and sheathed it, as well.

"I stand with Jaykriss. It is dishonorable to take any creature's life in this way. It serves no purpose. He is beaten. It is over."

The two of them stood before the queen, side by side.

One by one, the denizens of the Dead City began stomping their feet.

The rhythm grew moment by moment, *thud thud thud thud*, until it sounded as though the roof of the cavern was going to collapse. Even Zarg sat up and pounded his lone remaining fist upon the ground, again and again. The lights on the great tree had softened again, sending showers of light to wash over Marda and Jaykriss.

"What does this mean? Are we to be executed?"

Queen Bathrania smiled. "Quite the contrary, young man. You showed compassion—the mark of a true leader. You spared Zarg's life—and in so doing showed the depth of your character. They are showing you their support. You are indeed ready to face the Dark King."

Leaning upon his scimitar with his good arm, Zarg stood and shuffled over to join them. "You have won the allegiance of the Dead City. We will all fight on your behalf. Myself included," Zarg said.

Jaykriss glanced at Marda and grinned. Marda grinned back. Together, they locked arms and raised their clasped hands to acknowledge the crowd.

The roar at that moment was deafening.

36

They buried Archimedes in a shallow grave in the Dead City, in the deep forest just outside the entrance to the queen's cave. Zamarcus shed a few tears as he planted a small mulberry bush over the gravesite.

"Silkworms like mulberry leaves," he explained. "And Archimedes loved silkworms. So now he'll have a ready supply in the Otherworld."

"I'm sorry that I had to end his life," Zarg said as they walked back into the cavern. "He was a brave little bugger, taking me on like that."

"That was his nature. He was a survivor," Jaykriss said.

"I can respect that. He was a fierce warrior, that's for sure," Zarg said. Zarg's damaged left arm had been placed in a sling. He was a bit loopy on painkillers, which made him more talkative than usual and even a bit sentimental. The giant crocodilian actually wiped away a few tears when Zamarcus was burying poor old Archimedes.

The queen was certain that she could repair Zarg's arm using some medicines she had obtained from the Zeedezee.

"Just don't turn me into a tree, my queen. My apologies, but I don't know if I could handle being in one place all the time. We Stygians are wanderers by nature. I'd rather be dead."

"I promise we will not do that to you, Zarg. We won't let you take root," Bathrania said.

After they had packed their belongings (and there wasn't much to pack), the three of them walked back into the cavern for one final audience with Bathrania and Fyrdhom.

The cavern chamber was illuminated in a more subdued fashion this time. The greenish glow had returned; the white lights along the branches twinkled like the stars of some distant galaxy.

"So you're off, then," Fyrdhom said.

Zamarcus nodded. "We're leaving this morning. It's several days' journey to the Godswood. I prefer to travel by day. Some of the territory we shall have to cover can be a bit inhospitable," Zamarcus said.

"To say the least," said Fyrdhom.

"We came here originally in search of advice from you about the Mortal Challenge of the Priests. I understand that you were the youngest person ever to successfully complete it," Jaykriss said.

"The Mortal Challenge is nothing to be trifled with. I was a raw lad of nineteen when I completed it, full of vinegar and unwarranted pluck. There were five of us that year who attempted it, but I was the only one who lived. I only lived because one of the other four, a strapping young miller's son named Berrick, saved me from certain death, losing his own life in the process. A tragic thing—and a great loss. Berrick would have been one of the greatest warriors of all time. Why would you risk such a dangerous undertaking?" Fyrdhom said.

"My mother and sister have been taken hostage by the Godswood priests. Kranin, the war chief who suceeeded my father, wishes to marry my mother. I seek to use the Challenge to keep that from happening."

"Having a goal for the challenge bequest is a noble thing. I undertook the challenge simply because I was full of the hot blood of youth—and very nearly paid for that indiscretion with my life."

"But you became a legend!" Marda said.

Fyrdhom smiled. "And had I died, I would have been just another dead fool. When one takes a risk, one must always decide this one thing—is the potential reward worth the risk? If the answer is yes, then the challenge is worthy. If the answer is no, it is best to move on. You have heard the saying 'heroism has many faces,' have you not?"

Jaykriss and Marda both nodded. Both of their fathers had been fond of that adage.

"There is a lesser-known phrase I often cite, a saying from the Time Before: 'Discretion is the better part of valor.' That means that part of being a worthy person has to do with making the right choices. Keep that in mind at all times."

"So if I do decide to engage in the Mortal Challenge, what advice can you give me?" Jaykriss said.

"The Mortal Challenge is *solely* about making the proper decisions based on the data at hand. It is all about perception and response, and has very little to do with one's skills as an archer or swordsman. Pay attention to every detail. Weed out the unimportant and respond to the critical. That's all you need to know to pass the Challenge."

Fyrdhom paused for a moment before continuing. "Well, that and a little luck. Luck is always helpful," he said.

"Queen Bathrania, I have a question—if we need the assistance of the forces of the Dead City, how do we solicit your help?" Zamarcus asked.

"Why, you simply must ask for it," she said.

"We must physically come here?"

"Alas, Zamarcus, try as I might, I cannot come to you. I appear to be rooted rather deeply in this place, in case you have not noticed."

"Could we send an emissary?"

"You might—but the average messenger might not survive entrance into the Dead City. We have placed a few rather formidable obstacles in the path here to protect ourselves against the servants of the Dark King."

"This is something we are well aware of," Zamarcus said.

"There is a code of passage, however—a phrase known only to a select number who are friends of the Dead City. It could help an emissary gain safe passage into this place. The code word is the true name of the Dead City, a name long since lost to the ravages of time," said the queen.

"What is that name? Might we know it?" Jaykriss asked.

The queen seemed to lean forward. Waves of color coursed rapidly through her—saffron and green and blue and violet, blushing her trunk and painting the cavern walls with splashes of the rainbow. Her branches and leaves gleamed with a soft, gentle light.

"My dear boy, look up. It is carved directly above your head, in the old tongue," she said.

Jaykriss peered upward in the half-light.

The letters were clear and distinct. Jaykriss was not sure how he had missed them before. They were engraved in sharp relief into a set of marble blocks, moved into the cavern, and carefully placed over the entrance passageway in some earlier time—a tangible relic of the Time Before.

That name was chiseled into the rock by hands long since dead. He felt compelled to say the forbidden name aloud—as a charm, perhaps, an incantation to ward off the all-seeing eye of the dark King.

Atlanta Transit Authority, the words said.

"At Lanta," he murmured.

Bathrania smiled. "Atlanta," she said back to him.

✳ ✳ ✳

The journey back to the Godswood was long, but uneventful. Zamarcus spent some additional time cavorting with Ancalagon during their walk through the Valley of Shadows. Zarg remarked that he had never seen his dragon more taken with any human.

"She usually only likes to char and eat them," he said.

Their boat was exactly as they had left it, lashed to the wall at the Water Gate, and the queen was kind enough to suspend the vortex cycle until they had cleared the gate and made it back into the waters of the aqueduct. They spent one night in the boathouse at Dragon Lake, at the headwaters of the aqueduct, but the direwolves did not make a return visit to them this time around—a fact for which they were all three quite grateful. When they finally made it back to Zamarcus's home, it was a bit of a sad occasion, as there was no Archimedes there to chastise them.

"Cranky and insolent as he was, I'll miss the old thing," Zamarcus said as he turned on the hologram and locked up the place.

The old man had agonized about seeing Lineya once again after all of these years, but he felt he needed to be in the village to support Jaykriss in the Mortal Challenge, so he elected to come along with Marda and Jaykriss this time.

"I've been to the village a few times, you know. In disguise, mind you. I'm quite an expert at traveling incognito."

Jaykriss and Marda looked at the old man's bizarre multicolored traveling outfit and then glanced at each other. Marda raised one eyebrow and smiled. It was all they could do not to laugh, but they managed it somehow.

As the three of them approached the Godswood, Jaykriss could not help but be excited about seeing his mother and sister once again. He had missed them greatly. He had so much to tell them! Annya would be excited to know that he had met a real live queen—even if that queen was a tree.

That will bear some explanation, he thought.

They came to the last clearing before entering the Godswood. There was some commotion in the distance—an unexpected sound that disturbed the usual gentle susurration of forest breeze and babbling brook. It started as a low conversational murmur—the sounds of people talking—but then they heard other sounds: children squealing, bells tingling, and the sonorous clash of a gong.

"What is all of that racket?" Marda said.

The more noise they heard, the more concerned Jaykriss became. *What if there is an attack going on? A league of centurions, perhaps, looking to restore order after Kranin had let it slip further—or the Thrax, the gods forbid. What if the Thrax had returned?*

"I have to see what has happened," Jaykriss said. He started to sprint. Marda followed. Zamarcus called after them that he did not dare try to run at his age; instead, he would catch up with them once they entered the village.

It was obvious as they entered the village perimeter that the noise they had been so concerned about was not a battle. In fact, there was a celebration going on—a fair of sorts. Multicolored banners festooned the main roadway, jugglers were tossing things about, and the main village street had been showered with the petals of thousands of flowers. There was a band playing in the distance—a drum, a lute, and a trumpet, by the sound of it. Children were running about on the village green in their best clothes—chasing each other, laughing and screaming.

"What day is it? Is it a holiday?" Marda asked.

"I was not aware of any holiday coming up. Surely, we have not been away so long that they have created a new one in our absence," said Jaykriss.

At that moment, Beela darted by, her hair tied up in a ponytail. She was wearing a beaded sundress with bits of abalone shell sewn into the seams so that it sparkled in the sunlight. As usual, she zipped along like a hummingbird, darting here and there and never tarrying anyplace very long. Her ponytail flapped behind her like a flag.

"Beela!" Marda called.

Beela glanced at the two of them, and her eyes opened wide. She immediately flew over to them and alighted, grabbing onto Marda's arm with both hands.

"So *there* you are! Where have you been—off on some great hunting adventure?" She pulled back and eyed Marda and Jaykriss up and down. "You two look absolutely *terrible*—like you've plunged over a waterfall someplace. And you're not even dressed for the holiday. Of all people, Jaykriss, I figured that you would be in your best for the occasion."

"What occasion?" Jaykriss asked.

Beela laughed—a twittering sound—*teeheehee!*—that sounded like the mating call for some tiny forest songbird.

"Silly boy. After all, she is your *mother!*"

Jaykriss felt suddenly ill, as though he had eaten a bad piece of fish.

Beela had grasped Marda's hand and was dragging him toward the village green. Jaykriss followed.

As they rounded the corner where Sola's father kept his bakery, he saw what he had most feared. His heart sank like a stone in his chest.

"I'm too late, Marda. They've gone and done it."

Kranin was standing in all of the war chief's official finery on top of a gazebo in the center of the town square. His beard was adorned with silver, gold, and copper ringlets; his sword hung heavily at his side, sheathed in a bejeweled cermonial scabbard. Standing to his left was Annya, looking very pretty in her embroidered holiday dress. A garland of flowers was in her hair.

And standing to Kranin's right, in the usual bride's position, was Samaria. *My mother.*

She was wearing a jade necklace that Jaykriss did not recognize and was beaming broadly, a twist of jasmine woven gently through her hair.

And Samaria was wearing a brilliant white wedding dress.

"Newly married!" Beela said. "Isn't it grand?"

37

As Jaykriss approached the war chief's bain, it was as though he were coming to a replica of the place he grew up in. So much had happened since the last time he was here.

His mother saw him from the window while she was washing dishes. She sprinted out of the front doorway, drying her hands on her apron as she ran, her eyes moist with tears. She embraced threw her arms around him and kissed him on both cheeks.

"Look at you—gone just a few moons and already you look like a grown man! Why did you not tell me you were coming? We would have included you in the wedding!" she said.

Jaykriss scowled. "I would have declined that honor, Mama. How did this happen?"

"I told you about that in the High Priest's Bain, Jaykriss. One does what one must. And it is actually not as bad as you might think. Kranin is a gentle man."

"Is he here?" Jaykriss asked.

Samaria shook her head. "He's at the High Council meeting with High Priest Harros and the warrior brigade. Just like your father. It's always the day after Hunting Day, remember?"

Jaykriss had approached the war chief's bain with some trepidation. He wanted so badly to see his mother and sister, but anger boiled deep inside of him, like a teakettle left too long on the stove. He felt the pressure of it building in his temples.

If he had seen the drunkard Kranin sitting in his father's house, occupying his father's chair—and married to his *mother*, no less—Jaykriss was afraid that he would have simply exploded.

The jasmine over the doorway was deeper now, lusher, and it had been neatly trimmed. Samaria had not done that since Glyndich died. Jaykriss wondered if this had become Annya's job.

Surely she is not tall enough for that yet, he thought. *I have not been gone that long.*

But his younger sister *had* looked older as she stood next to Samaria and Kranin on the wedding dais. She did not seem quite like the little girl she had been anymore. Not a woman yet—but not still a pixie, either.

"Come inside. I can make you some hot tea."

Jaykriss hesitated. "Am I still welcome here?" he asked.

"Of course. It is your *home*, Jaykriss. My marriage does not change that."

"Kranin may not like it—another man, not his son, under his roof."

"Kranin would have no problem with it at all. He has no children of his own. As far as he is concerned, you are just as much his son as mine."

Jaykriss felt a flash of heat at the back of his neck. "I am *not* his son. Annya is *not* his daughter. And I wish you were not his wife."

Samaria stepped toward Jaykriss and clasped his hands in her own. "Come inside. The porch is not the place for such talk. We need some privacy." Samaria hugged her son again. "I've missed you, young man," she said.

"I can take care of myself," said Jaykriss.

She brushed the hair from his eyes. "A mother never stops worrying about her son."

He was surprised at how vividly he remembered her scent. It was floral and clean, like the jasmine that adorned the doorway. She smelled of comfort, of home and hearth.

The tears came quickly and unexpectedly, like a summer downpour. "I'm sorry, Mama. I was just so worried about you. I'm *still* worried. Mistress Lineya told me about how Kranin had always desired you, so much so that he never married, and I remember how Papa felt about him—a *drunkard*, he would say, always shaking his head."

"He's stopped drinking, you know. He stopped after your father died."

"That doesn't make him less of a lout. He wanted this house and so he *married* you, Mama. Does that not alarm you just a bit?"

"There's a lot you do not know about Kranin, Jaykriss. Perhaps you judge him too harshly."

"I know what Papa said about him—and Papa never led me astray."

"Did Papa ever tell you that he and Kranin were best friends once?"

Jaykriss looked at her, eyes wide. "What?"

"It's true. They were the two best warrior trainees at the Godswood School—and they were inseparable, like you and Marda, although they were not cousins. They were together constantly for years—sparring, hunting, fishing, you name it, from dawn until dusk."

"Papa never told me that. What happened? Why did Papa despise him so?"

"Your father didn't despise Kranin. There was one thing that came between them—something that they both loved, but that only one of them could have. It made them bitter rivals. Your father never got over it, and neither did Kranin. They just dealt with it in different ways."

Jaykriss gazed at his mother. "It was you, wasn't it?"

Samaria nodded. "Kranin and I were childhood companions. We grew up on adjacent farms outside the Godswood village; our parents were friends. Everyone always just assumed that we would marry—myself included. I'm sure Kranin felt the same way. But then Kranin introduced me to your father at a Warrior Games competition, and I was smitten. Glyndich did not set out to steal his best friend's girl, mind you. He didn't pursue me. But you know your father—and he was in rare form that day at the Games. He was really just Glyndich being Glyndich—a loud, funny, irreverent, charming rogue, larger than life in every respect. Still, I looked into his eyes once and simply *knew* that he was my soulmate. It did not hurt that he was the best-looking man I had ever seen in my life. Poor Kranin simply could not compete."

Jaykriss smiled as he remembered his father.

What Samaria was saying was, of course, deadly accurate. In his jovial, non-self-absorbed way, Glyndich had been a braggart of the first degree. Hyperbole was part of the fiber of his being, and Jaykriss, like everyone else, knew to take his bluster with a grain of salt. But Samaria had always been a quiet person, a woman very private about her feelings. Hearing this sort of talk from her was something else entirely, like having a wall in one's home torn down and seeing something both magical and just the slightest bit frightening hidden behind it. A unicorn, perhaps. But no dragons, certainly.

"Kranin was terribly distressed when your father and I married. He vowed never to marry another woman—and he kept that promise. But he never forgave your father fully for swooping in and taking me away from him like that. There was a deep-seated resentment there. They had been best friends forever—and, just like that, it was over, for good. All because of me. How would you like it if Marda just waltzed in and stole away that charming girl you drew those pictures of in your notebook. What was her name?"

"Sola," Jaykriss said. He felt his face flush.

"Sola. That's it. The baker's daughter, the snake-killer your father was so impressed with. How would you feel if Sola was married to Marda?"

Jaykriss thought back to the day of the archery competition, when Sola and Marda were feigning interest in each other. It had all been in jest, but Jaykriss had been green with jealousy.

I understand. "I'd probably feel terrible," Jaykriss said out loud.

I'd want to beat Marda to a pulp, he thought.

He realized that he had probably judged Kranin too harshly. He had relied too much on what his father had told him, not realizing that there might be another side to the story. And what had initially seemed merely sad—a great warrior subverted by his addiction to alcohol—took on new meaning. The trajectory of Kranin's life had been forever altered by the two people he cared most about falling in love with one another.

The revelation made Jaykriss ashamed of himself.

"You do seem happy," Jaykriss said.

"I *am* happy," Samaria said, smiling. "I'm happy for the very first time since your father died. Kranin is not Glyndich, mind you, and he knows that. Your father was the love of my life, and he can never be replaced. But Kranin is someone I have known since childhood. I know where he comes from. I can trust him. And I also know he loves me and would never do anything to hurt me. That means a lot to a girl."

"Well, I'm happy if you're happy," Jaykriss said.

Samaria hugged him again. "That means a lot to me, too," she said. "Now how about that tea?"

They went indoors. Annya heard them talking and came sprinting out of the back. She was wearing a simple white cotton shift, but the garland of flowers she wore at the wedding still adorned her head.

"Jay!" she squealed.

"Annie Bell!" he said, arms wide.

She leapt at him in full stride, from over three paces's distance, nearly knocking him off of his feet in the process.

"You've gotten taller!" he said.

"Have I? I thought I had. I'm taller than Sacha now, and I wasn't before, but we haven't measured. Did you see me at the wedding? I'm still wearing my fairy crown!"

She twirled around, splaying her dress out with her fingers, then curtsied, steadying her garland with one hand as she did so.

"Quite the little princess," he said. "I've missed you."

Annya hugged him again, pressing her head against her brother's chest and squeezing him tightly. "I've missed you, too," she said. She squeezed him again.

"Goodness, Annie Bell! You've gotten so strong! I can scarcely breathe!" Jaykriss said, laughing.

"Kranin has been teaching me exercise. He let me fight him with a wooden sword. Taught me how to row a rowboat and to shoot an arrow, too."

Good for him. Jaykriss did not want his sister to be some shrinking violet— and it looked as though she was going to be anything but that. He was grateful that Kranin was taking the time to get to know her better—and to teach her to fend for herself, like Mistress Lineya and Sola had learned to do.

"Sound bodies help make sound minds," Annya said. "That's what Kranin always says."

"A wise statement if I ever heard one," said a deep voice from outside the doorway.

"Kranin!" Annya exclaimed, running to hug him.

The Kranin that stepped through the doorway was nothing like the pot-bellied drunkard that Jaykriss had seen for years, red-eyed and red-faced, lying on various park benches, passed out under shade trees, and in the windowless holding cell at the village gaol. This Kranin was well-muscled, trim, and fit; his eyes were bright, and his grin was infectious.

"Well, well! The prodigal's come back home at last!" He clapped Jaykriss on the back. "How've ya been, Jaykriss? Are you hungry? We've got plenty of food here now. 'Twas a cryin' shame what the priests put your mother and sister here through after your father died, makin' 'em live on bread crusts and the like. They should have shown them more respect. Samaria was the wife of a noble war chief who had served the Godswood well."

He grinned again—a gap-toothed smile that was kind and genuine. "Lookin' at the space between my teeth, I see. Big enough to put an acorn into. Your papa knocked that one out with a wooden training sword when we were but twelve summers old. One devil of a swordsman, that Glyndich. I wish we could get the Bloodsword back for ya. An amazing blade, fit for a king."

"Someday," Jaykriss said.

"Someday *soon*! That's a promise, young man."

"Thanks, sir."

Kranin eyed Jaykriss up and down. "It's uncanny. You're the very image of your father at that age. It's like he opened his mouth and spit you out." Kranin extended a broad, calloused palm. Jaykriss took it. "Just so you know—I always admired your father. Glyndich was the greatest war chief in memory, and I'm not out to replace him. But someone had to stand up for your mother and sister after your father passed. I don't trust the Godswood priests. They're a crafty lot, filled with schemes and plots and other shenanigans. And they don't treat a woman well unless the woman belongs to a man. I love your mother, and I did not want them to make her leave her home. Eventually, they'd have sent Samaria and Annya off to some terrible service jobs in Capitus—polishing the armor of centurions, or perhaps something even worse. Their place is here, in the Godswood. And I meant to make sure they could stay here where they belong."

Samaria looked at Kranin and smiled.

It's good to see her smiling again. "Thank you for looking after them." Jaykriss said.

"This is your house, too, Jaykriss. I hope you know that. It was yours long before it was mine. As long as I live, you will have a place in this bain."

"I appreciate that, sir."

They shook hands again and sat down to drink a cup of hot tea.

"Tell me about everything you saw!" Annya said.

"Did I tell you that I met a queen?" Jaykriss said.

That night, as he drifted off to sleep in his old bedroom once again, he dreamt briefly of his father.

"Good night," Glyndich said, his eyes dancing like they always did, powerful arms folded across his chest.

And he was smiling.

38

It was strange, for both Marda and Jaykriss, to fall back into their old routine at the Godswood School once again. They talked about it on the archery range during their morning break.

"In some respects, it seems like we never left—like all of that was just a dream," Jaykriss said.

"If it was a dream, it was a pretty vivid dream," Marda said. He drew back an arrow on Fyrdhom's bow and let it fly. The arrow struck the target dead center with a *thwock!*

"You've changed the fletching on your arrows," Jaykriss said.

Marda nodded. "It's black and yellow. Fyrdhom's pattern. I figured that it was his bow, so I'd use his arrows."

"Impressive."

Thwock!

Another arrow struck the target, burying itself in the straw right next to the first.

"Strange to see Zamarcus in a master's robe, lecturing in a classroom," Jaykriss said.

Marda nodded, notching another arrow.

Zamarcus and Lineya had split the academic teaching duties—he was to take the sciences, she the humanities—and they were getting along famously. They ate lunch together every day, sitting close together under the shade of an overladen apple tree in the schooyard, and they could be heard cooing to one another like a mated pair of doves. He was living in her tiny, ancient house "for the time being." There was talk of an impending marriage.

"Are you planning to take Zamarcus's Dragonspeak class?" Jaykriss said.

"I was planning to, but Master Plewin wants me to take an advanced archery seminar. One on one, with just him. He has this compound bow design that he got from Zamarcus and is all excited about it. He built a prototype to try out. He offered the course to Sola as well, but she's going to be taking Dragonspeak with you."

"The priests have already spoken to Lineya about the 'new master.' Asking where he came from. She told them that he was a retired master from the Brightwood named Steeple," said Jaykriss.

"Don't you think they will check into that?"

"The odd thing is, Mistress Lineya says that there really *was* a retired master from the Brightwood named Steeple who moved to the Godswood after he retired a few years back. He was very old and had been quite ill. Knew Lineya from the Teachers' Academy. He said he was looking for some peace and quiet—and he found it, all right. Mistress called on poor old Steeple one morning and found him dead in bed with his nightcap on, like he was still sleeping."

"Stars! She didn't report it?"

"He had apparently asked her not to report his death when it happened. Something strange there—Steeple said he didn't want to cause a 'commotion,' whatever that means. Mistress Lineya buried the old codger herself, in the back yard of his house. The old cottage he lived in has now been taken over by the forest. It's just four walls and a bunch of weeds now, with an off-center chimney sticking up there like a crooked finger. You can see it in the edge of the forest if you go to the waterfall on the Brightwood Road."

"*That's* the creepy old run-down shack near the waterfall?"

"The very same."

"And there's actually a *dead person* buried in the back?"

Jaykriss nodded.

"I *knew* that place was haunted!" Marda said.

Afraid of the ghozim again, thought Jaykriss. "So anyway, to keep the story straight, we cannot call him Zamarcus in the classroom. It's 'Master Steeple.' Mistress Lineya accidentally called him Zamarcus one day but told everyone that it was a nickname."

Marda rolled his eyes. "This is way too complicated. How old would the real Master Steeple be right now if he were not dead already?"

Jaykriss snickered. "Over a hundred summers old."

"Stars. That's ridiculous," said Marda.

"Why do you keep saying 'stars?' I've never heard you use that phrase before," said Jaykriss.

Marda blushed. "It's something Beela says. We've spent a little time together lately."

"She's always liked you," said Jaykriss.

Marda shrugged, then picked out another arrow, and notched it. "She's all right," he said, as the arrow struck the target in the exact same place as the others.

The classroom at the Godswood Academy was packed. It was the first day back after the seven-day school break that had been called to celebrate the war chief's wedding, and the students were excited. The chatter in the wood-floored classroom was like the low hum of a beehive. It made Jaykriss smile. *I never realized how much I missed this place.*

"I heard there was a new master, from the Brightwood!" Beela said. She could not take her eyes off of Marda, who was trying his best to be nonchalant about her attentions.

"Oh, really? I'll bet he's old," said Marda.

"Old as dirt, from what I've heard," said Galabrel.

"I'll take that as a compliment, young man. With age comes wisdom," a voice said behind them.

Galabrel turned around, red-faced.

"I'm sorry, Master Steeple. I did not mean anything ill by that comment."

The master smiled. "No offense taken, Galabrel. None at all." He fished about in his robes, his hand clanking behind his Master's breastplate, and pulled out a pair of spectacles.

"Someone told me you might benefit from these," Master Steeple said, handing the spectacles to Galabrel.

Galabrel stared at the lenses, turning the spectacles over and over in his hands, before he finally spoke. "What do you...*do* with these?" he asked.

"You place the loops around your ears, and the glasses across your eyes. See how mine are arranged?"

Galabrel studied the master's face, then gingerly placed the wire loops around his ears. He then looked around the room, blinking. "Ye gods! I can *see!* It's a miracle!" he exclaimed.

"It's *not* a miracle, Galabrel. It's science," said Master Steeple, smiling.

Galabrel was so astonished at the revelations made possible by his sudden acquisition of visual acuity that he actually paid attention during every single moment of science class, which was something that no one could not ever remember him doing before.

Not even once.

The much-ballyhooed Dragonspeak class—a first in the history of the Godswood Aacdemy, by all accounts—was the very last class in the afternoon, beginning only an hour before the bell signifying the end of the day. Many of the academy students were already headed home to do chores by the time Master Steeple was to begin teaching it.

However, to Jaykriss, this did not explain the very small number of students who signed up—a grand total of three students. The only ones in the classroom were Jaykriss, Sola, and Sola's younger sister, Hopa.

"This is it?" Jaykriss asked.

"Are you complaining?" Sola asked. "I think it's great. I get a class with my sister and with *you.* How can that be bad?"

"I just feel sorry for Za—I mean for Master Steeple. He's new here, and I thought this class would generate more interest."

"Some of the kids wonder why anyone would want to take this class because they would never have the chance to speak to a dragon. Especially since no one in the village has ever even seen a dragon up close enough to talk to it and *lived,*" said Hopa.

"Except Jaykriss and Marda," Sola said.

Hopa rolled her eyes.

"OK. Except for your boyfriend and his Fyrdhom-clone shadow," she said.

Master Steeple, looking resplendent in his breastplate and Master's robes, closed the door with a flourish and called the class to order.

"Am I your boyfriend?" Jaykriss whispered.

"I guess so," Sola whispered back, batting her eyes at him.

"Good afternoon, students! Thank you for taking the 'Art of Dragonspeak' course. This is a skill that may come in handy if you ever run into a dragon of any sort, since their languages are all pretty much the same, with some minor species-related variations. Given that there are many fewer dragons left now than there once were, there are not many dragon-speakers left in the world, either. It is a dying talent. I commend you for being willing to take up the challenge!"

They spent the first lesson learning how to speak using only consonants. Dragonspeak was a sibilant tongue, full of tiny hisses, squeaks, and grunts—and there was no written language, so all of the instruction and feedback were entirely communicated in verbal fashion. By the end of the day, Jaykriss could say only, "Hello, Sir Dragon! My name is Jaykriss, and I am your friend. What are you called?" Only it came out sounding like, "Ssss Shhzzz Ghx Hxsss Nzzz."

Jaykriss could vividly imagine his mother telling him he was wasting his time. And perhaps she would be right.

But still, it *was* wonderful being back in a classroom with Sola. He enjoyed just having the opportunity to look at her. He had missed that greatly during his time away. Sitting behind her in class, Jaykriss frequently found his eyes tracing across Sola's slim shoulders, or lingering on hair at the nape of her neck.

Sometimes, he had to rub the sea- tripe gizzard stone he kept in his pocket just to get his mind back on the lesson at hand.

Sola picked up Dragonspeak incredibly quickly. Master Steeple /Zamarcus said that he had never seen anyone master it so well without having an actual dragon around to practice with.

"She's quite talented," Zamarcus said one day after class had dismissed.

"Who?" Jaykriss said.

"You know who I'm talking about, boy. Your girl. Sola."

"She *is* talented, in many ways. I think she's the smartest person in school. And she's an archer on a par with Marda. Beat him once in a head-to-head shooting competition, in fact."

"Did she? That's impressive," Zamarcus said. He packed up his things and hitched his pack up over one shoulder. "She's beautiful, too," he added as they locked up the school.

"I know," Jaykriss said.

They walked across the deserted archery range toward Lineya's cottage. A cool breeze played with Zamarcus's beard. They did not talk for a moment, listening instead to the songbirds as they twittered along the forest's edge.

"How are you and Lineya getting along?" Jaykriss said at last.

"Splendidly. It's as though I never left. We're like a pair of peas in a bean, the two of us."

"Pod."

"What?"

"Peas in a pod. That's how the saying goes—'peas in a *pod.*' 'Peas in a bean' makes no sense."

"Whatever. I'm not big on colorful colloquialisms," said Zamarcus.

Jaykriss walked with Zamarcus walked up the front steps to Lineya's formerly forlorn-looking cottage, remembering that terrible stormy night—not so long ago, although it seemed like a different lifetime—when he and Marda had clambered up those same steps seeking help from *anyone.*

"Wow," he said.

The desperate little home had been dramatically transformed. Zamarcus had planted a small vegetable garden out back, with beans and carrots and cabbage. He had hung new shutters on the windows, and there were flowers *everywhere.*

Lineya's cottage was so gloriously overgrown with plant life that it reminded Jaykriss of the area outside Queen Bathrania's cavern in At Lanta.

It's hard to still call At Lanta the "Dead City" when it is so full of life, Jaykriss thought.

Lineya came outside in a linen dress covered with a huge apron. Her hair was tied up in a ponytail and decorated with a single red rosebud. She was peeling a potato and smiled sweetly at them.

"Jaykriss! Come in! Come in! What don't you stay for dinner?"

She looks twenty years younger.

"I cannot, Mistress. I promised Mama that I would have dinner with her, Kranin, and Annya tonight."

"So everything's OK? I was worried about you."

"It's fine, Mistress. Everything's fine."

She smiled again. "I'm glad—for all of you. And as you might guess, everything is fine here, too."

"I can see that. And I'm glad for you, as well."

He left Zamarcus and Lineya standing in the doorway, kissing one another gently. It was a strange sight—but it warmed his heart.

That night, he had dinner at the family table with his mother, sister, and Kranin. He had not seen Samaria this lively since before Glyndich died—serving platas piled high with food, laughing like a schoolgirl. It was amazing to see her so transformed—a strange and wonderful alchemy, to be certain. It made him remember a poem he had read once, long ago. He could not remember the poet's name. Sola would have, of course. But at least he could recall the sentiment:

I came to see my maiden fair;
My love, my life, my every care.
Transfixed, transformed, we are a pair—
Two souls, as one, linked everywhere.

Jaykriss saw how happy his mother was now. He thought back to the contrast between Lineya before—an essentially kind but formidable woman, not someone anyone would characterize as soft or loving—and the Lineya he saw today, and a realization hit him: the scriptures were right. Human beings were meant to be in pairs. A solitary existence was an incomplete existence, doomed inevitably to at least some degree of disappointment.

And he decided, at that moment, that he would never give up Sola. Not for the sake of any prophecy or any divine decree. She was his soulmate, his better half. She meant the world to him—and he would risk his own death to save her from danger.

He was as certain of that as he was certain of anything.

39

Jaykriss was fast asleep, dead to the world, when the first explosion hit.

The blast blew him completely out of his bed and onto the floor. He struck his temple on the bedpost; it dazed him, causing him to see tiny sparkles of light at the corners of his eyes.

He stood up, rubbing the knot on his head. Glass from the window littered the floor. Something warm and sticky was dripping down his cheek.

He supposed it was blood.

He sprinted over to his bedroom door, opened it, and peered into the pitch-dark hallway. "Mama? Annya?" he called.

There was no answer. Barefoot, a stabbing pain in one heel, Jaykriss limped down the hallway and threw open the front door to the war chief's bain.

Flames were leaping over the roof of Galabrel's home a few hundred paces away. Black smoke was belching up into the sky. People were running about like frightened ants, their movements seemingly aimless. One wild-haired woman was rushing about carrying a chicken under one arm. A man with no shirt, his scalp smoking as if it had just been extinguished, limped by with one arm dangling uselessly by his side. A small child—Sheela, Beela's younger sister, a sprite not much bigger than a chicken herself—had wandered out into the roadway, a dazed expression on her little face.

"Hey, Sheela!" he yelled.

A tall black-clad rider wearing a grim metallic mask with curved edges thundered down the road on his black warhorse—a destrier, from the looks of it, heavy-legged but fast enough. The rider's left ear was missing; his scalp was scarred. The black rider was bearing down directly on Sheela, seemingly oblivious to her.

"SHEELA!"

The girl looked lost.

Jaykriss forgot about the pain in his foot and sprinted into the roadway, grabbing little Sheela around her middle in a single motion and hustling her out of the rider's path like a sack of grain.

When Jaykriss tried to put the little girl down, she clutched at him, trying to stay in his arms, shouting, "No, no, don't leave me with them. They hurt Daddy!"

Jaykriss knelt down. "Who hurt your daddy, Sheela?"

"The bad men. They hurt Daddy and burned down the house. Beela and I ran away because Mommy told us to. I was with Beela, but I got lost in the smoke, and then I saw the bad man again, and then you came."

"OK, Sheela. I'm Jaykriss. Do you remember me? I'm in school with your sister."

Sheela nodded. There were tears in her eyes; her face was smudged with soot.

"I'm going to find someone who can take care of you while I find help. Is that OK?"

She sniffed. "Just don't leave me with the bad men. They hurt my daddy."

Jaykriss hugged her and wiped her eyes.

"I won't. I promise. OK?"

Sheela nodded.

He picked her up and headed back across the road, to the war chief's bain.

Surely they are awake by now—and then a dread darkness stole over him, like an eclipse. *Unless...*

He rushed back into the house with Sheela clutched in his arms. He was in near panic mode now. *Where did that bomb go off? Beneath the house? Did Mama and Annya...*

He leapt up the steps to the war chief's bain in a single stride. Sheela's legs flopped in his grasp. She was trembling, clearly scared half out of her wits.

"Mama? Annya?" he shouted. He heard heavy footfalls bounding up the outside steps to the war chief's bain and whirled around quickly, half expecting to see the mysterious masked rider standing there, sword drawn, searching for the little girl he failed to kill the first time around.

But it was Kranin.

"I was looking for you—your window was shattered, and there was blood all over the floor, but you were gone. Are you OK?" Kranin said.

"I'm fine—just a few cuts here and there, and a bump on my noggin. Nothing serious. I saw this little girl in the street, and this black rider was bearing down on her, so I ran to move her out of the way, and then I saw you. Where are Mama and Annya?"

"I hid your mother and sister in the cellar. They're safe there, at least for now. Safer than out here, anyway."

He looked down the street at the rising flames, then turned back to Jaykriss.

"You saw a black rider? *Here,* on this street? When? Was he wearing a mask?"

Jaykriss nodded. "Just now. He was right there."

"Bad man!" Sheela said.

"This is Sheela, the blacksmith's daughter. She says that the bad men hurt her daddy."

"Let's get her into the cellar with Samaria and Annya. You should be there, too, come to think of it. You're not old enough for the brigades yet."

There was another explosion. The ground shook beneath their feet. Across the village, a fireball boiled up into the sky. Jaykriss could feel the heat of it on his face.

"I'm not staying in the cellar! I'm coming with you!" Jaykriss said.

Kranin fixed Jaykriss with a steely gaze and nodded. "Very well, then. Take the little girl back across to the cellar, get your bow and your short sword, and join me back out here. We're assembling on the village green."

Jaykriss took Sheela back across to the war chief's bain and opened the cellar door. Beneath it, he found his mother and sister unharmed.

"Mama, this is Sheela, the blacksmith's daughter. Their home was set on fire, and I found her wandering in the street. Could you watch her?"

"You're not coming in here? You're too young for the brigades."

"I'm going with Kranin."

"But you're only a child!"

He gazed down at his mother. "If Papa were alive, I would insist on joining him in this fight. And I will fight with Kranin. I must, for the sake of the village. I see no choice here. We are under attack, and the village needs the help of every able-bodied warrior to defend it."

There were tears in Samaria's eyes, but she nodded. "OK. Go. And remember I love you," she said.

"I love you, too, Jaykriss!" said Annya. "Safe hunting!"

"Safe hunting," Jaykriss said, kissing his fingertips and placing them over his heart.

With that, he closed the cellar door.

Jaykriss strapped on his sandals, picked up his weapons, and peered into the night to try to find Kranin. The roadway was a madhouse. People of all shapes and sizes—some bleeding, some blackened by soot and ash—were running hither and yon. A thin, whippet-like dog sprinted by, a terrified expression on its face. Clouds of viscid smoke, smelling strongly of sulfur, drifted through the air.

Jaykriss spied Kranin at the center of a knot of large, heavily armed men. He was barking out orders to them, pointing left and right.

He certainly doesn't look like a drunkard now.

"Are they safe?" Kranin asked.

"They are," said Jaykriss.

"Then let's head over to the green."

There was yet another explosion, this time to Jaykriss's right. Jaykriss felt the blast wave this time as it sucked his breath away and then gave it back to him again, white-hot. He felt his eyeslashes curling up as they burned and caught the distinct and awful odor of burning flesh. The two of them were pelted with a stinging rain of debris.

"Who is doing this? Who are the black riders?" Jaykriss asked.

"We don't know. They're outlaws, though—not centurions. They came like cowards in the middle of the night. Started by destroying the ironworks and the swordsmith's places, where most of our weapon reserves were. They have been riding through town wreaking havoc. We don't even know what their goals are here. This was all completely unexpected."

Jaykriss thought back to the black rider he had seen. There was something about him, something familiar...

And then it hit him. "They're Geshans," Jaykriss said.

"What?"

"The rider I saw had tusks curling out behind his mask and was missing his left ear. He was a huge guy, and he rode a destrier, the kind of horse normally used to carry armored men into battle. That's the sort of horse Geshans always use because they are so heavy. I'd be willing to bet that the rider I saw was Hammack. It looked just like him—big and ugly."

"Hammack, the murderer? I thought he was in Kingsguard prison."

"He's out. Marda and I saw him last month when we were confronted by his brother Honshul and a few other Geshans in the Brightwood, on the way to the Mist Valley. We actually put a few arrows into the lot of them. It made them pretty mad."

"Well," said Kranin. "That would explain a lot."

The brigade warriors had gathered at the village green. Master Plewin, divested of his master's robes, was now in full battle gear. He was outfitted head to toe in gleaming chain mail, with a helmet shaped like a dog's head. The helmet made him look positively fearsome and more wolf-like than ever. Plewin carried a huge quiver of arrows and was brandishing his new compound bow, a marvel of gears and pulleys. Marda was there as well, as Jaykriss had expected. He was dressed in an all-black outfit and had painted his face completely black as well, so that he looked like a living shadow. Marda carried his crossbow in one hand; his other hand had a death's grip on Icebreaker. Fyrdhom's great bow was strapped across his back.

And there, the lone girl among all of the men, was Sola.

She had her hair tied back in a ponytail. A quiver of arrows was draped over one shoulder, and a gleaming short sword was strapped to her side.

Jaykriss saw her and thought his heart was going to melt. *I can't let anything happen to her.* "You shouldn't be here."

"I *need* to be here. Same as you," she said.

"But what if you get hurt?"

"I can take care of myself. Surely you know that by now. And anyway, what would you have me do? Stay at the bakery and make pastries?"

Jaykriss shook his head, grinning. "You're just amazing," he said.

"OK, lovebirds, break it up. We've got a battle to fight," Marda said.

The brigade gathered around Kranin. "Men, we don't have much time. Half of the village is on fire already. If we don't act soon, it will burn to the ground. Anquel, I want you to activate the fire brigade. That will put the older men and children to work putting out the flames. Plewin, I need you to take most of the men and direct the engagement force. Jaykriss thinks that this is a band of Geshans, and I'm inclined to agree. That means that they will be fierce but stupid. We need to find their main body of warriors and engage them—but from a distance, with arrows. We don't want to fight them hand to hand. That's what they want you to do, but we need to battle them on our terms, not theirs."

"How do we find their main body of warriors?" Plewin said.

"By giving them something they want—what they came for, in fact."

"What's that?"

Kranin pointed with his sword at Jaykriss, Marda, and himself.

"Us."

"I don't understand," said Sola.

"The Geshans have a problem with authority. They always have. And they have a history of testing out any new war chief to see just what they can get away with. Glyndich kept them in check for years because they were afraid of him. But I'm new, and I have a reputation for drunkenness. They know that, so they've come to challenge me."

"We'll show them!" growled Plewin.

"Hold on. That's not all." Kranin gestured to Jaykriss and Marda. "These two were involved in a little skirmish with the Geshans earlier in the month— and from what I understand, Jaykriss and Marda somewhat embarrassed them."

"Mainly Marda," Jaykriss muttered.

Kranin glanced at Jaykriss and continued. "Now here's the deal: the Geshans are big on revenge. They don't like being perceived as weak. I think that's the other reason they are here—to seek these boys out. Like a herd of bulls on the loose, the Geshans are big, mean, and dangerous. But they are never cautious and can be easily deceived. We can use those tendencies against them—to draw them out. To force them to make a foolish error or two. And to defeat them."

Plewin nodded. "Sola, come with me," he said.

Sola shot Jaykriss a glance that said everything.

I love you, too, he thought.

And then the rest of the brigade was gone, leaving Jaykriss, Marda, and Kranin alone on the green.

"Time to fight the bulls," Kranin said. He lit three torches, handing one each to Jaykriss and Marda. The three of them strode to the center of the green. Each of them thrust their torches into the ground.

"It's more like 'time to call the pigs,'" Marda muttered.

The moon had come out from behind the trees and was trickling silver light down upon them, but the blood-orange glow at the edge of the village that they had seen earlier seemed to have burnt out. The air was still smoky and thick, and an odor of burning wood hung heavily in the air—a pungent, oaky scent that Jaykriss could actually taste on his tongue.

And in the middle of it all, Kranin began shouting, in a voice that seemed almost impossibly loud.

"Honshul! Hammack! We know you are here! Come out and show yourselves!"

A horse whinnied in the distance, beyond the treeline.

"I am Kranin, War Chief of the Godswood village! And I have the boys with whom you have had some...*differences*. They are willing to talk."

Jaykriss thought that he saw some movement at the treeline—as though the shadows had drifted somewhat, engaging and disengaging, moving in the darkness like some malevolent ghozim.

And then the shadows began moving.

They were all on horseback this time—ten Geshans, mounted on identical coal-black destriers, each one carrying a sword of some type. The largest Geshan had only one ear and brandished a curved scimitar whose cruel tip reached almost to the ground.

Hammack, Jaykriss thought.

"How do you like what we have done to your little village, Jaykriss? Feeling brave now? Feel like *dancing?*"

The Geshan who was speaking jiggled his butt in the saddle, evoking a low chuckle from his fellow horsemen.

"We know who you are, Honshul. You can remove the mask." Jaykriss said.

"The mask was not for you, Jackass. Isn't that your name? If not, it should be. The mask was for the women and children we frightened half to death. So they would know that when the black riders come, they should run and hide."

Honshul ripped off his mask and tossed it to the ground.

"Look around you, Jackass. Your village *burns*. Your poor father has been dead not even a year, and already the chickens have come home to roost. *Squawk! Squawk!*"

Honshul flapped his arms like a bird. Hammack laughed and shifted in his saddle, his chuckle a low-pitched *huh huh huh*.

"You need to leave the Godswood, Geshan," Kranin said, his voice brittle.

"Who are you to talk to me in that disrespectful tone, drunkard? What battles have *you* won?"

"I shall win this one," Kranin said.

Homshul spat on the ground.

"You? You're nothing. You couldn't even serve as a *squire* to Glyndich—much less as his replacement. As much as we hated your predecessor, and as much as we rejoiced when the Thrax took his head, we respected him as a warrior. But you? Any one of us could take you in a heartbeat."

In that moment, Jaykriss felt sorry for Kranin. *Always second to Papa in everything,* he thought.

"Bring it, then. Who is your best warrior? I'll fight him one on one."

Honshul chuckled. "This might actually be interesting. One on one, eh? No arrows?"

"No arrows."

"Then let's make it *really* interesting. One on one, no arrows—and if our man wins, we get to take these two pups and do with them what we will. You win, and we will leave here."

"I cannot agree to that. I am not in the business of wagering with the lives of children," Kranin said.

"Well, then. OK, how's this—if we win, we burn the Godswood Village to the ground, and you get to watch. Fair trade?"

"No," said Kranin.

Honshul shook his head. "Tsk, tsk. You are one *terrible* negotiator."

Jaykriss stepped forward. "We'll agree to your terms," he said.

Kranin glared at him, eyes wide. "*No*, Jaykriss. They will kill you."

"Torture *and* kill, most likely," said Honshul. "It's important to be accurate."

"I agree with Jaykriss," said Marda. "We'll go along with what you want—but only under one condition."

Honshul was distractedly picking at his tusks with a rapier blade. "What's that? You want our *women*? Geshan women are quite *skilled* at many things, you know. Only they would probably beat all of you in a fight!" Honshul said. He grinned and looked about at his comrades.

The Geshans chuckled at this. One of the destriers snorted and pawed the ground.

"If Kranin wins, you will leave the Godswood and never return. *Ever*," said Marda. He twirled Icebreaker in his grip so that it gleamed in the torchlight.

Honshul smiled. "See, Kranin? *That's* how you negotiate. Put something real on the table. Go big. Two boys' lives against a lifetime ban from your disgusting little cinder of a town."

Honshul stopped picking his tusks and glanced briefly at his own reflection in the blade, grimacing. The rapier slid cleanly into its leather sheath with a *sssst*.

"Of course, the point is all moot for us. Hammack will kill you before you can even get off a blow, little man. For you're no Glyndich."

He shot a glance at the giant Geshan to his right. "It's a deal, then. The fight is on. Hammack?"

Hammack removed his mask and dismounted, handing the reins of his destrier to his brother.

He's even uglier than I remember, Jaykriss thought.

Marda spoke up. "Remember the last time you faced a Godswood war chief in single combat, Hammack?" he said.

Hammack grunted.

"How did you lose that ear? That eye? Do you even remember? Or can Geshans not recall things that far back?"

Hammack struck his huge scimitar against the ground, making a clanging noise against the rocks.

"Can you even remember what you had for *breakfast*, Hammack?" Marda said.

Hammack threw his head back and roared, his curled tusks gleaming in the flickering torchlight.

"What are you *doing*?" Jaykriss whispered.

"I'm making Hammack mad. It always works against them. Makes them even more stupid than usual. You'll see," Marda whispered back.

Staring at the huge creature glaring at them across the green, Jaykriss was suddenly struck with an awful thought.

Mama is finally happy. If Kranin dies, after all she has been through, it would destroy her.

Jaykriss turned to Kranin. "Papa always said that he drew on the strength of his love for us in battle. You love my mother, do you not?"

"I do."

"Then draw on it. Feed on it. Beat this idiot, and let's go home."

Kranin nodded. "They underestimate me because of my past. But what is past is past," he said.

He turned to face Hammack, his eyes grim. "Let's fight, Geshan!" Kranin shouted.

Hammack charged like an enraged thrax, his evil-looking scimitar raised high. Kranin deftly stepped aside at the last minute and the Geshan rumbled past, stumbling forward as Kranin landed a glancing blow across one huge shoulder.

"What kind of a battle is this? Get in close and mix it up, Hammack!" Honshul said.

Hammack came in more slowly this time. He swung once and missed wildly, allowing Kranin to get another slice in across the big Geshan's forearm.

"Closer! Closer!" Honshul screamed.

Hammack came in tight. Kranin raised his arm to land a blow. Lightning-quick, the Geshan caught Kranin's sword arm in midair with his non sword hand, gripping it so tightly that Kranin's knuckles blanched. Jaykriss could see Kranin's fingers beginning to loosen and slip, his sword dangling at a precarious angle.

Ye gods, thought Jaykriss.

The Geshan flicked his wrist sharply.

"NO!" screamed Jaykriss.

Kranin's right arm snapped in two like a dry twig. His sword clattered uselessly to the ground.

"Hah! Finish him!" Honshul cackled.

Kranin's right humerus was protruding through his skin. His face was drawn and pale; beads of sweat had popped out across his forehead. He scrambled across the ground on three limbs like a wounded dog, holding his shattered right arm tightly against his chest. He looked frantic, his face twisted in agony.

Nonononononono, thought Jaykriss.

Hammack stalked the war chief on massive, tree-trunk legs. He looked like he might just stomp on poor Kranin and crush him, breaking his back.

"He's going to kill him, Marda," Jaykriss whispered.

"It's not over yet. Kranin's a fighter," Marda said.

Hammack cornered Kranin against a giant oak tree at the edge of the green. Unarmed, his fractured right arm flopped uselessly beside him, the war chief looked shrunken and desperate. His breath came in ragged gasps; his eyes were wide with fear.

"I can't watch," Jaykriss said.

"*Watch,*" said Marda.

Hammack swung hard and fast, the huge scimitar whistling as it cut through the air—right at the level of Kranin's head.

At the last possible moment, Kranin rolled out of the way and darted between Hammack's legs. The scimitar lodged in the tree and was stuck fast. As the Geshan pulled at it, trying to dislodge it, he failed to account for Kranin, who had recovered his sword with his left hand and had positioned himself behind the giant Geshan.

"Hammack! Look out!" Honshul screamed.

Hammack, his scimitar still lodged deep in the oak, started to turn but it was too late. Kranin had sliced cleanly through the giant's left calf. Hammack collapsed onto the ground, holding his left leg in agony. Kranin then leapt to the big Geshan's throat and held the blade's edge tight against Hammak's pulsating carotid.

"Yield," he said. "You are beaten."

"I yield," Hammack said.

Kranin removed the sword.

"NO!" Honshul shouted.

Honshul leaped from his destrier and in a heartbeat was bearing down on Kranin, twin swords raised.

Kranin whirled and met Honshul's thrust with a deft parry, twisting his sword so that the Geshan's wrist gave and the left-hand hand sword flew from his grasp.

"So now we're even." Honshul said, gasping. "We each have one sword—but I have my right, and you only have your left."

He drove in at Kranin, who parried the thrust easily once again.

"Ah, but that's where you're wrong. We're not even. It's not close *at all.*"

Kranin drove in then, disarming Honshul in seconds. He kicked the Geshan's feet out from under him and pounced, leveling his sword tip poised at the his throat in a matter of seconds.

"Yield, Honshul. It's over," Kranin said.

Honshul shot a glance at the nubbin of bone protruding from Kranin's upper arm.

"But how did you beat me? Hammack *broke* your sword arm."

Kranin smiled. "Ah. There's the deception. You see, I'm left-handed."

Kranin looked across the green at the remaining Geshans. They remained astride their horses, awaiting orders.

"Now call off your men, Honshul. Send them home. You've been beaten. We had an agreement."

Honshul glared at Kranin. The fury in his eyes was plainly visible.

"I refuse to accept it. You cheated."

"I did nothing of the sort."

Honshul looked at his men. They looked back at him, expectant.

"What are you fools looking at? *Attack!* Kill them all!"

The Geshans spurred their horses and charged, swords raised.

Suddenly, there was a whistling noise from all sides of the clearing. A hail of arrows rained down from the sky onto the advancing Geshan warriors. Every single Geshan was hit. Most fell from their horses; however, one horse galloped away with an arrow in its hindquarters, dragging a screaming, flailing, black-clad warrior behind it, his ankle completely wrapped up in the stirrup.

"Have you no honor at all, Geshan? Your force is beaten. Your men are down. You have lost," Kranin said.

Honshul spat a wad of bloody snot in Kranin's face.

Kranin merely blinked and gritted his teeth. "*Yield,*" he said.

He pressed his sword tip into the flesh at the base of the Geshan's neck deeply enough to draw blood. "Yield or die. I must warn you, I have no qualms about ending your sorry existence right here. You have caused enough trouble this night."

Honshul sighed and closed his eyes in resignation. "I…yield," he said.

"Well, then. You are not quite as stupid as you look," Kranin said, keeping the point of his sword firmly at the base of Honshul's neck.

Kranin glanced up at the rest of the Godswood brigade, who had clustered around him. "Good work, all of you. The Godswood will long remember this night. Is anyone injured?"

Sola, wide-eyed, gazed at Kranin's broken arm. "You are, sir," she said.

"Aye, I am. But the village is safe, and my wounds will heal," he said.

That's just the sort of thing my father would have said. His mother had been right, of course. Kranin *was* a good person—and, he had shown, a brave and resourceful warrior.

He is an excellent war chief, Jaykriss thought.

Somehow, he knew that Glyndich would agree.

After all of the arrows were removed from the Geshans, and their wounds were dressed by the village healers, Honshul and the rest of his crew were hauled off to jail by the warriors in the war brigade. Kranin's arm was set and bound by Zamarcus, who also displayed some unexpected talents at suturing and dressing the wound.

"This poultice will keep the infection down," he said, rubbing a yellow paste over the broken skin.

"You seem to have a great command of the healing arts, Master Steeple. We are blessed that you chose to move to the Godswood," Kranin said.

"I had some excellent teachers," Zamarcus said, glancing at Lineya.

Lineya beamed at him. "Give yourself a little credit, old man," she said.

The fire brigade had extinguished the last of the flames when Beela and Sola came running up to Marda. Beela's eyes were filled with tears.

"The black riders hurt my father, and my little sister is lost somewhere. I cannot find her!" Beela said.

"Sheela is safe. She's in the cellar of the war chief's bain, with my mother and sister," Jaykriss said.

Beela dabbed at her eyes with the hem of her dress.

"Really? Sheela's OK?"

Jaykriss nodded. "I can take you to her," he said.

"Oh, I'm so happy that I could kiss you!" Beela squealed.

And then, inexplicably, she kissed Marda. Full on the lips.

Marda looked at Jaykriss and shrugged his shoulders.

"Women," he said, grinning.

"You know I would have been jealous if she had actually kissed you," Sola said.

"You've got nothing to worry about," Jaykriss said.

Kranin, Jaykriss, Sola, Marda, and Beela walked back through the Godswood Village toward the war chief's bain just as the sun came up over the horizon. Most of the smoke had cleared, the village had been saved, and the birds were twittering their morning songs as though nothing had happened at all.

"It was an honor fighting alongside you today, Kranin," Jaykriss said, his heart swelling with pride.

"The honor was unequivocally mine, son. And I mean that with all my heart."

40

"They're getting *married?*"

Beela, her arms crossed and her tiny body covered in goosebumps, stood shivering beside the thundering waterfall.

"It's true. It's happening on the day before next Hunting Day, on the village green," said Sola, wrapping a towel around herself before tossing another one to Beela.

Beela caught the towel and began drying herself off.

"But they're *old*. People get married to have children. Why would two old people get married?"

"Perhaps they're going to have some old children," said Marda. He reached down, picked up a flat stone, and skipped it three times across the rippling pool at the base of the falls.

Jaykriss pulled himself out of the pool and sat upon a moss-covered rock at the pool's edge, dangling his feet in the cool water.

"Honestly, Marda, you are an idiot," he said, smiling.

The four of them had come to the edge of the waterfall for a picnic. Beela and Sola had brought apples and celery with bean paste, while Jaykriss had gathered up four boiled eggs. Marda had procured some smoked, cured deer meat from the storehouse—a rare delicacy in late summer, as it was supposed to be in storage for the winter months.

"Well, after all, it was *my* deer," he said, somewhat defensively, when Beela asked him about it.

"I think it's great," she said, smiling at Marda.

She thinks everything Marda does is great, thought Jaykriss.

After they had eaten, Sola proposed that they cool off with a swim before going back to the village. This was clearly premeditated; both girls were wearing their bathing costumes beneath their regular clothing.

"A plot," said Marda. But he swam anyway.

The conversation inevitably came around to the impending wedding of their two teachers, an event that had just been announced the day before. Beela had somehow completely missed that bit of news.

The courtship of Master Steeple and Mistress Lineya had been the talk of the Godswood School. It seemed to have gone almost too fast—the two of them met as Master Steeple began teaching, began spending a lot of time together at the school, and after a couple of months, he had moved into her place. Nobody really blamed him for that, as his little shanty seemed to be in a terrible state of disrepair, but the wedding announcement had rippled through the school like a small societal earthquake.

"Who cares about how old they are if they are happy?" Jaykriss said.

"I agree," said Sola. "That's what's important."

Of course, Jaykriss and Marda knew the real story—but for once, Marda was able to keep his mouth shut.

Zamarcus had only journeyed back to his place in the Mist Valley twice since the school session began—once to get some more clothing ("I can't wear the same robe every day," he said, leaving Jaykriss to ponder what sort of bizarre attire he was going to return with); and another time to bring back an advanced Dragonspeak textbook, because Sola was doing so well she was testing the limits of her teacher's knowledge. Otherwise, Zamarcus spent his days teaching and tending to the little vegetable and herb garden that he and Lineya farmed in the tilled area beside her cottage. Lineya seemed softer now; her lines were not quite as angular, her limp seemed less pronounced, and she actually fixed her hair at times. And Zamarcus seemed incredibly content.

In fact, Jaykriss thought that he had never looked happier.

Kranin, Samaria, Jaykriss, and Annya had settled into a routine at the war chief's bain, and Jaykriss had to admit that it was nice having another man in the house. He still missed his father greatly, but Kranin actually reminded Jaykriss of Glyndich in many ways. Most Hunting Days, while his arm was healing, Kranin would go with Jaykriss and Marda on the hunt. Kranin even taught the boys a few things about trapping rabbits that they did not know.

But this Hunting Day, his arm nearly fully mended, Kranin went out hunting alone.

Because Beela and Sola had planned a picnic.

Marda's first response had been to say no to this idea, of course. "A picnic? On Hunting Day? Why, I've never missed a Hunting Day in my life!" he said.

But it was Kranin, of all people, who had convinced him to go.

"Do you like this girl Beela?" he had asked.

Marda nodded.

"Then it's best that you do as she asks. Go on the picnic. My arm is strong. I can handle the hunt by myself for a week," he said.

Marda stood there, hesitant.

"Go on! If she's the right girl for you, it's best not to mess things up over a mere hunt!"

Now, Marda stood transfixed as he watched Beela, in her white bathing costume, dry off her arms and legs. She jutted out one hip, looked skyward, and wrung her her long hair out. Marda's mouth hung open like a barn gate.

"What are you staring at?" Beela asked, smiling.

"Nothing," he said, his face flushing crimson. Marda stared intently at at the ground, as if he had lost something, and picked up another stone—but when he tried to skip it, it sank without a trace.

"So the Hunting Day picnic idea is OK with you now?" said Jaykriss.

Marda grinned sheepishly. "Absolutely," he said.

The next week was a complete blur for everyone at the Godswood Academy—a mélange of sights, sounds, and whispers as the wedding day approached. Rumors drifted about like swarms of butterflies in summer. The girls spoke incessantly of flowers and wedding dresses and conjured up a cornucopia of sweet and delicate confections of romance. The boys had visions of rescuing fair damsels from the treacherous claws of dragons; theirs were heroic dreams, the vigorous dreams of innocent youth. Love was in the air—and in the water, food, and just about everything else.

Each day, Jaykriss spent most of the Dragonspeak class in a daze. He was enraptured simply listening to Sola's mellifluous voice as she effortlessly rolled through the multisyllabic hisses and grunts of the various dragon dialects.

"You are quite gifted at this, Sola," said Zamarcus, peering over the rims of his glasses.

"Thank you, Master Steeple," she replied.

Jaykriss worried just a little about what Zamarcus was going to wear. In the past, his sartorial taste had proved questionable at best.

His fears were unfounded.

Hunting Day came around sooner than they all expected. Kranin had done well on his own the week before; however, with Marda and Jaykriss to accompany him, this week's haul was positively prodigious—three dozen quail, eight fat rabbits, and a fine eight-point buck.

"This is truly a record hunt!" Samaria said as the three of them returned.

"We'll be able to prepare extra for the wedding feast!" Annya said.

Samaria hugged Jaykriss, whispering in his ear as she did so. "Thanks for accepting Kranin," she said. "It means a lot to him."

"He's earned it," Jaykriss whispered back.

His mother dabbed at her eyes with her sleeve.

"Are you all right?" Kranin asked. His bushy eyebrows were knitted tightly.

"I'm *fine*," Samaria said, red-eyed. She sniffled once and dabbed at her eyes onc again. "It's the wedding, of course. Nothing more," she said.

Dawn came the next day in brilliant fashion.

It seemed to Jaykriss that the sun rose a bit earlier than usual—as though it could not wait any longer. And the avian chorus that greeted the sunrise was even more vociferous than usual. Jaykriss thought he must be imagining things, but when Annya came to awaken him—only to find her brother already up— she seemed to notice it, as well.

"Why are the birds so loud in here?" she asked.

Jaykriss marveled at how quickly his sister was growing up. *She'll be a woman grown before very long,* he thought, *and quite the heartbreaker.*

He felt a pang of regret at that, for he knew how proud Glyndich would have been at the sight of his beautiful daughter. He imagined Glyndich holding Annya's arm on her wedding day, his beard in ringlets of gold and silver, grinning ear to ear.

"Mama says breakfast is ready," Annya said.

"What? No wrestling match? No panther attack?"

"The panther is tired," she said, yawning.

"So that's it. You're getting *old*, Annie Bell."

"Am not!"

"Are, too!"

"Race me, then!" he said, bounding toward the bedroom door.

The two of them pounded down the hallway in tandem.

Jaykriss let Annya win, as always.

The entire family ate breakfast together—boiled eggs and strips of crisp bacon, steaming piles of vegetable hash, and crisp slices of apple. Samaria beamed as she brought in the serving plata. The tantalizing odor of fried bacon filled the room, making Jaykriss's mouth water.

"This sure looks good, Samaria," Kranin said.

"I should hope so," she said. "It was dark out when I started making it. You were all sleeping like babies."

"Do you know what you're wearing today?" Kranin said, his mouth half full.

"Master Steeple and Mistress Lineya had asked that we wear our school robes. They wanted the school to be well-represented today, and some of the children do not have the sort of fine clothes that one would wear to a big, fancy wedding," Jaykriss said.

"That's an excellent idea. Nice that the two of them would think of that," said Samaria.

"Well, Mistress Lineya has had years to plan this. I'm sure every detail has been addressed," Jaykriss said.

"Why, whatever do you mean? The two of them just announced the wedding last week—and only met one another a few months ago. Quite unexpected, I'd say. I never thought that Mistress Lineya would ever marry. She seemed committed to life as a spinster schoolteacher."

Careful, Jaykriss, he thought to himself. He plunged a forkful of hash into his mouth, filling his cheeks, and smiled at his mother as he chewed.

The village green was festooned with multicolored banners and ribbons that undulated in the morning breeze. Twin rows of flowering palm trees, each abloom with myriad fragrant, lavender-colored blossoms, led to the elevated wedding dais in the center of the green. The dais itself was surrounded by a dense arc of flower banks that opened out toward the avenue created by the flowering palms. The sun was a brilliant orb hanging in a cloudless blue sky.

"It's *beautiful*," Sola sighed.

Jaykriss nodded.

The entire village, old and young alike, had turned out for the teachers' wedding. Children chased each other recklessly about, dogs barking at their heels. Men stood in tight groups of three or four, comparing the ceremonial weapons that they wore at their sides, and the women, their hair elaborately braided and interwoven with flowers, congregated in larger groups, segregated largely by age.

Master Plewin, in full academic regalia, was busy directing the students to their seats. The sun gleamed across his breastplate, which clanked loudly as he walked.

"Boys on the right, girls on the left. Come on, students! This is not your first wedding! Let's move along!" he said, clapping his hands.

The older people had already taken their positions near the front. Even the ancient crone who had told him about his mother and sister being taken to the Priestbain was there, dressed in a flimsy rag of a dress but with a loop of white flowering jasmine braided through her wiry hair. She grinned toothlessly as he walked past, waggling a bony finger at him.

"Redemption and salvation, young master," she whispered to him as he passed.

Jaykriss stopped.

"Pardon?" he asked.

"Redemption and salvation. You cannot hide from them. They will find you, sure as sunrise. You'll see, lad," she said.

"Yes, ma'am," Jaykriss said, walking on.

Galabrel was wearing his new spectacles and spotted Jaykriss far across the milling throng. He beckoned for him to join the other schooboys on the right side of the assembly. Galabrel stood next to Marda, who stood glowering with his arms crossed and his legs firmly planted apart, apparently trying to look about as fierce as one could possibly manage to look in a student's robe. He had his hand on the hilt of Icebreaker. As he came closer, Jaykriss realized that his friend was fully outfitted for battle—as if he expected the full contingent of Geshans to be released from the Kingsguard at any moment.

"I saw you all the way from over here," Galabrel said.

"Well really, Galabrel. You aren't blind anymore. Aren't you *something?*" Marda grumbled.

"What's up with you?" Jaykriss asked.

"It's nothing," said Marda.

Jaykriss rolled his eyes.

"Seriously, Marda. Why are you you angry? Is it Beela?"

He shook his head.

"What, then?"

He leaned over and whispered into Jaykriss's ear. "*My mother,*" he said. "She's drinking again. I couldn't get her to come today. I couldn't even get her out of bed this morning."

"I'm sorry, Marda. I really am."

Marda shook his head. "It's almost like both of my parents died when Papa went to the Otherworld. She has never been the same since. She just lies in her room in a stupor with the shades drawn and a bottle in her hand. Half the time she can't even talk to me."

Jaykriss unexpectedly found himself saying a silent prayer of thanks for Kranin.

As the guests assembled on the green, the rhythmic beat of a drum began sounding in the distance, beyond the treeline.

"They are coming, people! Please take your positions!" Master Plewin shouted.

Jaykriss strained his eyes at the east treeline, looking for the torches, but he could see nothing.

"There they are," said Galabrel, pointing.

Sure enough, Jaykriss gazed in the direction that Galabrel was pointing and could see it: the tiniest flicker of flame, like a spark meandering through the forest, as the Godswood priests wound their way along the Priestbain Road and headed toward the green.

The drumbeats grew louder. All conversation stopped. Everyone was looking expectantly at the treeline.

"They brought the centurions," Jaykriss whispered to Marda. He suddenly felt ill.

The priests filed out of the edge of the woods in double file—flanked on either side by an entire company of centurions, each armored in full battle gear.

Their snow-white helmets gleamed brilliantly in the morning sun; their capes fluttered in the breeze behind them.

Jaykriss had seen many weddings on the green. He had never seen the priests bring even a single centurion to one—much less an entire company of them.

They know, he thought, his heart sinking in his chest. *They'll arrest Zamarcus and take him away.* He shot a glance at Marda—whose expression had grown even more grim, if that was possible.

"I know what you are thinking, Marda. Don't do it," Jaykriss said.

"They'll kill him. You know that."

"And they would kill you, too."

"If we could create some sort of a distraction, perhaps one of us could get the two of them out of here," Marda said.

"Now how do you propose that we do that?" Jaykriss said.

Jaykriss felt a finger tap on his shoulder and nearly jumped out of his skin. Turning around, he saw the vulpine face of Master Plewin.

Plewin had an index finger to his lips and was shaking his head. "*Shh,*" he said.

Jaykriss nodded.

Harros was leading the priests as they approached. Two younger priests, carrying torches, stood at his sides. The centurions fanned out around the dais and formed a four-deep V-shape, taking positions four deep and ten across. By the time they had stopped marching, they flanked the entire crowd that had assembled on the green.

The torches were placed in torch-holders on either side of the dais. Harros alone ascended the steps and took a position at the top. The other priests stood behind him; the drummer—a young priest who did not look to be much older than Marda—marched to the front of the dais.

Harros raised his skinny arms and began to speak. "Greetings, people of the village of the Godswood! We meet here for a joyous occasion—the union of two of our esteemed teachers in the venerable Godswood Academy, Master Steeple and Mistress Lineya. And while it is an unusual union, as the bride and groom are both advanced in years, that does not make the occasion any less joyous! For man and woman were meant to be two individuals cleaving together as one—and as neither Master Steeple nor Mistress Lineya have ever been married, this wedding is acceptable and legal in the eyes of the gods and under the laws of Dhatzah-il, the God-King."

As Harros said the Dark King's name, everyone in the audience looked down and shielded their eyes with their right hands—everyone, that was, except the centurions, who stood as motionless as statues.

"And now, let me present the bride and groom," Harros said, beaming. He opened his arms wide.

The drummer began his rhythmic pace once again.

Mistress Lineya and Master Steeple came out of the thatched wedding hut that had been hastily constructed over the previous week. Lineya was wearing a diaphanous white wedding dress of a design that he had never seen. It seemed ancient, as of it had been put away a hundred years before and kept sealed in a box someplace, waiting for this day that might never come. Jaykriss found himself wondering if she had bought it before, when they were young, and had simply held onto it all of those years. She had honeysuckles in her hair and was wearing some sort of makeup, which was something that Jaykriss had never seen her do. And her limp was barely noticeable.

She's really pretty, Jaykriss thought.

Zamarcus, to Jaykriss's relief, was wearing his master's robes—but he had shaved his beard and teased his unruly mane of snow-white hair so that it appeared even more voluminous, like a great cumulus cloud floating about his head.

Priest Harros was staring at Lineya and Zamarcus/Steeple as they approached. He was smiling, but there was something bitter beneath his smile—as if the old priest had bitten into an unripe persimmon and had subsequently been forced to be cordial against his will.

Marda glanced at Jaykriss and tightened his grip on Icebreaker.

Jaykriss realized that his palms were sweating.

The drummer continued his insistent beat, oblivious to all of the drama.

When Lineya and Zamarcus had walked the avenue of palms and stood, at last, together in front of the dais, the old high priest gave an almost imperceptible nod to the drummer and the drumbeats stopped.

Harros cleared his throat.

"People of the Village of the Godswood! It is with great pleasure that I give you the marriage of Mistress Lineya and Master Steeple, here in the village green on this fine morning! The gods have been good to us!"

"The gods have been good to us!" the crowd responded in unison.

"Long live Dhatzah-il!" Harros said.

"Long live Dhatzah-il!" the crowd shouted back.

Harros gazed intently at Lineya. There was silence for a moment as he looked into her eyes.

"So today, in this place, with the entire Godswood village as witnesses, do you, Lineya, take this man, Master Steeple, to be your lawfully wedded husband, forsaking all others until the end of your days?"

Lineya smiled and glanced at Zamarcus. "I do," she said.

Harros turned his attention to Zamarcus. "And do you, Master Steeple, in this place and with the entire Godswood Village as witnesses, take this woman, Mistress Lineya, to be your lawfully wedded wife, forsaking all others until the end of your days?"

"I do," he said.

The priest took Zamarcus's left hand and Lineya's right and placed them together. He opened his mouth, started to speak, then stopped.

Harros then glanced at the centurion commander, who was standing beside the dais.

Jaykriss felt his gut clench.

"Tell, me, Master Steeple—do you have a brother?" Harrros said.

"What?"

"You look awfully familiar to me. Do you have a brother? A half-brother? A *cousin*? Because you look a good bit like someone I once knew, long ago."

Zamarcus shook his head. "My family's all dead, sir. I'm the last one left."

"What did your father do?"

"He was a simple farmer. In the Kingswood."

Harros kept his hand atop the two of theirs.

"I see," he said, his voice dripping with venom.

"You Grace, this is highly irregular," Lineya said.

"This entire *wedding* is highly irregular, don't you think? Two old people getting married? And especially one with *your* history, Mistress?"

"I have served the Godswood Academy loyally as an instructor for decades."

"And so you have. You've been exemplary. So why marry now?"

Lineya glanced at Zamarcus. "Because I love him," she said. There were tears in her eyes.

"That's touching. Only that sentiment does not have a stellar track record with you, does it, Lineya? The last man you loved was a traitor to your King."

Harros shot a nasty glance at Zamarcus. "So what about you, old man? A lifelong bachelor, retired from teaching and reportedly well on your way to the Otherworld, and now you're suddenly rejuvenated. A new job! Marriage! What is the secret of your re-invigoration?"

Zamarcus looked over at Lineya. He dried her eyes with the sleeve of his robe. "I love her, too," he said.

"So if I allow this marriage to take place, will the two of you share an oath of eternal loyalty to Dhatzah-il, the God King? Can you do that?" Harros said.

Lineya and Zamarcus looked at each other.

"We can," Zamarcus said.

Lineya nodded. "We can," she said.

"Well, then. That settles it."

Harros looked out at the crowd and beamed. "I now pronounce you man and wife!" the old priest shouted.

The crowd erupted in celebration—flower girls threw rose petals into the air, children danced, and everyone in the audience hugged the people around them.

Zamarcus took Lineya into his arms, kissed her gently, and wiped the damp hair from her red-rimmed eyes.

"We're married," he said quietly.

The two of them held each other tightly on the dais even as Harros gingerly descended the steps, assisted by two of the younger priests. The drummer pounded out an insistent rhythm, like the slow pulsation of an old man's heart. In unison, silent and emotionless, the company of centurions lined up in formation in preparation for the long march back to the Priest's Bain. Meanwhile, the crowd continued its raucous celebration.

Marda and Jaykriss stood shoulder to shoulder and watched the children dancing as the priests began their slow shuffle home. A ragtag band of minstrels from some village on the other side of the Mist Valley played an song called "The Honey and the Flower Fair" on a crooked old flute and an equally battered tambourine, while singing the old melody off-key.

Suddenly, Marda cocked his head to one side, listening.

"What's that?" he said.

"'The Honey and the Flower Fair,'" Jaykriss said.

One of the children did a passable somersault right in front of them. His flying feet nearly clipped Marda in the chin. But Marda ignored him, listening intently.

"Not that. I heard something," he said.

"What are you talking about? I can't hear anything except the bloody musicians," said Jaykriss.

And then, suddenly, he did.

The sound was a deep rumbling, like thunder from inside the earth. He knew it all too well.

"Ye gods," Jaykriss said under his breath, drawing out his short sword.

The next noise they heard was an ear-splitting screech, a sound that seemed to come from everywhere at once.

Grim-faced, Marda loaded and cocked his crossbow.

Jaykriss could feel his pulse throbbing, dull and insistent, in his temples.

The ground shook beneath them.

Galabrel pressed his palms over his ears but it was not enough. The unearthly screams tore into their eardrums like an icepick.

"What in the name of the gods *is* that?" screamed Galabrel.

"That, my eagle-eyed friend, is the Thrax," Jaykriss said, his jaw muscles clenched tight. His eyes narrowed. Something cold and deadly settled deep inside his chest. The taste of bile boiled up in his throat.

When Jaykriss spoke again, his words were like ice.

"It's come back."

41

Wider than the river, taller than the trees.
The Thrax is coming to look for me.
Dark as night,
Eyes so bright,
Children must hide from his cruel sight.
Run away! Run away!
Play again another day!
If a boy or girl should choose to stay.
The Thrax will eat their bones today.

Jaykriss had heard that nursery rhyme as long as he could remember. His mother had held him in her arms and rocked him to sleep next to the fireplace while murmuring it in his ear. They had sung it in class in nursery school and had danced around the Giving Tree while singing it back when he was a Little at the Godswood Academy. As he grew older, the creature became nothing more than a dark myth—a scary dragon story his friends told each other around campfires at night while roasting crawfish on a stick, no more real than the Green Ghozim or the Flying Man.

"Its teeth are as long as a broadsword," Marda would say.

"Its scales are as broad as a man's hand and cannot catch flame," Galabrel would chime in.

"My grandpapa said that the Thrax can eat an entire village at once, then pass the bones, timbers, and thatch out of its bottom in great lumps," Beela had once chimed in at a school picnic.

To her great consternation, Beela's statement caused a minor ruckus. It prompted two of the more squeamish girls to declare that they were no longer hungry, However, it caused great laughter among the boys, who then proceeded to concoct an impromptu scatological skit about an explorer hiking in the forest coming upon various and sundry things the Thrax had eaten, digested, and expelled.

But it was, after all, a joke. Ultimately, the older kids knew that the Thrax was something that could never hurt them because it was nothing more than a bedtime story for impressionable young children. The legends about it were simple confections of childhood, filled with empty words.

By the time Jaykriss was a teenager, he had come to the conclusion that the Thrax had never really existed at all.

Until the day that it killed his father.

And now, like a nightmare that Jaykriss could not wake from, the Thrax had returned once more—apparently to finish what it had started the year before.

The leviathan broke though the edge of the forest in full gallop, its clawed forelimbs shattering a pair of elm trees like toothpicks.

A lone pair of centurions, swords drawn, stood their ground against the beast. The sun gleamed off of their white armor for a fleeting instant before the great clawed foot of the Thrax stomped them both into the earth as if they were not even there. Seeing that, the rest of the centurions panicked, fleeing pell-mell into the forest and across the fields like so many snow-white insects.

Galabrel stood completely still, his mouth agape, bespectacled eyes open wide. He looked like he had been frozen.

Marda turned to Galabrel, grabbed his shoulder, and spun him so that they were face to face. They were so close that their noses were touching.

"Galabrel, listen to me. Get the girls and the younger children and go to the waterfall. You hear me? The *waterfall*."

Galabrel just stood there, unblinking.

Marda rapped him in the leg with Icebreaker.

"Ow! That hurt!" said Galabrel.

"Get the kids and the girls and head to the waterfall. You got that?"

Galabrel nodded, but his feet would not cooperate. He remained standing there, immobile, like some large and vaguely bovine shrub. His new spectacles had fogged completely over.

Marda pushed him in the direction of Mistress Lineya and Zamarcus, who were herding the younger children together under the shade of a large live oak tree.

"Go!" he screamed.

Galabrel stumbled off in the vague direction of the oak, his large feet plodding clumsily. He nearly trampled poor Beela, who at that very moment was darting toward Marda like a hummingbird.

Jaykriss glanced over to see the Thrax clamp its huge jaws around the edges of the flower-draped wedding dais. When the nightmare mouth snapped shut, the dais was crushed like a rosebud.

Thank the gods no one was there, thought Jaykkriss.

"Beela, you've got to get out of here!" Marda said.

"I want to fight! I want to stand with you!" she said.

Marda leaned down and kissed her gently on the lips. "Beela, listen to me. I need you to take care of the others. I'll do your fighting for you," he said.

Beela's eyes fluttered, but she simply nodded. Speechless and in full swoon, she drifted back over toward the growing knot of Godswood Academy students who had clustered under the wide-spread arms of the live oak.

The Thrax whipped its tail about as it crounched on the green, black scales reflecting the sunlight in dark rainbows. It huffed a hot, stinking breath through its cavernous mouth, the great head slowly moving right and left, red eyes blinking like embers.

"What is it doing?" Jaykriss said.

"Deciding the order we are to be eaten—who is to be the appetizer, first course, and the main course," said Marda, smirking.

"That's not funny." Jaykriss said. Looking at the tooth-studded maw of the dragon, Jaykriss could not help but think about his father, who had stared into that cruel mouth in his final moments.

And then he thought of the Bloodsword.

Glancing below the creature's mouth, he could actlly see it—still buried in the Thrax's shoulder, its ruby hilt gleaming like some exotic red star in a vast firmament of darkness. Something contracted in Jaykriss's chest. He thought of Glyndich again, bravely fighting a battle that he knew he was going to lose.

What did you think of, Papa, as you buried your sword in this thing in those final moments? Did you think of Mama, of me and Annie Bell?

He remembered Glyndich smiling, his great arms flexing with effort, as he practiced swordsmanship in the war yard out in the back of the war chief's bain.

"My primary job is to protect this village and everyone in it. That great responsibility is an honor—and, like all great responsibilities, it comes with a great potential price," Glyndich had said.

He stuck the tip of the Bloodsword into the earth before he knelt in front of the wooden horse that they used to teach riding to children. "Come here, son," he said.

Glyndich had wrapped his massive, sweat-slick arms around Jaykriss then. Jaykriss remembered the scent of him, an aroma of sea salt and freshly tilled earth. He felt a calmness surround him when his father was near that he could not explain. He always felt inordinately *safe* with Glyndich, as though nothing bad could ever happen to him.

"No matter what happens to me, remember this: I'll always love you, even from the Otherworld if that is what the gods will. And I will always be right here for you, as long as you live," Glyndich had said, tapping his temple with an index finger.

He had died the very next day.

Jaykriss was so lost in this thought that he did not even see the militia as they approached the creature. It was the shouts he heard first.

And then the screams.

Kranin, Master Plewin, and the other members of the Godswood village militia, fresh off of their triumphant defeat of the Geshans, had warily approached the creature on foot. They were now addressing it in shouts, brandishing their weapons to punctuate each and every shout.

The creature reared up, mouth opened wide. Row upon row of razor-sharp teeth gleamed in the sunlight. Saliva dripped from the corners of its mouth in great gobbets. And at the forefront of the militia, directly below the dragon's mouth, stood Kranin and Sola, side by side.

Ye gods, no, he thought. His heart was pounding in his chest. He absently rubbed the sea-tripe gizzard stone in an attempt to calm himself, but its magic seemed gone now. Nothing could make him think clearly in this moment; his thoughts were as muddled as the dark green waters of Great Marsh Creek.

He knew that if his mother lost Kranin, it would destroy her. She would go into the darkness and never come out again.

And if he lost Sola…

Jaykriss took off in a dead sprint.

"Where are you going?" asked Marda.

"If she dies, I die. I must be by her side," Jaykriss said.

Marda began running as well.

From the opposite side of the clearing, another man was running toward the militia—robes flapping, master's golden breatsplate gleaming in the sun. An older man, not a warrior. An unarmed man wearing little round sunglasses.

It was Zamarcus.

But the Thrax had its own schedule, its own agenda. It waited for no man. And so it reared up on its rear legs, opened its mouth wide, and screamed.

The force of that bellow nearly knocked Jaykriss down. He looked at Sola and Kranin, so tiny at the foot of the great beast, and wondered if he had come too late—or if it even mattered.

But then Master Plewin's arrow found its mark.

The arrow had streamed toward the creature in a graceful arc of flame.

Of course. He's aiming for the mouth. It's the only scale-free target.

When it struck the Thrax's palate, the arrow exploded, instantly wreathing the creature's massive head in a halo of smoke and ash.

In that instant, everything stopped.

The Thrax was stunned. Its eyes closed; its legs buckled. The great whip-lashing tail simply dropped to the ground.

Has he actually done it? Jaykriss thought.

And then the Thrax opened its eyes.

Enraged, it stomped its feet and bellowed more loudly than ever before. It now targeted Master Plewin, who was frantically trying to load another explosive arrow into his compound bow. The great beast leaned down toward him, opening its jaws wider and wider…

And then Sola jumped in front of Plewin, flashing her Thrax-scale necklace in the creature's face with both hands.

The Thrax stopped for a moment, staring at Sola with a look of genuine puzzlement.

From behind him, Jaykriss heard a human voice speaking impossibly loudly. Only it was not speech at all—at least not human speech. Instead, he heard a curious jumble of hisses and grunts and clicks that did not make any sense to him at first—until he realized who it was.

It was Zamarcus. And he was speaking in Dragonspeak.

The old man had somehow brought the loudspeaker to his own wedding—an admittedly odd selection of items for a wedding, but that was Zamarcus—and he was speaking directly to the Thrax in its own ancient language. Jaykriss could make out what he was saying. It was the same thing, over and over:

"Don't hurt us. We are not your enemies. We are no threat to your babies. We are just trying to protect our children as well."

The Thrax pulled back.

It looked around.

It saw the children huddled beneath the tree. And then it glanced down at Sola again. It leaned toward her, angling its great head to one side.

Sola, no. But then he realized that she was speaking to it. Jaykriss sprinted to Sola's side. His chest hurt, his muscles ached, and he was thoroughly out of breath.

"Are you crazy?" he said to her.

"Good to see you, too," she said.

She whistled and clicked and hissed another complex sentence in Dragonspeak. The Thrax hissed back.

"What does it want again?" Jaykriss said. "It's harder to understand when an actual *dragon* says it."

"It's a *she*, Jaykriss. And she has a nest in the Mist Valley—her first in forty seasons. She wants to be able to raise her babies in peace. She says that there are not many of her kind left. Humans have killed most of them. She calls the ones who have hunted and killed the dragons 'whiteshells.' I think she means the centurions. She hates them."

The Thrax whistled and grunted again.

"Oh, and there is one more thing: she would like someone to remove your father's sword from her. It hurts her."

Sola glanced at Jaykriss. "Would you do it?" she said.

Jaykriss nodded.

Sola said something else to the creature in Dragonspeak that Jaykriss could not fully understand.

The huge creature lay down across the green, spreading out like a huge dog. It dropped its head to the earth.

The Bloodsword was lodged between two scales just above the shoulder. The wound had festered; pus oozed from the angry flesh beneath.

Jaykriss walked up to the massive creature. He could feel its eyes—her eyes—tracking him as he approached.

Be with me, Father.

The beast was incredibly hot. Standing close to it was like standing next to a volcano. It was almost unbearable.

But then he was there, staring at the ruby-encrusted hilt of his father's sword. Grasping it with both hands, Jaykriss pulled on it—but the Bloodsword was stuck hard to the infected flesh and would not budge.

The Thrax whipped its tail high in the air and crashed it down again to the earth. It felt like a minor earthquake.

"Steady, old girl," Jaykriss found himself saying in Dragonspeak. "It's wedged in deep. I'm going to pull on it again. Are you ready?"

"*Yesssss,*" the Thrax said.

Jaykriss grasped the Bloodsword once again. The ruby hilt glittered in the sun.

Help me, Father, he thought again.

The sword came free easily this time, sliding out with almost no resistance at all.

The Thrax sighed. Its exhaled breath stank of sulfur and nearly blew Sola off of her feet.

"*Thank you,*" the Thrax said.

"You're welcome," said Jaykriss.

"*You and the girl can climb upon my neck if you like,*" the Thrax said.

Jaykriss looked at Sola, who nodded.

"We would be honored," Jaykriss said.

Jaykriss gave Sola a boost up and then climbed up himself. The Thrax then raised herself up to her full height.

The top of the Thrax's head towered above them, but the view from the vantage point of the creature's neck was simply incredible. Jaykriss could see the Mist Valley, the Dragon Lake and, beyond that, the bluish silhouettes of the Zephyr Mountains.

The Dead City is somewhere out there, too. But he kept those thoughts to himself.

"This is amazing! We're above the trees!" Sola said. Her eyes were as bright as new coins.

The two of them looked down at the Godswood Village. All across the green, people had dropped to their knees.

"What are they doing? Are they scared?" Sola said.

"I think they are in awe. We've tamed something they thought was untameable."

Jaykriss could feel the intense heat emanating from the scales of the creature beneath him. The wind whistled about his head. A pair of barn swallows darted past them.

He took a deep breath and sighed. *"This is incredible,"* Jaykriss said in Dragonspeak.

"Thank you for removing the pointy thing. It has made me quite ill," she said.

"I suppose we should go back to our people now," he said.

The Thrax lowered herself to the ground once again to allow Jaykriss and Sola to climb down.

Sola walked around to the front of the Thrax's head and patted her on the nose.

"We are also enemies of the whiteshells," she said in Dragonspeak. *"We want to help protect your children from them."*

"Then I will protect your village," the Thrax said.

Jaykriss walked up to stand beside Sola.

"Are you a king?" the Thrax said.

Jaykriss shook his head. "I am just a boy," he said.

The Thrax drew herself up to her full height. *"I have lived for hundreds of seasons. I have seen human kings come and go. You have the bearing of a king."*

Zamarcus came up beside Sola and Jaykriss.

"*He shall be king*," Zamarcus said in Dragonspeak. "*It has been written.*"

The Thrax surveyed the entire village, turning her head left and right.

What happened next was unexpected.

"He shall be king!" the Thrax said, in a voice that resonated throughout the Godswood.

"You can speak our language!" Zamarcus said.

"*Only a little*," the Thrax said, reverting back to Dragonspeak.

The people of the Godswood village watched in awe as the Thrax turned and left, plodding through the forest with footsteps that shook the earth. She angled her huge body carefully so that she did not inadvertently destroy any buildings or topple any more trees.

Kranin, Master Plewin, and Harros walked up to them.

"That was most impressive, you two. You saved the village," Kranin said.

"And you saved my life," Master Plewin said. He placed a hand on Sola's slim shoulder.

"We did what had to be done," Sola said.

"When did you learn Dragonspeak? I did not know that *anyone* knew that language anymore. Dragons are so scarce now," Kranin said.

"My father taught me, and I taught them," Zamarcus said.

"You *father*? I thought your father was a simple *farmer*, Master Steeple. How does a simple farmer from the Kingswood learn Dragonspeak?" said Harros, his eyes narrowed to slits.

Just then, Marda came sprinting up with Beela.

"That was awesome! I never realized that that Dragonspeak stuff could be so handy! Zamarcus, when you teach your next class, I want to be in it!"

Harros visibly stiffened.

"Zamarcus? Zamarcus, son of Zatharia?"

Jaykriss shook his head.

Marda, he thought.

"So it is *you* who have fomented this rebellion against Dhatzah-il! Once again, a traitor to the God Who Walks! And in league with dragons, no less!"

Harros turned to the two centurions who flanked him.

"Arrest this man for treason!" he said.

"But we've done nothing wrong!" Zamarcus said.

"Nothing wrong? You consort with dragons. You have a dragon declare this *boy* a king. You are, in word and in deed, a traitor like your father, a fugitive from justice, and you shall be exposed as the conspirator you are!" Harros said.

The centurions grabbed Zamarcus roughly by the arms.

Harros then turned to Jaykriss.

"And as for you, young man. I've had quite enough of your hubris. A king? Pah!"

Harros spat on the ground at Jaykriss's feet.

"No gods but the God Who Walks. No kings but the Dark King," the old priest said, pulling a razor-sharp ceremonial blade from beneath his cloak.

Jaykriss barely felt the knife as it slid between his ribs.

"You are nothing, Jaykriss, son of Glyndich. Nothing at all. And now you will go into the darkness—forever."

Jaykriss felt something warm spill down his tunic. He coughed and tasted blood on his breath—a spent, metallic taste, like rust. His breath tightened up; each successive attempt to inhale was more difficult than the last. He pulled his hand away from his chest and stared at the crimson stain on it with a puzzled expression. Black spots pulsated behind his eyes, coalescing, growing larger by the minute.

So this is it.

It was the last conscious thought Jaykriss had.

42

When Glyndich came for Jaykriss, it was still dark outside.

"Hurry up. We'll miss the ferry," Glyndich said.

"What happens then?" Jaykriss said.

A thin smile crossed Glyndich's lips. "Nothing, son. We'd just catch the next one."

The stars spilled across the sky like diamond dust. Jaykriss stood at the door of the war chief's bain and gazed up at at them as a breeze drifted in from the forest, carrying with it the sweet scent of jasmine.

Jaykriss laced up his leggings and picked up the Bloodsword. It felt firm and substantial in his grip. He admired the way that the candlelight gleamed along the edges of the silvery blade.

"You won't be needing that after the crossing. Best that you leave it here," Glyndich said.

Jaykriss cocked his head. "But I went through so much to get it back. It seems a shame to just leave it."

"It's OK, son. Don't get me wrong, now; I'm proud of you for getting it back. But it is just a thing. And things can stay."

Jaykriss blew out the candle, plunging the room into darkness. "Where are Mama and Annya?"

"They'll be along later. It's not their time yet."

The ferry arrived just as the sun was climbing over the horizon. It was a nondescript battered wooden dinghy encrusted with barnacles and seaweed, rowed by a solitary boatman—a thin man, dressed in a diaphanous gray shroud.

"Come on," croaked the boatman.

Jaykriss tried to make out the boatman's face but he couldn't. The man's features *wavered,* as if he were made of smoke.

Glyndich got into the ferry, which was bobbing about in the waves at the river's edge. Jaykriss saw shadows drifting about in the deep and an occasional static flash of blue-green light.

Anglerfish. I've seen those fish before.

"Are you coming or not?" the boatman rasped. "I'm on a schedule."

Jaykriss looked at his father. "Should I go with you, Papa?"

"That is up to you."

"Where does this ferry travel?"

"Why, I thought you knew," Glyndich said.

Jaykriss shook his head.

"It goes to the Otherworld, boy. You didn't know that?" the boatman said.

Jaykriss shook his head.

"On or off, then. Make up your mind," said the boatman.

Glyndich, standing in the back of the boat, was holding out his hand.

Jaykriss thought for a moment. But only for a moment.

His only notion was a single, pervasive one: *Sola.*

It was all the argument he needed in the world.

"No," he said. "It's not time. Not yet."

"You're not going?" said Glyndich.

"I can't, Papa. There's a girl."

Glyndich arched his generous eyebrows and grinned. "Very well, then. You should stay. There's no better reason than that," he said.

"I have not disappointed you, Papa?"

Glyndich shook his head. He was smiling.

"You've never disappointed me, son," he said.

The boatman pushed away from the shoreline. Jaykriss stood and watched as the little craft moved slowly away, silhouetted against the burnt orange horizon. At some point—he was not sure when—he could no longer see them, but he knew that Glyndich was still out there someplace.

He could *feel* it, deep in his marrow.

Goodbye, he thought.

The sun had waxed brilliant now, scattering flecks of gold across the broad expanse of the river. The far side of the riverbank was shrouded in mist. Part of him wanted to journey there, to unravel the mystery that was on the other side. But Jaykriss turned his back on it, at least for now. There was too much yet to do.

He clambered back up the moss-covered steps to the war chief's bain and picked up the Bloodsword once again.

"Papa, tell them I'm coming home," he said.

And then everything went black.

When Jaykriss opened his eyes, he was looking at Sola. She was stroking his hair and gazing absently into space—her mind someplace far, far away.

"Hey," he said.

The word tasted like dust in his mouth.

She glanced down at him. Her face blossomed into an enormous smile. She kissed him on the forehead, both cheeks, and on the lips.

"Wow," he said. "I should take naps more often."

"I've missed you *so* much!" she said. She clasped his hand in hers, not daring to let go for fear of losing him again. "Marda! Zamarcus! He's awake!"

Jaykriss tried to sit up, but the black spots returned. He felt as weak as rainwater. "How long have I been asleep?" he asked.

"Too long," Sola said. "Far too long."

Marda ran into the room in full battle gear, still clutching Icebreaker. "How long has he been awake?" he said.

"A minute. He just woke up."

Marda knelt by Jaykriss's bed and tousled his hair. "I'd kiss you if you were a girl," he said.

"Please don't," said Jaykriss, smiling.

Lineya, Zamarcus, and Beela came in next. All three of them were covered in flour.

"We were baking," explained Zamarcus.

"Biscuits with honey butter," added Beela.

"How do you feel, Jaykriss?" asked Lineya.

"OK. Tired, and weak, but OK."

He looked around the room. It was windowless; the walls seemed carved out of living rock. His bed was shoved up against one wall; there was a bedside table covered with clear glass jars filled with blue, reddish-orange and black liquids. A lantern flickered on the bedside table; two more were mounted on iron sconces located on the opposite wall.

"Where is this place?" Jaykriss asked.

"The Dead City," said Zamarcus. "It's the only place we knew that you'd be safe after Harros stabbed you."

Harros.

Jaykriss had forgotten all of that somehow. Now, it all came rushing back.

He traced his fingertips along his right side. He could feel the scar, a long one along his lower ribs, where the priest's blade had cut him.

"Can someone get me a mirror?" he said.

Sola found picked up a handheld mirror from the bedside table and handed it to Jaykriss.

"Can you hold it?" she asked.

He nodded.

He looked at his face first. It was drawn and thin. His skin was very pale; his lips were dry and cracked. There were dark circles around his eyes. And he looked *older* somehow, if that was possible. He then angled the mirror so that he could see the scar. It was a raised, reddish thing, twisted along his rib cage like a serpent, well-healed but terribly long. Another small round scar was just below it.

"What's this one?" he asked.

"Chest tube. We put it in to re-expand your lung. The tube's been out a few weeks now."

"A few *weeks?*"

Jaykriss looked at his belly. He was very thin, without an ounce of fat left. Another tube extended directly into his abdominal wall. It was hooked up to a bottle of milky liquid suspended beside the bed.

"What's this? Another tube?" he said, pointing to the tube.

"We had to feed you. You were not able to eat. Zamarcus read about this in a medical book from the Time Before. He figured that it was your only chance."

"So I had a chest tube that has been out for weeks, a tube placed in my stomach because I could not eat anything by mouth, and you somehow got me all the way to the Dead City without me being aware of any of this."

Everyone nodded.

"How long has it been, exactly?"

Sola looked at Zamarcus. "Seven moons," she said.

"*Seven moons!*"

"You nearly died, Jay. Bathrania and her potions helped quell the infections. Zamarcus learned to do surgery from a book. And that first night, with all of the centurions coming on the flying ship from Capitus, was a nightmare," said Marda.

"Centurions from Capitus? The flying ship? But why?"

"They wanted to make certain that you stayed dead," Zamarcus said.

"*Stayed* dead? But I never died!"

"Everyone in the Godswood saw you collapse. There was blood all over you. Your face was gray, and your eyes were rolled back in your head and to them, you were dead. You had that tension pneumonia…" Marda said.

"Pneumothorax," said Zamarcus.

"Whatever. And then we got you down on the ground and Zamarcus saw what was going on and put the tube in your chest and everything was better all of a sudden, a *lot* better. But as far as everyone else was concerned, the people of the Godswood all saw you die. We told Harros and the others that you were gone. And Harros called in the centurions to make certain that you stayed that way—that no one could take away your body and say that you had survived. After the Thrax spoke, the people were already calling you a king. Some even said that the whole thing with the Thrax was a miracle, and that you were a god-sent emissary."

"Which is why Harros wanted you dead," said Zamarcus.

"So the high priest stabs and tries to kill a teenage boy, right out there in public, and gets away with it?" Jaykriss said.

"He claimed that you had used dark magic to control the Thrax, and that the whole village was in danger because of it. He felt that he had to kill you to save the village," said Marda.

"That's ridiculous! Who has even heard of dark magic, anyway?"

Everyone's hand shot up.

"Zamarcus taught us about it," said Sola. "It's real."

"We had lots of spare time after we got here. He's been educating us," Beela said.

"He does that sometimes," Jaykriss said, smiling. He looked at Zamarcus and Lineya. "How did the rest of you get away? The last I remember, Harros was trying to arrest you."

"Kranin. There was a 'jailbreak.' Someone left the doors to our cells open, and all the guards were given sleeping flakes, like the ones you took the night you went into the Library of Souls. Truly amazing how things work out sometimes," Zamarcus said.

At that moment, Jaykriss had a horrible thought—a thought that made him feel ill.

"Do my mother and sister know that I am not really dead?" he asked.

Zamarcus nodded. "I got word to them shortly after we left the village. And we've kept them updated about your progress. No one else in the village knows, though—not even Kranin. He's still war chief, at least technically, so his ties to the priests and the Dark King are close enough that he could be in danger if they thought he knew something."

"Why do you say that he's 'technically' war chief? Is there someone else?"

"After you 'died,' Harros feared an insurrection might arise as a result of your demise, so he brought in an entire garrison of centurions led by an ill-tempered brute named Uzo, a centurion commander," said Zamarcus.

"Uzo the Ugly," said Marda. "He smells like urine."

"Marda!" Beela said, giggling.

"Well, he does!"

"Anyway, Uzo imposed martial law over the entire Godswood. He really runs it now. Kranin is just a figurehead. But they need Kranin's help to keep things peaceful."

Jaykriss felt dizzy. He was not certain if it was the medication, the information, or simply being weak after seven moons of inactivity, but he felt as though the world was spinning too fast—as though he might just fly off into space, ending up someplace near Jupiter or Mars or one of those other planets that Zamarcus had taught him about long ago.

"This is all too much," he said.

Zamarcus glanced over at Sola, then at Marda and the rest of them. "Well, there is one more thing," he said.

"Can it wait? I'm really tired."

A worried look creased Sola's face. "Perhaps we should. It's his first day back. Can't they wait a day?" she said.

"Of course. Jaykriss should rest. We can show him the dragons tomorrow."

Jaykriss sat up. The black spots returned for a moment, but they dissipated quickly. "*Dragons?* As in the plural?"

Zamarcus nodded. "Vashoong had her babies," he said.

"Vashoong?"

"That's the Thrax's real name. The centurions were hunting her after Uzo showed up, so we brought her here from the Mist Valley. Her babies hatched a few months ago. But I suppose they can wait until tomorrow," Zamarcus said. His bushy eyebrows arched over the rims of his spectacles.

"Unhook me. *Now.* I want to see them," said Jaykriss.

"Are you sure?"

Jaykriss nodded.

Zamarcus disconnected the feeding tube, and Marda picked Jaykriss up out of the bed. He had carried Jaykriss about twenty paces before Jaykriss said, "Put me down."

"You're weak."

"I feel OK. I want to try to walk."

Marda looked at Zamarcus.

"Let him try," Zamarcus said.

Jaykriss's legs trembled. He held tightly onto Marda's shoulder, but he was able to put one leg in front of another and walk slowly across the room to the door.

"How far is it?" he asked.

"Not too far. We have to keep them in another part of the cavern," said Zamarcus.

It was much further than they had implied. The hallway was long, dark and seemingly interminable. Its walls were slimy and cool to the touch—and Jaykriss had to touch them *a lot,* steadying himself, trying to keep his wobbly feet beneath him. But after a few minutes' walk, they came to a broad oaken door bound up with iron reinforcements. The door was heavily padlocked, but Zamarcus carried a skeleton key on a leather lanyard draped around his neck.

He opened the door and swung it open.

The cavern was almost impossibly huge. Jaykriss could barely make out the far side of it. But it was open to the sky, and sunlight streamed down in a golden column to illuminate the broad expanse of the cavern floor.

"Where is she?" Jaykriss said.

"She is in hibernation mode. It makes her one with the rock, invisible to our eyes."

There was an ominous rumble from the far side of the cavern. The cave's stony wall seemed to undulate slowly, and a pair of red eyes appeared, blinking twice.

"I'm here," Vashoong said.

The Thrax moved toward them with an elegance that belied her prodigious bulk. Incandescent sunlight ignited her myriad dark scales as she crossed the cavern. When she reached their group, she leaned down, canting her massive head down to look at Jaykriss.

He could not help but notice her knifelike teeth.

"The young king has awakened at last. We are grateful," she said.

"Your human speech has improved," Jaykriss said.

"That sort of thing comes from being around humans," she said.

Jaykriss could have sworn that she was smiling. "Where are your babies? I heard that they had been born."

"They are out hunting. I can call them for you if you'd like."

Jaykriss nodded. "I'd love to see them."

The Thrax raised her head toward the cavern roof and let out an unearthly cry. It began with a guttural, bone-shaking growl that seemed to start out some-place deep in her throat and ended with an urgent, ear-piercing screech that could have shattered glass—a cry so loud that Jaykriss thought the stalactites hanging from the ceiling might come crashing down upon them.

The first dragon—a beautiful sapphire-blue creature with reddish-purple wings—swooped in directly through the gap in the roof and stopped, hovering in midair as it sized up the humans in the room.

"*It's OK*," said Vashoong in Dragonspeak. "*They are our friends.*"

The blue dragon, which was about the size of a cow, flapped over to a place near Zamarcus before landing. It nuzzled the old man with its broad, horn-tipped head.

"Arius," Vashoong said. "My baby girl."

A moment later, a second dragon—about the same size as the first, but completely red with the exception of an iridescent, sky-blue head—dove headlong into the cavern. This dragon did not hesitate for a second. Pulling into a spiral after entry, it barrel-rolled toward its mother, careening perilously close to the wall before righting itself. It then somehow pulled up into a dead stop before alighting gently next to Vashoong.

The red dragon's chest heaved. He seemed slightly out of breath.

"Bexath," Zamarcus said, rolling his eyes. "An incorrigible show-off."

Bexath folded his wings and shuffled over toward Zamarcus. He seemed to be looking for something.

"I'm all out," Zamarcus said, extending his palms.

The young dragon raised his head and screeched, then belched a forty-foot gout of flame.

"You don't scare me, Bexath. I'll get you some later, but we have company right now, and I'm not going to be rude to them," Zamarcus said.

Bexath dropped his head. He seemed to be pouting.

"He likes me to bring him fish," Zamarcus explained. "Especially salmon. He absolutely *loves* salmon."

"So is that all?" asked Jaykriss.

"Not hardly," said Zamarcus.

Suddenly, a vast shadow eclipsed the opening in the cavern roof.

The creature that hovered above the cavern opening was as black as night. His eyes were crimson, like his mother's, as were the spiked horns on his gargantuan head. He was so large that he looked like he would barely fit through the gap in the cavern's ceiling.

"Coriander," Zamarcus said. "The biggest of them all."

The black dragon suddenly folded its leathery wings and simply *dropped* through the opening, extending them again once he was inside so that he could catch himself. He flapped vigorously, each beat nearly blowing Jaykriss off of his feet, for a few moments as he surveyed the scene below him.

"He's cautious, that one—and quite intelligent. He already can speak human very well. The others are just learning. And his hunting range is huge. That's why he was the last to get here. He'll fly a hundred miles or more in search of food."

Coriander folded up his wings again and landed on both clawed feet with a resounding *thud*.

"He always does that," Zamarcus said. "It's his thing. Likes to stick the landing."

Jaykriss turned to Vashoong.

"They're all beautiful," he said in Dragonspeak. "And they can fly."

"Their father could fly."

"Are they all fire-breathers?"

"Yes. We don't know where that came from. But they all three can do it. Still learning control, though," Vashoong said.

"It's all part of their training," Zamarcus said.

"They're in training?" asked Jaykriss.

"Why, yes. I thought you understood that."

"In training for what?"

"For your return to the Godswood, Jaykriss. So that we can take back what is rightfully ours," said Zamarcus.

"So that we can drive out the whiteshells and make the world safe once again for my children," said Vashoong.

"So that we can fulfill the Prophecy of Ramallah, end the reign of the Dark King once and for all, and avenge our fathers," said Marda.

Jaykriss felt his heart racing. His palms were moist; his mouth felt like cotton. He glanced over at the old man.

"I'm not ready for all of this, Zamarcus," he said.

The old man opened his cloak and pulled out a twine-bound package wrapped in ragged oilcloth. He unwrapped the twine and shucked off the oilcloth.

The Bloodsword gleamed in the shaft of sunlight that poured in from the ceiling. Zamarcus handed the sword to Jaykriss.

"Feel this," he said.

Jaykriss appreciated the finely balanced heft of the ancient weapon as it sat in his hand. The Bloodsword seemed filled with energy, as though it were alive. He could feel it thrumming in time with his heartbeat. The ruby in the sword's hilt pulsated, its blood-red eye peering directly into the depths of Jaykriss's soul.

"It *knows* you, Jaykriss," Zamarcus said.

There was a spiritual connection between Jaykriss and the Bloodsword. It was a sensation far deeper than a son wrapping his palm and fingers around his dead father's sword. There was something tangible in all of it that linked past, present, and future.

It's my destiny, Jaykriss thought, in spite of himself.

Zamarcus fixed him with a steady gaze. "You're *not* ready, Jaykriss. Not yet. But you *will* be."

Made in the USA
Charleston, SC
06 March 2014